John Sandford is the pseudonym of Pulitzer-prize winning journalist John Camp. He is the author of sixteen PREY novels, and four KIDD novels. He lives in Minnesota.

Also by John Sandford

Sudden Prey

Certain Prey

Easy Prey

Chosen Prey

Mortal Prey

Hidden Prey

NakedPrey

Kidd Novels

The Fool's Run

The Empress File

The Devil's Code

The Hanged Man's Song

Published by Pocket Books

Secret Prey

JOHN SANDFORD

POCKET
BOOKS

LONDON • SYDNEY • NEW YORK • TORONTO

First published in Great Britain by Headline Book Publishing, 1998
This edition published by Pocket Books, 2004
An imprint of Simon & Schuster UK Ltd
A Viacom Company

1 3 5 7 9 10 8 6 4 2

Simon & Schuster UK Ltd
Africa House
64-78 Kingsway
London WC2B 6AH

www.simonsays.co.uk

Simon & Schuster Australia
Sydney

A CIP catalogue record for this book is available
from the British Library

ISBN 0 7434 8420 7

Printed and bound in Great Britain by
Bookmarque Ltd, Croydon, Surrey

Secret Prey

Chapter One

The chairman of the board pulled the door shut behind him, stacked his rifle against the log-sided cabin, and walked down to the end of the porch. The light from the kitchen window punched out into the early-morning darkness and the utter silence of the woods. Two weeks of nightly frost had killed the insects and had driven the amphibians into hibernation: for a few seconds he was alone.

Then the chairman yawned and unzipped his bib overalls, unbuttoned his pants, shuffled his feet, the porch boards creaking under his insulated hunting boots. Nothing like a good leak to start the day, he thought. As he leaned over the low porch rail, he heard the door opening behind him. He paid no attention.

Three men and a woman filed out of the house, pretended not to notice him.

'Need some snow,' the woman said, peering into the dark. Susan O'Dell was a slender forty, with a tanned, dry face, steady brown eyes and smile-lines around her mouth. A headlamp was strapped around her blaze-orange stocking cap, but she hadn't yet switched it on. She wore a blaze-orange Browning parka, snowmobile pants, and carried a backpack and Remington .308 mountain rifle with a Leupold Vari-X III scope. Not visible was the rifle's custom trigger job. The trigger would break at exactly two-and-a-half pounds.

'Cold sonofabitch, though,' said Wilson McDonald, as he slipped one heavy arm through his gun-sling. McDonald was

1

a large man, and much too heavy: in his hunting suit he looked like a blaze-orange Pillsbury dough-boy. He carried an aging .30–06 with open sights, bought in the '30s at Abercrombie & Fitch in New York. At forty-two, he believed in a certain kind of tradition – his summer car, a racing-green XK-E, was handed down from his father; his rifle came from his grandfather; and his spot in the country club from his great-grandfather. He would defend the Jaguar against far better cars; the .30–06 against more modern rifles; and the club against parvenus, hirelings, and, of course, blacks and Jews.

'You all ready?' asked the chairman of the board, as he came back toward them, buttoning his pants. He was a fleshy, red-faced man, the oldest of the group, with a thick shock of white hair and caterpillar-sized eyebrows. As he got closer to the others, he could smell the odor of pancakes and coffee still steaming off them. 'I don't want anybody stumbling around in the goddamn woods just when it's getting good.'

They all nodded: they'd all been here before.

'Getting late,' said O'Dell. She wore the parka hood down, and the parka itself was still unzipped; but she'd wrapped a red-and-white kafiyah around her neck and chin. Purchased on a whim in the Old City of Jerusalem, and meant to protect an Arab from the desert sun, it was now protecting a third-generation Irishwoman from the Minnesota cold. 'We better get out there and get settled.'

Five-forty-five in the morning, opening day of deer season. O'Dell led the way off the porch, the chairman of the board at her shoulder, the other three men trailing behind.

Terrance Robles was the youngest of them, still in his mid-thirties. He was a blocky man with thick, black-rimmed glasses and a thin, curly beard. His watery blue eyes showed a nervous flash, and he laughed too often, a shallow, uncertain chuckle. He carried a stainless Sako .270, mounted with a satin-finished Nikon scope. Robles had little regard for tradition: everything he hunted with was new technology.

James T. Bone might have been Susan O'Dell's brother: forty, as she was, Bone was slim, tanned, and dark-eyed, his face showing a hint of humor in a surface that was hard as a nut. He brought up the rear with a .243 Mauser Model 66 cradled in his bent left arm.

Four of the five – the chairman of the board, Robles, O'Dell and Bone – were serious hunters.

The chairman's father had been a country banker. They'd had a nice rambling stone-and-redwood home on Blueberry Lake south of Itasca, and his father had been big in Rotary and the Legion. The deer hunt was an annual ritual: the chairman of the board had hung twenty-plus bucks in his forty-six years: real men didn't kill does.

Robles had come to hunting as an adult, joining an elk hunt as a thirtieth-birthday goof, only to be overwhelmed by its emotional power. For the past five years he'd hunted a half-dozen times annually, from Alaska to New Zealand.

O'Dell was a rancher's daughter. Her father owned twenty square miles of South Dakota just east of the Wyoming line, and she'd joined the annual antelope hunt when she was eight. During her college years at Smith, when the other girls had gone to Ivy League football games with their beaux, she'd flown home for the shooting.

Bone was from Mississippi. He'd learned to hunt as a child, because he wanted to eat. Once, when he was nine, he'd made soup for himself and his mother out of three carefully shot blackbirds.

Only McDonald disdained the hunt. He'd shot deer in the past – he was a Minnesota male, and males of a certain class were expected to do that – but he considered the hunt a pain

3

in the ass. If he killed a deer, he'd have to gut it. Then he'd smell bad and get blood on his clothing. Then he'd have to do something with the meat. A wasted day. At the club, they'd be playing some serious gin – drinking some serious gin, he thought – and here he was, about to climb a goddamned tree.

'Goddamnit,' he said aloud.

'What?' The chairman grunted, turned to look at him.

'Nothing. Stray thought,' McDonald said.

One benefit: if you killed a deer, people at the club attributed to you a certain common touch – not commonness, which would be a problem, but contact with the earth, which some of them perceived as a virtue. That was worth something; not enough actually to be out here, but something.

The scent of wood smoke hung around the cabin, but gave way to the pungent odor of burr oaks as they pushed out into the trees. Fifty yards from the cabin, as they moved out of range of the house lights, O'Dell switched on her headlamp, and the chairman turned on a hand flash. Dawn was forty-five minutes away, but the moonless sky was clear, and they could see a long thread of stars above the trail: the dipper pointing down to the North Star.

'Great night,' Bone said, his face turned to the sky.

A small lake lay just down-slope from the cabin like a smoked mirror. They followed a shoreline trail for a hundred and fifty yards, moved single-file up a ridge, and continued on, still parallel to the lake.

'Don't step in the shit,' the woman said, her voice a snapping break in the silence. She caught a pile of fresh deer droppings with her headlamp, like a handful of purple chicken hearts.

'We did that last week with the Cove Links deal,' the chairman said drily.

The ridge separated the lake and a tamarack swamp. Fifty yards further on, Robles said, 'I guess this is me,' and turned off to the left toward the swamp. As he broke away from the group, he switched on his flash, said, 'Good luck, guys,' and disappeared down a narrow trail toward his tree stand.

The chairman of the board was next. Another path broke to the left, toward the swamp, and he took it, saying, 'See you.'

'Get the buck,' said O'Dell, and McDonald, O'Dell and Bone continued on.

The chairman switched on his flash and followed the narrow beam forty-five yards down a gentle slope to the edge of the swamp. The lake was still open, but the swamp was freezing out, the shallow pockets of water showing window-pane ice.

One stumpy burr oak stood at the boundary of the swamp; the kind of oak an elf might live in. The chairman dug into his coat pocket, took out a long length of nylon parachute cord, looped it around his rifle sling, leaned the rifle against the tree, and began climbing the foot spikes that he'd driven into the tree eight years earlier.

He'd taken three bucks from this stand. The county road foreman, who'd been cleaning ditches in preparation for the snow months, told him that a twelve-pointer had moved into the neighborhood during the summer. The foreman had seen him cutting down this way, across the middle of the swamp toward this very tree. Not more than two weeks ago.

The chairman clambered into the stand fifteen feet up the tree, and settled into the bench with his back to the oak. The stand looked like a suburban deck, built of preservative-treated two-by-sixes, with a two-by-four railing that served as a gun rest. The chairman slipped off his pack, hung it from a spike to his right, and pulled the rifle up with the parachute cord.

The cartridges were still warm from his pocket as he loaded

the rifle. That wouldn't last long. Temperatures were in the teens, with an icy wind cutting at exposed skin. Later in the day, it would warm up, maybe into the upper 30s, but sitting up here, early, exposed, it would get real damn cold. Freeze the ass off that fuckin' O'Dell. O'Dell always made out that she was impervious to cold; but this day would get to her.

The chairman, wrapped in nylon and Thinsulate, was still a little too warm from the hike in, and he half-dozed as he sat in the tree, waiting for first light. He woke once more to the sound of a deer walking through the dried oak leaves, apparently following a game trail down to the swamp. The animal settled on the hillside, behind him.

Now *that* was interesting.

Forty or fifty yards away, no more. Still up the ridge, but it should be visible after sunrise, if it moved again. If it didn't, he'd kick it out on the way back to the cabin.

He sat waiting, listening to the wind. Most of the oaks still carried their leaves, dead brown, but hanging on. When he closed his eyes, their movement sounded like a crackling of a small, intimate wood fire.

The chairman sighed: so much to do.

The killer was dressed in blaze-orange and moving quietly and quickly along the track. Dawn was not far away and the window of opportunity could be measured in minutes:

Here: now twenty-four steps down the track, 1–2–3–4–5–6–7–8–9–10–11–12–13–14 . . . 23–24. A tree here to the left . . . wish I could use a light.

The oak tree was there, its bark rough against the fingertips. And just to the right, a little hollow in the ground behind a fallen aspen.

Just get down here . . . quietly, quietly! Did he hear me? These leaves . . . didn't think about the leaves yesterday, now it sounds like I'm walking on cornflakes . . . where's that log, must be right here, must be . . . ah!

From the nest in the ground, the fallen aspen was at exactly the right height for a rifle rest. A quick glance through the scope: nothing but a dark disc.

What time? My God, my watch has stopped. No: 6:17. Okay. There's time. Settle down. And listen! If anybody comes, may have to shoot . . . Now what time? 6:18. Only two minutes gone? Can't remember . . . two minutes, I think.

There'd be only one run at this. There were other people nearby, and they were armed. If someone else came stumbling along the track, and saw the orange coat crouched in the hole . . .

If they came while it was dark, maybe I could run, hide. But maybe, if they thought I was a deer, they'd shoot at me. What then? No. If someone comes, I take the shot then, whoever it is. Two shots are okay. I can take two. It wouldn't look like an accident anymore, but at least there wouldn't be a witness.

What's that? Who's there? Somebody?

The killer sat in the hole and strained to hear: but the only sounds were the dry leaves that still hung from the trees, shaking in the wind; the scraping of branches; and the cool wind itself. Check the watch:

Getting close, now. Nobody moving, I'm okay. Cold down here, though. Colder than I thought. Have to be ready . . . The old man . . . have to think about the old man. If he's there, at the cabin, I'll have to take him. And if his wife's there, have to take her . . . That's okay: they're old . . . Still nothing in the scope. Where's the sun?

Daniel S. Kresge was the chairman of the board, president and chief executive officer of the Polaris Bank System. He'd gathered the titles to him like an archaic old Soviet dictator. And he ran his regime like a dictator: two hundred and fifty banks spread across six Midwestern states, all wrapped in his cost-cutting fist.

If everything went exactly right, he would hold his job for another fifteen months, when Polaris would be folded into Midland Holding, owner of six hundred banks in the South Central states. There would be some casualties.

The combined banks' central administration would be in Fort Worth. Not many Polaris executives would make the move. In fact, the whole central administrative section would eventually disappear, along with much of top management. Bone would probably land on his feet: his investments division was one of the main profit centers at Polaris, and he'd attracted some attention. O'Dell ran the retail end of Polaris. Midland would need somebody who knew the territory, at least for a while, so she could wind up as the number-two or -three person in Midland's retail division. She wouldn't like that. Would she take it? Kresge was not sure.

Robles would hang on for a while: a pure technician, he ran data services for Polaris, and Midland would need him to help integrate the separate Polaris and Midland data systems.

McDonald was dead meat. Mortgage divisions didn't make much anymore, and Midland already had a mortgage division – which they were trying to dump, as it happened.

Kresge turned the thought of the casualties in his head: when they actually started working on the details of the merger, he'd have to sweeten things for the Polaris execs who'd be putting the parts together, and the people Midland would need: Robles, for sure. Probably O'Dell and Bone.

McDonald? Fuck him.

Kresge would lose his job along with the rest. Unlike the

others, he'd walk with something in the range of an after-tax forty million dollars. And he'd be free.

In two weeks, Kresge would sit in a courtroom and solemnly swear that his marriage was irretrievably broken. His wife had agreed not to seek alimony. In return for that concession, she'd demanded – and he'd agreed to give her – better than seventy-five percent of their joint assets. Eight million dollars. Letting go of the eight million had been one of the hardest things he'd ever done. But it was worth it: there'd be no strings on him.

When she'd signed the deal, neither his wife nor her wolverine attorney had understood what the then-brewing merger might mean. No idea that there'd be a golden parachute for the chairman. And his ex wouldn't get a nickel of the new money. He smiled as he thought about it. She'd hired the wolverine specifically to fuck him on the settlement, and thought she had. Wait'll the word got into the newspapers about his settlement. And it *would* get in the newspapers.

Fuck her.

Forty million. He knew what he'd do with it.

He'd leave the Twin Cities behind, first thing. He was tired of the cold. Move out to LA. Buy some suits. Maybe one of those BMW two-seaters, the 850. He'd been a good gray Minnesota banker all of his life. Now he'd take his money to LA and live a little. He closed his eyes and thought about what you could do with forty million dollars in the city of angels. Hell, the women alone . . .

Kresge opened his eyes again with a sudden awareness of the increasing cold: shivered and shook the stiffness out. Looking to the east, back toward the cabin, he could see an unmistakable streak of lighter sky. There was a ruffling of leaves to his right, a steady trampling sound. Another deer went by, a shadow in the semi-dark as the animal picked its way through a border of finger-thick alders at the fringe of the swamp. No antlers that he could see. He watched until the deer disappeared into the tamarack.

He picked up the rifle then, resisted the temptation to work the bolt, to check that the rifle was loaded. He knew it was, and working the bolt would be noisy. He flicked the safety off, then back on.

The last few minutes crawled by. Ten minutes before the season opened, the forest was still gray to the eye; in the next few minutes, it seemed to grow miraculously brighter. Then he heard a single, distant shot: nobody here on the farm.

Another shot followed a minute later, then two or three shots over the next couple of minutes: hunters jumping the gun. He glanced at his watch. Two minutes. Nothing moving out over the swamp.

Through the scope, the target looked like an oversized pumpkin, fifteen or twenty feet up the tree. His body from the hips down was out of sight, as was his right arm. The killer could see a large part of his back, but not the face. The crosshairs of the low-power scope caressed the target's spine, and the killer's finger lay lightly on the trigger.

Gotta be him. Damn this light, can't see. Turn your head. Come on, turn your head. Look at me. Have to do something, sun's getting up, have to do something. Look at me. There we go! Keep turning, keep turning . . .

Thirty seconds before the season opened, the crackle of gunfire became general. Nothing too close, though, Kresge thought. Either the other guys were holding off, or nothing was moving beneath them.

What about the deer that had settled off to his left?

He turned on the bench, moving slowly, carefully, and looked that way. In the last few seconds of his life, Daniel S. Kresge first saw the blaze-orange jacket, then the face. He recognized the killer and thought, *What the hell?*

Then the face moved down and he realized that the dark circle below the hood was the objective end of the scope and the scope was pointed his way, so the barrel . . . ah, Jesus.

Jesus went through Kresge's mind at the same instant the bullet punched through his heart.

The chairman of the board spun off the bench – feeling no pain, feeling nothing at all – his rifle falling to the ground. He knelt for a moment at the railing, like a man taking communion, then his back buckled and he fell under the railing, after the rifle.

He saw the ground coming, in a foggy way, hit it face-first, with a thump, and his neck broke. He bounced onto his back, his eyes still open: the brightening sky was gone. He never felt the hand that probed for his carotid artery, looking for a pulse.

He would lie there for a while, head downhill, would Daniel S. Kresge, a hole in his chest, with a mouthful of dirt and oak leaves. Nobody would run to see what the gunshot was about. There would be no calls to 9–1–1. No snoops. Just another day on the hunt.

A real bad day for the chairman of the board.

Chapter Two

Looking as though he'd been dragged through hell by the ankles, a disheveled Del Capslock stumbled out of the men's room in the basement of City Hall, fumbling with the buttons on the fly of his jeans. Footsteps echoed in the dark hallway behind him and he turned his head to see Sloan coming through the gloom, a thin smile on his narrow face.

'Playing with yourself,' Sloan said, his voice echoing in the weekend emptiness. Sloan was neatly but colorlessly dressed in khaki slacks and a tan mountain parka with a zip-in fleece liner. 'I should have expected it; I knew you were a pervert. I just didn't know you had enough to play with.'

'The old lady bought me these Calvin Kleins,' Dell said hitching up the jeans. 'They got buttons instead of zippers.'

'The theory of buttons is very simple,' Sloan began. 'You take the round, flat thing . . .'

'Yeah, fuck you,' Del said. 'The thing is, Calvin makes pants for fat guys. These supposedly got a thirty-four waist. They're really about thirty-eight. I can't get them buttoned, and when I do, I can't keep the fuckin' things up.'

'Yeah?' Sloan wasn't interested. His eyes drifted down the hall as Del continued to struggle with the buttons. 'Seen Lucas?'

'No.' Del got one of the buttons. 'See, the advantage of buttons is, you don't get your dick caught in a zipper.'

'Okay, if you don't get it caught in a button hole.'

Del started to laugh, which made it harder to button the

12

pants, and he said, 'Shut up, I only got one more . . . maybe you could give me a hand here.'

'I don't think so; it's too nice a day to get busted for aggravated faggotry.'

'You can always tell who your friends are,' Del grumbled. 'What's going on with Lucas?' He got the fly buttoned finally and they started up the stairs toward Lucas' new first-floor office.

'Fat cat got killed,' Sloan said. 'Dan Kresge, from over at Polaris Bank.'

'Never heard of him.'

'You heard of Polaris Bank?'

'Yeah. That's the big black-glass one.'

'He runs it. Or did, until somebody shot his ass up in Garfield County. The sheriff called Rose Marie, who called Lucas, and Lucas called me to ride along.'

'Just friends, or overtime?'

'I'm putting in for it,' Sloan said comfortably. He had a daughter in college; nothing was ever said, but Davenport had been arranging easy overtime to him. 'Great day for it – though the colors are mostly gone. From the trees, I mean.'

'Fuck trees. Kresge . . . it's a murder?'

'Don't know yet,' Sloan said. 'This is opening day of deer season. He was shot out of a tree stand.'

'If I was gonna kill somebody, I might do it that way,' Del said.

'Yeah. Everybody says that.' Davenport's office was empty, but unlocked. 'Rose Marie's in,' Sloan said, as they went inside. 'Lucas said if he wasn't here, just wait.'

As Lucas stood up to leave, he asked Rose Marie Roux, the chief of police, why she didn't do something simple, like use the Patch.

''Cause I'd have to put patches all over my body to get enough nicotine. I'd have to put them on the bottom of my feet.'

She was on Day Three, and was chewing her way through a pack of nicotine gum. Lucas picked up his jacket, grinned faintly and said, 'A little speed might help. You get the buzz, but not the nicotine.'

'Great idea, get me hooked on speed,' Roux said. ''Course, I'd probably lose weight. I'm gonna gain nine hundred pounds if I don't do something.' She leaned across her desk, a woman already too heavy, getting her taste buds back from Marlboro County. 'Listen, call me back and tell me as soon as you get there. And I want you to tell me it's an accident. I don't want to hear any murder bullshit.'

'I'll do what I can,' Lucas said. He stepped toward the door.

'Are you all right?' Roux asked.

'No.' He stopped and half-turned.

'I'm worried about you. You sit around with a cloud over your head.'

'I'm getting stuff done . . .'

'I'm not worried about that – I'm worried about you,' she said. 'I've had the problem – you know that. I've been through it three times, now, and doctors help. A lot.'

'I'm not sure it's coming back,' Lucas said. 'I haven't tipped over the edge yet. I can still . . . stop things.'

'All right,' Roux said, nodding skeptically. 'But if you need the name of a doc, mine's a good guy.'

'Thanks.' Lucas closed her office door as he left and turned down the hall, by himself, suddenly gone morose. He didn't like to think about the depression that hovered at the edge of his consciousness. The thing was like some kind of rodent, like a rat, nibbling on his brain.

He wouldn't go through it again. A doctor maybe; and

maybe not. But he wouldn't go through it again.

Del sat in one of Lucas' visitor's chairs, one foot on Lucas' desk, blew smoke at the ceiling and said, 'So what're you suggesting? We send him a fruitcake?'

Lucas' office smelled of new carpet and paint, and looked out on Fourth Street; a great fall day, crisp, blue skies, young blonde women with rosy cheeks and long fuzzy coats heading down the street with their boyfriends, toward the Metrodome and a University of Minnesota football game.

Sloan, who was sitting in Davenport's swivel chair, said, 'The guy's hurting. We could . . . I don't know. Go out with him. Keep him busy at night.'

Del groaned. 'Right. We get our wives, we go out to eat. We talk the same bullshit we talk at the office all day, because we can't talk about Weather. Then we finish eating and go home with our old ladies. He goes home and sits in the dark with his dick in his hand.'

'So what're you saying?' Sloan demanded.

'What I'm saying is that he's all alone, and that's the fuckin' problem . . .' Then Del lifted a finger to his lips and dropped his voice. 'He's coming.'

Lucas stepped into the office a moment later, with the feeling he'd entered a sudden silence. He'd felt that a lot, lately.

Lucas was a tall man, hard-faced, broad-shouldered, showing the remnants of a summer tan. A thin line of a scar dropped through one eyebrow onto a cheek, like a piece of fishing line. Another scar slashed across his throat, where a friend had done a tracheotomy with a jackknife.

His hair was dark, touched by the first few flecks of gray, and his eyes were an unexpectedly intense blue. He was wearing a black silk sweatshirt showing the collar of a French-blue shirt beneath it, jeans, and a .45 in an inside-the-pants rig. He carried a leather jacket.

He nodded at Del, and to Sloan said, 'Get out of my chair or I'll kill you.'

Sloan yawned, then eased out of the chair. 'You get your jeans dry-cleaned?' he asked.

'What?' Lucas looked down at his jeans.

'They look so crisp,' Sloan said. 'They almost got a crease. When I wear jeans, I look like I'm gonna paint something.'

'When you wear a tuxedo, you look like you're gonna paint something,' Del said.

'Mr Fashion Plate speaking,' Sloan said.

Del was already wearing his winter parka, olive drab with an East German army patch on one shoulder, an Eat More Muffin sweatshirt, fire-engine-red sneaks with holes over the joints of his big toes, through which were visible thin black dress socks – Del had bunion problems – and the oversized Calvin Kleins. 'Fuck you,' he said.

'So what's happening?' Lucas asked, looking at Del. He circled behind the desk and dropped into the chair vacated by Sloan. He turned a yellow legal pad around, glanced at it, ripped off the top sheet and wadded the paper in his fist.

'We're trying to figure how to snap you out of it,' Del said bluntly.

Lucas looked up, then shrugged. 'Nothing to do.'

'Weather's coming back,' Sloan said. 'She's got too much sense to stay away.'

Lucas shook his head. 'She's not coming back, and it doesn't have anything to do with good sense.'

'You guys are so fucked,' Del said.

'You say "fuck" way too much,' Sloan said.

'Hey, fuck you, pal,' Del said; joking, but with an edge in his voice.

Lucas cut it off: 'Ready to go, Sloan?'

Sloan nodded. 'Yeah.'

Lucas looked at Del: 'What're you doing here?'

'Seeking guidance from my superiors,' Del said. 'I've got an opium ring with fifty-seven members spread all over Minneapolis and the western suburbs, especially the rich ones like Edina and Wayzata. One or two in St Paul. Grow the stuff right here. Process it. Use it themselves – maybe sell a little.'

Lucas frowned. 'How solid?'

'Absolutely solid.'

'So tell me.' Lucas poked a finger at Del. 'Wait a minute . . . you're not telling me that fuckin' Genesse is back? I thought he was gone for fifteen.'

Del was shaking his head. 'Nah.'

'So . . .'

'It's fifty-seven old ladies in the Mountbatten Garden Club,' Del said. 'I got the club list.'

Sloan and Lucas looked at each other, then Sloan said, 'What?'

And Lucas asked, 'Where'd you get the list?'

'From an old lady,' Del said. 'There being nothing but old ladies in the club.'

'What the hell are you talking about?' Lucas asked.

'When I went over to Hennepin to get my finger sewed up after the pinking shears thing, this doc told me he'd treated this old lady junkie. She was coming down from the opium, but she thought she had the flu or something. It turns out they've been growing poppies for years. The whole club. They collect the heads at the end of the summer and make tea. Opium tea. A bunch of them are fairly well hooked, brewing up three or four times a day.'

Lucas rubbed his forehead. 'Del . . .'

'What?' Del looked at Sloan, defensively. 'What? Should I ignore it?'

'I don't know,' Lucas said. 'Where're they getting the seeds?'

'Seed stores,' Del said.

'Bullshit,' Lucas said. 'You can't buy opium seeds from seed stores.'

'I did,' Del said. He dug in his parka pocket, pulled out a half dozen seed packets. Lucas, no gardener, recognized the brand names and the envelopes.

'That's not . . .'

'Yes, it is. They got fancy names, but I talked to a guy at the University, and brother . . .' He tossed them on Lucas' desk. '. . .them's opium poppies.'

'Aw, man.' Now Lucas was rubbing his face. Tired. Always tired now.

'The hell with the old ladies,' Sloan said. 'Let's get out of here.'

'I'll talk to you later,' Lucas said to Del. 'In the meantime, find something dangerous to do, for Christ's sakes.'

Lucas and Sloan took Lucas' new Chevy Tahoe: Kresge's body, they'd been told, was off-road.

'I'm not gonna push you about being fucked up,' Sloan said. 'Just let me know if there's anything I can do.'

'Yeah, I will,' Lucas said.

'And you oughta think about medication . . .'

'Yeah, yeah, yeah . . .'

'Is . . . How's Weather?'

'Still in therapy. She's better without me, and gets worse when I'm around. And she's making more friends that I'm cut off from. She's putting together a new life and I'm out of it,' Lucas said.

'Christ.'

'When she moved out,' Lucas said, 'she left her dress in the closet. The green one, three thousand bucks. The wedding dress.'

'Maybe it means she's coming back.'

'I don't think so. I think she abandoned it.'

Much of the trip north was made in gloomy silence, through the remnants of the autumn's glorious color change; but the end was coming, the dead season.

Jacob Krause, the Garfield County sheriff, was squatting next to the body, talking to an assistant medical examiner when he saw Lucas and Sloan walking down the ridge toward them. They were accompanied by a fat man in a blaze-orange hunting coat and a uniformed deputy leading a German shepherd. The deputy pointed at Krause, and turned and went back toward the house

'Is this him?' Krause asked.

The AME turned his head and said, 'Yeah. Davenport's the big guy. The guy in the tan coat is Sloan, he's one of the heavyweights in homicide. I don't know the fat guy.'

'He's one of ours,' the sheriff said. He had the mournful face of a blue-eyed bloodhound, and had a small brown mole, a beauty mark, on the right end of his upper lip. He sighed and added, 'Unfortunately.'

A few feet away, two crime-scene guys were packing up a case of lab samples; up the hill, two funeral home assistants waited with a gurney. The body would be taken to Hennepin County for autopsy. Krause looked a last time at Kresge's paper-white face, then stood up and headed back up the path. He took it slowly, watching as Davenport and Sloan and the fat man dropped down the trail like Holmes and Watson on a Sunday stroll with Oliver Hardy. When they got closer, Krause noticed that Davenport was wearing loafers with tassels, that his socks were a black-and-white diamond pattern, and that the loafers matched his leather jacket. He sighed again, the quick judgment adding to his general irritation.

'Hello. I'm Lucas Davenport . . .' Lucas stuck out his hand and the sheriff took it, a little surprised at the heft and hardness of it; and the sadness in Davenport's eyes. 'And detective Sloan,' the sheriff finished, shaking hands with Sloan. 'I'm Jake Krause, the sheriff.' He looked past them at the fat man. 'I see you've met Arne.'

'Back by the cars,' the fat man said. 'What do we got, Jake?'

'Crime scene, Arne. I'd just as soon you don't come up too close. We're trying to minimize the damage to the immediate area.'

'Okay,' the fat man said. He craned his neck a little, down toward the orange-clad body, the AME hovering over it, the crime-scene boys with their case.

'Accident?' Lucas asked.

Krause shrugged. 'C'mon and take a look, give me an opinion. Arne, you better wait.'

'Sure thing . . .'

On the way down to the body, Lucas asked, 'Arne's a problem?'

'He's the county commission chairman. He got the job because nobody trusted him to actually supervise a department or the budget,' Krause said. 'He's also a reserve deputy. He's not a bad guy, just a pain in the ass. And he likes hanging around dead people.'

'I know guys like that,' Lucas said. He looked up at the tree stand as they approached the body and asked, 'Kresge was shot out of the stand?'

'Yup. The bullet took him square in the heart,' Krause

20

said. 'I doubt he lived for ten seconds.'

'Any chance of finding the slug?' Sloan asked.

'Nah. It's out in the swamp somewhere. It's gone.'

'But you think he was shot out of the tree stand,' Sloan said.

'For sure,' Krause said. 'There's some blood splatter on the guard rail and threads from his coveralls are hanging from the edge of the floor boards up there – no way they should be there unless they snagged when he fell over the edge.'

Lucas stepped over next to the body, which lay face up a foot-and-a-half from a pad of blood-soaked oak leaves. Kresge didn't look surprised or sad or any of the other things he might have looked like. He looked dead, like a wadded-up piece of waste paper. 'Who moved him?'

'The first time, other members of the hunting party. They opened up his coat to listen to his heart, wanted to make sure he wasn't still alive. He wasn't. Then me and the doc here . . .' Krause nodded at the AME, '. . . rolled him up to look at the exit wound.'

Lucas nodded to the assistant medical examiner, said, 'Hey, Dick, I heard you guys were coming up,' and the AME said, 'Yup,' and Lucas said, 'Roll him up on his side, will you?'

'Sure.'

The AME grabbed Kresge's coat and rolled him up. Lucas and Sloan looked at the back, where a narrow hole – a moth might have made it – was surrounded by a hand-sized blood stain just above the shoulder blade. Lucas said, 'Huh,' and he and Sloan moved left to look at the entry, then back at the exit. They both turned at the same time to look at the slope, then at each other, and Lucas said, 'Okay,' and the AME let the body drop back into place.

Lucas stood and brushed his hands together and grinned at the sheriff. The grin was so cold that the sheriff revised his earlier, quick, judgment. 'Good one,' Lucas said.

'What do you think?' Krause asked.

'The shooter got close,' Lucas said.

'You wouldn't get that angle through the body, upward like that, unless the shooter was below him,' Sloan explained. 'And if the shooter's below him . . .' They all looked back up the slope. '. . . he couldn't have been more than thirty or forty yards away. Of course, we don't know how Kresge was sitting. He could have been looking out sideways. Or he could have been leaning back when the slug hit.'

Krause said, 'I don't think so.'

'I don't either,' Lucas said.

'So it's a murder,' Krause said. He shook his head and looked from the body to Lucas. 'I wish you'd keep this shit down in the Cities.'

'Mind if I check the tree?' Lucas asked the crime-scene cops.

One of them said, 'We're done, if it's okay with the sheriff.'

'Go ahead,' Krause said.

Lucas began climbing the spikes, looked down just as he reached the platform and asked, 'What about motive?'

Krause nodded. 'I asked those people down at the cabin about that. Instead of a name, I got an estimate. Fifteen hundred, maybe two thousand people.'

Sloan said, 'Yeah?'

'There's this merger going on . . .'

Lucas listened to Krause's explanation of the merger as he carefully probed the backpack hung on the tree. He remembered seeing bank-merger stories in the *Star-Tribune*. He hadn't paid much attention – more corporate jive, as far as he could tell.

'Anyway, he was up here hunting with a bunch of big-shots from the bank,' Krause said, unwinding his story. 'Some of them, maybe all of them, are set to lose their big-shot jobs.'

'Those are the people we saw down at the cabin?' Lucas asked. He'd finished with the backpack, left it hanging where he found it, and dropped back down the tree.

'Yeah,' Krause said sourly. 'They filled me in on the merger business.'

'Shooting him seems a little extreme,' Sloan said.

'Why?' Krause asked. The question was genuine, and Sloan glanced at Lucas and then looked back at the sheriff, who said, 'Close as I can tell, he was about to mess up the lives of hundreds of people. Some of them – hell, maybe most of them – will never get as good a job again, ever in their lives. And he was doing it just so he could make more money than he already had, and he had a pile of it. Shooting him seems pretty rational to me. Long as you didn't get caught.'

'I wouldn't express that opinion to the press,' Lucas said mildly. He went back to the body, knelt on one knee and began going through Kresge's pockets.

'I never say anything to the press that I haven't run past my old lady,' Krause grunted, as he watched. 'She hasn't turned me wrong yet.' A second later, he added, 'There is one other possibility. For the shooting. His wife. He's right in the middle of a divorce.'

'That could be something,' Lucas agreed. He squeezed both of Kresge's hands through their gloves, then stood up and rubbed his hands together.

'These folks at the cabin said the divorce is signed, sealed and delivered, that the wife really took a chunk out of his ass.'

'Makes it sound less likely,' Sloan said.

'Yeah, unless she hates him,' Lucas said. 'Which she might.'

Sloan opened his mouth to say something, then shut it,

thinking suddenly of Weather. Krause asked, 'Find anything new in the backpack?'

'Couple of Snickers, couple packs of peanut M&M's, half-dozen hand-heater packs.'

'Same thing I found,' Krause said.

'Do you deer hunt, sheriff?' Lucas asked.

'Nope. I'm a fisherman. I was gonna close out the muskie season this afternoon, beat the ice up. I was loading my truck when they called me. Why?'

'It gets as cold on a tree stand as it does on a November day out muskie fishing,' Lucas said.

'Colder'n hell,' Krause said.

'That's right. But he hadn't eaten anything and hadn't used any heat packs, even though he brought them along and must've intended to use them,' Lucas said. 'So he was probaby shot pretty soon after he got to the stand.'

'Did anyone hear any early shots?' Sloan asked.

'I asked the other people about unusual shots, but nobody said anything was out of order. Bone said he thought either Kresge or one of the other guys, a guy named Robles, had fired a shot just after the opening. But Robles said he didn't, and his rifle is clean, and so's Kresge's.'

'How long had they been sitting?'

'About forty-five minutes.'

Lucas nodded: 'Then that was probably the killing shot. He'd still have been pretty warm up to that point.'

They talked for a few more minutes, then left the AME with the body and headed back through the woods toward the cabin. As they passed the mortuary attendants, now sitting on the gurney, Krause said, 'He's all yours, boys.'

'Been a nice month, up to now,' the sheriff said, rambling a bit. 'No killings, no rapes, no robberies, only a half-dozen domestics, a few drunk-driving accidents and a couple of small-time burglaries. This sort of blots the record.'

Lucas said, 'The killer had to find the place in the dark – so he had to know where it was, exactly.'

'Unless he came after daylight,' Krause said. 'That's possible.'

'Yeah, but when we were coming in, your deputy – the one with the dog? – pointed out where this Robles guy was sitting, and generally where the other people were. So the killer would have to take a chance on being seen, unless he really knew the layout.'

'And if he knew all that, he'd probably be recognized by the others,' Sloan said. 'Which means he probably came in when it was dark.'

'Unless he's one of these guys,' Krause said. 'These guys would have all the information, plus an excuse for walking around with guns ... and they'd know that nobody would come looking at the sound of a shot.'

'It could be one of these guys,' Lucas said. 'But it'd take guts.'

'Or a crazy man,' Sloan said.

At the end of the track they could see a half-dozen people sitting and standing on the cabin porch, a man in a red-plaid shirt talking animatedly to the others. A short man in a blue suit sat apart from them.

'What's the situation with these people?' Lucas asked, as they started down the slope toward the cabin. 'Who questioned them?'

'I did, and one of our investigators, Ralph – that's Ralph in the blue suit.'

'Is he good?' Lucas asked.

The sheriff thought for a minute and then said, 'Ralph couldn't pour piss out of a boot with the instructions written on the heel.'

Sloan asked, 'So how come . . . ?'

'I try to keep him out of the way, but he was at the office and answered the phone this morning.'

'Did he collect all the guns?' Lucas asked.

'No, but I did,' Krause said. 'Two of them had been fired – both people had deer to show for it. The others look clean.'

'I saw the deer hanging down by the cabin . . .' Lucas said. Then: 'Get your crime-scene guys to check their hands and faces for powder traces. And count shells – find out what they claim to have fired, and do a count.'

'I'm doing all that, except for the shells,' Krause said. He looked up at Lucas. 'I'm going by the book. The whole book. My problem is more along the lines of interrogation and so on. Expertise.'

Lucas tipped his head at Sloan: 'Sloan is the best interrogator in the state.'

Sloan grinned at the sheriff and said, 'That's true.'

'Then we'd like to borrow you for a while,' Krause said. 'If you got the time.'

'Fine with me,' Sloan said. 'Overtime is overtime.'

'Is there any possibility that you could do some running around Minneapolis for me?' Krause asked.

Sloan looked at Lucas. 'I've got a couple of things going . . . Sherrill is doing research on that Shack thing, but she's not getting much. Maybe she could do some running around.'

Lucas nodded. 'I'll call her this afternoon, on my way back. Anything you break out of these guys, call it down to her. I'll have her talk to Kresge's wife, check for girlfriends . . .'

'Or boyfriends,' Sloan said.

'Or boyfriends. And I'll have her start talking to people in his office – secretaries and so on.' Lucas looked at Krause. 'I don't want to take over your investigation . . .'

'No, no, no, don't worry about that,' Krause said hastily. 'The more you can do, the better. My best guys are busier'n two-dick dogs in a breeding kennel . . . And my other guys would have a hard time finding Minneapolis, much less anybody in it.'

'Sounds like you have some problems,' Sloan said. 'First Arne, then Ralph . . .'

'We're going through a transitional period,' Krause said grimly. Then: 'Look, I'm the new guy up here. I was with the highway patrol for twenty-five years, and then last fall I got myself elected sheriff. The office is about fifty years out of date, full of deadwood, and all the deadwood is related to somebody. I'm cutting it down, but it takes time. I'll take any help I can get.'

'Whatever we can do,' Lucas said.

Krause nodded. 'Thanks.' He'd been prepared to dislike the Minneapolis guys, but it hadn't turned out that way. Actually, he sort of liked them, for city people. Sloan, especially, but even Davenport, with his shoe tassels and expensive clothes. He glanced at Davenport again, quickly. From a little bit of a distance you might think *pussy*. You didn't think that when you got closer to him. Not after you'd seen his smile.

He added, 'I don't think I'm gonna get too far up here. Matter of fact, I don't think I'm going to get anywhere – everything about this shooting was set up in the Cities.'

They were coming up to the porch, and Sloan said, quietly, 'So let's go jack up these city folks. See if anybody gets nervous.'

Chapter Three

The four surviving hunters sat on the porch in the afternoon sunlight, in rustic wooden chairs with peeling bark and waterproof-plastic seat cushions. They all had cups of microwaved coffee: Wilson McDonald's was fortified with two ounces of brandy. James T. Bone sat politely downwind of the others, smoking a cheroot.

The sheriff's investigator perched on a stool at the other end of the porch, like the class dummy, looking away from them. If one of the bankers suddenly broke for the woods, what was he supposed to do? Shoot him? But the sheriff had told him to keep an eye on them. What'd that mean?

And the bankers were annoyed, and their annoyance was not something his worn nerves could deal with. He could handle trailer-home fights and farm kids hustling toot, but people who'd gone to Harvard, who drove Lincoln and Lexus sport-utes and wore $800 après-hunt tweed jackets, undoubtedly woven by licensed leprechauns in the Auld Country – well, they made him nervous. Especially when one of them might be a killer.

'Davenport is the bad dog,' Bone said from downwind, as they watched Krause lead his parade down through the woods toward the cabin. He bit off a sixteenth-inch of the cheroot and spit it out into the fescue at the bottom of the porch. 'He oughta be able to tell us something.'

'Mean sonofabitch, by reputation,' O'Dell said. She said it casually, looking through the steam of the coffee. She wasn't impressed. She was surrounded by mean sonsofbitches. She might even be one herself.

'Just another cop,' Robles stuttered. Robles was scared: they could smell it on him. They liked it. Robles was the macho killer, and his fear was oddly pleasing.

'I talked to him a couple of times on the transfers with his IPO – you all know he used to be Davenport Simulations?' Bone said. They all nodded; that was the kind of thing they all knew. 'He sold the company to management and walked with better'n ten, A-T.' He meant ten million dollars, after taxes.

'So why doesn't he quit and move to Palm Springs?' Robles asked.

''Cause he likes what he does,' Bone said.

'I wish he'd get his bureaucratic ass down here and do what we have to do; I wanna get back to town,' McDonald grumbled. Back to a nice smooth single-malt; but he'd stay here as long as the others did. Sooner or later, they'd start talking about who'd be running the bank. 'No point in keeping us here. We've told them everything we know.'

'Unless one of us killed him,' Bone said lazily.

'Gotta be an accident,' Robles said, nervously. 'Opening day of deer season . . . I bet there're twenty of them. Accidents.'

'No, there aren't,' Bone said. 'There are usually one or two, and most of the time, they know on the spot who did the shooting.'

'Besides, it wasn't an accident,' O'Dell said positively.

'How do you know?' McDonald asked. He finished the loaded coffee and rubbed his mouth with the back of his hand. He could use another.

'Maybe she did it,' Robles said. He tried to laugh, but instead made a small squeaking noise, a titter.

O'Dell ignored him. 'Karma's wrong for an accident,' she said.

'Great: we're talking karma,' McDonald said. 'Superstitious hippie nonsense.'

Bone slumped a little lower in his chair and a thin grin slipped across his dry face: 'But she's right,' he said. 'Dan was a half-mile onto his own property. Who's going to shoot him through the heart from more'n half a mile away? Nope. I figure it was one of us. We all had guns and good reasons.'

'Bullshit,' McDonald said.

As they watched the parade approaching, O'Dell said, 'We should decide who'll speak for the bank. The board'll have to appoint a CEO, but somebody should take over for the moment. Somebody in top-management.'

'I thought Wilson might do it – until a decision is made on a CEO,' Bone said. He looked over at Wilson McDonald, whose eyes went flat, hiding any reaction; and past him at O'Dell. The top job, Bone thought, would go either to himself or O'Dell, unless the board did something weird. Robles didn't have the background, McDonald wasn't smart or skilled enough. 'If you think so,' McDonald said carefully. This was the moment he'd been waiting for.

O'Dell had done her calculations as well as Bone, and she nodded. 'Then you've got it,' she said. She put her battered hunting boots up on the porch railing, and looked past McDonald at Bone: 'Until the police figure out if one of us did it. And the board has a chance to meet.'

After a moment's silence, Robles said, 'My gun wasn't fired.'

Bone rolled his eyes up to the heavens. 'I'll tell you what, Terry. It would take me about three seconds to figure a way to kill Kresge and walk out of the woods with a clean weapon.' He took a final drag on the cheroot, dropped the stub end on the porch, ground it out with his boot, and flipped it out into the yard with his toe. 'No sir: I figure a fired weapon is purely proof of innocence.'

He was breaking Robles' balls. Bone and O'Dell had the two dirty rifles, while McDonald and Robles were clean. Usually, Bone wouldn't have bothered: Robles wasn't much sport. But Bone was in a mood. Davenport and the others were dropping the last few yards down the trail to the clearing around the house and Bone muttered to the others, 'Bad dog.'

Lucas led the parade up the porch steps, with Krause and Sloan just behind, and the four bankers all stood up to meet them. Lucas recognized Bone and nodded: 'Mr Bone,' he said. 'Did Sally get the Spanish credit?'

Bone's forehead wrinkled for a second, then he remembered, and nodded, smiling: 'Sure did. She graduated in June . . . Are you running things here?'

'No, I was just about to leave, in fact. Sheriff Krause runs things up here. We'll be cooperating down in Minneapolis, if he needs the backup.'

'So why did you come up?' O'Dell asked. She put a little wood-rasp in her voice, a little annoyance, so he'd understand her status here.

Lucas grinned at her, mild-voiced and friendly: 'Mr Kresge carried a lot of clout in Minneapolis, so it's possible the motive for the shooting will be found there. Quite possibly with the bank, from what I hear about this merger. Detective Sloan . . .' Lucas looked at Sloan, who raised a hand in greeting, '. . . has been assigned to help Sheriff Krause with his interviews, so we can get you folks on your way home.'

'Are you s-s-sure it wasn't an accident?' Robles stuttered.

Lucas shook his head and Krause said, 'He was murdered.'

'So that's it,' O'Dell said, and the bankers all looked at each other for a moment, and then Bone broke the silence: 'Damn it. That'll tangle things up.'

McDonald, ignoring Krause, asked Lucas, 'Do you think . . . one of us . . . ?'

Lucas looked at Krause. 'We have no reason to think so, in particular. Since we know you were here, we've got to talk to you,' Krause said. 'But we've got no suspects.'

Sloan suggested that he would prefer to talk to the four of them individually, inside, while the others waited on the porch. 'Nice day, anyway,' he said, pleasantly. 'And it shouldn't take long.'

'Let me go first,' McDonald grunted, pushing up from his chair. 'I want to get back and start talking to the PR people. We'll need a press-release A-S-A-P. God, what a disaster.'

'Fine,' Sloan said. He turned to Lucas. 'You gonna take off?'

'Yeah. The sheriff'll send you back with a deputy.'

'See you later, then,' Sloan said. 'Mr McDonald?'

McDonald followed Sloan and Krause into the cabin. When they'd gone, Bone said to Lucas, 'I'd feel better about this if you were running things.'

'Krause is a pretty sharp cookie, I think,' Lucas said. 'He'll take care of it.'

'Still, it's not something where you want a mistake made,' Bone said. 'A murder, I mean when – you're a suspect, but you're innocent.'

'I appreciate that,' Lucas said. He glanced at the other two, then took a card case from his jacket pocket, extracted four business cards and passed them around. 'If any of you need any information about the course of the investigation, or need any help at all, call me directly, any time, night or day. There's a home phone listed as well as my office phone. Ms O'Dell, if you could give one to Mr McDonald.'

'Very nice of you,' O'Dell said, looking at the cards. 'We just want to get this over with.'

'You shot one of the deer, didn't you?' Lucas asked her. The two gutted deer were hanging head-down from the cabin's deer pole in the side yard.

'The bigger of the two,' she said.

'I like mine tender,' Bone said drily. 'Always go for a doe.'

'Good shot,' Lucas said to O'Dell. 'Broke his shoulder, wiped out his heart; I bet he didn't go ten feet from where you shot him.'

She didn't feel any insinuation; he was just being polite. 'Do you hunt?' she asked.

He smiled and nodded: 'Quite a bit.'

When Lucas had gone, O'Dell said to Bone, 'That's not a bad dog. That's a pussy cat.'

Bone took another cheroot out of his jacket pocket, along with a kitchen match, which he scratch-lit on the porch railing; an affectation he acknowledged and enjoyed. 'He's Hied four or five guys, I think, in the line of duty. He built a software company from nothing to a ten million A-T buyout in about six years. In his spare time. And I'll tell you something else . . .'

He took a long drag on the cheroot, and blew a thin stream of smoke out into the warming afternoon air, irritating O'Dell. 'What?'

Bone said, 'When we did the transfers on the IPO, I talked to him for ten minutes. While we were doing it, my daughter called on my private line, from school. All upset. She was having a problem with a language credit, and she was afraid they'd hold up her graduation. I mentioned it to him, in passing – just explaining the phone call. This was seven months ago. He remembered me, he remembered Sally's name and he remembered the language she was taking.'

Bone looked at O'Dell. 'You can take him as lightly, if you

want. I wouldn't. Especially if you pulled the trigger twice this morning.'

'Don't be absurd,' she said. But she looked after Lucas, down by the parking area, just getting into his truck. 'Nice shoulders,' she said, thinking the comment would irritate just about everybody on the porch.

The truck was very quiet without Sloan: Lucas didn't need the quiet – in the quiet, his mind would begin to churn, and that would lead . . .

He wasn't sure where it would lead.

He was tired, but he needed to be more tired. He needed to be so tired that when he got back home, he could lie down and sleep before the churning began. He put a tape in the tape player, ZZ Top, the greatest hits album, and turned it up. Interference. Can't churn when there's too much interference.

The killing at the hunting camp was not particularly interesting: one possible motive, the bank merger, was already fairly clear. Others of a more personal nature might pop up later – Kresge was in the process of getting a divorce, so there might be other women. Or his wife might have something to do with it.

Routine investigation would dredge it all up, and the killer would either be caught or he wouldn't. Whichever, Lucas felt fairly distant from the process. He'd been through it dozens of times, and the routine greed, love and stupidity killings no longer held much interest.

Evil was interesting, he would still admit; this a residue from his term in Catholic schools. But so far he detected no evil in the killing. Spite, probably; stupidity, possibly. Greed. Anger. But not real evil.

He rode mindlessly for a while, the winter fields and woods rolling by, holsteins out catching a few uncommon November rays, horses dancing through hillside pastures; a few thousand doomed turkeys ... Then he glanced out the side window, caught the almond-shaped boles on an oak, recognized them, shivered. Turned up the tape.

He'd been dreaming again, lately; he hated the dreams, because they woke him up, and when he woke, in the night, his mind would begin running. And the dreams always woke him ...

One dream had an odd quality of science fiction. He was being lowered, on some kind of platform, into a huge steel cylinder. Nearby was a steel cap, two feet thick, with enormous threads, which would be screwed into place after he was inside, sealing him in. The process was industrial: there were other people running around, making preparations for whatever was about to happen. He was cooperating with them, standing on the platform obviously expectant. But for what? Why was he about to be sealed inside the cylinder? He didn't know, but he wasn't frightened by the prospect. He was engaged by it, though. He'd start thinking about it, and then he'd wake up, his mind churning ...

The other dream was stranger.

A man's face, seen from a passing car. There were small beads of rain on the window glass, so the view was slightly obscured; in his dream, Lucas could not quite get a fix on the face. The man was hard, slender, wore an ankle-length black coat and a snap brim hat. Most curious were the almond-shaped eyes, but where the surfaces of his eyes should be – the pupils and irises – there were instead two curls of light maple-colored wood shavings. The man seemed to be hunched against a wind, and the drizzle; he seemed to be cold. And he looked at Lucas under the brim of the hat, with those eyes that had curls of wood on their surfaces.

Lucas had begun to see the almond shapes around him on

the street. See them on the faces of distant men, or in random markings on buildings, or on trees. Nonsense: but this dream frightened him. He would wake with a start, sweat around the neckline of his t-shirt. And then his mind would start to run . . .

He turned up the ZZ Top yet another notch, and raced toward the Cities, looking for exhaustion.

An hour after Lucas had passed that way, James T. Bone hurtled down I-35 in a large black BMW. As he crossed the I-694 beltline he picked up the cell phone and pushed the speed-dial number. The other phone rang three times before a woman answered it, her voice carrying a slight whiskey burr. 'Hello?'

'This is Bone. Where are you?'

'In my car. On my way back from Southdale.'

'I'm coming over,' he said. 'Twenty minutes.'

'Okay . . . you can't stay long. George is . . .'

'Twenty minutes,' Bone said, and punched off. He pushed another speed-dial button, and another woman answered, this voice younger and crisper: 'Karin.'

'This is Bone. Where are you?'

'At home.'

'Dan Kresge's been killed. Shot, probably murdered. Had you heard yet?'

'No. My God . . .'

'I'll be at the office in an hour, or a little more. If you have the time . . .'

'I'll be there in ten minutes. Can I get anything started before you get there?'

'Names and phone numbers of all the board members . . .'

They talked for five minutes, then Bone punched out again.

A three-car fender-bender slowed him a bit, but he pulled into the downtown parking garage a little less than a half hour after he made the first call. He'd gotten out of his hunting clothes, and was wearing a Patagonia jacket with khakis and a flannel shirt. He pulled the jacket off as he rode up in the elevator.

Marcia Kresge met him at the door in a blue silk kimono. 'You like it? I bought it a hour ago.'

'I hope you're not celebrating,' he said.

He said it with an intensity that stopped her: 'What happened?'

'Your soon-to-be ex-husband was shot to death up at the cabin this morning. I'm undoubtedly one of the suspects.'

Kresge looked mildly shocked for a quarter-second, then slipped a tiny smile: 'So the fucker's dead?'

'I hope to Christ you didn't have anything to do with it.'

'Moi?' she asked mockingly, one hand going to her breast.

'Yeah, Marcia, you're really cute; I hope you're not that cute when the cops show up.'

'The cops?' Finally serious.

'Marcia, sit down,' Bone said. Kresge dropped onto a couch, showing a lot of leg. Bone looked at it for a moment, then said, 'Listen, I know you think you fucked over Dan pretty thoroughly. You're wrong. Last week the board granted him another 250,000 options to buy our stock at forty, as a performance award. If the merger goes through, and it's botched, the stock'll be worth sixty in a year. If the merger is done exactly right, it could be at eighty in a year. That's ten million dollars, and if it's held for a year, you'll take out eight after taxes.'

'Me? I . . .'

'Marcia, shut up for a minute. The options have value. They become part of his estate. You'll inherit. You'll also get the rest of his estate, that you didn't get in the divorce. No taxes at all on that. In other words, Dan gets murdered, you get ten million. I'm up there with a gun, and guess who's fucking Marcia Kresge?'

'Jesus,' she said.

'I seriously doubt that he's involved.'

'But they can't think I . . . ?'

'You didn't, did you? You know all those crazy nightclub characters . . .'

'Bone: I had not a goddamned thing to do with it. I really *did* think I'd taken him to the cleaners . . . and I mean, I didn't like him, but I wouldn't kill him.'

He knew her well enough to know she wasn't lying. He exhaled, said, 'Good.'

'You honest-to-God thought . . .'

'No. I didn't think you went out and hired some asshole to kill him,' Bone said. 'What I was afraid of, is, you'd mentioned to one of your little broken-nosed pals that if Dan died, you'd get another whole load of cash.'

'Well, I didn't,' she said. 'Because I didn't know that I would.'

'Okay . . . I don't think it would be necessary to mention to the police that we've been involved,' he said drily.

'Good thought,' she said, matching his tone precisely.

'All right,' he said. He stood up and started toward the door. 'I've got to get down to the bank.'

'The bank? God, when you called, I thought maybe . . .' She'd gotten up and come around the couch.

'What?' He knew what.

'You know.' She slipped the belt of the kimono; she was absolutely bare and pink beneath it. 'I just got out of the shower.'

'I thought George was coming over.'

'Well, not for a couple of hours . . . and you gotta at least tell me what happened.'

'Take off the kimono.'

She took it off, tossed it on the couch. He was staring at her, like he always did, with an attention that both disturbed and excited her.

'What?' She unconsciously touched one arm to her breast bone, covering her right breast as she did it. Bone reached out and pushed her arm down.

'Put your hands behind you,' he said. 'I want to look at you while I tell you this.'

She blushed, the blush reaching almost to her waist. She bit her lower lip again, but put her hands behind her back.

'We started out like we always do, walking back into the woods. You know how that trail goes back around the lake . . .'

As he told the story, he began to stroke her, his voice never faltering or showing emotion; but his hands always moving slowly. After a moment she slowly backed away, and he stepped after her, still talking. When her bottom touched the edge of a couch table, she braced herself against it, closed her eyes.

'Are you listening?' he asked; his hands stopped momentarily.

'Of course,' she said. 'A few minutes before six and the shooting started.'

'That's right,' he said. He pushed her back more solidly into the couch table and said, 'Spread your legs a little.'

She spread her legs a little.

'A little more.'

She spread them a little more.

'Anyway,' he said, gently parting her with his fingertips. 'Any one of us could have killed him. It was just a matter of climbing down from the tree, sneaking back up the path . . .'

'Did you do it?' she asked.

'What do you think?'

'You could have,' she said. And then she said, 'Oh, God.'

'Feel good?'

'Feels good.'

'Look at me . . .'

She opened her eyes, but they were hazy, a dreamer's eyes, looking right through him. 'Don't stop now,' she said.

'Look at me . . .'

She looked at him, struggled to focus on his dark, cool face. 'Did you kill him?'

'Does the thought turn you on?'

'Oh, God . . .'

Susan O'Dell's apartment was a study in black and white, glass and wood, and when she walked in, was utterly silent. She pulled off her jacket, let it fall to the floor, then her shirt and her turtle-necked underwear, and her bra. The striptease continued back through the apartment, through her bedroom to the bathroom, where she went straight into the shower. She stood in the hot water for five minutes, letting it pour around her face. When she'd cleaned off the day, she stepped out, got a bath towel from a towel rack, dried herself, dropped the towel on the floor, and walked back to the bedroom. Underpants and gray sweatsuit.

Dressed again, warm, she walked back the apartment to the study, stood on her tiptoes, and took a deck of cards off the top of the single bookshelf.

Sitting at her desk, she spread the cards, studied them.

She'd once had an affair, brief but intense, with an artist, who'd taught her what he called Tarot for Scientists. A truly strange tarot method: business management through chaos theory, and he really knew about chaos. An odd thing for an artist to know, she'd thought at the time. She'd even become suspicious of him, and had done some checking. But he was a legitimate painter, all right. A gorgeous watercolor nude, which nobody but she knew was O'Dell herself, hung in her bedroom, a souvenir of their relationship.

When she realized the value of the artist's tarot method, he'd bought her a computer version so she could install it on her computer at work – the cards themselves were a little too strange, and a little too public, for a big bank. They'd done the installation on a cold, rainy night, and afterwards had made love on the floor behind her desk. The artist had been comically inept with the computer. He'd nearly brought down the bank network, and would have, if she hadn't been there to save him. But she could now access electronic cards at any time, protected with her own private code word.

Still. When she could, she preferred the cards themselves: the cool, collected flap of pasteboard against walnut. Hippie-like, she thought. McDonald referred to her as a hippie, but she was hardly that. She simply had little time for makeup, for indulgent fashion, or for the flattering of men – all the things that Wilson McDonald expected from a woman. At the same time, she obviously enjoyed the company of men, and her relationship with the artist and a couple of other men-about-town had become known at the bank. And she was smart.

As McDonald had thumbed through his box of mental labels, he'd been forced to discard *housewife* and *helpmeet, lesbo* and *bimbo.* When word had inevitably got around about the tarot, McDonald had relaxed and stuck the *hippie* label on her. The label might not explain the hunting, or the manner in which she'd cut her way to the top at the bank . . . but it was good enough for him.

Fuckin' moron.

O'Dell laid out the Celtic Cross: and got a jolt when the result card came up: The Tower of Destruction.

She pursed her lips. *Yes*.

She stood up, cast a backward glance at the spread of cards, the lightning bolt striking the tower, the man falling to his death: rather like Kresge, she thought, coming out of the tree stand. In fact, exactly so . . .

She shivered, pulled a cased set of books out of the bookcase, removed a small plastic box, opened it. Inside were a dozen fatties. She took one out, with the lighter, went out to her balcony, closing the glass doors behind her. Cold. She lit the joint, let the grass wrap wreaths of ideas around her brain. Okay. Kresge was dead. She'd wanted him dead – gone, at any rate, dead if necessary, and lately, as the merger deal crept closer, dead looked like the only way out.

So she'd gotten what she wanted.

Now to capitalize.

Terrance Robles hovered over his computer, sweating. He typed:

'Switch to crypto.'

You're so paranoid, and crypto's boring.

'Switching to crypto . . .'

Once in the cryptography program, he typed:

'What have you done?'

'*Why?*'

Oh shit. 'Somebody shot Kresge today. I'm a suspect . . .'

'*My, my . . .*'

Even with the crypto delay, the response was fast. Too fast, and too cynically casual, he thought. More words trailed across the screen.

So, did you do it?

Robles pounded it out: 'Of course not.'

But you thought I did?

He hesitated, then typed, 'No.'

Don't lie to me T. You thought I did it.

'No I didn't but I wanted you to say it.'

I haven't exactly said it, have I?

'Come on . . .'

Come on what? The world's a better place with that fucking fascist out of it.

'You didn't do it.'

A long pause, so long that he thought she might have left him, then *Yes I did.*

'No you didn't . . .'

No reply. Nothing but the earlier words, half-scrolled up the screen.

'Come on . . .'

A label popped up: *The room is empty.*

'Bitch,' he groaned. He bit his thumbnail, chewing at it. What was he going to do?

Looking up at the screen, he saw the words,

Yes I did.

Marcia Kresge opened her apartment door and found two uniformed cops standing in the hallway.

'Yes?'

'Mrs Kresge?' The cops looked her over. Late thirties, early forties, they thought. Very nice-looking in a rich-bitch way. She was wearing a black fluffy dress that showed some skin, and was holding a lipstick in a gold tube. She had a lazy look about her, as though she'd just gotten out of bed, not alone.

'Yes?'

They kept it straightforward: her husband had been killed in a hunting accident.

'Yeah, I heard,' she said, leaning against the doorpost. Her eyes hadn't even flickered; and to the older cop they looked

43

so blue he thought he might fall in. 'Should I do something?'

The cops looked at each other. 'Well, he's at the county medical examiner's office. We thought you'd want to make, er, the funeral arrangements.'

She sighed. 'Yeah, I suppose that would be the thing to do. Okay. I'll call them. The medical examiner.'

The older of the two cops, his experience prodding him, tried to keep the conversation going. 'You don't seem too upset.'

She thought about that for a moment. 'No, I'd have to say that I'm not. Upset. But I'm surprised.' She put one hand on her breast, in a parody of a woman taken aback. 'I thought the asshole was too mean to get killed. Anyway, I just don't . . . mmm, what that's colorful redneck phrase you policemen always use in the movies? I don't give a large shit.'

The cops looked at each other again, and then the younger one said, 'Maybe we got this wrong. We understood . . .'

'Yeah, I'm his wife. In two weeks we would've been divorced. We haven't lived together for two years, and I haven't seen him for a year. I don't like him. Didn't like him.'

'Uh, could you tell us where you were . . . ?'

She smiled at him sleepily. 'When?'

'Early this morning?'

'In bed. I was out late last night, with friends.'

'Could anybody vouch for you being here last night?' The older cop was pressing; once you had somebody rolling, you never knew what might come out.

But she nodded: 'Sure. A friend brought me home.'

'I'm talking about later, like early this morning.'

'So am I,' she said. 'He stayed.'

'Oh, okay.' Neither one of them was a bit embarrassed, and she was now looking at him with a little interest. 'Could we get his name?'

'I don't see why not. Come on in,' she said. 'I'll write it down.'

They followed her into the apartment, noted the polished wood floors, the oriental carpets, the tastefully colorful paintings on eggshell-white walls.

'You haven't asked me how much I'd get from him, if he died before the divorce,' she said over her shoulder.

The older cop smiled, his best Gary Cooper grin. He liked her: 'How much?'

'I don't know,' she lied. 'My attorney and I took him to the cleaners.'

'Good for you,' he said. She was scribbling on a notepad, and when she finished, she brought it over and handed it to him. 'George Wright. Here's his address and phone number. I'm going to call him and tell him about this.'

'That's up to you,' the older cop said.

'That's my number at the bottom, in case you need to interrogate me. It's unlisted,' she said. She looked at him with her blue eyes and nibbled on her lower lip.

'Well, thanks,' he said. He tucked the slip of paper in his shirt pocket.

'Do I sound like a heartless bitch?' she asked him cheerfully. And as she asked, she took his arm and they walked slowly toward the door together.

'Maybe a little,' he said. He really did like her and he could feel the back of his bicep pressing into her breast. Her breast was very warm. He even imagined he could feel a nipple.

'I really didn't like him,' she said. 'You can put that in your report.'

'I will,' he said.

'Good,' she said, as she ushered him out the door. 'Then maybe I'll get to see you again . . . You could show me your gun.'

45

The cops found themselves in the hallway, the door closing behind them. At the elevator door, the younger one said, 'Well?'

'Well, what?'

'You gonna call her?'

The older one thought a minute, then said, 'I don't think I could afford it.'

'Shit, you don't have to *buy* anything,' the young one said. 'She's rich.'

'I dunno,' the older one said.

'Take my advice: If you call her, you don't want to jump her right away. Get to know her a little.'

'That's very sensitive of you,' the older one said.

'No, no, I just think . . . she wants to see your gun?'

'Yeah?'

'So you wanna put off the time when she finds out you're packin' a .22.'

'Jealousy's an ugly thing,' the older cop said complacently. As they walked out on the street, to the car, he looked up at the apartment building and said, 'Maybe.'

And even if not, he thought, the woman had made his day.

Audrey McDonald, coming in from the garage, found her husband's orange coveralls on the kitchen floor, and just beyond them, his wool shooting jacket and then boots and trousers in a pile and halfway up the stairs, the long blue polypro underwear.

'Oh, shit,' she said to herself. She dropped her purse on a hallway chair and hurried up the stairs, found a pair of jockey shorts in the hallway and heard him splashing in the oversized tub.

When Wilson McDonald got tense, excited, or frightened, he drank; and when he drank, he got hot and started to sweat.

He'd pull his clothing off and head for water. He'd been drunk, naked, in the lake down the hill. He'd been drunk naked in the pool in the back yard, frightening the neighbor's daughter half to death. He'd been in the tub more times than she could remember, drunk, wallowing like a great white whale. He wasn't screaming yet, but he would be. The killing of Dan Kresge, all the talk at the club, had pushed him over the edge.

At the bathroom door, she stopped, braced herself, and then pushed it open. Wilson was on his hands and knees. As she opened the door, he dropped onto his stomach, and a wave of water washed over the edge, onto the floor, and around a nearly empty bottle of scotch.

'Wilson!' she shouted. 'Goddamnit, Wilson.'

He floundered, rolled, sat up. He was too fat, with fine curly hair on his chest and stomach, going gray. His tits, she thought, were bigger than hers. 'Shut up,' he bellowed back.

She took three quick steps into the room and picked up the bottle and started away.

'Wait a minute, goddamnit . . .' He was on his feet and out of the tub faster than she'd anticipated, and he caught her in the hallway. 'Give me the fucking bottle.'

'You're dripping all over the carpet.'

'Give me the fucking bottle . . .' he shouted.

'No. You'll . . .'

He was swinging the moment the 'no' came out of her mouth, and caught her on the side of the head with an open hand. She went down like a popped balloon, her head cracking against the molding on a closet door.

'Fuckin' bottle,' he said. She'd hung onto it when she went down, but he wrenched it free, and held it to his chest.

She was stunned, but pushed herself up. 'You fuck,' she shouted.

'You don't . . .' He kicked at her, sent her sprawling. 'Throw you down the fuckin' stairs,' he screamed. 'Get out of here.'

He went back into the bathroom, and she heard the lock click.

'Wilson . . .'

'Go away.' And she heard the splash as he hit the water in the tub.

Downstairs, she got an ice compress from the freezer and put it against her head: she'd have a bruise. Goddamn him. They had to talk about Kresge: this was their big move, their main chance. This was what they'd worked for. And he was drunk.

The thought of the bottle sent her to the cupboard under the sink, to a built-in Lazy Susan. She turned it halfway around, got the vodka bottle, poured four inches of vodka over two ice cubes, and drank it down.

Poured another two ounces to sip.

Audrey McDonald wasn't a big woman and alcohol hit quickly. The two martinis she'd had at lunch, plus the pitcher of Bloody Marys at the club, had laid a base for the vodka. Her rage at Wilson began to shift. Not to disappear, but to shift in the maze of calculations that were spinning through her head.

Bone and O'Dell would try to steal this from them.

She sipped vodka, pressed the ice compress against her head, thought about Bone and O'Dell. Bone was Harvard and Chicago; O'Dell was Smith and Wharton. O'Dell had degrees in history and finance; Bone had two degrees in economics.

Wilson had a B.A. from the University of Minnesota in business administration, and a law degree from the same place. Okay, but not in the same class with O'Dell or Bone. On the other hand, his grandfather had been one of the founders of Polaris. And Wilson knew everyone in town, and was a member of the Woodland Golf and Cricket Club. The vice-chairman of Polaris, a jumped-up German sausage-maker who never in a million years could have gotten into the club on his own, was now at Woodland, courtesy of Wilson McDonald. So Wilson wasn't weaponless . . .

She heard him thumping down the stairs a minute later. He stalked into the kitchen, still nude, jiggling, dripping wet. 'What'ya drinking?' he asked.

'Soda water,' she said.

'Soda water my ass,' he snarled. Then his eyes, which had been wandering, focused on the cold compress she held to her head. 'What the fuck were you taking my scotch for?'

'Because we've got things to think about,' she said. 'We don't have time for you to get drunk. We have to figure out what to do with Kresge dead.'

'I already got his job,' he said, with unconcealed satisfaction.

'What?' She was astonished. Was he that drunk?

'O'Dell and Bone agreed, I could have it,' he said.

'You mean . . . you're the CEO?'

'Well . . . the board has to meet,' he said, his voice slurring. 'But I've already been dealing with the PR people, putting out press releases . . .'

She rolled her eyes. 'You mean they let you fill in until the board meets.'

'Well, I think that positions me . . .'

'Oh, for Christ sakes, Wilson, grow up,' she said. 'And go put some pants on. You look like a pig.'

'You shut the fuck . . .'

He came at her again and she pitched the vodka at his eyes. As he flinched, she turned and ran back into the living room, looked around, spotted a crystal paperweight on the piano, picked it up. Wilson had gotten the paperweight at a Senior Tour pro-am. When he came through the doorway after her, she lifted it and said, 'You try to hit me again and I swear to God I'll brain you with this thing.'

He stopped. He looked at her, and at the paperweight, then stepped closer; she backed up a step and said, 'Wilson.'

'All right,' he said. 'I don't want to fight. And we gotta talk.'

He looked in the corner, at the liquor cabinet, started that way.

'You can't have any more . . .'

She started past him and he moved, quickly, grabbed her hand with the paperweight, bent it, and she screamed, 'Don't. Wilson, don't.'

'Drop it, drop it . . .' He was a grade-school bully, twisting the arm of a little kid. She dropped the weight, and it hit the carpet with a thump.

'Gonna fuckin' hit me with my paperweight,' he said, jerking her upright. 'Gonna fuckin' hit me.'

He slapped her again, hard, and she felt something break open inside her mouth. He slapped her again, and she twisted, screaming now. Slapped her a third time and she fell, and he let her go, and when she tried to crawl away, kicked her in the hip and she went down on her face.

'Bitch. Hit me with, hit me, fuckin' bitch . . .'

He went to the liquor cabinet, opened it, found another bottle. She dragged herself under the Steinway, and he stooped as though he were going to go in after her, but he stumbled, bumped his head on the side of the piano, caught himself, said, 'I'm the goddamned CEO,' and headed back up the stairs to the tub, his fat butt bobbling behind him.

Audrey sat under the piano for a while, weeping by herself, and finally crawled out to a telephone, picked it up, and punched a speed-dialer.

'Hello?' Her sister Helen, cheerful, inquiring.

'Helen? Could you come get me?'

Helen recognized the tone. 'Oh, Jesus, what happened?'

'Wilson's drunk. He beat me up again. I think I better get out of the house.'

'Oh, my God, Aud, I'll be right there ... hang on, hang on ...'

Chapter Four

Lucas arrived at the office late Monday morning, neatly dressed, neatly shaved, dead tired. The simpler things in life could be done on automatic pilot: take the clothes to the cleaners, shower, shave, and eat. Anything more complicated was difficult. Exercise took energy, and a heavy workout was impossible after a month without sleep.

He'd been the route before. The last time over the edge, he hadn't recognized what was happening, hadn't seen it coming, and it'd almost killed him. This time, the process felt slightly different. He could feel it out there – the depression, the break-down, the unipolar disorder, whatever the new correct name for it was – but it didn't seem to be marching on him with the same implacable darkness as last time.

Maybe he could fight it off, he thought. But he still dreaded the bed. The minute his head touched the pillow, the brainstorm would begin. Sleep would come only with exhaustion, and then not until after daylight . . .

In the winter just past, Weather Karkinnen, the woman he'd been about to marry, had been taken hostage by a killer looking for revenge against Lucas. Weather had managed her attacker: she'd talked him into surrender. She'd given him guarantees. But nobody on the outside knew.

When Lucas closed his eyes at night, he could see the two of them walking down the narrow hospital corridor toward him, Weather in front, Dick LaChaise using her as a shield, with a pistol to her head. He could also feel the pressure at his back, where a hidden police sniper, a kid from Iowa, was looking at LaChaise though a rifle scope.

Lucas's job was to talk the gun away from Weather's head, if only for half a second. If he could just get LaChaise to move the muzzle . . . And he did. The Iowa kid was cold as ice: Dick LaChaise's head had been pulped by the mushrooming .243 slug.

Weather, whose face was only inches away from LaChaise, had been showered with bone, brain and blood. She had recovered, in most ways. She could work; she could even forget about it, most of the time. Unless she saw Lucas. They tried to pull the relationship back together, but three months after Dick LaChaise died in a hospital hallway, she was gone.

Gone for good, he believed.

And Lucas was staring into the darkness again.

'Hey, Lucas?'

Lucy Ghent, a secretary, was calling down the hall from the chief's office door. She was one of the older women in the office, who competed with her peers on hair-dos. 'Chief Roux is down in Identification. She wants to see you right away.'

'Trouble?'

Ghent flopped a hand, dismissively. 'Just . . . weirdness.'

Rose Marie Roux was sitting at a cluttered desk in the Identification, chewing Nicorette, paging through a document Lucas recognized as the departmental budget. She looked up when Lucas came in and said, 'I swear to God, if you killed the smartest guy on the city council, the average IQ in Minneapolis would go up two points. Don't quote me.'

'What happened?'

'The York case.'

'Yeah?'

Morris York, two years on the force, found with a half-ounce of Mexican bud in a Marlboro box behind his patrol-car visor. His marijuana habit had been detected by a departmental mechanic who claimed he was getting a contact high off the car's upholstery. Internal affairs made movies of York getting mellow on the job.

'Tommy Gedja says this morning, at the council meeting, if that's all we're doing in our cars, why do we need new cars? I think he was serious. I think they're gonna try to pull twelve cars out from under us.'

Lucas shrugged: 'Life sucks and then they cut your budget. What're you doing down here?'

'More budget problems.' A piece of white paper, wrapped in a plastic folder, lay on the desk's otherwise empty typewriter tray. She picked it up and handed it to him. 'Came in the mail, first thing this morning.'

Dear Chief of Police Roux:

One week ago, Mr Kresge sent a memo to Susan O'Dell which said that her department would not be allowed to continue with a planned expansion because of budget constraints. Mrs O'Dell has worked on the expansion for a long time and when she got the memo, her quote was, 'God Damn him, I'm going to kill him.' There were three people in the room at the time: Sharon Allen (assistant to the vice-president) Michelle Stephens (executive secretary) and Randall Moss, assistant head cashier. I can't tell you my name, but I thought you should know.

'Not much here,' Lucas said. He snapped the paper with his index finger. 'We could interview Stephens to see how serious she thinks it is. Or if she's just trying to torpedo O'Dell.'

'Stephens?' Roux had the gene that allowed her to lift one

eyebrow at a time, and her left brow went up.

Lucas nodded. 'She's probably the one who sent it – sounds like somebody who actually heard O'Dell say it, but she misuses the word "quote," which means not a lot of education. On the other hand, everything is spelled right, and secretaries spell things right. She's very aware of titles and refers to Kresge as Mister, which means she saw him as somebody with a lot more status than she has: not an associate. She wouldn't put herself first on the list, because that would make her nervous. And an assistant head cashier probably has a college education.'

'So how's she dressed, Sherlock?'

Lucas smiled, but a droopy, tired smile. 'Navy jacket and skirt or tan jacket and skirt with an older but neatly ironed white shirt and some kind of tie. Practical heels. Single mother. Tense. Anxious. Angry with O'Dell for personal reasons. Hurting for money.'

Roux said, 'Smart ass.' She turned and shouted into a closet-sized office: 'Beverly! Bring the other thing out so Sherlock Holmes can take a look.'

The department's document specialist, a dark-haired woman with a faint Moravian accent, bustled out of the closet with another slip of paper wrapped in plastic.

'Also in the mail,' Roux said. 'Beverly's checking for fingerprints.'

'There are none,' the woman said. 'Not on the letter or the envelope. Standard twenty-pound copier paper, no watermark. Printed with a laser printer.' Lucas took the paper.

Chief Roux:

Daniel S. Kresge was shot by Wilson McDonald, who was hunting with Kresge when the shooting occurred. I have known Wilson McDonald for many years and I believe that he has killed two other people to further his career. These people were:

A man named George Arris, who was killed about 1984, in a shooting outside a restaurant in St Paul.

Andrew Ingall, who was killed in a boating accident in 1993 on Lake Superior. (He was from North Oaks and his wife still lives there.)

I hope you catch him on this one. He can't go on like this.

A Concerned Citizen

Lucas looked at Roux, and she caught the small light in his eye. 'Interesting?'

'More than the first one,' Lucas admitted. 'No waffling about the presentation. He gets right to it: Daniel S. Kresge was shot by Wilson McDonald.'

'You think a man wrote it?'

Lucas hesitated for a minute, then said, 'Maybe not. Could be a woman.'

'When I read it, I assumed it was a woman. I don't know why,' Roux said.

'Something about the wording,' said Beverly. 'I think it's a woman, too.'

'Would you look into it?' Roux asked Lucas. 'Sort of . . . carefully? Lot of rich people involved.'

Lucas said, 'Sloan and Sherrill are on it.'

'Sloan is working on the Ericson killing. That's getting complicated. Sherrill's doing the routine for the sheriff up there. I'd just like you to look at this letter: It sounds so . . . sure of itself.'

'You want me to look into it because you think it's necessary?' Lucas asked. 'Or because you're worried that I'm going crazy?'

Roux nodded: 'Both. It'd be nice if we could catch whoever killed Kresge.'

'Are you getting pressure?'

'No, not really. Kresge was divorced, no family around here, not all that well-liked. But I mean, hey, it's what we're supposed to do, right?'

'The paper this morning said that McDonald would be speaking for Polaris, at least until the board of directors meets,' Lucas said. 'The in-fighting could get pretty intense; something could fall out. In fact . . .' He tapped the first letter with the second. 'Something already has.'

'So catch up with Sherrill, tell her you'll take this angle. Get away from your desk.'

Lucas nodded: 'Okay; I'll look at it. And listen, I'm gonna send Del Capslock around with a problem.'

'That goddamn Capslock *is* a problem,' Roux grunted.

'Good cop,' Lucas said.

'Yeah, but I can't stand to look at him: I keep wanting to give him a buck, or send him out to get his teeth fixed . . . What's the problem?'

'He turned up an opium ring.'

'Drugs can't handle it?'

'You might want to think about it first,' Lucas said. Again, the droopy grin: 'I suspect most of the members are friends of yours.'

Sloan was drinking a Cherry Coke and reading a *Star-Tribune* story about sex in the workplace when Lucas wandered in, carrying Xerox copies of the two letters. Sloan dropped the newspaper in the waste basket, leaned back and said, 'You know what the thing is about you?'

'What?' Lucas pulled another chair around.

'You can't have an adulterous affair, because you're not married. So if you go down to Intelligence, say, and pick out some single chick and fuck her brains loose, well, that's just what bachelors do. But if I did it, that would be adultery and the *Star-Tribune* thinks I should be fired.'

'If you did it, your old lady'd kill you anyway, so you wouldn't need a job.'

'I'm talking in theory,' Sloan said.

'Did you pick out the guilty guy on Saturday? In theory?'

Sloan shook his head. 'They're a pretty tough group. Robles was in a sweat, but I think he might sweat everything. Bone seemed to think that Kresge getting murdered was mildly amusing; he was cooperative, though. And he had to stop to think at all the right places. O'Dell was almost too busy figuring out the consequences to talk to me about whether she did it . . . and that made me think she didn't. If she had, she'd have already figured out the consequences. I had a harder time getting a reading on McDonald. He acted like the whole thing was a plot to personally inconvenience him.'

'Cold? Sociopathic?'

'Mmmm.' Sloan scratched his chin. 'No . . . If he is, he covers it,' he said after a minute. 'I'd say he's more like . . . unpleasant. Arrogant.'

'So what's it all mean?'

'If Robles did it, we might get him, eventually. If it's one of the others, forget it. Unless the guy does something really stupid, like tell somebody else about it. Or if it was a group effort. But that's . . .'

'Unlikely,' Lucas said.

'More like ridiculous.'

'Perfect crime?'

'Just about,' Sloan said. 'Lots of people probably heard the shot, but nobody thought anything about it. Nobody was looking for the shooter. Once he was off the scene . . . there's no way we're gonna get him. The only chance to get him was to have somebody see it happen, and recognize the shooter. That was it.'

'But we know some stuff,' Lucas said. He leaned back in the chair and put his feet on the edge of Sloan's desk. 'The shooter knew his way around there, in the dark. And he knew which tree stand Kresge would be in. That means that he was either close to Kresge or he worked for him, maybe out at the cabin. Is Krause checking any employees out there?'

'Yeah. There were only two or three people – a handyman who'd do maintenance work around the place, an old guy who patrols some of the cabins, just checking on them two or three times a day. And some guy who plows out the driveway in the winter. None of them had any apparent problem with Kresge. The sheriff doesn't think they're suspects.'

'If this was a movie, the handyman would have done it,' Lucas said, staring blankly at the ceiling. 'He'd be like a Stephen King character, a secret psycho who everybody thinks is retarded . . .'

'. . . but who's really pretty smart, but only behaves the way he does because he couldn't get a date to the prom, which is why he burned down the high school.'

'How about Sherrill? Is she around?'

'I don't know. She was working yesterday, but I haven't seen her today. I know she was going to try to nail down people in Kresge's office, and talk to the ex-wife.'

'All right . . .'

'But suppose it is somebody close to Kresge,' Sloan said. 'Suppose we find a guy who hated Kresge, but knew the farm, knew where the tree stand was, knew Kresge would be in it, and we can prove that he has a rifle, is a great shot, and has no alibi for opening day. You know what? We got all that, and we still ain't got shit.'

'There might be one more way,' Lucas said.

'Like what?'

'We build a pattern around him.'

'Good luck.'

'Rose Marie got some mail this morning,' Lucas said. He leaned forward and slid the Xerox copies across Sloan's desk. 'One letter nominates O'Dell, the other one McDonald.'

Sloan read them slowly, then read the McDonald letter a second time, and finally looked up at Lucas: 'Two more dead ones, huh? But we'd need more than a pattern. We'd have to push him out in the open.'

'That could be done,' Lucas said. 'If it's McDonald.'

'Are you buying into the case?' Sloan asked.

'Rose Marie asked me to take a look . . . if you don't mind. If Sherrill doesn't mind.'

'I don't mind,' Sloan said. 'I've got the Ericson file. I could use some extra time.'

'I thought the boyfriend did it – the Ericson thing. I thought he admitted it.'

'Not exactly,' Sloan said. 'He says he might have. He doesn't deny it. But we can't come up with any physical evidence, and he was so fucked up at the time he can't remember anything. And I'm wondering, if he was so fucked up – and he was, he had enough chemicals in him to start a factory – what'd he do with his clothes? They had to have blood all over them.'

'You've got nothing physical? No hair or semen . . .'

'No semen. And he had no blood on him, under his nails or in his hair. And the problem is, she was killed on the bed and he slept there every night and half the day. So he's all over the place . . . but so what? He's gonna be. And I'm really worried about the clothes. He says he's not missing any, and I think he might be telling the truth. He doesn't have all that much to begin with. Couple pairs of jeans, couple t-shirts, a coat, some sneaks.'

'Huh. Check the drains in the bathroom? Maybe he was naked . . .'

Sloan nodded: 'Yeah. The lab looked at it. No blood.'

'Okay. So I'll take the McDonald thing,' Lucas said. 'I'll talk to Sherrill about it.'

'She'll go along,' Sloan said. He said it with a *tone*.

'Yeah?'

'She's got the great headlights,' Sloan said.

'Not exactly a key criterion for a police investigation.'

'Yeah, but . . .'

'You've been married too long, all you can think about is strange tits and adultery complaints,' Lucas said.

'Not true. Sometimes I think about strange asses . . . Seriously, I heard them talking about you – some of the women. The idea was, don't rush him, let him get a little distance away from Weather.'

'Fuck 'em,' Lucas said, pushing away from Sloan's desk. 'I'll take McDonald. I'd like to see the interviews you did Saturday . . .'

'Krause tape-recorded them, he's getting a transcript made. Probably today. He said he'd shoot a copy down as soon as it's ready.'

'All right,' Lucas said. 'Ship it over.'

'And you'll talk to headlights? I mean, Sherrill?'

Lucas grinned. 'Yeah. If you see her, tell her I'm looking for her; I'll be around later in the day.'

Chapter Five

D amascus Isley was a very smart fat man with a taste for two-thousand-dollar English bespoke suits that almost disguised his size. Lucas spotted him at a back table at the Bell Jar, hovering over a chicken-breast salad that had been served in what looked like a kitchen sink. Lucas told the maître d', 'I'm with the fat guy,' and was nodded past the velvet rope.

'Lucas,' Isley said. He made a helpless gesture with his hands, which meant, *I'm too fat to get up.* 'Are you coming to the reunion? Gina asked me to ask.'

Lucas shook his head, and took a chair across from Isley, who was sitting on the booth seat. 'I don't think so. I've busted too many of them.'

'Mary Big Jo's gonna be there,' Isley said.

'Fuck Mary Big Jo.'

'I certainly did,' Isley said cheerfully 'Made all the more glorious by your abject failure to do the same.'

Lucas grinned: 'No accounting for taste,' he said. Isley was six-five, a bit taller than Lucas. He'd once been a rope instead of a mountain, a basketball forward when six-five was a big man; Lucas had been hockey, and they'd chased several of the same women through high school and college.

A waitress stepped up behind Lucas, slipped a menu in front of him, and said, 'Cocktail, sir?'

'Ah no, I just want . . .' He thought for a second, then said, 'Hell, give me a martini. Beefeaters, up, two olives.'

'I could give you three olives, if you need more vegetables in your diet,' the waitress said.

'All right, three,' Lucas said; she was pretty in a dark-Irish way.

The waitress went to get the drink, and Isley, following her with his eyes, said, 'The way she looked at you, something would be possible. Maybe you'd have to come back a couple of times, get to know her, but it'd be possible.' He looked down at the vast salad, the chunks of chicken breast, avocado, egg, tomato, cheese and lettuce, covered with a bucket of creamy herb dressing, then back up at Lucas. 'You know how long it's been since that was possible with me? With all this fuckin' . . .' He couldn't say *fat*. '. . . lard?'

Lucas tried to put him off. 'So you work out for a couple months.'

'Lucas . . . when I was playing ball, my last year, I weighed two-oh-five. So I go to this fat doctor and say, "Give me a diet I can stay on, something simple, that'll get me back to two-oh-five." He says, "Okay, do this: go to lunch every day and eat one Big Mac with all the fixings. And as much popcorn as you want, all day. Nothing else." I say, "Jesus Christ, I'll starve." He says, "No, you won't, but you'll lose a lot of weight." '

Isley looked at Lucas. 'You know how long he said it would take to get to two-oh-five?' Lucas shook his head. 'A year and a half. A fuckin' year and a half, Lucas . . .'

'I'll tell you what, Dama,' Lucas said bluntly. 'You're either gonna lose it, or you're gonna die. Simple as that.'

'Not that simple,' Isley said.

'Oh, yeah it is,' Lucas said. 'After all the bullshit, that's what it comes down to.'

'I don't even like food that much . . . and I'd like to live a while longer,' Isley said wistfully. 'I'd like to quit the company, go to London and study money . . . find out what it really is.'

'Money.'

'Yeah, you know. *Money*,' he said. 'Not many people really know what it is, how it works. I'd like to spend some time finding out.'

'So start hitting the McDonald's,' Lucas said.

'Fat chance.'

The waitress arrived with the martini, and Isley's wistfulness disappeared, replaced by the steel-trap investment banker. 'So what's going on? Starting another business?'

'No.' Lucas sipped the martini. 'When you took my company public, we ran some of the money stuff through Jim Bone over at Polaris. You seemed to know him pretty well. He was hunting with Kresge when Kresge got shot, and I need a reading on him. Bone, I mean. And Susan O'Dell, if you know her. And Wilson McDonald.'

Isley's face went cautious. 'Is this official?'

'No, of course not. I'm just trying to get a reading. Nobody'll be coming back to you.'

Isley nodded. 'Okay. I know them all pretty well – socially and business, both. Either Bone or O'Dell has the guts to shoot Kresge, but I don't think either one did. These people are very smart and very serious. If they'd wanted to lose Kresge badly enough, they would have done it another way.'

'What about Robles or McDonald?'

'Robles is a software genius. He does the math. But he's more of a technician than a manager. He also doesn't have the motive. With his math, he could go about anywhere. McDonald . . .' Isley looked away from Lucas, pursed his fat lips, then turned back. 'There are McDonalds who are good friends of mine – same family. Not Wilson, though. There've been rumors . . .' Again, he paused.

'What?' Lucas asked.

'No comebacks?'

'No comebacks.'

'There're rumors that he occasionally beats the shit out of his wife,' Isley said. 'I mean, she goes to the hospital.'

'Huh.'

'Alcohol, is what you hear,' Isley said. 'He's a binge drinker. Sober for two months, then has to take a few days off.'

'Smart?'

'Pretty smart. Not world-class, but he got through law school with no problem.'

'I didn't know he was a lawyer.'

'He never worked at it. He's always been a salesman, and a damn good one. Knows everybody. *Everybody.* Access to all the old money in town – his family built a mill over on the river, hundred and some years ago, and eventually sold to Pillsbury to go into banking and real estate. Like that.'

'Okay,' Lucas said. 'So here's another question. Everything I've heard about him says McDonald's rich, he comes from an old family, and all that. Why would he kill Kresge, just 'cause Kresge's gonna merge the bank? He's got all the money in the world anyway.'

'No, not really,' Isley said. He dabbed at his lips with a linen napkin, tossed the napkin aside, and made a steeple out of his fingers. After a moment of silence, he said, 'He's maybe worth . . . seven or eight million. The older generation was a lot richer, relatively speaking, but there were a lot of kids, and a lot of taxes, and the money got cut up. After taxes, and including his after-tax salary, I'd imagine his real expendable income is something in the range of a half million. If he doesn't dip into his capital, and assuming he puts aside enough to cover inflation.'

'Well, Jesus, Dama, that just about *is* all the money in the world,' Lucas said.

'No, it's not. It's a lot by any normal standard, but having ten million dollars is nothing compared to being the CEO of a major corporation. Being an American CEO is like being an old English duke or earl.' He paused again, his eyes unfocusing as he looked for the right words. 'Say you have a spendable income of a half-million a year, and your wife likes to fly first class to Hawaii or Paris every so often. You can spend fifteen thousand after-tax bucks flying a couple first class to the Islands. You go out of town a half-dozen times a year – Hawaii, the Caribbean, Europe – you can spend a hundred and fifty grand, no trouble. And it's all out of your own pocket. Plus you've got big real estate taxes, you're probably running a couple of fifty-thousand-dollar cars . . . I mean, you can spend a half-million a year and feel like your collar's a little too tight. But if you run a business the size of Polaris, screw first class – you've got your own Gulfstream waiting at the airport. You've got several thousand people kissing your ass day and night. You've got people driving your cars, running your errands. From everything I can tell by watching it, this all must feel better than anything in the world . . .'

'So even if he had a lot of money, a guy might have reason to waste old Kresge.'

'Especially McDonald. Bone, O'Dell and Robles are essentially hired guns. They are very good at what they do, but they're *here* mostly by chance. They could go anywhere else. But everything Wilson McDonald is, is tied to the Twin Cities. In New York or L.A. or even Chicago, they could give a rat's ass about a Wilson McDonald.'

'Do you think Bone would talk to me about McDonald? Off the record?'

Isley shrugged: 'Maybe. If the idea appealed to him. He played a little ball at Ole Miss.'

'Yeah?'

'Yeah. Good quick guard. Probably not pro quality, but he would've been looked at. Called him T-Bone, of course. If you want, I could give him a ring. Just to say you asked about him, tell him you're okay.'

Lucas grinned. 'Maybe I'm not.'

Isley said, 'Ah, you're okay . . . if he's innocent. And I'm pretty sure he is.'

'Anybody mourning Kresge?'

Isley had been about to stuff a slice of chicken in his mouth, and stopped halfway to the target. Shook his head. 'Not a single person that I know. He spent his life fucking people in the name of efficiency.' He stuck the chicken in his mouth, chewed, swallowed. 'Why would you do that?' he asked. 'I know all kinds of people who do, but I can't figure out why.'

'Make money.'

'Hell, Lucas, I've made a pile of money, and I don't fuck people. You made a pile, and your ex-employees think you're a hell of a guy. But why would you do things in a way that you'd end up in life with a pile of money, but not a single fuckin' friend?'

'Maybe you figure that if you get enough money, you could buy some.'

Isley nodded, gloomily. 'Yeah, probably; that's the way they think.'

Lucas finished the last of the three olives, and the last of the pleasantly cool martini, and said, 'Listen, Dama. I got a pickup game once a week, bunch of cops, couple lawyers. You start eating those Big Macs and I'd like to get you out there.'

'Goddamnit, Lucas . . .'

'Feel good, wouldn't it? Playing horse in the evening. Down on 28th?'

Isley tossed his fork in the salad bowl. 'Get out of here, Davenport.'

Lucas stood up. 'Call Bone for me?'

'Yeah, yeah, soon as I get back.' He looked at his Patek Philippe. 'Give me twenty-five minutes.'

Lucas got back to the office, stuck his head into Administration, and said, 'Got anything for me?' The duty guy said, 'Computer's down.'

'How long?'

'I don't know, it's not just us. Some state road guys cut a major fiber-optic. Half the goddamn city's down.'

'Road guys?'

'Shovel operators.'

James T. Bone's secretary suspected Lucas of making sport of her. When she told him, peremptorily, on the phone, that Mr Bone was making no new appointments, and Lucas had answered, 'Go tell Mr Bone right now that a deputy chief of police wants to talk to him, and if he says no, I'll have to come down and shoot him.'

'I beg your pardon?'

'I think you heard me,' Lucas said. He almost added 'Sweetheart,' but decided that might push it too far.

She went away for a moment, then another voice came on, feminine, cool: 'Mr Davenport? This is Kerin Baki, Mr Bone's assistant. Can I help you?'

'I need to talk to Mr Bone.'

'When?'

'As soon as possible.'

'Come over, and we'll get you in,' she said.

Baki was a chilly northern blonde, with an oval face and pale-blue fighter-pilot eyes. She met him without any softening smile: In the spring, Lucas thought, she probably had genetic dreams of turning her tanks toward Moscow...

She led him though into Bone's office, said, 'Mr Bone, Mr Davenport,' and left them, shutting the door behind her.

Bone was dressed in a subdued single-breasted wool suit with a crisp white shirt and an Italian necktie; but somehow the ensemble came off as a wry comment on Yankee banker-tude. He had a telephone to one ear, and a foot propped on the N–Z volume of the *New Shorter Oxford English Dictionary*, which lay flat on his desk. He waved Lucas in, and as Lucas dropped into a bent-oak chair across the desk, said into the phone, 'Two? That's as good as you can do? Last week it was one and seven... Yeah, yeah, yeah. I'll get back to you, but I think we might have to talk to Bosendorfer or Beckstein. Yeah, yeah. By four.'

He hung up, made a notation on a legal pad and said, 'I can give you all the time you'd need this evening, but if you gotta talk now, you gotta talk fast. And this is all off the record at this point, right?'

Lucas nodded. 'Yes. If we need an official statement, we'll send you a subpoena and get a formal deposition.'

Bone leaned forward. 'So?'

'So do you think McDonald did it?'

'If one of us did it, it was McDonald. I didn't do it. Robles, no motive, O'Dell, too smart. Unless I'm missing something. And to tell you the truth, I don't think it's McDonald. Way down at the bottom, I don't think he's got the grit to pull it off.'

'Then why's he running the place?'

'He's not. He's only speaking for it. And that'll only last until O'Dell and I get the board sorted out. Then it'll be one of us.'

Lucas said, 'Huh,' and then, 'Have you ever heard of George Arris? Does the name ring a bell?'

'Yes, of course. He was a famous case around here, around the bank. He was murdered – this must've been a few months or maybe a year or so before I came here. Must've been back in '85.'

'How was it famous? The name doesn't ring a bell with me . . .'

'It was over on the St Paul side of the river. Somebody started shooting white guys who were walking in the black areas . . . there were like three or four of them in a few weeks, shot in the back of the head.'

'Ah, jeez, I remember that,' Lucas said. 'Never solved. And Arris was one of them?'

'Yup.'

'What'd he do here?'

'Worked with the trust department, setting up portfolios for rich folk.'

'Would he have worked with McDonald?'

Bone said, 'Probably. I'd have to look up the exact dates, but they probably overlapped. They certainly both went through that department. I don't really know the details. I wasn't here yet. I just heard about the killing later.'

'Okay. How about Andrew Ingall?'

'Andy. He was a vice-president, also in the trust department, but he died a few years ago in a boating accident up on Superior. You think Wilson had something to do with it?'

'Why would he?' Lucas asked.

Bone leaned back, then spun his chair in a circle, stopped it with one foot, reached into a desk drawer where he apparently had a stereo tuner hidden. A Schumann piano piece, simple, easy, elegant and sweet, sprang into the office, and Bone said, 'Schumann,' and Lucas said, 'I know – *Scenes from Childhood*,' and Bone said, 'Christ, we're so cultured I can't stand it,' and Lucas said, 'A friend of mine used to play them. Why would McDonald do Andy Ingall?'

'Because they were both candidates to run the operation. Then Andy sailed out of Superior Harbor one day, just moving his boat up to the Islands. He never got there. No storm, no emergency calls, nothing. Just phhht. Gone. The theory was that he had a leaky gas tank – he had some kind of old gas engine, an Atomic, or something like that – and gas leaked into the bilge, and he fired up the engine out on the water somewhere, and boom. He was gone before he could call for help. That was the theory, but nobody ever knew for sure. No wreckage was ever found.'

'So McDonald got the job.'

'Well, no. When Andy disappeared, everything was screwed up for a while, then we had a general shuffling around, and McDonald wound up as a senior vice-president in the mortgage company.'

'Huh,' said Lucas, and Bone said, 'Yeah,' and asked, 'Can't you get this stuff from the FBI or somewhere?'

'Probably not. Besides, the computer's down.'

'You, too? Christ, it's chaos downstairs . . .'

'Did you ever hear that McDonald might whack his wife around from time to time? Pretty seriously?'

Bone nodded. 'I heard it. I went out with a lawyer lady for a while, old family, she knows that whole country-club bunch, and she said something to me about it. She might have some details . . . you could talk to her if you want.'

'That'd be good . . .'

Bone scratched a name and phone number on a piece of notepaper and pushed it across the desk. 'Sandra Ollson, two ll's. That's her office phone over at Kelly, Batten.'

'What kind of law?'

'Estate planning, wills, trusts.' He looked at his watch and said, 'Listen, I've got to go to a meeting, but I can talk to a

71

guy who's gonna be there, and find out if there was anything between Wilson and Arris.'

Lucas said, 'Thanks,' stood up, and as they shook hands, said, 'I understand you used to play a little ball.'

'Yeah, a little,' Bone said.

'How well do you know Dama Isley?'

'Reasonably well – I heard he played for the Gophers, back when. Hard to believe.'

'Yeah. Listen, next time you see him, take a couple of minutes and talk a little ball, old-time stuff, like college days.'

Bone shrugged. 'Sure. Why?'

'Private project,' Lucas said. 'You still play?'

Bone, grinning, said, 'I still shoot around a little bit on Saturdays. Always a couple of kids trying to take advantage of me.'

Lucas said, 'A banker? Playing for money?'

'Good grief, no,' Bone said. 'Not for money. That'd be illegal.'

On the way out, Lucas paused in the open door of Bone's office, saw Kerin Baki talking to the secretary, and said, loud enough for her to overhear, 'I'm probably going to want to talk about McDonald again.'

Bone, already settling back into his desk, distracted, missed the double-directed comment, nodded, said, 'Okay,' and Lucas pulled the door shut. He smiled at Baki on the way out and said, 'Thank you.'

By the time the elevators reached the bottom floor, he thought, the word on McDonald would be out. If Baki was as efficient as she looked, she could never pass on the chance to screw one of her boss's competitors.

Like Bone, Sandra Ollsen was really too busy to talk to Lucas; but he mentioned Bone's name and was admitted to the mahogany offices of Kelly, Batten, Orstein & Shirinjivi. Ollsen was a tall, coordinated woman who looked as though she might once have played some ball herself.

'How's Jim?' she asked casually, as Lucas settled into the chair across her desk.

'Looks fine; something of a power struggle going on over there,' Lucas said.

'Yes. With Susan O'Dell. I hope she kicks his butt.'

'Really?' Lucas asked.

'Really,' she said. Lucas, bemused, watched her for a moment, waiting, and then she said, 'He sort of dumped me.'

'Ah. I know the feeling,' Lucas said.

She looked him over. 'I don't think so,' she said after a minute.

'You'd be wrong,' Lucas said. 'Anyway . . . he seems to think of you as a friend.'

'Right.' She rolled her eyes. 'Actually, I don't think he was actually looking for friendship when he started squiring me around. He was looking . . .' She grinned at him, not a bad smile at all. 'Why am I telling you this?'

'Because of my open face and genuine curiosity?'

''Cause you're a trained interrogator, that's why. When I was in college, we called you pigs.'

'When I was in college, I called us pigs,' Lucas said. 'So what was he looking for when he started taking you around?'

'Sex,' she said, ingenuously. 'Any place, any time . . . some of the girls around the bank call him The Boner, if you know what I mean.'

'All right,' Lucas said. 'Listen, the reason I came by . . .'

'Bet nobody would ever call you that,' Ollsen said. 'The Boner.'

'Only 'cause I carry a big leather sap in my pocket,' Lucas said. 'I'd beat the tar out of them.'

'Oh, it's a sap. And I just thought you were happy to see me.'

Lucas held up his hands: 'All right, you win the war of wits,' and they both laughed. 'But listen, the real reason I came around: You know about the Kresge killing, of course. We're investigating it, and I'm wondering how well you know Wilson McDonald?'

A sudden wariness appeared in her eyes, and she put a hand to her throat. 'You think Wilson did it?'

'No, we don't think anything, just yet. But he was one of the four people up there when Kresge . . .'

'Bit the bullet?'

'Exactly the words I was looking for,' Lucas said. 'Anyway: how well do you know McDonald?'

'My parents knew the family quite well . . .'

'Does Wilson McDonald beat his wife?'

'Ah, Jesus,' she said, softly. 'I wondered what Jim told you. What are you going to do, blackmail him with it? Wilson?'

'Domestic violence is not my department,' Lucas said. 'I'm just trying to get a reading on him, what kind of a guy he is.'

Again, she hesitated, and Lucas added, 'This is all informal. There won't be any record of what you say.'

'But you could subpoena me.'

'If it got to that point, you'd be morally obliged to tell us anyway,' Lucas said.

She thought about that for a moment, then said, 'I was at a pool party last summer – Rush and Louise Freeman, he runs Freeman-Hoag.'

'The advertising agency.'

'Yes. Wilson got drunk. He was getting loud and he went into the pool with his clothes on – Audrey said he fell, but I saw it, and he looked like he was jumping in. Anyway, we got him out, and Audrey walked him around the house out toward their car, and they started arguing. And Louise went over to Rush – I was talking to Rush – and she said something like, "Rush, you better go around, they're starting to argue." Something about the way she said it. So Rush went around the house, and I followed around, and we both came around the corner just in time to see Wilson hit her right in the head. He just swatted her and knocked her down. Rush ran over and they started arguing and I thought Wilson was going to fight him. But Audrey got up and said she was all right and I got between the two guys. And they went off.'

'Nobody called the police?' Lucas asked.

'No.'

'I thought that was the correct thing to do,' Lucas said. 'I mean with the lawyer-doctor-advertising set. No violence.'

She nodded. 'I'll tell you what, buster. If any guy ever hit me like that, his ass would be in jail ten minutes later. But . . . sometimes things are more complicated. Audrey didn't want it. She said he was drunk and didn't mean anything.'

'So that was the end of it.'

'Yes. Then, anyway. I was talking to Louise afterwards, and she said that he'd beaten her up before. A couple of times a year.'

'And she'd know?'

'Yes . . . she's a little younger. Louise is. She's Rush's second wife, used to be his secretary. She knows Audrey's younger sister pretty well, I don't know how. The sister told Louise that Wilson beats up Audrey a couple of times a year. Sometimes pretty badly.'

'Do you think Wilson McDonald could have killed Kresge?'

'Yes,' she said. 'Not just because I saw him hit Audrey. I was always a little afraid of him. I knew him when I was little – he was five or six years ahead of me at Cresthaven, and my

75

brother knew him. He's big and fat and mean, he's got those little mean eyes. He's a goddamned animal.'

Lucas nodded: 'Okay.'

'Even if he did it, you won't get him. He's pretty smart, but most of all, he's a McDonald,' she said. 'The McDonalds . . . they've got this family thing. They don't care what a family member does, as long as he doesn't get caught at it.' She stopped: 'No, that's not quite right: they don't care what he does, as long as he's not convicted of it. In their eyes, not being convicted is the same as not doing it. That comes from way back. The first McDonalds were crooks, they stole from the farmers with their mill. The second or third generation were still crooks, and they made millions during the Depression with real-estate scams that they ran through Polaris. And they're still crooks. And they've got very good legal advice.'

'But don't quote you.'

'Subpoena me first,' she said. 'Then you can quote me.'

'Do you think Louise Freeman would talk to me?'

'Probably. She's the kind who'd have all the dirt, if I do say so myself.'

Chapter Six

A grim-faced Helen Bell steered her Toyota Camry into the driveway at her sister's house and said, 'Audrey, you're crazy.'

'It's all right,' Audrey McDonald said sharply. She had a small black circle under her left eye, now covered heavily with makeup, where one of Wilson McDonald's blows had landed. 'He must be sober by now. He had to work today.'

'He could have gone to work this morning and be drunk all over again,' Bell said. She was four years younger than her sister, but in some ways, had always been the protective one. 'That's happened.'

'I'll be okay,' Audrey said.

'You'll never be okay until you leave him,' Helen said. 'The man is an animal and doesn't deserve you. Even the police know it, now – you said so yourself.'

'But I love him,' Audrey said. On the drive over, Helen had gotten angrier and angrier with her sister, but now her face softened and she patted Audrey on the thigh.

'Then you're going to have to see a doctor, together,' she said. 'There's a name for this – codependency. You can't keep going like this, because sooner or later, it won't just be a slap, or a beating. He's going to kill you.'

'You know what he's said about that, about a doctor,' Audrey said. 'They don't go to psychiatrists in the McDonald family.'

'But it'd all be confidential,' Helen protested. 'Times have changed . . .'

'After this bank thing is done with,' Audrey said, as she pushed open the car door. 'Maybe then.'

Bell watched her go. She hated McDonald. She'd never liked him, but over the years, distaste had grown into this curdling, bitter-tasting hatred. Audrey would never remove herself from McDonald. Somebody else would have to do it for her, like a surgeon removing a cancer.

She liked the metaphor: Dan Kresge had been a cancer on the bank, and he'd been removed. Good for the bank and everybody employed there. McDonald was a cancer on her sister: the sooner he was cut out, the better.

Audrey eased into the house, moving quietly, wary of an ambush. Was he in the tub again? In the study? She stepped into the kitchen, and the board that always squeaked, the one she'd sworn two hundred times to fix, squeaked.

'Audrey? Is that you?' He was in the study; he sounded sober.

'It's me,' she said tentatively.

'Jesus Christ, where have you been? I've been calling Helen, but nobody ever answers.' He'd been lurching down the hall as he spoke, a yellow legal pad in his hand, and when he turned into the kitchen, he spotted the black eye and pulled up. 'Holy cow. Did I do that?'

She recognized the mood and moved to take advantage of it: 'No, of course not,' she said sarcastically. 'I've been hitting myself in the face with a broomstick.'

'Aw. Jesus . . .' That was all she'd get. He went on, 'But Jesus, we gotta talk. I got a cop following me around. And the board's gonna meet on Wednesday, but probably won't make a decision. They're talking about a search, for Christ's sake.'

'A search? That's just a way of slowing everything down.'

'I know that. It's me or O'Dell or Bone.'

'Have you talked to your father?'

'Just for a minute, to ask him to stay out of it for the time being. I thought it might be a little too obvious if he got out there. At this point.'

'Good thought . . . What about the cop?'

'It's this fuckin' Davenport,' McDonald said impatiently. 'He was talking to Bone today, and the word is, he's asking about me.'

'What's he asking?' Audrey asked. 'He doesn't think you . . .'

'I don't know; I'm finding out. He could be a problem.'

'How can he be a problem? You didn't shoot anybody.'

His eyes slid away from hers: 'I know . . . but he could be a problem.' He looked back: 'I mean, Jesus, if there's a search, you think they're gonna pick a guy who the cops are investigating?'

'Okay.'

'And the thing is, the sheriff up there, Krause, he's just about signed off on the thing, from what I hear. He's dead in the water. If it wasn't for Davenport, it'd be pretty much over with.'

'Maybe that's something your father could help with right now.'

'Come on in here,' Wilson said, and turned back toward the study. The study was a large room with a window looking out on the front lawn, and two walls of shelves loaded with knick-knacks, travel souvenirs, and small golf and tennis trophies going back to Wilson's days in prep school and college. Framed photos of Wilson and Audrey with George Bush, Ronald Reagan and, in much younger days, with a tired-looking Richard Nixon, looked down from the third wall. Wilson dropped into the brown-leather executive's chair behind the cherry desk, while Audrey perched on a love seat below Nixon's worn face.

'So call your father on Davenport. On the board, we can call Jimmy and Elaine,' Audrey said. 'Elaine is very close to Dafne Bose and Jimmy's been trying to get into the trust department's legal work *forever* . . .' Dafne Bose was on the board. 'If we can get to Dafne, we're halfway there.'

'You know who else?' He looked down at the legal pad. 'We're carrying two million bucks in land-and-attachments paper on Shankland Chev, which they couldn't get a half million anywhere else. And Dave Shankland . . .'

'. . . is married to Peg Bose.' Peg Bose was Dafne's daughter. 'We couldn't use that right away, it'd look too much like blackmail. But if we got in a squeak . . .'

'Here's the list I've got so far,' Wilson said. He passed the legal pad to Audrey. 'Seventeen board members, so we need nine. Four I can count on – Eirich, Goff, Brandt and Sanderson. If we can get Dafne, we can probably get Rondeau and Bunde, 'cause they pretty much do what she suggests. Then we'd need two . . .'

'How about Young? You know he wants to get into Woodland.'

'Oh, man, I don't know if I could swing that,' Wilson said doubtfully.

'We need a black member anyway, because of that government thing, and who'd be better than Billy Young? His father was a minister and he's really pretty white. And he must be worth . . .'

They began working down strings of possible supporters, analyzing relationships, working out who knew whom, who owed who, who could be bought, and with what.

Later, getting coffee, Audrey, without thinking, brushed her cheek, and flinched at the sudden lancing pain. The black eye: she'd forgotten about it, and Wilson had never really paid any attention to it anyway. The excitement of conspiracy, she decided: some of their tenderest moments had occurred in the study, working over legal pads . . .

Marcus Kent was an assistant vice-president in corporate operations, working for Bone; he sat on one end of Susan O'Dell's couch. Carla Wyte, who technically worked for Robles in the currency room, lounged on the other end. Louise Compton, wearing blue jeans and a Nike sweatshirt, sat cross-legged on the floor.

'. . . either Bone or me,' O'Dell was saying. She was on her feet, as though she were a junior exec making a presentation to the board of directors. 'McDonald can't get more than six. He's the obvious first-thought, because of his family, but twelve members would be dead-set against him. When that becomes obvious, things will start to move. I can see myself with eight votes; and I can see eight for Bone, but only a couple are solid for each of us. Everything is very fluid . . . So I think we're gonna have to start maneuvering here.'

'How about Robles?' Wyte asked.

'No chance,' O'Dell said. 'It's gonna be Bone or me.'

'Bone is good,' Wyte said. 'His division makes the big bucks.'

'Most of it by me,' Kent said.

O'Dell looked at Kent: 'But it's his division, not yours. He gets the credit.'

Kent said, 'Before we get any further in this, let me ask . . . What do we get out of it? Carla and Louise and me? We know what you get.'

O'Dell said, 'You get Bone's job. He won't stay around long if I'm picked for the top spot. And Carla's eventually

81

going to move into Robles' slot. But right away and I mean right away – she gets money.'

'How much?' Wyte's eyebrows went up.

'Fifty more. Fifty is the number I had in mind.'

'Fifty is a nice number,' Wyte said.

'And it'll be twice that when Robles leaves.'

Compton said, 'How about me?'

'You're gonna be my executive assistant. You're gonna be my ears. My intelligence department. You'll do real well – in terms of clout, if not in title, you'll be Number Two in the bank.'

'So how do we do this?' Wyte asked. 'What do we do . . . assuming we're all in.'

O'Dell looked around the room. After a second, Kent said, 'I'm in,' and Compton said, 'Yeah.' Wyte nodded.

'So . . .' O'Dell said. 'I'm going to start putting together a pitch for the board. It's got to be good, and it'll take time. And I'll start working the board: that's something I have to do personally.'

'To some extent, it's gonna be like a political campaign, but with fewer voters,' Compton said. She'd come to the bank from the state capitol. 'One thing we can do is, we can make the point with the newspapers that you'd be the first woman ever to run a major bank in Minnesota. Or anywhere, as far as I know. Any other major bank CEOs are women?' She looked around, then answered herself. 'No. Okay. I'll check that out, but I can also start working the papers.'

'That's good,' O'Dell said. 'But we've got to get it going. How long before we could see it on the news?'

Compton looked at her watch: 'I've got time today. I'll have to talk to a couple of people, but we should see some action by tomorrow morning. When they call, you've got to be modest and all that . . . you know, the board has to make a decision.'

'I know,' O'Dell said. 'I can do that.'

Kent leaned forward, took a cinnamon candy out of a bowl on the coffee table, peeled off the crinkly cellophane wrapper, and popped the candy into his mouth: 'Speaking of negative campaigning . . .'

'Were we speaking of that?' Compton asked, with a quick, cynical smile. They would have come to it, sooner or later.

'We are now,' he said. 'We all know Bone's weakness.'

'Women.'

O'Dell shook her head. 'That won't help. We just don't have the time – even if we could find somebody willing to dig into it, it'd take weeks.'

Kent was shaking his head. 'Not really. Not if the cops look into it and if somebody tips the papers that the cops are looking into it.'

'Why would they?' Wyte asked.

''Cause of the woman,' Kent said, sitting back, savoring his little nugget.

'Marcus . . .' O'Dell said.

'James T. Bone is fucking Marcia Kresge. And has been for a while.'

O'Dell's mouth had literally fallen open. 'You're kidding me.'

Kent shook his head: 'Nope. I saw her one night at Bone's place – I was in the ramp, I'd been over at Casper Allen's, about his idiot trusts . . .'

'Casper lives right downstairs from Bone,' O'Dell said to the others.

'. . . and she'd been fuckin' *somebody,* believe me. And as she's getting into her car, who should come out after her, carrying something? James T. Bone.'

'The cops need to know that,' Wyte said, with an effort at sincerity. 'I mean, even if we weren't trying to . . . to . . . help Susan, they'd need to know that. Dan's death is worth millions to her, and opens the top job for her lover.'

'That's what I thought,' Kent said, leaning back on the couch, sucking on the cinnamon.

Two hours later, O'Dell ushered Compton into the elevator, the last of them to go, and stepped pensively back into her apartment. Kent was a rat: she'd have to remember that. Starting now. The other two should be okay . . .

She spotted her rifle case, dumped in the corner Saturday morning. The case was empty: the Garfield sheriff still had the rifle. She picked it up, carried it back to a storage closet, and slipped it inside. Stuck on the wall of the same closet was an instant-open gun safe. Acting on impulse, she jabbed at the number pads, rolling her hand like a piano player, and the door popped open. Inside lay an Officer's Model Colt. She took it out, pulled the magazine, pulled the slide back to make sure the chamber was empty, let it slam forward.

She moved slowly through the apartment, dry-firing the pistol from various hiding spots and corners; corny, but fun. After ten minutes, she carried the pistol back to the safe, reseated the magazine, and shut the safe door.

She'd have to get out to the range one of these days; she was losing her edge.

Marcia Kresge was getting comfortable on James T. Bone's couch: 'Are you going to get the job?'

'I don't know. O'Dell's pretty strong.'

'How about McDonald?'

'We can handle McDonald.'

'Good. He's an asshole. O'Dell, you know, smokes dope.'

'So what?' Bone said. 'So do you.'

'I'm not trying to get to be a bank president,' Kresge said.

'I don't think that's enough to disqualify her,' Bone said.

'It would if she was arrested for possession,' Kresge said. 'The board wouldn't touch her with a ten-foot pole.'

'You'd really wish that on her?' Bone asked with real curiosity.

'I'd like to see you get the job,' Kresge said. 'And I could fix the bust.'

'How?'

'We've got the same dealer,' Kresge said.

Bone laughed despite himself. 'How'd that happen?'

She shrugged, not seeing anything funny in the coincidence. 'You know, we all hang out at the same places, and word gets around. This guy, Mark, used to be a waiter at The Falls. He's working his way through college.'

'Selling grass?'

'Grass, speed, acid, coke, heroin, ecstasy. PCP, probably. Anyway, he deals to Susan. If somebody tipped off the police, maybe they could catch him making a delivery. You know, socialite dope ring. The cops would like that.'

'What if they got your name?' Bone asked.

She shrugged. 'I'd get rid of everything before I tipped them, and I wouldn't buy any more. What're they going to do? If they even got my name, I'd sue their butts off if they let it out.'

'Listen,' Bone said, now serious, leaning toward her: 'Forget it. I swear to God, Marcia, if anybody tips off the cops about Susan, I'll whip your ass.'

'Ooo . . . that could be fun,' she said lightly.

'No. It wouldn't be fun,' he snapped.

Sometimes he frightened her, just a bit, she thought. But a bit more than she found pleasant. 'You're not gonna get this job by looking pretty, you know,' she snapped back.

'I know that. I'm working on it,' he said.

'I could talk to a couple of people.'

'Anything you could do I'd appreciate . . . but let me know first.'

'Hey: if I go into banker's-wife mode, I could probably deliver two or three votes off that board. That damn Jack O'Grady has been trying to get my pants off for fifteen years: I bet he could pull a couple votes for you.'

'I think Jack's already with me,' Bone said. 'But encouragement would be good.'

'Even if I have to take my pants off?'

'How big a change would that be?' he asked.

A pause. Then Kresge, smiling prettily, said, 'Really great fuckin' thing to say, Bone.'

'Tell you the truth, I'm surprised the police haven't spent more time with you. You're not the most discreet person in the world and you weren't divorced when Dan was killed.'

'I can be discreet when I wanna be,' she said. 'Look at us.'

'Okay.'

'Besides, a woman cop *did* come around and talk to me – Sherrill, her name was. Last name. She had that big-tit look you go for. And hell, I told her everything.'

'But not about us.'

'She didn't ask.'

Bone stood up, turned. 'Anyway. I think McDonald's in trouble. We know O'Dell's gonna get a certain number of votes, and I'll get mine, but it's McDonald's that are up for grabs.'

'How's McDonald in trouble?'

'This cop – Lucas Davenport, assistant chief . . .'

'I know him, actually.'

'He thinks McDonald's involved. I've talked to him a couple of times and he's a smart guy. He's talking to

McDonald's pals and the word is getting out. If there's even a whiff of involvement, the board'll drop him like a hot rock.'

'So anything that would encourage Davenport to look at McDonald . . . that would help.'

'As long as it didn't turn back on us.'

'I'll see what . . .' The doorbell rang, and Kresge turned her head.

Bone stepped across the room and opened the heavy paneled door. Kerin Baki was there, struggling with an over-sized briefcase. As she brought it in, her glasses slipped down her nose, and she jabbed them back, as though they'd mutinied. She saw Kresge on the couch and said, 'Mrs Kresge. Have you spoken to Mr O'Grady?'

'We were just talking about that,' Kresge said pleasantly. 'Your boss was giving me a very hard time.'

Baki turned, said, 'Mr Bone, you should listen to Mrs Kresge on this.'

'Christ, you're conspiring against me,' he said.

'*Working* for you,' Baki said. 'I printed everything I could find on the mortgage company performance since McDonald took over. There are a few things we can use – not necessarily his fault, but you know how mortgages have been per-forming . . .'

'Let me get a Coke,' Bone said. 'What would you like, Kerin? Marcia already has a . . .'

'Bloody Mary,' Kresge said. 'And it's all gone. I'll help you . . .'

'Just sparkling water,' Baki said. She began spreading her papers on a coffee table as Bone and Kresge went to the kitchen to get drinks. When Baki finished with the papers, she heard Kresge laugh, a low, husky laugh with a little sex in it; she could see them moving around Bone's small kitchen, inside each other's personal space, casually bumping hips.

Their relationship had been clear to Baki for a while, now; she wouldn't tolerate it much longer. She got so deep into that calculation – the end of Bone's relationship with Marcia Kresge – that she almost didn't notice them walking toward her.

'Kerin?' Bone said curiously. 'Are you home?'

He was standing next to her, holding out a glass and a bottle of lime-flavored Perrier. 'Oh. Sure. Pre-occupied, I guess.' She pushed the Perrier aside and went to the papers. 'This stack of papers is the annualized return on . . .'

Bonnie Bonet dyed her hair black, the dense, sticky color of shoe polish. She dressed in black from head to toe, wore blue lipstick and carried thirty-five extra pounds. But she was almost smart and could write poetry in Perl-5. She sat across the table from Robles and said, 'Because the motherfucker was going to kill a couple of thousand people, that's why.'

'I know you're lying,' Robles said. He'd broken a sweat.

'No, you don't. I'm not lying.'

'So tell me what kind of a gun you used,' he said.

'My father's .30–30.'

'Bullshit. You never fired a gun in your life.'

She sneered at him: 'You think I couldn't figure out a gun? Every redneck in Minnesota can shoot a gun, but I can't?'

'I'm gonna tell the cops about this,' Robles said.

'Go ahead,' she said. 'You've got no proof.'

'Jesus Christ, Bonnie. I know you're lying, but you're pushing me into a corner. You get this fantasy going, you'll tell somebody else, like one of your fuckin' novels . . .' Bonet laughed, but looked away. Robles said, 'Oh, Jesus, who'd you tell?'

'He doesn't believe me, either.'

'You told goddamned Dick . . .'

'Well, you started it . . . the whole fantasy thing.'

'I was joking,' Robles insisted. 'I didn't want him dead . . .'

'You got him.'

'But I was joking . . .'

'Too late now. You tell the cops about me, I'll tell them about you.'

Robles left the bar, sweating, half-drunk. Okay, she was lying. But she'd never admit it. She was crazy. Almost for sure . . .

Terrance Robles had made just shy of a half-million dollars the previous year, and he'd spent only a small part of it. With his access to information, he could grow his stake at twenty to thirty percent per year, on top of earnings. If he could hang on for another five years, he could quit. Get out. Buy an old used Cray computer somewhere, and do some *serious* shit.

But he had to hold on.

He could turn Bonet in. Or, alternatively, he could kill her – nothing else would shut her up. She was having too good a time.

Robles bit on a thumbnail, stumbled along the street.

Late night: the mixed smells of vinegar and gasoline, one pungent, one metallic; the combination smelling like blood. The vinegar went into the wash tub, and down the drain, followed by a steady stream of water that would carry it away.

A glass cutter: this had been in the book, which went on to say that it was probably unnecessary, but why take chances? Deep scored lines up and down the bottle, then more, horizontally, until the bottle was checkered with shaky, intersecting lines. Then the bottle sprayed with Windex, carefully and meticulously wiped with paper towels. No fingerprints here.

Now the gasoline, mixed in the bottle with two four-ounce

cans of chainsaw oil. A strip of old t-shirt for a wick.
The bottle was heavy; a little better than seven pounds.
But it wouldn't have to be thrown far.
Just far enough.

Chapter Seven

'Now we're getting some heat,' said Rose Marie Roux. She was drinking coffee from a bone china cup; a matching saucer sat on her desk, and on the saucer, a wad of green chewing gum. 'Harrison White called, and said if you need to interview Wilson McDonald, or if you would like to bring him before a grand jury, McDonald will come over anytime and testify. Without immunity. He will answer any questions, without reservation. Under oath.'

'And if we don't need him to do that?' Lucas asked. He was facing Roux's window, the sun streaming in. Another good day. Cold.

'Then knock off the innuendos – the snooping around asking other people about him. White says the snooping could cost McDonald the top job at the bank, and if it does, he'll see that the city picks up the difference in what he makes now, and what he would have made in twenty-some years as bank president. He thinks it might be forty or fifty million.'

Lucas grinned. 'Would we have to pay it all up front?'

Roux smiled back: 'He didn't say. But he also talked to a couple of people on the city council, and McDonald's father has been calling around . . . but fuck them. Do what you need with McDonald. I thought you should know that glaciers are starting to move.'

'Thanks,' Lucas said.

'And, of course, what White says is true. McDonald could be completely innocent, and we could be screwing him out of his lifetime job. In fact, we could even have been set up to do it, with the letter.'

'Tell you what,' Lucas said. 'Let me talk to White. I wanted McDonald bumped, I wanted him nervous, but I don't need to push much harder. We could back off a bit.'

'Whatever you think,' Roux said. She finished the coffee, peeled the gum off the saucer, and popped it back in her mouth. 'Nicotine,' she said. 'Too expensive to throw away before I chew it out.'

'So I'll . . .' Lucas was getting to his feet.

'Sit down,' Roux said. She probed her desk for a moment. 'We have a couple of things to talk about. First, the opium ring . . .'

'Oh, shit,' Lucas groaned.

'And then Capslock has put in for thirty hours accumulated overtime for investigating it.'

'Rose Marie . . .'

'He's your guy, goddamnit. Now, this thirty hours. He took the thirty hours when he was supposedly on disability leave after the pinking-shears incident. Now what I'm trying to figure is how . . .'

'Aw, Rose Marie, c'mon . . .'

Roux was amusing, and he laughed with her, and convinced her to sign off on the thirty hours. But the laughter was like a water-bug on a pond, skating across the surface of his mind. He was amused and he laughed but nothing was deeply funny; life was simply stupid most of the time. Going downhill, again, he thought. He walked back to his office, tired, a little unnerved by the overnight rattling in his brain, and found Sherrill waiting for him.

Sherrill was lanky and dark-eyed, with short black hair and – Sloan's words – the good headlights. Her estranged husband had been killed by a crazy outlaw, who was himself killed by Lucas in a close-quarters firefight in the middle of a freak blizzard. It all happened just minutes before the cold-eyed Iowa boy had blown up both Dick LaChaise and Lucas' marriage prospects. Last winter had been a bad one.

'There you are,' Sherrill said. 'Want to come detect?'

'Detect what?'

'An anonymous caller phoned the Garfield sheriff's office and said that a US West lineman saw the killer, or might have seen him. The lineman was working on an exchange box near Kresge's place. Said that he was talking about it in a bar, thought about calling the cops but didn't because he didn't want to get involved. So the sheriff tracked him down, and guess what?'

'He confessed and threw himself on the mercy of the court.'

'Nope. He's down here. They sent him to an NSP warehouse to pick up a bunch of splicer-things . . . the sheriff talked to him and called me. He's the only eyewitness we have so far. I'm going over.'

'How far?'

'Ten minutes?'

'Let's go,' Lucas said.

Sherrill had a city car parked at the curb. They took I-394 west, falling into routine cop chitchat that covered a vaguely uncomfortable tension between them. Sherrill was at least somewhat available, and, rumor had it, would not be averse to exploring possibilities with Lucas. At the same time, word was around that Lucas hadn't quite recovered from the loss of Weather, and nobody wanted to be the first woman afterwards.

Lucas, on the other hand, with a small reputation as a womanizer, had been expected to make a run at Sherrill ever since her marriage began going bad. He'd never done that.

There lingered about them the sense that somebody ought to make a move, almost as a matter of common politeness.

'Did you get anything good out of Kresge's office?' Lucas asked after a while.

'Naw. But there are some newly humble secretaries and assistants around the place, I'll tell you,' Sherrill said cheerfully. 'Especially around Bone and O'Dell and McDonald. Everybody thinks one of them will get the job.'

'What about the merger?'

'That's apparently on hold.'

'Hmph. So if somebody shot Kresge to stop the merger, it worked.'

'Yup. For the time being, anyway.'

'And this telephone guy . . .'

'Harold Hanks.'

'. . . saw the killer.'

'Maybe. But there's something odd about the whole thing. Whoever called, the sheriff's office said she heard him talking in a bar. Harold Hanks is a hardshell Baptist. He told the sheriff he hadn't been in a bar for fifteen years, since he was born again. But he did see somebody, just like the caller said. But he never connected whoever he saw with the killing.'

'The caller was a woman?'

'Yeah.'

'They knew where the call came from?'

'A pay phone off I-35. I wrote it down, it's up north somewhere.'

'Nothing there, then.'

'Nope.'

'Both letters to Rose Marie were probably written by women – one of them for sure, and the one pointing at McDonald has a female feeling to it . . .'

'Yeah, it does,' Sherrill agreed. 'So we've got somebody

out there who knows a lot more than we do, and she's leading us in.'

'Which makes you wonder . . .' He looked out the window.

'What?'

'McDonald's wife,' Lucas suggested.

'Hmm.'

'He beats her up,' Lucas said.

'Yeah?' Old story.

'Something to look into,' he said.

They rode in the slightly tense silence for another few minutes, then Sherrill blurted, 'Seeing Weather at all?'

'No. The shrink thinks we ought to spend some time apart.' Everybody in the department knew about the shrink.

'But eventually get back?' Sherrill asked.

'Maybe,' Lucas said moodily. Three teenagers in reflective vests were peering through a surveying total station just off the Interstate. All three wore their hats backwards.

'You know,' Sherrill said, plowing ahead, 'You've really got your head up your ass in a lot of ways. You walk around with this cloud over you, mooning over her. Why don't you do something to get her back?'

'I'm afraid it's more complicated than that,' Lucas started, a distinct chill in his voice.

'Oh, bullshit, Lucas. If you love her, get her back. Don't wait for her to work it out – plot something. Suck her in. The thing is, if she gets a little freaky when she sees you, then you've got to hang around more. Screw the shrink: the thing is, life goes on, and if you're around all the time, and life keeps going on . . . the freakiness will go away. It'll get boring. Tiresome. And if she basically loves you, and you love her . . .'

'Can we knock this off? You're bumming me out.'

'Jesus, what a crock,' Sherrill said, angry now.

Lucas was just as angry: 'It's a crock, all right. I should

trick her back? How would I do that? Huh? Get somebody to set up a blind date, and it's me? Hide in her closet, and pop out when she goes to iron a blouse?'

Sherrill rolled her eyes and nearly took the car into the on-coming lane; Lucas flinched and she jerked it back to the right. 'Lucas, this is Marcy Sherrill you're talking to. I was there when you suckered John Mail, remember? I helped you track the LaChaise women. I heard you order up a traffic stop, that you knew would never be made, so when we wasted them, our asses would be covered with the press. I was there, for Christ's sake. I heard you work it out. So don't tell me you couldn't work out some little scheme to get close to her. When it came time to finish off John Mail, you didn't get moody . . .'

'Shut the fuck up,' Lucas said.

'Fuck you.'

'There's US West,' Lucas said, pointing to the right.

'Maybe you don't want her back,' Sherrill said. She missed the turn.

'You missed the goddamned turn,' Lucas fumed.

'I'll make the goddamn turn,' Sherrill said, and she braked, looked quickly left, then did an illegal U, bouncing across a median strip.

'Jesus Christ,' Lucas said, startled, bracing himself, as the muffler dragged over the curb.

'You want the fuckin' turn, I'll make the fuckin' turn,' Sherrill snarled, and ignoring a red light, turned left across two lanes of traffic into the US West parking area. They lurched to a stop in a visitor's space.

'Satisfied?' she asked.

'Yeah,' Lucas said. 'Really.'

Sherrill was out of the car, steaming toward the warehouse entrance. Lucas trailed behind, deflected the door as it slammed on his face, and finally caught her at the service counter, where she flashed her ID at a guard and said, 'We're here to see Harold Hanks.'

'Oh, yeah,' the guard. 'He's waiting, up in the canteen on two.'

'Second floor?'

'Take those elevators.'

She steamed on back to the elevators. 'Like you're Miss Social Life,' Lucas said at her back.

Then she was suddenly calm: 'Lucas, I have an active social life. You just don't see it.' A blatant lie, and they both knew it. The elevator went 'ding' and they got inside.

'Maybe Weather and I don't recover quite as quickly as you do,' Lucas said, as the doors slid shut.

'That's a horseshit thing to say,' Sherrill shouted, really angry now. 'You take that back.'

'I take it back,' Lucas said meekly.

'I'd already signed off on Mike when he got killed,' she shouted.

Now he just wanted to quiet her down. 'I know, I know . . .'

'Jesus, what a jerk.'

The elevator doors opened, and a short, rotund man in a brown suit was staring at them owlishly; he'd obviously heard the shouting. 'Is there a problem?'

'Yeah, him,' Sherrill said, tossing her thumb at Lucas, who hovered, embarrassed, in the doorway.

'There are some police officers coming up,' the man ventured.

'We are the police officers,' Sherrill said. 'We're looking for a man named Harold Hanks.'

'The canteen . . . that way, left around the corner.'

They went left around the corner and Lucas said, 'That was really cute.'

'Shut up,' she said.

Harold Hanks was a gangly, raw-boned man who wore a billed hat over plaid shirt, jeans and boots, and though he'd spread out on a couch, he looked as though he'd be even more comfortable standing in a ditch somewhere. He was drinking a Welch's grape soda from the can, while he paged through a copy of *Guns & Ammo*.

'Anything good?' Sherrill asked, tipping her head to look at the magazine cover.

'Some. But it's mostly pistol bullshit . . . you're Miz Sherrill.'

'Yes. And this is Chief Davenport. Sheriff Krause says you saw somebody up by the Kresge place.'

'Yeah, I guess – but I didn't tell anybody about it in no bar.'

'Did you tell anybody about it at all?' Lucas asked.

'No, I never did,' Hanks said. 'No reason to. Just somebody in the woods during deer season. Only saw him for a minute. And, see, I was up on the south side of Kresge's place, way around from the driveway. I didn't even think of it being up that far . . . I never put it together.'

'So what'd he look like? The guy you saw?'

''Bout what you'd expect at that time of day, that day of the year. Blaze-orange hat and coat. Carrying a rifle.'

'Couldn't see his face?' Sherrill asked.

'Nope. He was wearing a scarf.'

'A scarf?'

'Yeah. Covered the whole bottom part of his face. His hood covered the top part of his face, down to his forehead, and the scarf came right up to his eyes.'

'Wasn't that a little weird?' Sherrill asked.

'Nope. It gets damn cold out there, sitting in a tree.'

'Big guy?' Lucas asked.

Hanks thought for a minute. then shook his head: 'Mmm, hard to tell. I only saw him from about the waist up, walking along back in the trees. Not real big. Maybe average. Maybe even smaller than average.'

Lucas looked at Sherrill: 'Have you seen McDonald?'

She shook her head. 'Not yet.'

'Six-three, six-four, maybe two-sixty.'

'Wasn't anybody that big,' Hanks said, shaking his head. 'With them coveralls and the blaze-orange coat, a guy that big would look like a giant.'

'Did you hear a shot before you saw him?'

'Heck, it was a shooting gallery out there. I was wearing blaze-orange myself, just to stand in a ditch. I was happy to get out of there alive. But there was a shot, sort of closeby, and in the right direction. About five, ten minutes before I saw him.'

'That'd be right,' Lucas said to Sherrill.

Sherrill nodded and went back to Hanks. 'But that's all. Just a guy in orange. Nothing distinctive?'

Hanks shrugged. 'Sorry. I told the sheriff I couldn't help much.'

'Didn't see any cars coming or going?'

'There were a couple of trucks and maybe a car or two. I don't know. I wasn't paying any attention.'

'What were you doing out there anyway?' Lucas asked. 'Six-thirty, on a Saturday morning?'

'Aw, there's this place called Pilot Lake, full of city people. They got maybe fifty phones around the lake, and some idiot put their exchange right on top of a spring. About once a month, the whole damn place goes down and then they all raise hell until somebody fixes it. It's a priority for us, until we can redo the exchange.'

'When did they go down?'

'About ten o'clock Friday night.'

'Including Kresge's place?'

'Nope. He'd be the next exchange up the road. Like I said, I was on the south side . . .'

'Okay.' Lucas thought for a moment, then asked, 'What'd the scarf look like? Black? Red?'

'Red,' Hanks said. He scratched his jaw, thinking about it. 'Or pink.'

'What else? Was it wrapped on the outside, or inside . . . ?'

'Inside – like he covered his face, then pulled the hood up over.'

'Okay . . .'

They dug for another five minutes, running him through it again, but came up with nothing more, until they both stood up. Then Lucas asked, 'Where would this guy have been walking to? Assuming he had a car?'

'I don't know,' Hanks said. His eyes drifted off to the ceiling. 'Probably . . . well, he could have been heading back to the Kresge cabin. He was sort of going that way, in a round-about way.'

'Could he have been going anywhere else?'

'Not that I know of.'

'How about this Pilot Lake place?'

'Nope. I was on that corner and he was walking . . .' He made a hand gesture, like a time-out signal. 'This way to the access road.'

'Perpendicular,' Sherrill suggested.

'Yeah. Like that,' Hanks said.

'You didn't hear a car start?'

'Nope. But I was quite a way from the house, and I was wearing my hat with ear flaps . . . So I probably wouldn't have.'

'Pink scarf,' said Lucas.

'Pink scarf,' Hanks said.

'What's the pink scarf?' Sherrill asked, after they let Hanks go. They were sitting alone in the canteen, eating Twinkies from the coin-op.

'Susan O'Dell wears a kafiyah as a scarf. It's pale red and white – she was wearing it when I saw her Saturday.'

'What's a kafiyah?'

'You know, one of those head wraps like Arabs wear,' Lucas said. 'Like what's-his-name, the Palestinian guy always wears.'

'Oh, yeah. Him. But his is black-and-white.'

'There's another kind that's red and white. And it would look pink from a distance, or pink and white.'

'He said pink.'

'O'Dell said she never left her tree before seven-thirty, when she shot her buck,' Lucas said. 'Then she gutted him and dragged him up to the trail and sat down next to her tree to wait until nine, which was the agreed-on time to take a break. Didn't go anywhere.'

'I think it's the car that's interesting. If there wasn't a car, it almost had to be one of those guys. Whoever it was, had to know the Kresge place pretty well, and there's no way you could walk in from very far away.'

'Yeah, but he's pretty shaky on that car stuff,' Lucas said. 'O'Dell would have been walking *away* from her tree stand if she was going in the direction Hanks said she was. She was definitely at her tree when Bone came by to pick her up at nine o'clock.'

'Maybe we push Miz O'Dell,' Sherrill said. 'See which way she goes.'

'Not yet,' Lucas said. 'I want to go back up there, to Kresge's, look around. And we need to know more about the bank merger idea – of the three realistic candidates to run the bank, we have accusations against two of them, McDonald and O'Dell. All the accusations come in anonymously, from women. At least, we think the accusation pointing at McDonald came from a woman ... So the question is, are they legit? Or are they meant to drag O'Dell and McDonald into an investigation that would eliminate them from contenders to run the bank.'

'You mean, by Bone? Or somebody working with Bone?'

'I'd hate to think so,' Lucas said, 'Because I kinda like the guy. But all of them are smart and tough. And the stakes are pretty big. Bone would be looking for an edge.'

'So we push Bone.'

'Let's wait before we push anyone. Just a day or two ... Let me get back up north.'

'Want me to come?'

Lucas looked at her as he finished his Twinkie. 'If you want to. If you stay out of my goddamned life while I'm trapped in the car.'

She flushed and said, 'I meant what I started out to say, before we got sidetracked. If you still want her, you've got to get off your ass and go after her. If you don't, you'll just ... drift away. And you'll never know for sure that it's over. If you go after her, you'll know pretty soon whether there's any hope.'

'I'll think about it,' he said.

'So when are we going up north?'

'Tomorrow,' Lucas said, looking at his watch. 'We should have some biographical stuff about the people McDonald supposedly killed. Let's take a look at that.'

They were six blocks from police headquarters when Sherrill's telephone chirped. She fumbled it out of her jacket pocket one-handed, said, 'Yeah?' and then passed the phone to Lucas. 'Sloan,' she said.

Lucas took the phone: 'What's going on?'

'I solved the Kresge case,' Sloan said laconically. 'I had a little break from the Ericson thing, and I thought I might as well clean it up.'

'That's good,' Lucas said. 'It's a burden off my mind.'

Sloan's tone of voice changed: 'Terrance Robles just walked in and said he may know who did it.'

Lucas, uncertain, and not wanting to bite too hard, said, 'You're kidding.'

'I'm not kidding. He's out sitting at my desk. Where are you?'

'About two minutes away.'

'See you in two minutes,' Sloan said.

Chapter Eight

Robles was sitting at Sloan's desk when Lucas and Sherrill arrived at homicide. He was talking to Sloan, and Lucas watched for a minute. Robles was crossing and recrossing his ankles under his chair, twisting his hands together, rubbing the back of his neck, squirming in the chair. Serious stress, Lucas thought. Lucas walked up behind him, trailed by Sherrill, and when Sloan looked up, Robles turned, then got to his feet.

'D-d-detective Davenport,' he stuttered. 'I've b-b-been talking to Detective Sloan, he thinks you should know about this.'

Lucas took a chair and Sherrill pulled one out of a nearby desk.

'So . . . you think you know who did it?' Lucas asked.

'No. I know somebody who says *she* did it, but I don't think she really did. But if I didn't tell you, I thought . . . I don't know what I thought.'

'So?' Lucas grinned at him and made a 'what?' gesture with his hands.

Robles had a friend, he said, a woman, a computer freak he'd met in an Internet chat room, and then in person, when it turned out that she lived in Minneapolis. When the news hit the papers that Polaris was considering a merger, and a large number of administrative and clerical personnel in Minneapolis could lose their jobs, she called him to ask him if the merger could be stopped.

104

'Her mother works at Polaris, routine clerical stuff, exactly the kind of job that would probably be wiped out,' Robles said.

'And you told her that the merger couldn't be stopped.'

'Not exactly. I told her that nobody much wanted it except Kresge and a small majority of board members, and the only reason the board was going for it was the stock premium . . .'

'Explain that,' Sherrill said. 'I don't understand stocks.'

'Well, see, Midland has offered to buy all the outstanding Polaris shares by trading with their shares, one to one. When they made the offer, they were trading in the sixties – sixty-plus dollars per share – and we were trading in the upper thirties. Their stock dropped on the offer, down to about fifty-three right now. But ours went to forty-six right now, and the closer we get to the merger, and the more certain it looks, the more ours will go up. If we finally merge, and nothing else happens, it'll probably be around fifty dollars a share. Polaris needs ten board members to okay the deal. If you look at how many board members own how much stock, the tenth biggest holder . . .' Robles looked at Sherrill, who seemed to be having trouble following the explanation. 'What I'm saying is, of those ten members needed to approve the merger, the one with the smallest holding is Shelley Oakes. He has ninety thousand shares, plus options for fifty thousand more at an average price in the thirties. If the sale goes through at fifty bucks, he'll make a couple of million bucks over what the stock was worth before the merger talk started.'

'Ah,' Sherrill said, as though she understood.

'The biggest holder, Dave Brandt, has better than four hundred thousand shares, plus God only knows what he has in stock options, which he could exercise before the deal goes down. He'll make tens of millions. Literally tens of millions.'

'So the board and Kresge make millions, and everybody else gets fired,' Lucas said.

'No, not exactly. Some people would make it. There're rumors that the investment division will be kept intact, that Midland wants the division. Then there are other executives who could make a stink, but most of them have stock options.'

'Do you have options?' Lucas asked.

'Yeah, yeah. I've got options on five thousand shares at a bunch of different prices that average out to about thirty-five, so if it goes to fifty, I'd make seventy-five thousand. But I'll tell you what, that's about six weeks' pay for me. And the government would get most of it anyway. I mean, it's nothing.'

'Nothing,' Sherrill said.

'Nothing.'

'Jesus, I make forty thousand a year,' Sherrill said. 'And I've been shot for it.'

'For your bigshots, forty ain't a salary,' Sloan said from behind Robles. 'It's more like the price tag on something they might buy next week.'

'Okay, okay,' Lucas said. 'So this woman . . .'

'Bonnie Bonet.'

'. . . told you she killed Kresge, and she has some motive.'

'Yes.'

'Why'd she tell you?'

'Ah, God. Because I asked her.' He twisted his hands nervously, and Lucas noticed that he seemed to sweat all the time, and copiously. 'See, the thing is, when she came on the 'net and asked if the merger could be stopped, I told her, not unless we killed Kresge. I didn't mean it, we were just joking on the 'net. But she came right back and said, "Let's do it." '

'And you said . . .'

'I said maybe we could figure a way to blow his car up,' Robles said.

'Blow his car up,' Sloan said, repeating the phrase as though he were astonished.

'I was *joking*. I really was – I'd never hurt anyone, it was just all bullshit. We went back and forth about ways to kill him, all ridiculous, like sci-fi stuff, and then . . . we stopped.'

'Stopped?' Sherrill's eyebrows went up.

'Yeah. It never came up again,' Robles said. 'It was like, a couple of nights, then we wore the subject out, and it never came up.'

'Until somebody killed him,' Lucas said.

'Why didn't you tell me this on Saturday?' asked Sloan.

'Because I didn't think there was any chance she'd done it. And if she hadn't done it, talking about it could only get me in trouble. So I wanted to check with her. I came back, and I couldn't find her on-line, and I didn't know where she lived. She's unlisted, and I'd only gotten together with her at Uncle Tony's. That's a bar . . .'

'We know,' Sherrill said. 'The one with the porno on computers.'

'Porno? You mean the TV3 story? That was all bullshit . . .'

'Yeah, yeah, yeah,' Lucas said. 'Go ahead.'

'Anyway, when I did find her, yesterday, I asked her if she's heard about it, and she said yeah. She'd done it,' Robles said.

'But you don't believe her.'

'No. She's never fired a gun. She doesn't even go outside, for Christ's sake. She's white as a sheet . . . she doesn't know about walking around in the woods. Her old man's got something wrong with his bowel or something, and never worked, and they never went anywhere when she was growing up. She said she shot him with her father's .30–30, and I bet she doesn't even know what a .30–30 looks like or that he has one.'

'Could be the right kind of rifle,' Lucas said. 'The medical examiner says Kresge was killed with a large caliber rifle, which around here probably means thirty caliber...'

'That's why I decided to tell you,' Robles said plaintively. 'I'm ninety-five percent sure she didn't do it – but I'm five percent not sure.'

'And you don't know where she lives,' Sloan said.

'No, but she uses her driver's license as an ID, and I figured you could get that.'

'Bonnie Bonet?'

'B-o-n-e-t,' Robles said, spelling it out. 'Is this gonna be in the newspapers?'

Sherrill looked at Lucas: 'Want me to pick her up?'

'Yeah. Do that. Get some uniforms to back you up. Call me when you've got her.' When Sherrill had gone, Lucas turned back to Robles, looked at him for several seconds, then said, 'We'll need a statement. Detective Sloan will take it.'

And to Sloan: 'Read him his rights on the tape.'

'My rights?' Robles threw his head back to peer at Lucas. 'To a lawyer? Do I need a lawyer?'

Lucas shrugged: 'Purely up to you ... Anyway, talk to Sloan.' And to Sloan: 'I'll be down at my office. I've got some paper to look at.'

Two files were waiting for him: files on the people mentioned in the anonymous letter as victims of Wilson McDonald.

Lucas took off his jacket, hung it on an antique oaken coat rack, dropped in the chair behind his desk. He picked up the first file, put his heels on his desk, and leaned back. And then let the file drop to his lap for a few seconds. He was not particularly introspective, but he was suddenly aware that the constant mental grinding in the back of his head – the grinding that had gone on for weeks, a symptom of the beast prowling around him – was fainter, barely distinguishable.

A book project, he thought: *Serial Murder: A Cure for Clinical Depression?* by Lucas Davenport.

George Arris was killed on a rainy night in September, 1984, while walking down St Paul's Grand Avenue toward a restaurant-bar generally regarded as a meat rack. Somebody unknown had fired a single shot from a .380 semi-automatic pistol into the back of Arris' head, and left him to die on the sidewalk.

St Paul homicide investigators had torn the city apart looking for the killer, because Arris was only the last of four nearly identical killings, spaced about two weeks apart.

All the victims were younger white men, all relatively affluent, all walking alone at night. All of the killings were within twenty blocks of each other. A racial motivation was suspected, and black gang members were targeted as the primary suspects.

Four different pistols had been used in the killings. Two of the guns had been found.

The first, a .22-caliber Smith & Wesson revolver which had been used in the second killing, was found by a city work crew trying to open a clogged storm sewer a half-mile from the killing. That set off a general inspection of storm sewers, and the second pistol, a .25-caliber semi-auto was found three blocks from the .22. Neither of the other two pistols was found.

The lead detective on the case was George Jellman.

Jellman was retired, and it took two phone calls to locate him. 'He's out back,' his wife shouted. 'I'll go get him.' She must have been shouting, Lucas mused, because they lived in Florida, which was a long way from Minnesota.

Jellman came to the phone a second later: 'Davenport, you miserable piece of shit. I never thought I'd hear from you again.'

'How are you, Jelly?'

'Well, I'm looking out at my back yard,' he said. 'There are two palm trees and two orange trees and a lime tree – Denise makes key lime pie from it. It's just a bit shy of eighty degrees right now, and I can smell the ocean. About an hour from now, I'll be hitting golf balls on the greenest golf course you ever saw in your life . . . How's it up there?'

'Cool, but nice.'

'Right. Nice in Minnesota means the snow's not over your boots yet . . . So what's happening?'

'You remember a bunch of killings you handled back in '84, four guys shot in the back of the head?'

'Oh, hell, yes,' Jellman said. 'Never got the guys who did it.'

'I'm interested in the last one – George Arris.'

'Why him?'

'We got an anonymous letter with the name of the supposed killer.'

'I bet it ain't no goddamn Vice Lord,' Jellman said.

'Why is that?'

'Is it? A Vice Lord?'

'No. It's a bank vice-president.'

'Hah. I knew it. Trust the letter, Lucas – if it was a bullshitter, he would've said it was a Vice Lord, 'cause that was on all the media. The Vice Lords did the other three, but that fourth one, that was a copycat.'

'Are you sure?'

'Pretty sure. That was the word on the street, though nobody had any names for us. But the word was, the fourth one came out of the blue. That the Vice Lords who'd done the shooting had split for Chicago before the fourth one ever happened.'

'So it was pretty much street talk about the fourth one.'

'There was something else, too – the first three were all up there in the colored section. But the last guy was down on Grand Avenue. You look on a map, it looks pretty close, but you don't see many blacks over there. Not walking on the street – especially not then, not as tight as everybody was about the first three shootings. And there's Wylie's Market used to be over there. You remember Wylie's?'

'Sure.'

'They had a surveillance camera in the back of the store, looking at the cashier's cage and the front door, get people's faces coming in. Anyway, on the film, you can see the street through the window, and we picked out Arris strolling down the street, just a minute or so before he was shot. But there weren't any blacks, either before or after.'

'Huh. Is the tape still around?'

'Yeah, someplace. Since the case is still open . . .'

'Did you ever look at the people around Arris? Friends and co-workers?'

'Oh, sure. Went over to that bank where he worked, came up empty. He'd been dating a few women, but hadn't had anything serious in a couple of years. All he did was work: that's what everybody said. Wasn't interested in pussy, gambling, booze. Just interested in work.'

'Huh. And he was dead when they found him.'

'Yup. Never knew what hit him. Probably never saw it coming. Entry wound right below the bump on the back of his head, exit wound right between his eyes.'

'Exit wound? So how'd you know it was a .380 – was there a shell?'

'Yeah, we found it in the grass next to the curb. There was a partial print, but really partial – not enough even to start looking for a match.'

'Slug fragments?'

'Yeah, one piece. Hollowpoint of some kind, nothing that would identify a pistol.'

'Not much of anything, then.'

'Nope. Listen, if you want, I'll call Doug Skelly over in St Paul and get him to run down that tape for you.'

'Thanks, Jelly. Wish you were still on the job.'

'Wish I was too, man. I hate this fuckin' place.'

The file on Andrew Ingall consisted of one sheet: his boat had been reported missing on Superior on a clear, fine day with good sailing winds. The Coast Guard, the Civil Air Patrol and the local sheriff's departments in adjacent Minnesota and Wisconsin counties had done a search. Nothing was ever found, not even a life jacket.

An address and phone number were listed in the town of North Oaks. Lucas punched the number in, got an answering machine, a woman's voice. He hung up, dialed dispatch, had them check the cross-reference index for numbers on both sides of that address, dialed the first one.

'Hello?' Another woman.

'Yes, my name is Lucas Davenport and I'm with the Minneapolis Police Department. I'm trying to get in touch with Annette Ingall, but all I get at her home is an answering machine.'

'Oh, my God, nothing happened to Toby?'

'No, no, I just need to talk to her about her husband. Do you know if she works? Where I could call her?'

'Well she has a bridal-wear boutique downtown . . .'

The bridal shop was a brisk ten-minute walk from City Hall, among a cluster of boutiques on Marquette Avenue. Annette Ingall was a tall woman with auburn hair and pale-blue eyes; motherly, Lucas thought later, though she was probably five

112

years younger than he was. She did a smiling double-take when he walked into the store, and when a clerk came over and he asked for her, she said, 'That would be me. Can I help you?'

He stepped closer and pitched his voice down: 'I need to talk to you privately for a moment. I'm with the Minneapolis Police Department – nothing happened with your boy, it's a completely different matter.'

Her hand went to her throat as the smile died on her face. 'How do you know about my son?'

'Because I called one of your neighbors to find you, and she said, "Oh my God, nothing happened to Toby?" '

'Oh. Okay.' The smile flickered back. 'Why don't you come back to my office.'

Ingall led the way through a door into the back of the store, to a small office cubicle that stuck out into a stock-storage area. There were two chairs inside, and she sat behind her desk and crossed her legs.

Lucas sat down and said, 'I'm investigating the death of Daniel Kresge.'

'Yes? I read about it.'

Lucas picked up the tone. 'You didn't like him?'

'No. Not especially. He once made a pretty heavy pass at me, when he and his wife were still together. This was after my husband died, and I was feeling pretty vulnerable.'

Lucas nodded: 'I'm actually here because I want to know more about your husband. I have an abstract of a Douglas County file about his disappearance, but there's not much in it.'

'There wasn't much to say.' Her lower lip trembled as she said it; she was twisting a ring on her finger and Lucas noticed that it was a wedding ring. 'He just got on the boat and vanished.'

'But there isn't any doubt that the boat sank?' Lucas asked.

'What? Have you found out something?'

'No, no, no. Just . . . your tone of voice.'

'Well . . .' Again, the trembling lip. 'It's been almost impossible to put this behind me, because nothing was ever found. No body, no boat debris, nothing. After he disappeared, all kinds of inspectors went to the bank and they came and questioned me, to make sure he hadn't taken off with some money. I mean, every time I get a phone call at home, that I'm not expecting, I halfway think it's going to be his voice.'

'But you really think the boat sank.'

'Yes.' She nodded firmly. 'In fact, I even think I know what happened. Do you sail, Mr Davenport?'

'I have. I'm not particularly good at it.' Weather was a sailing fanatic, as her father had been, and they'd gone out almost every warm weekend, and for a long two weeks in the Caribbean.

'When a boat goes down, there's almost always lots of debris,' Ingall said. 'You know the enormous amount of stuff sailors carry around with them – books and logs and guides and all kinds of paper. Andy had even more of it than most people. Business papers and references and so on. Plus the boat had a lot of wood. So if it had blown up, like some people thought, they'd have found *something*. But they didn't find anything. So you know what I think?'

'What?'

'What I think was, it was a cool day, and Andy had the autopilot on and he'd gone below. While he was down there . . . the keel fell off,' she said.

'The keel?'

'Yes. The keel on our boat was about 4,000 pounds of lead, held in place with four huge steel bolts. You normally couldn't even see the bolts, without pulling up parts of the sole – the flooring.'

'Yeah.' He knew what a sole was.

'Anyway, I think the nuts worked off the bolts, from vibration, and then, with some sudden strain, the keel simply fell off,' she said. 'If that happened, the boat would have turned turtle just instantly, and water would have started pouring down the companionway and the whole thing would have sunk in a minute or two. There are cases known like this. They're rare, but it sort of explains everything. There wouldn't have been time for life jackets or anything, and the inflow of water would have kept everything inside. It would've been just . . . glug.'

'But that's a rare thing.'

'Yes – But.'

'But.'

'We kept the boat in Superior, and there's this old guy up there who pretty much lives on his boat. Not technically, because they don't allow that, but he's around day and night. When I was up there during the search, he told me that Andy'd had somebody working on the boat the night before he disappeared. He didn't pay much attention, but he said he'd noticed the guy had pulled up the sole and stuck it in the cockpit, out of the way of whatever he was doing. He assumed the guy was working on the plumbing, but he could have been working on the bolts. Maybe there was something wrong with them. Or maybe he did something that messed them up.'

'Huh. Was your husband there that day? When the work was being done?'

'No, not that day.'

'Did he often hire people to do work when he wasn't there?'

'From time to time. I mean, good boat repair people are like plumbers or electricians. They'll schedule you for some work, but something happens on another job and it gets stretched out, or they get free earlier than they think. So lots of times we just give them the key and the go-ahead to do the work whenever they can get there.'

'Did you know that work was being done?'

'No. But sometimes he didn't tell me. The boat was more Andy's thing than mine.'

'Did anybody ever talk to the guy who did the work?'

'Nope. We looked around, but nobody ever figured out who it was. We had a guy we'd used quite a bit, but he said he didn't know anything about it. And nobody ever really saw the guy doing the work. He did it in the evening, mostly after dark. And he wasn't there very long – so that made me think it wasn't the plumbing, which would take a while. The only thing I could think of, that you'd pull up the sole for, and wouldn't take long, would be the bolts.'

'Look,' Lucas said, 'I don't want to upset you, but . . . was there any possibility of suicide?'

'No.' She said it positively.

Lucas said, 'Okay.'

'Andy was a happy guy,' she said. 'He was doing great in his job, he was up for a promotion, we were talking about putting a big garden in behind the house, we were talking about another child. I was supposed to bring Toby up to the islands the next day, and we were all going sailing, and Toby was all excited . . . No. He didn't commit suicide. And he didn't take off with any money or anything. He was just a heck of a good guy and well-adjusted and his folks are nice and my folks liked him and they liked him at the bank . . .'

'This promotion,' Lucas said. 'Who got it? After he died.'

'Well . . . Wilson McDonald.'

'Would Andy have gotten the promotion if he hadn't died? For sure?'

'*He* thought so. He said he'd aced Wilson out of the slot. I mean, it's never for sure until it's done, and Wilson has

116

all those family connections . . . why?'

'We're just trying to run down all possibilities,' Lucas said vaguely.

She was too smart for that. One hand went to her throat and she leaned toward him and said, 'Oh my God, do you think Wilson McDonald killed Andy to get promoted, and then shot Dan Kresge? He got Dan's job, didn't he?'

'Temporarily. There seems to be some doubt about it in the long run . . .'

She pointed a finger at him, excited: 'Do you know about George Arris?'

'Yes . . .'

'Wilson got his promotion, too.'

'I haven't been able to establish that. Not clearly.'

'Believe me, George would have gotten the job. My God, this never occurred to me,' she said. She pushed the palm of her hand against her forehead. 'How could I have missed it? It's so obvious.'

'There's probably nothing to it,' Lucas said.

'Oh, bull . . . feathers, Mr Davenport. Three people dead and Wilson gets all the promotions? My God, he murdered Andy!'

'No, no, no. There's no evidence of that at all.'

'Then why'd you bring it up?'

'Because I'm checking everything . . .'

'Wilson McDonald,' she marveled. 'Who would've thought.'

'Please, Mrs Ingall . . .'

He halfheartedly tried to talk her out of the sudden conviction that Wilson McDonald had killed her husband, then said good-bye.

He was out the door and on the sidewalk when she called after him: 'Mr Davenport?'

'Yes?' He turned and she came down the sidewalk to him.

'If this was murder – just say it was, that somebody loosened up the bolts on the keel, okay? They couldn't have taken them all the way off, because then the only thing that would be holding it on would be some adhesive and sealer. Then, with a good bump, the keel might have fallen off in the harbor.'

'Yeah?'

'So they had to leave the bolts part way on, expecting them to work off, which they eventually would have. But they couldn't know *when*. Toby and I usually went up with Andy, so whoever it was . . . it wasn't just killing Andy,' she said. 'If Andy'd made the islands, we'd have been on the boat the next day, and it might of fallen off with us aboard. This guy, whoever it is – he was willing to kill all three of us.'

Lucas had last seen Sherrill when she'd left to pick up Bonnie Bonet, Robles' friend. When he got back, Sherrill and a uniformed cop were marching a young woman down the hall, her hands cuffed behind her back. Lucas caught up with them, said, 'Bonet?'

'Yeah,' Sherrill said.

Bonet snarled, 'Who the fuck are you?'

'Sit her down in homicide,' Lucas said. 'I'll be there in a minute.'

'She wants an attorney,' Sherrill said.

'Got any money?' Lucas asked.

Bonet shook her head defiantly. 'No. You gotta appoint one.'

Lucas nodded: 'So call the public defender,' Lucas told Sherrill. 'I'll be right back.'

He dumped his coat and the file on Ingall in his office, and made a quick call: 'I want everything we can find on Wilson McDonald. Everything.'

* * *

Back at homicide, Bonet was sitting next to Sherrill's desk, while the uniform cop lounged at another desk between her and the door. She'd been uncuffed and Sherrill was scratching notes on a legal pad.

When Lucas walked in, Bonet looked up and said, 'I want the attorney. I'm not answering any questions without an attorney.'

'I called. Somebody's walking over,' Sherrill said.

'I'm not going to ask you a question, Ms Bonet,' Lucas said. 'I'm gonna make a little speech. Mr Robles says you told him you shot Daniel Kresge because you thought Kresge was setting up a bank merger and your mother would lose her job. But he says he really doesn't think you shot him, that you're making a grandstand play, because you like the attention. For the experience of it. To fuck us over. Do you know the first thing that will happen when the word of your arrest gets out? The bank's gonna fire your mother.'

Bonet, naturally pale, went a shade paler. 'They can't do that. That's discrimination . . .'

Lucas was shaking his head. 'No. There's no union at the bank. They can fire her for any reason they want, as long as the firing isn't illegal – because of race or religion or like that. If her daughter is accused of murdering the bank president on her behalf . . . you think that's not a reason? I'll tell you what: your mother's gonna be on the sidewalk in about half an hour, as soon as the *Star-Tribune* guy checks out the day's arrest reports. And they check every couple of hours.'

Bonet looked at Sherrill, who nodded, then back at Lucas. 'But I didn't shoot him,' she blurted.

Sherrill dropped her pencil and said, 'Oh, shit.'

Lucas said, 'Again, I'm not going to ask you any questions, but I'll say this: If there's anything that would prove that you didn't shoot him, this would be a good time to mention it.'

'Friday night,' Bonet said. 'I was at a friend's house until almost four in the morning, we were on-line, gaming.'

'How many people?' Lucas asked.

'Four . . . three besides me.'

'She'd still have time to drive up there,' Lucas said.

'It'd be tight,' Sherrill said.

'But she could make it,' Lucas said.

'I didn't shoot anybody,' Bonet wailed. 'I don't even know where the asshole lived.'

'You were never up there?'

'Never. Why would I be?'

'After you left your friends, you went right home? Did you see anybody who knew you?'

'No . . . well, I bought some Pepsi at the gas station, but they don't know me there. Maybe they'd remember me.'

'What gas station?'

'It's an Amoco down off 494, like 494 and France.'

'Did you pay with cash or a credit card?'

'Credit card!' Her face brightened. 'The goddamn credit slip has the time and location on it. And it comes on my statement – I bet you can call Amoco and find out.'

Lucas nodded, and said, 'Why'n the hell did you tell Robles that you shot McDonald?'

'Just to jerk his chain,' Bonet said. 'He called me up and he pretended to be all freaking out and worried, and the next thing I know, he's turned me in.'

'He pretended to be freaking out?'

'Yeah. Pretended. He's a cold fish,' Bonet said. 'I'll tell you what, I wouldn't be surprised if he did it, and he deliberately set me up with that talk on the 'net about how to kill McDonald. I mean, he started it, I didn't. And then he fed me to you.'

'Why do you think he might have done it?' Sherrill asked.

'Because of the way he plays with guns all the time,' she said. 'I think if you pretend to be killing people long enough, pretty soon, you want to try it. Don't you think?'

Lucas' and Sherrill's eyes locked: they'd both killed people in gunfights. 'I don't know,' Lucas said finally. 'Maybe.'

Sherrill said, 'What do you mean, plays with guns?'

'He's always out shooting. You know, rifles and pistols and sometimes he goes out to Wyoming and shoots prairie dogs He calls them prairie rats. Or prairie pups. And he does that whole paintball thing. You know, runs around in the woods in camouflage clothes with some other guys and they shoot each other.'

'Robles,' Lucas said.

'Yeah. He doesn't come off that way, does he?'

'Have you ever done the paintball thing with him?'

'No – he doesn't even know that I know about it. But I know a friend of his, and he saw us together, and he told me. I thought it was weird.'

'Huh.' Lucas rubbed his chin, then looked at Sherrill. 'What do you think?'

'I think I should check with Amoco,' Sherrill said. 'And then maybe start talking to people about Robles.'

Lucas pointed a finger at Bonet: 'If this checks out, we'll forget about it. But you keep your mouth shut about what happened. And what you told us. You don't talk to Robles about it, or anyone else. And remember what's at stake, here. I'm talking about your mom.'

'Okay,' she said, solemnly. A tear started in one eye.

'Okay,' Lucas said. And to Sherrill: 'Call Amoco.'

On the way back to his office, Lucas bumped into an assistant public defender heading toward homicide. She was carrying two briefcases, apparently full of briefs, which bumped alternately against her thighs as she walked. Her hair stood out from her round face in an electrocution halo. Her face was drawn with lack of sleep.

'On your way to see Bonny Bonet?' Lucas asked.

She stopped and said, 'Yeah. But if you're not done with the rubber hoses, I could wait. Maybe catch a nap.'

'We're all done. We beat the truth out of her and she's innocent,' Lucas said. 'We're turning her loose in a few minutes.'

'Really?' The lawyer yawned and said, 'God, I've gone to bed with men who've said less pleasant things to me.'

'Yeah, well . . . sleep tight.'

'Won't let the bedbugs bite,' she said with another yawn, and humped the briefcases on down the hall toward homicide. Had to see for herself.

Lucas sat in his office, his feet on his desk, and added up the accusations. After a while be picked up the phone and called Sherrill. 'All done?'

'Yeah. She checked out with Amoco. She's gotta do some paperwork, then she's outa here.'

'Who's loose? Besides you.'

'Tom Black is sitting in a corner, reading *Playgirl*,' she said. From somewhere behind her, her regular partner shouted, 'I am not.' Black was gay, but still mostly in the closet.

'Why don't you guys come on down? I'll tell you about it,' Lucas said.

'Almost time to quit.'

'It'll take ten minutes, and we won't do anything until tomorrow.'

Black, pretending to be disgruntled, slumped in one of Lucas' two visitor chairs, while Sherrill looked out the window at the street.

Lucas was saying, '. . . if somebody accused say, Sloan, of deliberately setting out to murder somebody, and actually doing it, I'd say, "Nope, he couldn't do that." The idea might occur to him, but someplace along the way, he just wouldn't do it.'

'So?' Sherrill asked.

'We've got too many people to worry about, all of them with motives. So what we do is, we go around to people who know them well, and ask for a confidential assessment. Could they do it? Would they do it? What would have to be on the line for them to do it?'

Black cocked his head to one side and thought about it for a moment: 'That's weird.'

'And it could ship us off in a completely wrong direction,' Sherrill said. 'You've already decided Bone didn't do it, because you like him.'

'No,' Lucas said, shaking his head. 'I do like him, but I haven't decided anything about him.'

'But if you like him, you're sort of predisposed not to believe bad stuff.'

Black ticked a finger at her: 'Psychobabble,' he said.

'Sorry,' she said. Then, 'What about O'Dell and the kafiyah? Who's gonna check that?'

'I'll ask her,' Lucas said.

'Tomorrow?'

'Yeah.' He yawned. 'Tomorrow.'

Chapter Nine

M ary Washington called at nine-thirty, and when Weather
Karkinnen picked up the phone, Mary said, 'Oh, good,
you're still up,' and Weather rolled her eyes and lied: 'Just
barely.'

'Henri asked about you again today. He's interested,'
Washington said.

'Oh, my God, Mary, why don't *you* go after him?' Exasperation, but also a little tingle of pleasure?

''Cause I'm "Let's have a couple beers and go bowling,"
and Henri's "Let's have a couple of glasses of champagne and
talk about monoclonal antibodies." '

'Well, thanks for the news,' Weather said.

'Would you go out with him if he called?'

Henri was six-three and had big eyes and long black
eyelashes, was thin as a bean pole, balding, and spoke with a
French accent. People who knew him well said he was almost
too smart: Weather liked him. 'I don't know, Mary,' she said.
'I'm still pretty messed up.'

'I think I'm gonna suggest he give you a ring,' Washington
said.

'Mary . . .' Like being trapped in a high-school locker room.

'Then maybe you can introduce me to one of those cops
you know; somebody who bowls.'

Weather had been reading the *Wall Street Journal* when Mary
called. When she got off the phone, she yawned, tossed the

paper in the recycling pile, and headed for the bedroom.

Weather was sleeping again, finally. Her problem had been no less difficult than Lucas', but hers had less to do with errant brain chemicals. Her problem was plain old post-traumatic shock. She'd pulled the academic studies up on MedLine, knew all the symptoms and lines of treatment, recognized the symptoms in herself – and was powerless to do anything about them.

The unbreakable barrier was Lucas Davenport.

She'd never really been in love with anyone before Lucas. But she'd been in love with him, all right – she'd recognized all those symptoms, too. Then the shooting . . .

There'd always been something in Lucas that was hard, brutal, and remote. She'd been sure she could reach it, smooth it out. He needed that as much as she did: he didn't know it, but his taste for the street, his taste for violence, was killing him, in ways that weren't obvious to him. But she'd been wrong about reaching him: the violence was essential to him, she now believed.

The shooting in the hallway, which Lucas had set up, had all the earmarks of that immutable trait. He'd risked his own life, he'd risked hers, and he'd absolutely condemned Dick LaChaise to death, all on his own hook, without consulting anyone, without even much thinking about it. He'd just *done* it. When the Lucas Davenport machine was in gear, nobody had a way out – and when LaChaise had agreed to walk down the hall with Weather, he was dead no matter what else happened.

Weather could never quite put her finger on exactly how she objected to the killing of Dick LaChaise. Intellectually, she knew that she might easily have been killed by LaChaise if Lucas hadn't done what he'd done. Further, LaChaise was an undoubted killer, who deserved anything he got. She could say to herself — intellectually — *all right. It worked.*

Which had nothing to do with her emotional state.

Something had turned in her, the instant the bullet tore through LaChaise's skull. She couldn't talk to Lucas without experiencing the flash of terror when the gun went off, followed by the horror of the death. There, in the hallway, with LaChaise slumping to the floor, with the pistol spinning down the hallway . . . She was actually *wearing* LaChaise, the dead and dying remnants of the part of LaChaise that actually made him human . . .

She'd gotten past the pills now. She was still talking to her shrink, Andi Manette, and Manette was pushing her to consider and reconsider Lucas.

But Weather wasn't doing that anymore. She'd realized that however deeply she'd loved him before the shooting, that feeling was dead. And the psychological flashes that carried her back to the killing were no longer tolerable. Lucas brought them on. The sight of his face, the sound of his voice.

She'd learned that she could live without him. She was going to do that. And she was beginning to suspect that sooner or later, she'd even start enjoying herself again. If she could keep him away . . .

She hadn't yet told this to Manette, much less to Lucas. She dreaded the idea: but the time was coming. Time to get on with her life.

Weather went to bed early, as most surgeons did: she was staff at three separate hospitals now, and the work load was increasing. She was operating five or six times a week, starting at seven in the morning. She'd be in bed by ten-thirty, up by six in the morning, walking into the women's locker room by six-forty-five.

Went to bed every night, feeling cool and lonely. But sleeping again.

She was in the very pit of the night when her subconscious picked up the sound of a car rolling to a stop outside the house, a subtle change from those few cars that simply rolled on by. In her dreams she thought, *Lucas?*, though when awake she'd never remember the thought. But she was there, just rising to the cusp of consciousness, when the front window blew out.

SKEEEEEEEEEEEE

The explosion shook her out of bed: she was up in an instant, not quite awake, but on her feet and moving; and as she moved, the smoke alarm in the living room went SKEEEEEEE.

She lurched into the hallway toward the living room; she was first aware of the light, then the heat, then the realization that she was staring into a fireball.

'No! No!'

And all the time: SKEEEEEEEEEEE.

Weather moaned, registered her own moan as though she was standing out-of-body, then ran back down the hall to the bedroom, snatched up the bedside telephone and punched in 911. She got an immediate answer, and said. 'My house just blew up. It's burning, I'm at . . .' And she dictated the address and said, 'I've got to get out.'

'Get outside immediately,' the cool voice said. 'Just drop the phone and . . .'

And the kitchen smoke alarm triggered, a slightly lower, less energetic note than the first, but just as loud: SKAAAAAAAAAAAA

She'd dropped the phone, almost stumbled over a pair of loafers on the dark floor, slipped them on, hit a light switch, was rewarded with lights. She padded back down the hall. The fireball seemed to have receded, or to have pulled back within itself. The flames were confined to the front room, to an area not much longer than her couch. There wasn't yet much smoke, although the fire was roaring ferociously.

Weather moved in three quick steps to the kitchen, pulled a fat semi-professional fire extinguisher from under the sink, pulled the pin as she walked back to the living room, aimed the nozzle at the flames, and squeezed the trigger. Whatever kinds of chemical were in the extinguisher blew out in a fog, and the fire seemed to cave in, but just for a second, and then it was back: no matter how much of the chemical extinguisher she poured on, the fire would only retreat and spring up on another perimeter.

SKEEEEEEE/SKAAAAAAAA . . .

She stepped closer, working the chemical, felt it slackening in force. To her right, she felt the photos of her parents and grandparents staring down from the walls, black and white and hand-tinted photos she'd grown up with, memories she'd imported from her former home in the North Woods. With the extinguisher chemical almost gone, she tossed the container behind her, turned to the wall and started pulling down the photos. Behind her, the fire burned with new authority, and she could feel the heat on her back and legs. She ran with the photos to the kitchen, fought her way back into the living room, tore open the low buffet, and took out a half dozen photo albums and a box of photos she'd always meant to put in more albums.

And that was all she could do. The fire was growing quickly now, and she ran through the kitchen, well out onto the back lawn, dropped the albums, ran back inside – the smoke was heavy now, and she coughed, staggered – found the framed photos, and carried them through the smoke out back.

SKEEEEEEEEEEEEEEE/AAAAAAAAA

She could hear sirens: the nearest fire station was no more than three-quarters of a mile away. She started back inside one last time, unaware that she was panting, that her hair was frizzing and uncurling with the heat, that she'd taken spark-burns on her hands and arms, that she'd walked on broken glass and cut her feet. She felt it all as discomfort, but she wanted to save the last things, some dishes her mother gave her . . .

She couldn't reach them. The rug in the living room had ignited, and thick gray smoke was rolling through the house. She staggered back through the door just as the first of the fire engines arrived. She ran around the house as the firemen hopped off the truck and yelled, 'The front room . . .'

The noise never stopped: SKEEEEEEEEE/SKAAAAAAAAAA

Weather sat on the curb and watched the fireman knock down the front door.

And after a minute, she began to cry.

Chapter Ten

Ten o'clock in the morning was an early hour for a man to be recalcitrant, Lucas thought, especially if he wasn't a cop, but Stephen Jones was recalcitrant.

'Of course I'd like to help, but I have the damnedest feeling that if I talk to you, it's going to find its way into a gossip column.'

'Not from me, it won't,' Lucas said.

A piece of art hung from the wall behind Jones' desk. The print was colorful and maybe even beautiful, though it resembled a woman hacked up with a pizza cutter. Lucas, who knew almost nothing about fine art, suspected it was a Picasso.

'. . . And the thing is, if it does, I'd be severely damaged . . .'

'I can assure you it won't happen,' Lucas said patiently.

Jones rubbed the back of his neck and said, 'All right. If somebody absolutely pushed T-Bone up against the wall, when the only option was kill or be kill, he'd kill. But this situation isn't like that. He's already got a lot of money and he's good enough that he could go somewhere else in a top job. So I don't see it.'

'Assume that somehow, we don't know how, he was pushed to the wall. Emotionally, psychologically, or maybe he gambles and we don't know it.'

Jones shook his head. 'Even then . . . he's the kind of guy who'd always figure he could recover. Always get back. The thing is, he grew up poor. Did you know that?'

'No.'

'Yeah, some cracker family down south somewhere, Louisiana, Mississippi, Alabama. He made it all on his own. He's a guy who figures he can always do it again. I don't think he'd . . .'

His voice died away.

'What?' Lucas asked.

'You know . . . If you come at this from another angle . . . We're talking about whether he'd cold-bloodedly kill someone because he'd lose money or his job; and I don't think he would. But I can see him killing somebody if the other person had something on him,' Jones said. 'Blackmail, for instance. If Kresge had something really serious on him, and threatened to use it, for some reason, I can see Bone killing him for that reason. Not to keep it from being used, but because the threat, or the extortion, would . . . besmirch his honor.' He mused over the thought, then jerked his head in a nod: 'Yep. That would do it. That's the only way I see Bone deliberately killing somebody. But it would have to be deadly serious, and it would have to be deadly personal.'

'What about Terrance Robles?'

'I don't know him well enough to answer. I really don't.'

'Susan O'Dell?'

'Susan couldn't do it. She's crusty and calculating and all that, but she's got a soft interior.'

'I've seen a deer that would disagree with you,' Lucas said.

'You mean, the hunting? That's cultural,' Jones said. 'People from out there, out on the prairie, farmers, have a whole different attitude toward the life and death of animals than they do the life and death of people. I really don't think she could kill anyone. I'm not even sure she could do it in self-defense, to be honest with you. Nope. You're barking up the wrong tree with Susan.'

'Wilson McDonald.'

Jones frowned. 'I can see him killing somebody, but it'd be in hot blood, not cold blood. If he was drunk and angry, he might strike out. He's got a violent streak, and he can be sneaky about it. But as for pulling off a calculated killing . . . I don't think so. Actually, I think he'd be chicken. He'd start imagining all the things that could go wrong, and, you know, being thrown in prison with a bunch of sodomites. I don't think so.'

'What about the moral equation – would it be . . .'

'Oh, it wouldn't be a moral problem for him. He'd just be chicken. Wilson McDonald's a classic bully, with all the classic characteristics of a bully: he's a coward at heart.'

Lucas met Sherrill in the skyway off City Center and she was shaking her head as she came up. 'They're all innocent,' she said. 'What happened with Louise Freeman?'

Louise Freeman was the gossip mentioned by Bone's attorney friend Sandra Ollsen. 'She and her old man went to New York,' Lucas said. 'She's back on Friday. I talked to Jones instead.'

'How about Black? Did he get anything?'

'Haven't talked to him yet. He's supposed to call when he's done talking with Markham. So: You'll take Bennett, and I'll take Kerr.'

'Why don't we go over to Saks first,' she suggested. 'You can buy me something expensive.'

'I've got about twenty dollars on me,' Lucas said.

'So let's go to the bank and you can take out a bunch of money.'

'Give me a break, huh? I don't . . .' The phone in Sherrill's purse buzzed, and Lucas said, 'Probably Black.'

Sherrill fished the phone out of her purse, said, 'Hello,'

listened and passed the phone to Lucas. 'Dispatch, looking for you.'

Lucas took the phone: 'Yeah?'

The dispatcher said, 'Lucas, a woman named Andi Manette is trying to get you. She says it's about a personal friend of yours and it's extremely urgent. You want the number?'

'Oh, Jesus,' Lucas said. Andi Manette was Weather's shrink. 'Hang on.' He patted his pockets, found a pen and a slip of paper, and said, 'What is it?'

He copied the number, punched the power button, punched it again, and dialed.

Manette picked it up on the first ring. 'Yes?'

'Andi? This is Lucas.'

'Lucas, I need to tell you something, but I don't want you running off to help. Nobody needs help.'

'What? What?'

'Weather was . . . somebody firebombed Weather's house last night. She was singed a little, and has some small cuts, but she's not badly hurt. She's going to be staying with us for a while, until this is straightened out.'

'Firebombed! What do you mean, firebombed? Where is she?'

'The thing is, it would be best if you didn't go looking for her. She's pretty freaked out and having you around, with all the associations, won't help.'

'Well, Jesus Christ, Andi, what happened? Do I get to know that?'

'Nobody knows what happened. It's being handled by the Edina police.'

'You don't mean just an explosion or something, you mean somebody threw a firebomb through her window.'

'That's exactly what happened,' Manette said. 'Somebody threw a firebomb through her picture window.'

'Andi, I swear to God I won't come after her, but where is she? Tell me that. Just tell me.'

'She's at my house, taking a nap right now. She's had a couple of sedatives, she's feeling better. But we figured that people would let you know, and that I'd better talk to you.'

'Let me know? My God, Andi, I'm probably a suspect. And even . . . I gotta call those guys.'

'Don't call . . .'

'Not Weather. I've got to call Edina.'

'Okay. But please don't come out, okay?'

'Okay.'

'Thanks. You know I'm trying to bail this out for the two of you, and I'm bailing as hard as I can.'

'Hey listen,' Lucas said. 'Thanks for calling me.'

He punched off and Sherrill said, 'Weather? Firebombed?' She looked perplexed.

'Yeah. Last night. Listen, you go after these other guys. I'm running out to Edina.'

He called first: The chief's name was Peter Hafman and Lucas barely knew him.

'Don't have much to show you,' Hafman said. 'Somebody walked up last night and pitched a gallon jug of gasoline through the front window. We've got bits of the wick, looks like a piece of ordinary cotton cloth, I'm told. There is one odd thing . . .'

'What?'

'The bottle was scored so it'd break easier. Scored with a glass cutter. The guys out here says that sounds like a pro.'

'I never heard of that,' Lucas said. 'Look, could I come out and talk to your guys?'

'Come on ahead.'

He rang off and handed the phone back to Sherrill, and it

immediately beeped again. She answered and handed it back: Dispatch again.

'You've got another call coming in. They say this one is urgent, too.'

'Put it through.'

There was a *click*, and a woman said, 'Chief Davenport?' She had a purring voice, a little smoky.

'Yes, this is Davenport. Who is this?'

'Did you know that Jim Bone was sleeping with Dan Kresge's wife? For a long time? And now she'll get all those options that used to be worthless?'

And the phone went dead. Lucas looked at it, looked at Sherrill.

'Now what?'

'That was our woman, I think.'

'Really? What'd she say?'

'She said Jim Bone is sleeping with Kresge's wife. And that she's gonna get a pile of stock options now that he's dead.'

Sherrill's eyebrows went up: 'Any more goddamn clues and we'll have to get a secretary to keep track of them.'

'Jim Bone,' Lucas said. 'Huh.'

When Weather had left Lucas, she'd stayed with the Manettes for a couple of weeks, then taken over the lease on a small house being vacated by a University Hospitals surgical resident. Lucas had cruised it in city cars a half-dozen times, hoping to get a glimpse of her. He never had, but he knew the house.

Now he cruised it again, a ranch-style house of stone and clapboard that reminded him of his own house. It looked much the same as it always had, except that the front picture window, which looked out across the flagstone walk, was covered by a piece of unpainted plywood; and the eaves over the window were stained with soot.

He pulled into the driveway, got out, walked up to the front of the house and peered through the small windows that flanked the center window. He was looking in at the front room: the place was a jumble of scorched furniture and carpeting, with burned drywall panels hanging down from the ceiling, books scattered across the floor in sodden clumps. He could smell the smoke and the water and the burnt fiberglass insulation. No gasoline.

He stepped back, and as he turned to leave, noticed a woman watching from next door: she wasn't hiding, and didn't pretend to be doing anything else. She'd come outside to watch him. He headed toward her, dug out his identification.

'Hello. I'm Deputy Chief of Police Lucas Davenport from Minneapolis; I'm a friend of Weather's.'

The frown on her face eased a bit, and she tried on a smile. 'Oh, good. I've been trying to keep an eye on the place since last night.'

'Thanks. I, uh, I'm on my way to talk to your police chief out here, and I thought I'd take a look . . . Listen, do you know if anybody saw anything last night? Or heard anything?'

'Nobody in my house heard anything until the fire engines, but Jane Yarrow across the street heard the window break. She said she didn't know it was a window breaking until later. She just heard *something*. And then she heard a car door slam, but she didn't get up until she heard the sirens. And that was about it – nothing like this ever happened here before.'

The chief was out when Lucas arrived at Edina, but he was routed to a detective James Brown. Brown was a tall, shambling man with a shock of white hair; he wore a rough tweed sportcoat with suede elbow patches, a blue Oxford cloth shirt and khakis with boat shoes. He looked like a professor of ancient languages.

'Not *the* James Brown?' Lucas asked.

'Why, yes, I am,' Brown said modestly. 'This is my disguise: keeps the groupies off.'

'Excellent strategy,' Lucas said. He dropped into a chair beside Brown's desk.

Brown looked down at a file open on his desk, sighed, and said, 'I understand you have a personal relationship with Weather Karkinnen.'

'Had one; she broke it off,' Lucas said. 'I can't prove to you where I was at three o'clock this morning, 'cause I was home at bed, alone. But . . .' He shrugged. 'I didn't do it.'

'And even if you did, that's a pretty goddamn unbreakable alibi,' Brown said.

Lucas said, 'Hey . . . I didn't do it.'

Brown sighed again and asked, 'The chief told you about the scoring on the bottle?'

'Yeah. He said it looked like a pro job.'

'That's what the fire guys say. You get a regular bottle, it might bounce, it might not even break. But with the scoring, it explodes when it hits the floor. Very fast, very efficient. What we think is, the bomber came in from the north, idled to a stop in front of the house, got out, leaving the car door open, walked up to the front of the house with the jug, flashed the wick with a cigarette lighter, and heaved it through the window. The whole thing, I timed it, would be ten to fifteen seconds, walking, from the time he got out of the car to the time he got back in. Then he rolled off down the street, around the corner, four blocks down to the highway, and back to Minneapolis. He was on the highway before Ms Karkinnen even called 911.'

'Who owns the place?'

'A couple named Bartlett – they're down in Florida. They'd rented it to a doctor for the past eight years, and then to your friend. Strictly an income property for them.'

'Any reason they might want to torch it?'

'Nothing obvious – it's a good neighborhood, they could probably sell it for a lot more than they'd ever get from insurance. And they're pretty reputable people.'

'Shit,' Lucas said.

'All that stuff that was in the paper last winter . . . The LaChaises . . .'

'Yeah. That's what I'm afraid of,' Lucas said.

Brown tapped his desk: 'But one thing doesn't fit with that. Whoever did this wasn't trying real hard to kill her. I mean, if it was a pro job. They didn't even come close. She was in the back bedroom, ran out when she heard the window break, saw the fire, called 911, and if she hadn't tried to save her pictures, she wouldn't have been hurt at all.'

'She was hurt?' Lucas sat up, angry now. 'I was told she wasn't . . .'

'Not bad, not bad,' Brown said. 'She got a couple of small cuts on her feet from broken glass, and her hair was singed, and she got some small spark burns on one hand. But she told us she has some operations tomorrow and she expects to do them.'

Lucas took it slow driving back to the Minneapolis, pulling threads together. Black checked in on Lucas' car phone: 'I had to do some psychotherapy on this Markham asshole, but the bottom line is, he thinks O'Dell couldn't do it.'

'All right. You got another one yet?'

'L.Z. Drake,' Black said. 'Went to school with McDonald.'

'Call when you get done.'

'Yeah. Hey, you know about Weather?'

'Yeah. How'd you hear?'

'They had some pictures of the house in a news brief . . . Markham had his TV on the whole time I was talking to him. They said she was okay.'

'Yeah, yeah . . .'

'You think there's any chance it's another comeback from LaChaise?'

'I don't know what to think.'

'All right,' said Black. 'I'll call you after I talk to Drake.'

Sloan and Franklin were waiting outside Lucas' office when Lucas got back. Both of them had been involved in the shootout that killed the two LaChaise women the winter before, though Sloan hadn't fired his weapon and hadn't been a direct target of the reprisal attacks. Franklin, on the other hand, had been shot in his own driveway.

'We've been talking, man,' Franklin said in his booming voice. Lucas was large; Franklin dwarfed him. 'We gotta look into this, unless there's some motive for somebody hittin' Weather.'

'How'd you hear about it?'

'It's all over the department, it's been on TV,' Sloan said.

'You think I oughta call my folks, get them out of the house?' Franklin asked.

'I don't know,' Lucas said. They were milling in the hall, and he saw Sherrill starting down toward them. 'I don't know what's going on. Nobody's got a motive that I can figure, and there's a possibility that it was a pro job.'

'Why a pro job?' Sloan asked. As Sherrill came up, Franklin said to her, 'Could've been a pro job.'

'You're sure?' Sherrill asked.

Lucas told them about the scored bottle. 'That's it,' Franklin said, 'I'm putting the old lady in a motel.'

Black arrived as they were talking about it, stood on the edge of the discussion: he hadn't been in the shootout, hadn't been a target.

'I think what we need to do before we panic, is we need to get everybody we got out on the street,' Lucas said. 'I'll talk to intelligence and narcotics and the gang people, I'll talk to St Paul, and every one of us has got people . . . Let's get out there and dig for a few hours. If this is a group, somebody'll know.'

'Loring's got the good biker contacts,' Franklin said. 'He's been working nights, he's probably home asleep. You want me to roust him?'

'Get him moving,' Lucas said.

'I'll find Del, get him started,' Sloan said.

'I'm outa here,' said Franklin.

As the group started to break up, Black said, 'Lucas, I talked to this guy Drake about McDonald.'

'Oh, yeah.' Old news; he wasn't thinking about McDonald anymore.

Black continued: 'I had to push him, but he says he knew McDonald all the way through school, and he has a real violent streak. Bottom line was, Drake thinks he could kill somebody if he decided it was necessary. He said McDonald was a big guy, played a little high-school football, and he and a couple of other guys stalked another kid for a couple of years, a little wimpy guy, beat him up a half dozen times just because they knew they could make him cry in front of the girls . . .'

'Yeah, yeah,' Lucas said impatiently. 'We can pick that up later.'

And as Black left, Sherrill who'd been drifting away, said, from down the hall, 'You were gonna talk to O'Dell today . . .'

'No time now,' Lucas said. He remembered the phone call

about Bone sleeping with Kresge, but pushed the memory away. 'Let's get out on the street.'

Chapter Eleven

The Polaris Bank tower was a rabbit-warren of meeting, training and conference rooms, but only one of them was The Room.

The Room was on the fortieth floor, guarded by two thick oaken doors.

No Formica here, no commercial carpeting or stainless steel. The conference table was twenty feet long and made of page-cut walnut; the chairs were walnut and bronze and plush crimson cushions; the lighting was subtle and recessed. The floor was oak parquet, accented with Quashqa'i rugs.

An alcove at one side of the room contained a refrigerator stocked with soft drinks and sparkling water. A small bar was tucked discreetly away under a counter-top, and a coffee maker kept fresh three flavors of hot coffee, as well as hot water for anyone who wanted to brew tea. A Limoges-style sugar-bowl and creamer waited next to an array of delicate cups and small serving plates. On the counter-top itself was a tray of sandwiches cut into equilateral triangles, cookies, and a freshly opened box of Godiva chocolates.

Constance Rondeau probed the box of chocolates, her sharp nose probing up and down like a bird going after a worm. O'Dell watched her work over the box, and realized that she recognized individual types among the Godiva variety, and was picking out the good ones.

O'Dell pulled herself back: she was drifting. Oakes was talking.

'. . . do agree that somebody had to take the reins. We've got too much going on, and it's too dangerous out there right now. And somebody's got to work with Midland . . .' If Rondeau looked like a bird, Shelley Oakes looked like a pork pie – all puffy and round-faced.

'But my point is,' said Loren Bunde, 'We can't take forever finding someone. We don't have the time, with this merger going on. We probably ought to go over to Midland and get one of their mechanics, and just pull the thing together.'

'Where would his loyalty be?' asked Bone. 'It'd have to be with Midland, because that'll be the successor bank. He'd find a way to screw us: hell, that'd be his job. I definitely think we should go with the merger: but on our terms. They need us. We don't really need them. We've got the fifty-dollar price in play, but if everything shakes out right, we'll get seventy-five.'

'Nobody ever mentioned seventy-five,' said Rondeau, looking up from the Godiva chocolates with a light in her eye.

'I think that would be a minimum. I don't know what was going on between Midland and Dan Kresge, but something was going on,' Bone said. 'Fifty dollars is ridiculous. One-for-one is ridiculous. We should get cash as well: I don't think a hundred is out of the question.'

'I think it is,' O'Dell said bluntly. 'I think seventy-five is on the outer edge of any sane possibility.'

'You don't know what you're talking about,' Bone said.

O'Dell ignored him, and looked around at the other board members: 'Listen: We *must* reconsider the possibility of continuing as an independent,' she said. 'An immediate merger on the proposed terms would turn some quick profits for all of us, myself included. But the merger talk alone has pushed the stock price, and we'll keep most of that whether or not we merge. So that much is locked in. And the fact is, if the new

143

management were to take what I think is a proper view of the board and its duties, and the top management and its duties, then additional compensation would be provided anyway. There are also benefits available to board members and top management that we will lose in a merger, no matter how much money we got right away.'

After a moment of silence, somebody asked, 'Like what?'

O'Dell smiled and said, 'There's quite a wide range of possibilities . . . a little research on what other boards get as compensation could point to some interesting alternatives. Tax-free alternatives, I might add.'

McDonald sat at the far end of the table, where Kresge had always sat, watching the talk, struggling to keep up with it. Bone and O'Dell were clearly at odds, Bone pushing for the proposed merger, O'Dell resisting.

'All these possibilities should be explored,' he ventured ponderously. 'But I do think that we should consider Polaris' position as a major community asset. We've been here for a hundred years and more, and a lot of us wouldn't be where we are today if we hadn't had the ear of some friendly people at Polaris . . .'

He droned on, losing most of the board immediately. John Goff had the right to buy almost forty thousand shares of Polaris at prices ranging from twelve dollars a share to forty-one dollars, most of it at the lower end. Using a scratch pad and a pocket calculator, he began running all the option prices against Bone's suggestion that they might get a hundred.

Dafne Bose was drawing an airplane on her scratchpad. The bank had a small twin-prop, mostly used for flying audit and management teams to small banks out on the countryside. But what if the bank were to buy something really nice – a small jet – and what if it were available to the board? It probably should be, anyway. A plane like that would be worth tens of thousands of dollars a year, none of it visible to the IRS. O'Dell said there were other possibilities. Bose underlined the plane and looked up at O'Dell, who smiled back.

'Yeah, yeah, that's all fine,' Goff said, when McDonald appeared to be running down. 'So we've all got a lot to think about. I would propose that we leave everything as is: Wilson speaks for us, but we ask Susan and Jim each to prepare a report on their respective ideas, deliverable before Friday noon to each of us. That's quick, that's only a couple of days, but we gotta move on this. I further suggest that we meet again next Monday to consider the reports. We'd want a complete discussion of all the, uh, options, and at that time we can consider how to go forward.'

He looked around, got nods of assent. For just a fleeting, tiny part of a second, O'Dell and Bone locked eyes. Only two of them were left. McDonald had just been cut out. Whoever's report was adopted would be running the place in a week.

McDonald didn't understand that yet. He harumphed, allowed that the reports were probably a good idea, and after a few more minutes of talk, the board adjourned.

O'Dell ordered Carla Wyte and Louise Compton to her office as soon as she got out of the meeting. Marcus Kent, her other major ally, was too exposed to meet with her publicly, since he technically worked for Bone.

'Everything I said was true,' O'Dell told Wyte and Compton. 'The trouble is, it's not money in hand. I need exact, specific examples of the kind of payoff we can deliver to board members and top management if they adopt my approach.'

She turned to Wyte: 'You're the numbers person. I want you to nail down the numbers on this stuff, so they'll know what they'll get, and how much it'll cost the bank, and what the tax consequences will be. Do you know Pat Zebeka?'

Wyte was scribbling on a yellow pad: 'I've heard of him. A lawyer.'

'Tax guy, one of the best, and he's done a lot of compensation work. Get with him – on my budget, I'll fix it – and get a laundry list of everything we can offer, that will provide tax advantages.'

And to Compton, who never took notes on anything, because if you never took notes, nobody could subpoena them: 'I want charts from you. Get the details from Carla, and put them together in a package. It's gotta be good, and it's gotta be clear. Not so simple they'll be insulted, but they've got to see what they'll get. It has to be as real as the dollars they'd get from a merger. And another thing – there are some pretty big advantages to being on the Polaris board. We need to put together a list of those advantages. Social status stuff.'

'Good. What about polling the board?' Compton asked.

'I'm talking to them, the ones I can get. And I've got to talk to McDonald. Tonight, if I can. I'm not sure if the idiot knows he's out of it, but he's got to find out sometime.'

'From you? Do you think that's smart? He might be insulted.'

O'Dell shook her head: 'Has to be done. I've got to get to him before Bone, and I can make him an offer Bone can't.'

'What?' Wyte asked.

'I'm president and CEO, but he's board chairman. Talking is what he does best anyway. In a couple of years, when the bank's mine . . .' She flipped a hand dismissively. '. . . he can go away.'

'Why couldn't Bone offer him . . .' Compton stopped herself, shook her head. 'Sorry. Stupid question. If Bone gets it, the bank's gonna go away.'

* * *

Bone told Baki to coordinate a graphics package on how much money would be available through the merger: he would provide the details. 'If you do this right, Kerin, and by that, I mean if you do this perfectly . . .'

'What?' Kerin Baki was like a piece of blonde ironwood, he thought, brutally efficient, great to look at, but cold. Distant. A Finn, he'd heard. Sometimes she was so chilly he could feel the frost coming off her. He couldn't see her with a Southern boy, but thought she might go well with somebody like, say, Davenport.

'You'll be the most important person in the bank, since I can't do shit without you.' She disapproved of extraneous vulgarities, which is why he sometimes used them. And what she did next surprised him – almost shocked him. She sat down across his desk and crossed her legs. Good legs. Maybe even great legs.

'I hope you've talked with the board members. Privately, I mean,' she said.

'I've started . . .'

'You've got to do better than start,' she said. 'This is a campaign, not a party.'

'Well, I'll . . .'

'Have you talked to McDonald?'

'No. He's out of it . . .'

'I know. But he's got friends on the board. He can possibly throw them to O'Dell. So you've got to talk to McDonald and do it soon. Call Spacek at Midland and find out if they can find some kind of figurehead job for him after the merger. Vice-chairman of the merged banks, or something . . .'

Bone nodded: 'Good idea. I'll do that.' He looked at her, gauging the change in their relationship, then took the step: 'What else?' he asked.

'I've only got one more thing – well, two more things.

First, your old pal Marcus Kent works for O'Dell. Everything you tell him, goes to her.'

Bone's eyebrows went up. 'Since when?'

'Since he decided he wanted your job, which was about two minutes after you hired him.'

'Little asshole,' Bone grumbled, not particularly surprised. 'I'll take care of him later. You said two things. What's the other one?'

'I want you to do me a favor.'

'Sure. What?'

'I'll tell you when you're given the job. All you have to do now is promise to do me a favor.'

'You mean . . . blind? You won't tell me what favor?'

She nodded. She was so serious, so cool, so remote, that he nodded in return. 'All right. I hate to do it blind, but if it's anything like rational, I'll do you a favor.'

She nodded once again, quickly, ticking the commitment off some mental list.

'I mean, money? A title?' he asked.

'I'll tell you later,' she said. And for a fraction of a second, he thought she almost smiled. 'Now: I can get a graphics guy to actually put our presentation together, but we might also want some kind of short video presentation from Midland, from Spacek himself, probably. That means we'll need to check the VCR up in The Room.'

Bone slapped his forehead: 'That's great. I'll talk to Spacek as soon we're done here.' He looked at his watch. 'Plenty of time.'

'What else?' she asked.

'I need to talk to a guy named Gerry Nicolas. Today. He runs the state pension fund, I don't know the formal name.'

'I'll get it,' she said. 'May I ask why? Just so I can stay current, and see how you're thinking?'

Oddly enough, Bone thought, he trusted her: 'Because his constituents don't know anything about the stock market, but they know he hasn't gotten them fifteen percent on their money this year, and they want to know why. He's feeling a little shaky, and he also happens to own almost six million shares of our stock which, until the merger talk started, had been sitting in his portfolio like a brick. He's now up sixty million, and due to go up quite a few more if the merger goes through. If it doesn't, he's sucking wind again.'

'So if you tell him the board is thinking about backing out . . .'

'He'll be on the phone to the board. And he's got some serious clout when it comes to electing board members.'

'Good. That's exactly how we've got to think.' She stood up. 'I know this changes our relationship somewhat, Mr Bone, but I really think you'll have a much better chance at this job if you listen seriously to my proposals. And I'll critique yours.'

'Of course,' he said.

'Don't dismiss me like that,' she snapped. 'I'm as smart as you are. I might not know as much about investments, but I know a lot more about the way this place really works. If I'm going to save my job, you've got to listen to me.'

He laughed despite himself, and again, was somewhat shocked: 'Is that what this is all about? Saving your job?'

'That's half of it,' she said.

'What's the other half?'

'The favor you're going to do me – that's the other half.'

As she was going out the door, he said, 'Maybe you better start calling me Jim.'

She stopped, seemed to think for a minute, pushed her glasses up her nose and said, 'Not yet.'

'They're gonna screw you,' Audrey McDonald shouted. Wilson

was in the den, staring at a yellow pad. Audrey had gone to the kitchen to get a bowl of nacho chips and a glass of water; she snuck the vodka bottle out of the Lazy Susan, poured two ounces into the glass, gulped it down, took a pull at the bottle, screwed the top back on, put it back on the Lazy Susan, turned it halfway around, and shut the cupboard door. Then she stuffed a half-dozen nachos in her mouth to cover any scent of alcohol, got a full glass of water and the bowl of chips, and carried them back to the den.

'If they were gonna give you the job . . .'

'I heard you, I heard you,' Wilson McDonald snarled. 'I heard you a dozen fuckin' times. You're so full of shit, sometimes, Audrey, that you don't even know you're full of shit. I'm running the board – I chaired the meeting today – I can handle them.'

'Yeah? How many board members have you talked to, who were willing to commit?'

He was shoving a fistful of chips into his mouth, chewed once, and said, 'Eirich and Goff and Brandt . . .'

'You told me that Brandt . . .'

'I know what I said,' he shouted. 'I'll get the fucker. That sonofabitch.' Brandt had equivocated.

'You can't count on . . .'

The phone rang, and they both turned to look at it. 'Did you talk to your father?' Audrey asked.

'Yes.'

'Huh.' She stood up, took two steps, picked up the phone. 'Hello? Yes, this is Audrey.' She turned to look at Wilson. 'Why, yes, he's here, somewhere. Let me call him.'

She pressed the receiver to her chest and said, 'It's Susan O'Dell. She said she needs to talk to you right away.'

'Okay. Jesus, I wonder what she wants, right away?'

'It won't be good news,' Audrey said. She was seized by a

sudden dread, looking at her husband's querulousness. This wasn't going right.

Wilson took the phone. 'Hello?' He listened for a moment, then said, 'Sure, that'll be okay. Give us an hour . . . okay, see you then.'

'What?'

'She's coming over. She wants to cut a deal.'

Audrey brightened: 'If we can cut a deal, we knock Bone right out of contention. For that, we could offer her quite a bit.'

'That's right. And we basically agree on . . .' The phone rang again, and he turned and picked it up, expecting to hear O'Dell's voice again. 'Hello?'

Again, he listened, and finally, 'Really can't until about, say, ten o'clock. We've got guests . . . okay, we stay up late anyway. See you then.'

He hung up and Audrey raised her eyebrows.

'Bone,' he said. 'And *he* wants to cut a deal.'

Audrey smiled, almost chortled: 'My my. Aren't we popular tonight. Aren't we popular . . .' The half-glass of vodka was brightening the world, right along with the phone calls. 'We've got some planning to do.'

O'Dell came and went.

Bone came and went.

McDonald went up to the bedroom, found a bottle of scotch he'd hidden in the closet, ripped off the top and took a long pull. 'Jesus fuckin' Christ,' he bellowed. 'What's wrong with me? What the fuck is wrong?'

Audrey cowered in the doorway. 'Are they right? Are they right, Wilson?' She'd been back to the Lazy Susan, this time for a full glass of the vodka.

'That mother-fucking Brandt, that traitor,' McDonald

screamed. He took another long pull at the bottle, two swallows, three, four. When he took the bottle down, he seemed stunned. 'How could the fuckers do that?'

And suddenly he was blubbering, his face red as a stop sign, the bottle hanging by his side.

'Call your father,' Audrey offered. 'Maybe he . . .'

'Fuck that old asshole,' McDonald screamed. 'I'm dying. I'm fuckin' dying.' He began pulling off his shirt, and when it came off, threw it in a wad on the floor. Audrey retreated to the hall, saw him trot into the bathroom, heard the water start in the oversized tub. A moment later, his trousers flew out the door, followed by his shorts.

'Wilson, we really don't have time for this. We've got to get ourselves together. Just because they said . . .'

'They were right, you stupid fuckin' cow,' McDonald screamed. And he ran out of the bathroom, nude now, his penis bobbing up and down like a crab-apple on a windy day. 'I'm gone. I'm out of it. I'm dead in the fuckin' water . . .'

He spun around, looking for booze, found it in his hand. He was already drunk: he'd finished half a fifth downstairs before he ran up to get the new bottle. Audrey, desperate, tried to rein him in. O'Dell and Bone couldn't be right. The job couldn't be gone . . . He couldn't be out of it.

'Maybe O'Dell's offer, the chairmanship . . .'

'I'd be out of there in a month,' he shouted. 'I'd be nothing . . .'

'Wilson, I think if we . . .'

'And you, you bitch.' McDonald turned, his small eyes going flat as he moved toward her. 'You sure as shit didn't do anything to help. *"We've got some planning to do,"* ' he mimicked, quoting her from early in the evening. ' *"We've got yellow pads to fill up . . ."* And then they waltz in and tell me I'm done.'

'They're wrong.'

'Shut up,' he bellowed, and he hit her, open-handed. The blow picked her up, smashed her head against the doorjamb, and she went down, dazed, tried to crawl away. 'You fuckin' come back here, you're gonna answer for this.' He kicked her in the buttock, and she went down on her stomach. He stooped, nearly fell, caught himself, grabbed one of her feet and dragged her toward the bedroom.

'Wilson,' she screamed. She rolled and tried to hold onto the carpet, then the doorjamb. 'Don't, please don't.' Tried to distract him. 'Wilson, we've got to work.'

'Shut up,' he screamed again, and he dropped her foot and grabbed the front of her blouse. Made powerful by the booze, he picked her bodily off the floor and hurled her at a wall. She hit with a flat *smack*, and went down again. 'Crazy fuckin' bitch . . .' he mumbled, and he took another pull at the bottle. 'When I get fuckin' finished with you, you won't be able to fuckin' *crawl* . . .'

Chapter Twelve

Very early in the morning. Cold, damp, with the sense that frost was sparkling off exposed skin.

Loring wore a suit that was almost exactly lime-green, with a yellow silk shirt and tan alligator shoes, with a beige ankle-length plains duster worn open. On someone else, the outfit might have looked strange. On Loring, who was slightly larger than a Buick, it was frightening.

'Now just take it easy in there,' Loring rasped. 'Everything is cool with everybody.'

They were in an alley on the south side, walking toward a clapboard garage with silvered windows. 'Whose garage?' Lucas asked.

'A friend of Cotina's. The guy's straight, they rode together before Cotina got wild. He's the only guy in Minneapolis that Cotina knew who'd loan them a spot to meet with the cops.'

'Could've fuckin' done it downtown,' Lucas grumbled.

Loring shook his head. 'He's got those warrants out and he's paranoid. He says he's gonna turn himself in.'

'Right,' Lucas said.

'But he's got some shit to do first.'

'Like peddling a ton of ice to make bail and pay legal fees.'

'Probably; but it ain't like the warrants are any big deal. Assault and shit like that.'

'All right,' Lucas said. They walked up to the garage and Loring banged on an access door. A man opened it, peered out.

'Just the two of you?'

'Yeah, just the two,' Loring said.

The man let them in: he was thin, wore a t-shirt with bare arms, despite the chilly weather. A leather jacket hung on a single chair that sat in the middle of the garage, while a jet-black Harley softtail squatted against the overhead door, ready to run.

Lucas looked around: 'So where is he?'

'Be here in a minute,' the man said.

'Who're you?'

'Bob,' the man said. He'd taken a cell phone out of the jacket pocket, punched in a number, waited a minute and spoke: 'Yeah, they're here. Yeah. Okay.' He punched off and said, 'They're just gonna cruise the neighborhood for a minute, then they'll be here.'

Lucas turned and looked out the windows – the silver film was one-way, so anyone inside could see out, but people outside would see only their own reflection – and after a few seconds of silence, Bob asked Loring, 'You still ride?'

'Yeah, when I can. My old lady's kind of gone off it, though.'

'You been to Sturgis lately?'

'Went this year,' Loring said. 'Pretty decent.'

'Not like the old days, though.'

'No. Everybody gettin' old.'

'That's the truth. Everybody's got gray hair. We look like the Grateful Dead.'

Loring nodded: 'Half the people out there brought their bikes in vans, just rode in the last five miles.'

'Were you there the year we burned the shitters?'

'Yeah, that was good,' Loring said.

Lucas broke in: 'This is them? Two red bikes?'

Bob leaned sideways to look out the window. Two bikers in

jackets, sunglasses and gloves were rolling slowly toward the garage. 'That's them,' Bob said.

The bikers coasted to the side of the alley, killed the engines, climbed off, a little stiff, maybe a little wary. Lucas dropped his hand in his pocket around the stock of his .45, which he'd cocked before they went in. His thumb found the safety and nestled there. Loring's hand drifted to his hip: Loring carried a Smith .40 in the small of his back. A second later, the door popped open, and Charlie Cotina slouched through the door, pulling off his gloves. He was dressed in a plain black leather jacket and jeans, with black chaps and boots. His escort wore Seed colors with a red bandana. Cotina looked quickly at Loring, nodded, then at Lucas, at Lucas' hand, and then back to his face.

'Is that a gun?'

'Yeah.'

'Bet you can get it out of there fast,' he said.

'I took the jacket to a tailor and had him fix the pockets,' Lucas said.

Cotina nodded, looked at Loring. 'This was supposed to be friendly.'

'This is friendly, if you've got anything to say,' Lucas said.

'I ain't got much,' Cotina said, looking back to Lucas. 'Just this: We didn't have nothin' to do with that firebomb. Nobody in the Seed is looking for the cops. Whatever happened to LaChaise and his friends is their business. They was out of the group when they come after you. None of us have nothin' against you, and we're stayin' away.'

'Maybe you've got some crazy in the group,' Lucas said.

But Cotina was shaking his head, again looking at Loring: 'You know this bunch of fuckin' hosers: if anybody threw a bomb through this broad's window, it'd be all over town in fifteen minutes. Nobody's said shit, which means to me, that nobody we know did it. And I been askin'.'

Lucas looked at him for ten seconds without speaking, and Cotina stared back, eyes small and black, like a fer-de-lance. Finally, Lucas nodded, put his free hand in his opposite coat pocket, pulled out a business card, and handed it to Cotina. 'If you hear anything, call us. Might be worth something to you someday . . . if you ever go to court.'

'Do that,' Cotina grunted. And he turned and left, his escort pulling the door shut behind them.

Lucas relaxed a notch, and Bob said, 'It'd be polite to give them a minute to get out of here.'

'Fuck 'em,' said Lucas. But he handed a card to Bob as the bikes fired up: 'Same thing applies to you. If you hear anything, it could be worth something in the future.'

Bob took it: 'Get out of jail free?'

Lucas said, 'Depends on what you're in for. But could be.'

'Good deal,' Bob said. He tucked the card in his hip pocket.

Lucas nodded and Loring led the way through the door, squinting in the brighter light outside. Cotina and his escort were just disappearing around the corner, leaning into the curve. Lucas bent over and picked up his card where Cotina had dropped it. 'Must not want to get out of jail,' Lucas said.

'He had to do it; he'd have faced problems if he kept it,' Loring said. As they walked back to the city car, Loring asked, 'What do you think?'

'You're the expert,' Lucas said.

'I think he was telling the truth.'

Lucas nodded. 'So do I. Which creates some problems. Like, who the fuck bombed Weather?'

They met Sloan and Del at a Northside diner, and Sloan pushed the business section of the *Star-Tribune* across the table at Lucas.

'The bank deal has people freaking out – turns out three or four public pension funds own a big piece of Polaris, and if this merger caves in, so does the stock price,' Sloan said. 'I don't know if that could have anything to do with Kresge.'

'Don't see how,' Lucas said. He took the paper and scanned the article. Bone was quoted as saying the merger was still on track, and the bank was continuing to work toward the merger. Further down in the article, an unidentified executive said that the merger was being 'reconsidered.'

'Snakepit,' Sloan said.

'Yeah, they're setting up for a fight over there,' Lucas said. He pushed the paper back to Sloan and picked up a menu. Everything featured grease. 'I bet Susan O'Dell is the unidentified executive.'

'Whatever. But this sounds like pretty heavy pressure to keep the merger going; which would piss off the killer if he was trying to stop it.'

Lucas had been preoccupied by the firebombing, but now looked up from the diner menu and said, 'Bone's the main guy behind keeping it moving . . . which is sort of odd, when you think about it.'

'Why?'

'Because most of those kinds of guys dream about being at the top. Running something. If this goes the way the papers have it outlined, and Bone gets the job, he'll be putting himself out in the cold in a few months.'

'With about a zillion dollars,' Del said.

'Yeah, there's that . . . the thing is, should we put a watch on him? If some goofball is roaming around out there, trying to stop the merger, he'd be the next target.'

'Maybe talk to him, anyway,' Sloan said.

Lucas took a call on the car phone, transferred in from

Dispatch: 'Why haven't you arrested Wilson McDonald?' A woman's voice, angry, but under tight control.

He said, 'Who are you? Who is this?' and in the passenger seat beside him, Del took a phone out of his coat pocket and started punching in a number.

'A person who is trying to help,' the woman said. 'He almost beat his wife to death last night. You've got to arrest him before he kills someone.'

Click. She was gone. Del was talking to Dispatch, but Lucas said, 'She's off,' and Del said into the phone, 'So do you have a number?'

They did. 'Find out where it came from.'

Pay phone. Up north, off I-694. Nothing there.

'Who is it?' Lucas asked Del. 'She knows everything.'

'Who'd know that Wilson McDonald beat up his wife last night? Especially if they both try to keep it quiet?'

Lucas thought about it, then said, 'Somebody in the family, maybe – and then there's Mrs McDonald herself.'

'Anonymous calls – she doesn't take the rap if her old man finds out about them.'

'Yeah ... you remember Annette what's-her-name?'

'Honegger. I was thinking the same thing. And what happened to her.'

'Yeah.' Lucas bit his lip. 'They ever find her hands and feet?'

'Not as far as I know.'

Shirley Knox wasn't a particularly good receptionist, but she did know a cop when she saw one. As Lucas and Del climbed out of Lucas' Porsche, she muttered, 'Oh, shit,' picked up the telephone, pushed the intercom button and said, 'Mr Knox – Mr Johnson is here to see you.'

Out in the warehouse, Carl Knox was standing next to a foot-tall pile of illegally imported Iranian rugs. He looked up at the speaker as his daughter's voice died away, said, as she had, 'Oh, shit,' and then, 'Wonder what they want?' To the man standing next to him, he said, 'I'll slow them down, you throw the rugs back in the box. If you got time, put a couple nails in the lid. Hurry.'

Carl Knox didn't know exactly how it had happened, but over the years he'd become the Twin Cities answer to the Mafia – or to organized crime, at any rate. He'd gotten his start twenty-five years earlier, stealing Caterpillar earth-moving equipment, a line which he still pursued with enthusiasm. Half of the Caterpillar gear north of the 55th Parallel had gone through his hands, as well as most of the repair parts when they broke down.

He'd done well stealing Caterpillar. So well, in fact, that he'd piled up a couple hundred thousand unexplainable dollars, which inflation – this was back in the late seventies – began eating alive. Then he'd met a man named Merchant, who explained to him the street need for quick untraceable cash, which led Knox to becoming the Cities' largest prime-lending loanshark. He didn't actually shark himself, he simply loaned to sharks . . .

And that led to his introduction to gambling, and it occurred to him that you could run a pretty sizable book with the computer equipment he was using to locate the Caterpillar equipment he was planning to steal . . . and pretty soon one of his subsidiary partners was running the Cities' largest sports book. But he'd never put any hits out on anyone, and while the occasional broken bone didn't necessarily make him queasy – especially when the bone wasn't his own – his Twin Cities attitude toward violence was, 'Damn it, that sort of thing shouldn't be necessary.'

Carl Knox hustled his skinny butt into the showroom. A nice rehabbed Caterpillar 966 wheel loader was on display, with fresh yellow paint job, just outside through the big front windows where he could admire it. As he walked in, he saw Del Capslock slouching toward the reception desk, where Shirley was concentrating on her gum-chewing. Capslock was followed by another man, bigger and darker. Knox knew both the face and the name, though he'd never met him.

'Mr Capslock,' he called, a smile on his face. The smile was almost genuine, because Capslock usually wanted nothing more than information. Del spotted him, and drifted over, in the odd street-boy sidle of his.

'Mr Knox,' he said. He lifted a thumb over his shoulder to the dark man behind him. 'This is Mr Davenport.'

'Mr Davenport – Chief Davenport – I've heard much about you,' Knox beamed.

'And I've heard about you,' Lucas said.

'What can I do for you gentlemen?' Knox asked. 'A D9 for that gold mine, maybe?'

'We need you to call up your assholes and have them ask about a firebomb thrown through the window of Weather Karkinnen over in Edina last night,' Lucas said. His voice was friendly enough, and Knox presumed.

'My assholes? What . . .'

'Don't pull my weenie, Knox,' Lucas said, and the friendliness was gone – snap – without transition. 'This is a serious matter, and if I have to pull down this fuckin' warehouse with a crowbar to convince you it's serious, I'll call up and get some crowbars.'

The hail-fellow disappeared from Knox's face: 'How the fuck am I supposed to know about somebody gets a bomb?'

'You saw it on TV?' Del asked.

'Saw it on Channel Three, they were talking about the Seed coming after your asses again. I got nothin' to do with the Seed . . .'

161

'We're off the Seed,' Lucas said. 'We're looking for a new angle. So we want you to call up all your particular jerk-offs and tell them to start asking around. You can call me at my office in say . . . four hours. Four hours ought to be enough time.'

'Jesus Christ, I'd need more time than that,' Knox said. 'I can't do nothing in four hours . . .'

'We don't have any time. We want to know where this is coming from, and why,' Lucas said.

'So I can ask . . .'

'Ask,' Lucas said. He held out a business card, and Knox took it. 'Four hours.'

'We're spinning our wheels,' Lucas said as he settled behind the wheel of the Porsche.

'You know what you gotta do?' Del asked.

Lucas shook his head and started the car.

'You gotta talk to Weather,' Del said. 'We gotta know that it's not coming from her direction, instead of ours.'

'Can't do it,' Lucas said.

'Get Sherrill to do it,' Del said. 'Another woman, that oughta be okay.'

'I'll think about it,' Lucas said.

'Gotta do it, unless something comes up,' Del said. 'I told the old lady to hang out at her mom's tonight. Until we find out.'

Del had an improbably good marriage, and Lucas nodded. 'Good . . . Goddamnit, I can't go see Weather.'

Del didn't answer. He simply stared out the passenger-side window, watching the darkening fall landscape go by. 'Hate this time of year, waiting for winter,' he said finally. 'Cold coming. Wish it was August.'

* * *

Cops were wandering in and out of Lucas' office – nobody had anything – when Knox called back.

'You owe me,' Knox said. 'I came down on everybody, hard.'

'I said four hours, it's been six,' Lucas said.

'Fuck four hours,' Knox said. 'I had to take six, because in four I wasn't getting anything.'

Lucas sat up: 'So what'd you get in six?'

'Same thing: nothing,' Knox said. 'And that makes me think that whoever did it is nuts. This isn't a *guy*, this is some freak. Bet it was a neighborhood kid has the hots for her, or something like that. 'Cause it's coming out of nowhere.'

'Thanks for nothing,' Lucas said.

'Hey: I didn't give you nothing,' Knox objected. 'I'm telling you serious: there's nothing on the street. Nothing. Zippo. This was not a pro job, not a gang job, not bikers. This had to be one guy, for his own reasons. Or we woulda heard.'

Lucas thought about it for a minute, said, 'Okay,' and dropped the phone on the hook.

'What?' Sherrill asked. She was parked in a chair across the desk and looked dead tired.

'Knox got nothing, says there's nothing on the street.'

'He's right.'

'Damn it.' He turned in his chair, staring out the window at the early darkness.

'Want me to talk to Weather? Del mentioned something . . .'

'Damnit . . .' He didn't answer for a moment, then sighed and said, 'I'm gonna do it.'

'Want me to come along?'

'No . . . well, maybe. Let me talk to her shrink.'

Andi Manette was angry about the interview: 'You're not helping anything.'

Lucas' anger flashed right back: 'Not everything can be resolved by counseling, Dr Manette. We've got somebody throwing firebombs, and I've got cops hiding their wives and kids. They're afraid it's another comeback from the crazies. I gotta talk to her.'

After a moment: 'I can understand that. Weather's probably at her house right now, salvaging what she can – there's smoke in everything. It'd be better if you talked to her here, at my place.'

'All right. When? But it's gotta be soon.'

'I'll call her. How about . . . give us two hours.'

'Do you want me to bring another cop? I can bring Marcy Sherrill if that'd help – maybe it'd make it seem more official and less personal. If that'd be good.'

'I don't know if it'd make any difference, but bring her along. Maybe it'll help.'

He hadn't seen Weather in almost a month, and when Lucas walked in the door of Andi Manette's house, trailed by Sherrill, the sight of her stopped him cold. She was curled in a living-room chair, a physical gesture that he knew too well. She was a small woman, and often curled in chairs like a cat, her feet pulled up, her nose in a book – and when she turned toward him, she smiled reflexively and it was almost like everything was . . . okay.

Then the smile faded, and Sherrill bumped him from the back. He stepped forward and nothing was okay.

'How've you been?' he mumbled.

'Well: the firebomb . . .'

'Sorry; stupid question. But you know.'

'I know: I've been okay.' The smile was long-gone now, and her face was tense, her voice controlled. 'But the firebomb – do you think it might be the Seed?'

Lucas shook his head, found a chair, sat down. Sherrill was wearing a leather jacket, and she pulled it off to reveal a very large cherry-stocked .357 magnum in a black leather shoulder rig. She looked like a masochist-magazine's cover girl. 'Not the Seed,' Lucas said. 'I talked to their head guy, and we've had feelers out everywhere. It's not the Seed.'

'A crazy man?'

'That's the consensus right now.'

'Unless you've got something going on that we don't know about,' Sherrill interjected. 'Have you had any serious problems with unhappy patients, or relatives of unhappy patients, or maybe state cases from the psycho hospitals . . . like that?'

Weather frowned, thought for a moment, then shook her head: 'Not that I know of.'

Sherrill leaned forward a bit: 'I only know you a little bit, and I don't want to step on either your feet or Lucas' feet. But how about new relationships? Or men who think you might be interested, who you blew off? There's usually some kind of emotional basis for a nut attack.'

Weather was shaking her head: 'Nothing like that.'

'Any kids?' Lucas asked. 'Any teenage boys trying to cut your grass for you, water your lawn? Just hanging around?'

'No . . . Lucas, I've been racking my brains trying to think of anybody who might do this. Any hint. People from back home, people from the hospital, from the University, cops, but . . . There's nobody. Not to just come walking up some evening and throw a bomb through the window.'

'Goddamnit,' Lucas said.

'My best idea was that somebody was trying to get at you through me,' Weather said. 'Remember that newspaper article after the thing with Andi and John Mail? "The Pals of Lucas Davenport?" Maybe somebody who goes way back read that article – maybe somebody in prison at the time – and decided to come after me. There'd be no way for an outsider to know that we'd broken off the relationship. So . . . I think you might look at your past, more than mine. That is, if it's not just some random crazy man.'

'How about the landlords. Would they . . .'

'Oh, God, Lucas, no. They're the nicest people in the world. I called to tell them about the house, and they were worried about *me*. No. Not them.'

'All right.' Lucas looked at Sherrill: 'Anything else?'

'Not if she's sure she's not the target. But Weather, if you think of *anything* . . .'

'I'll call Lucas the next minute,' she said.

'So is that it?' Andi Manette asked.

Lucas looked at Weather for a long five seconds, then to Manette: 'Yeah, that's it.'

Outside on the sidewalk, with the door closing behind them, Sherrill pulled on her jacket and said, 'Whew.'

'What?'

'She said that thing about breaking off the relationship, and you never even flinched. And she just said it like . . .'

'It was done.'

'Yeah.'

'I flinched,' Lucas said.

'God,' Sherrill said. Then, after a while, 'Bad day.'

Real bad day.

That night, a little after ten-thirty, Wilson McDonald was shaking his hand in James T. Bone's face, sputtering, 'Vice-chairman. That's nothing! Nothing! You're treating me like a piece of shit.'

Bone said, 'Look, Wilson – you're not gonna get the top spot. You're just not. I can commit to leaving you as top guy in the mortgage company. I can get you the vice-chairman's job with the merged bank. But I can't say what'll happen after the merger.'

'Not gonna be any fuckin' merger,' McDonald said. He'd never taken off his coat. He headed for the door, turned when he got there and said, 'And you're never gonna run the goddamned bank. Maybe I can't get it myself, but I can fuck you up.'

And he was gone.

Kerin Baki said, 'If they go to O'Dell, we may have a problem.'

Bone shook his head. 'Not necessarily. O'Dell needs ten. I can't see more than seven or eight. And frankly, I don't think McDonald can swing votes. Why should people swing on his say-so? He's gone.'

'It's not all power and money equations,' Baki said. 'Some of it's family and friendship. And all he has to do is swing maybe two votes . . .'

'I don't think he can do it,' Bone said.

'You're underestimating O'Dell,' Baki said.

'No. I just know what I'm willing to do, and what I'm not. If she gets it – so be it. But I don't think she will.'

Real bad day.

Susan O'Dell took a small red diabetic candy from a bowl on her coffee table, unrolled the cellophane with her finger tips, popped the candy in her mouth and said, 'I'm sure about Anderson, Bunde, Sanderson, Eirich, Sojen and Goff. If you can give me Spartz, Rondeau, Young and Brandt, then we've got it: we've got ten.'

'We can. Wilson talked to his father today, and he's got Rondeau's commitment. Spartz, Young and Brandt have already committed to whatever Wilson wants to do,' Audrey

McDonald said. Audrey was sitting on a love seat, her feet squarely on the floor, her purse squarely on her lap. Her whole body hurt, but nothing had been broken. When Wilson beat you, he did it carefully. Thoroughly, but carefully.

'We've got to be sure,' O'Dell said.

'I'll get written commitments if you wish,' Audrey said stiffly. She hated O'Dell, but this was necessary.

'That's absurd,' O'Dell said. 'Nobody would do that. And it's not necessary. No – I want to talk to them. It'll all be very pleasant, but we have to talk.'

'I'll arrange it,' Audrey said. 'But we do want your commitment in writing. We won't be able to show it to anyone, of course, if you go through with your end . . . but if you don't do what you say, we'll . . . hurt you with it.'

O'Dell shook her head. 'Can't do it.'

'You can if you want the job,' Audrey said. She twisted slightly, trying to ease a cramp in her back. He really *had* hurt her.

O'Dell sat silently for a moment. Then, 'Can I call you tomorrow? First thing?'

'First thing,' Audrey said. 'There's not a lot of time left.'

Audrey looked old, O'Dell thought, looking after her as she scuttled away toward the elevator. They were of an age, but already Audrey was bent over, stiff.

O'Dell worked out, both for strength and flexibility. She was a long-range planner, and had every intention of living to a nice ripe ninety.

After letting Audrey out, O'Dell went to the refrigerator, got a bottle of Dos Equis, popped the top, and sat down on the couch to think about it. Five minutes later the telephone burped from the end table, a single half-ring. She waited, but whoever it was had rung off. She took a couple of sips of the beer, leaned sideways and picked up the phone, punched in Louise Compton's number.

Compton picked it up on the third ring, and O'Dell said, 'Audrey McDonald was just here. She said she can deliver Spartz, Rondeau, Young and Brandt. But there are some conditions.'

'Like what?'

'Like they want a written statement: I'm president and CEO but Wilson gets the chairman's job. He'd just be a figurehead but the salaries would be the same.'

'That sounds . . .'

'Illegal. It might be.'

'Why don't you see if you could commit yourself with a couple of witnesses – maybe a couple of the board members – rather than putting it in writing. Then in a couple of years, when we've got the place under control . . .'

'We bump him off.'

'Exactly.'

'I like your thinking,' O'Dell said. The doorbell rang, and she turned, frowned. 'Somebody at the door. Hang on.'

O'Dell hopped off the couch and hurried across the living room, looked through the peephole into the hallway, frowned and opened the door.

'I . . .' Then she saw the muzzle of the gun. 'No,' she said.

In the narrow space of the reception hall, the shot sounded like the end of the world and, for O'Dell, it was. The slug hit her in the eye, and knocked out the back of her skull.

She went down on her back, and a second later another shot hit her in the forehead: but she was already dead.

The telephone lay on the couch, and a tiny, tinny voice screamed, 'Susan? Susan, what was that? Susan?'

A real bad day for Susan O'Dell.

Chapter Thirteen

Lucas stepped out of the elevator, brushed past a couple of uniformed cops in the hallway, stopped in O'Dell's door and looked down at the body. She was lying flat on her back, her feet toed in, her nose pointed straight up. Her face had been ruined by the two gunshots; a small blood stain was visible in the carpet below her skull. He could smell the blood.

'What the fuck is this?' Lucas asked in anger and utter disgust. 'What the fuck is it?'

An older plainclothes cop named Swanson was sitting in a ladderback chair, flipping through an appointment book. 'Same old shit,' he said. Swanson had seen maybe 600 murders in his career. 'Watch your feet, nothing's been processed.'

His partner, who was named Riley, said, 'We got that McDonald woman coming over. She was here just before the shooting.'

'Audrey McDonald? How do we know that?' Lucas asked. He was walking around O'Dell, peering down at the body as though a clue might be written on it.

'O'Dell was on the phone with a friend from the bank when she was killed. The friend – uh, let me see, Louise Compton – called us, called 911. But anyway, just before O'Dell was killed, she told this Compton that Audrey McDonald had just left. We understand you've been talking to her. Audrey McDonald.'

'Never laid eyes on her,' Lucas said. 'Talked to her

170

husband.' He squatted next to O'Dell, picked out the powder burns on her face. Small- to medium-caliber pistol, fired from a few inches away, he thought. 'Got a slug?'

Swanson pointed a pistol at an entry-way wall. 'Right there . . . we'll get it. And it looks like maybe the second shot was fired when she was already down, so it might be right under her head. Wooden floors.'

'What about this friend? Compton?'

'She's on her way – ought to be here any minute, actually.'

'Let's get something over her, then,' Lucas said. 'Cover her up.'

'I'll get it,' Riley said.

'What time we got?' Lucas asked.

'Compton called 911 at eleven-oh-four,' Swanson said. 'She says she was on the phone, heard the shots, and when O'Dell didn't come to the phone after she screamed for a few seconds, she called. So we figure it was a minute or two after eleven o'clock.'

'You know, Sloan and Sherrill have already interviewed everybody involved,' Lucas said. 'Maybe you ought to get them up here.'

'All right. I'll give 'em a ring.'

'Christ, what a mess,' Lucas said, turning away from the body. 'She opens the door and bang. That's all.'

'That's about the way we see it . . . We called you because you're up-to-date on this bank thing – we figured if it's a goofball knocking off the top guys . . .'

'Doesn't make sense,' Lucas said. 'She's the wrong one to get shot.'

'Huh?'

'We thought Kresge was shot because he was pushing a merger with a bigger bank. But O'Dell was going after his job on the basis of *stopping* the merger.'

Swanson said, 'Maybe the merger doesn't have anything to do with it. Maybe they were killed for some bank reason, but nothing to do with the merger.'

Lucas said, 'I don't know.'

'Whatever happened with the firebomb business?' Swanson asked.

'Nothing. Just fuckin' nothin',' Lucas said. His mind switched tracks to the firebomb: and Knox, the Caterpillar man, was probably right, he thought. A kid in the neighborhood who liked to watch fires. But not a street action.

Riley pulled a rubber sheet over O'Dell's body and stood up and turned. People in the hall. Then Wilson McDonald stepped through the door, jerked to a halt when he saw the figure on the floor, and said, 'My God, is that her?' Audrey McDonald followed reluctantly, a foot or two behind, and peeked around her husband at the covered body. She reminded Lucas of a small, brown hen.

Swanson was just punching off his cell phone: Sloan was on the way. 'Who're you?' Swanson asked.

'Wilson and Audrey McDonald . . .' McDonald spotted Lucas emerging from the kitchen hallway. Lucas had taken a quick tour of the apartment after talking to Swanson, but had found nothing that meant anything to him. 'Officer Davenport . . . what happened?'

'Somebody shot O'Dell,' Lucas said flatly. He examined McDonald, then his wife, then said, 'Where were you tonight at eleven o'clock?'

McDonald flushed: 'Are you questioning me?'

'Do you have an answer to the question?'

McDonald looked at his wife, then said, 'I was driving home. I'd just left Jim Bone's place.'

'Your wife was here, and you were at Jim Bone's?'

'Yes. We were trying to put together a deal on the succession to Dan Kresge. We needed to talk to the two of them simultaneously.'

Lucas shifted his gaze to Audrey: 'And you were driving home as well.'

'Yes.' She touched her throat. 'I was.'

Her voice touched a memory cell : 'How long were you here?' Lucas asked. 'And what did you decide?'

'We were arranging . . .' Wilson McDonald started, but Lucas waved him down.

'Please let your wife answer,' Lucas said.

McDonald looked down at Audrey, who said, falteringly, 'Well, we were arranging . . . talking about . . . votes on the board of directors. The board appeared to be split three ways, and if we could arrange an alliance with one or the other of them . . .' She shrugged.

And Lucas recognized the voice as the woman on the telephone earlier that day. He wasn't absolutely positive, but he would have bet on it. The timbre of her voice, and the pacing of the words, were very close.

'Did you see anyone in the hall when you left? Or downstairs?' Swanson asked, swerving off the topic.

'There were some people downstairs, but nobody I recognized,' Audrey said. 'There wasn't anybody up here. The hallway is short . . .' She pointed back to the hallway through the open apartment door. 'There're only two apartments.'

Lucas pulled them back to the meeting. 'What did you decide. Did you get your alliance?'

'Well . . .' Audrey looked at her husband, whose lips were pressed tight in anger.

'This has nothing to do with who killed Susan O'Dell, does it?' he asked. 'You're trying to screw me so your pal Bone gets the CEO's job.'

'He's not my pal,' Lucas snapped back.

'No? Who handled the money for your IPO and the management buyout? And you were in his office last week talking about me. I haven't done anything and you've been spreading rumors that are killing me.'

Lucas shook his head: 'Routine . . .'

'Bullshit. My lawyer used to be a cop, and he says it's nothing like routine.'

'So get your lawyer down here if you want,' Lucas asked. 'But I want an answer: did you strike a deal with Susan O'Dell?'

Wilson McDonald looked down at his wife, who stared back, then nodded almost imperceptibly. Wilson turned back to Lucas. 'Yes, we had. Between the two of us, we had the votes. She becomes president, I become chairman. I work on strategic issues, she works on day to-day matters.'

'How about Bone?'

He shook his head: 'Bone is committed to the merger. We couldn't talk.'

'So, if O'Dell hadn't been shot, you'd have had the job.'

'And Bone would have been out,' McDonald said. 'Why don't you go ask your pal about that one?'

Swanson stepped in: 'Mr McDonald, we're gonna ask you to step out into the hallway while we talk to your wife. No big problem, you can take a chair if you wish, but we need a statement from her, a sort of blow-by-blow account of everything that happened.'

'I thought she had a right to an attorney,' McDonald blustered.

'She does,' Swanson said, 'And if she wants one, we can wait until you get somebody here. But we're not accusing her of anything at all. We just want to hear what happened.'

'Then why can't I stay?'

'Because you have a way of answering her questions for her. We've been through this before, and we've just gotten to the point where we ask the spouse to step outside. An attorney's fine, if she wants one now, or she can ask for one at any time.'

McDonald looked at his wife for a moment, as if weighing the possibility that she would say something strange under questioning, then looked back at Swanson and nodded. 'I'll take a chair.' And to Audrey: 'The minute they push the wrong button, you come get me, and we have Harrison get up here.'

'Okay,' she said, swallowing nervously. 'Don't go far away.'

When Wilson McDonald had gone, Lucas said, 'Detective Swanson is going to talk to you for a few minutes, then Detective Sloan will want to ask a few questions – Detective Sloan has already spoken to your husband . . .'

'Up at Dan's cabin, he told me about it,' Audrey said. She seemed more assertive when her husband wasn't around.

'I have to leave in a minute or two, but I'd like to talk to you privately just for a moment, you and I,' Lucas said. He looked at Swanson. 'I just need to speak to her for a second.'

'Sure.'

Lucas escorted her into O'Dell's kitchen, lowered his voice: 'I believe I spoke to you earlier today.'

'What?' Was she really surprised, he wondered? There was an instant of surprise in her eyes. 'I don't believe so.'

'Mrs McDonald, you have a rather nasty bruise on your leg, just above your ankle. Is that new?'

'I just . . .' She looked away, groped for a word. '. . . bumped myself.'

'No, you didn't,' he said. 'Your husband beat you up last night. Would you like a call from the domestic intervention people?'

'No, no, we only had a little argument.'

'If we took you downtown and had one of our policewomen take a look at you, she'd find a lot of bruises, wouldn't she?'

'That's illegal. I want to see my husband.'

'Okay.' Lucas raised his hands. 'Like I said, this is just between you and me. If you don't want to make a complaint, I'm not going to insist on it. But you should. It never gets better, it always gets worse.'

'Things will get better. Wilson's been under a lot of stress. This job . . .'

'Just a job,' Lucas said.

'Oh, no.' She was shocked. 'This . . . this is everything.'

Before he left, Lucas took Swanson aside: 'Treat her very carefully. Get as much as you can on her – personal history, everything – and tell Sloan that I want her wrung out, but not scared. Don't push her into getting an attorney.'

'Are we trying for anything in particular?' Swanson asked. He turned half-sideways to look at Audrey, who was perched on a chair in O'Dell's home office.

'If we can do it – very gently – it'd be nice to get a wedge between her and her husband. Don't be obvious, but if the opportunity comes up, it'd be good to let her know that her interests and her husband's are not necessarily the same.'

Back in his car, Lucas picked up the car phone and called St Anne's College, which was located a few blocks from his house in St Paul. He told the St Anne's operator that he knew it was late, that nuns commonly don't take calls from men in the middle of the night, that this was an emergency and perhaps a matter of life and death, that he was with the police department . . . and he got his nun.

Sister Mary Joseph, a psychology professor and childhood friend he'd always known as Elle Kruger: 'Lucas? Is somebody hurt?' A sharp, somewhat astringent voice, becoming more so as they got older.

'Nothing like that, Elle. I'm sorry to disturb you, but I have a couple of questions on a case.'

'Oh, good. I was afraid . . . anyway, have you read the *Iliad* lately?'

'Uh, no, actually.' He looked at his watch. Had to get to Bone's place.

'Have you ever read it?'

'That's the one . . . no, that's the *Odyssey*. I guess not. Same guy, though, right?'

'Lucas . . .' She sounded exasperated. 'I keep forgetting you were a jock. Listen, go down and get the *Iliad*, the one that's translated by Robert Fagles, that's the one I'm reading now, and I'll tell you what parts to read if you don't want to read the whole thing.'

'Elle . . .'

'The thing is, this translation is much coarser in all the right places, than the old ones – my goodness, the Trojan War resembled one of your gang wars. That was always obscured by the language of the other translations, but this one . . . the language is brilliantly apt.'

'Elle, Elle – tell me later. I'm calling from my car and I've got a serious question.'

She stopped with the *Iliad*: 'Which is?'

'If a woman is routinely beaten by her husband, is it likely that she might betray him behind his back, while defending him when he was around?'

'Of course – wouldn't you if you were in her shoes?'

'No.'

'No, you probably wouldn't. You'd probably go after him with a baseball bat . . . But yes, a woman might do that.'

'I'm not talking about some kind of pro-forma defense.

I'm talking about really believing in the defense. But at the same time, betraying him to the police anonymously, then denying it even to the police.'

'This isn't a theoretical question.'

'No.'

'Then you're dealing with a badly abused woman who needs treatment – if it's not too late for treatment. Some people, if they're abused badly enough, will identify and even love their abusers, while another side of their personality is desperately trying to get out of the relationship. Just to use a kind of layman's terminology, you could say you have a condition of . . . mmm . . . stress-induced multiple-personality disorder. The part of her personality that sincerely defends her husband may not even know that the other part of her personality is betraying him.'

'Shit . . . excuse me,' Lucas said. 'So even if I broke her out from her husband in, say, a murder case, she could be impeached as being nuts.'

'Nuts is not accepted terminology, Lucas,' she said.

'But she could be impeached . . .'

'Worse than that. If she were required to testify in the presence of her husband, she might flip over and start defending him – lying – because he so dominates her personality.'

'All right.'

'Will I be meeting this woman?'

'Probably not, Elle. I'll tell you about it next time we talk. Right now, I'm running.'

'Take care.'

'You, too.'

Bone lived in a high-security building much like O'Dell's, and not more than a five-minute walk away. Lucas dumped the Porsche in a no-parking zone outside the glass front doors, and when a security guard came to the doors, flashed his ID and was admitted to the lobby.

'I need to talk to James T. Bone,' Lucas said.

'Don't know if Mr Bone is in. He often goes out at night,' the guard said, moving behind the security console.

'Ring him and let it ring about fifty times,' Lucas said.

The guard did that: and after a few seconds, said into the phone, 'Mr Bone, this is William downstairs. I'm sorry to bother you, but there's a police officer here asking to see you; yes, Deputy Chief Davenport, and he says it's urgent. Yes, sir.'

He hung up the phone: 'Mr Bone is on fourteen,' he said. 'Take the elevator on the right.'

Bone was waiting in the hallway outside his apartment door: as Lucas got off the elevator, he realized that this hallway also had only two doors, as had O'Dell's. Something ticked at the back of his mind, but the thought was gone as Bone stepped out and said, 'What's going on?'

Bone was wearing jeans and a t-shirt, but was barefoot.

'You alone?'

'No, actually, I have a friend here . . . come on in. What happened?'

Lucas stepped inside. A woman, about Bone's age, was sitting on the couch.

'This is Marcia Kresge, Dan Kresge's wife. We were just talking strategy.'

'Was Wilson McDonald here an hour ago?' Lucas asked.

Bone looked at his watch: 'Well, more than an hour. He left here probably at ten-thirty or ten forty-five.'

'Ten-thirty. Have you been here ever since?'

'Yes . . . Marcia got here about . . .'

'About eleven-twenty,' said Kresge.

'So what happened to McDonald?' Bone demanded.

'Did you make a deal with McDonald?' Lucas asked, ignoring the question.

Bone looked at Kresge, then back at Lucas: 'No. What's he done?'

'So you're out of the job. Because he made a deal with Susan O'Dell.'

'Oh, no, I'm not out of it at all,' Bone shook his head. 'Wilson thinks he can deliver several votes to Susan. He doesn't know it, but he can't. Well, maybe one. The rest are still up for grabs. Now what the hell happened?'

Lucas looked at Kresge, then back at Bone, interested in their reactions. 'A couple of minutes after eleven o'clock, somebody rang the doorbell at Susan O'Dell's apartment, and when she opened the door, shot her twice in the head with a handgun. O'Dell's dead.'

And they were, as far as Lucas could tell, stunned. Astonished.

Bone, who didn't seem given to sputtering, sputtered, 'That's not possible. I just talked to her tonight.'

'What time?'

'Seven o'clock or so.' He looked at Kresge. 'About the Community College deal.'

Kresge was solemn: 'You know what? It's a crazy man. We could be next.'

'Mr Bone, I don't want to imply anything, but you're the obvious beneficiary of all this – the top job is opened up by a murder, then the main competition is eliminated. Again, I don't mean to imply anything, but we really have to pin down where you were, and what you were doing all evening.' He turned to the woman. 'And the same with you, I'm afraid.'

'Do you really think I'd do this?' Bone asked. He sounded more curious than afraid.

Lucas thought for a moment and then said, 'I don't know you well enough to say. But even if I didn't, I have to make sure. If McDonald left here a little after ten-thirty, and you were here alone, and the woman didn't get here until eleven-thirty . . . who has an alibi?'

'I wasn't alone,' Bone said. 'I'm sorry, I should have said so . . . My assistant, I think you met her at the bank, the blonde? Kerin Baki? She was here . . . We were working on a presentation for the board.'

'When did she leave?'

'A few minutes after Wilson – she was heading down to the bank. She's probably still there,' Bone said. 'And between the time she left, and the time Marcia got here, I made a half-dozen phone calls. There must be some way to get at phone records.'

Lucas nodded. 'We'll get those.'

And Bone said, 'I'll tell you something else: we know exactly how many votes I've got, which is nine. And we know how many Susan had, which is seven. I'm one vote away. At least three votes are uncommitted, and we were just working out ways to get one of those three. Because when we get one, all the others will come.' He hopped off the couch, and started to prowl the apartment as he talked. 'So what I'm saying is, I think I had the top job. This might knock me out – or slow things down. If the board thinks there's the slightest chance that I'm implicated, I'm dead meat. Better to hire somebody else, and apologize to me later, if I'm innocent, than get stuck with a CEO who turns out to be a killer.'

'You know who the real beneficiary is?' Kresge said. 'Wilson McDonald.'

'He made a deal with her,' Lucas said.

Kresge made a rude noise: 'She might have made a tactical agreement with him, just to grab the top slot. But after she'd gotten rid of Bone and a few other people, she'd have gotten rid of McDonald. She and Jim were actually friends, in a way – but she hated McDonald.'

'But everybody says McDonald's out of it.'

'Not if there's nobody else left,' Kresge said. She looked at Bone. 'Jim, darling, I'd be very careful if I were you. Very careful.'

Bone and Kresge agreed to stay at Bone's apartment until Sloan got there. Lucas talked to Sloan by phone, and Sloan said he was nearly done with the McDonalds.

'What do you think?' Lucas asked.

'When I talked to Mrs McDonald alone, she's pretty straight,' Sloan said. 'When I get her around her old man, she's a fucking ventriloquist's dummy.'

'I talked to Elle Kruger about that. She said severely abused women can get like that.'

'We need to give McDonald a good look,' Sloan said. 'Something tells me he's involved. I don't know if I think that because he's really involved, or because I just don't like the sonofabitch.'

'Listen, when you get to Bone's . . . get him aside and talk to him about his sex life. Who he's screwing. Because I think that tip about him sleeping with Kresge is right. You'll understand what I mean when you see them together. And find out if he's screwing his assistant. She's a little chilly, but that's probably just me. Maybe Bone can warm her up.'

'I'll do that,' Sloan said.

'And you'll need to talk to the assistant. I'll give you her name and you can call her, and get her over to Bone's.'

'Where're you going?'

'Home to make a list,' Lucas said. 'This fuckin' thing is starting to confuse me.'

Chapter Fourteen

Lucas lived in a ranch-style house in St Paul, on a road that ran along the top of a Mississippi River bluff. From his front window he could see the lights of Minneapolis across the river. The neighborhood was quiet, fine for walking, and he and Weather had walked a lot when they were together.

Weather.

Why would somebody hit Weather? The Edina cops had exactly nothing. Zero. Zip. No likely neighborhood kids. One of the Edina guys had checked on Lucas – would he do it, why wouldn't he do it. He'd been told emphatically that Lucas would not, and he'd gone away.

But Lucas couldn't accept it as a nut case. Nut cases didn't pick out random houses to bomb, or if they did, the chances of hitting someone with Weather's history were . . .

Impossible. Not just slim. Impossible.

He'd once converted the master bedroom to use as a den, but after Weather arrived, he'd converted it back to a bedroom, and moved his drawing table into one of the smaller bedrooms. He hadn't worked on a commercial game for years now: everything had gone to computers, and while he might still develop ideas and scenarios, he was rapidly moving away from game development.

Too much money, he thought sometimes. He'd made too much money, almost inadvertently, as sometimes happened in the computer age. He'd drifted from writing table-top war games, to writing game scenarios which a University of

Minnesota computer freak turned into games, to writing simulations of police emergencies to be played out on police computers. And his company had simply grown, first run out of his hip pocket, then with the computer freak, and finally by a professional businessman who'd taken the company public.

And now that he really didn't need to write games, didn't need to sit up until three in the morning thinking of new sci-fi beasts to challenge computer geekdom . . . he didn't. He missed it, but he didn't do it.

Now he sat at his drawing table, cleared away detritus from earlier skull sessions, pulled out a sheet of heavy paper and started making a chart.

The situation at the bank was too complicated. There were too many suspects, and all of them had motives. He needed to simplify and clarify.

But the firebombing prowled around the edge of his consciousness: that's what he needed to settle. The bank killings were almost technical problems, problems that cops solved. The firebombing was personal. What if it was aimed at him, rather than Weather? But why would it be?

What if Weather had a new boyfriend, a freak of some kind? Naw. That wasn't Weather. She had a built-in bullshit detector, and nobody would get past that. Maybe she'd snubbed somebody . . .

Goddamnit. Work. The suspects:

Wilson and Audrey McDonald. What appeared to be a possibly explosive relationship; who knew what might be brewing in that little perfecta? And the more he thought of it, the more he thought that Audrey McDonald was the woman who'd called him – who was pointing the finger at her own husband.

Jim Bone. And Marcia Kresge and Kerin Baki.

He chewed on the end of his pencil. Baki was a little thin –

what would she get out of the killings? Her job? An assistant's job didn't seem heavy enough, but hell, it might to the assistant. Bone, of course, had that reputation as a ladies' man, and supposedly had been sleeping with Kresge's wife. What if he was also sleeping with the assistant? And if he was, so what? There might be some kind of twisted connection between an illicit relationship between Bone and Marcia Kresge, and the killing of Dan Kresge, but even if they had a relationship, how could that lead to the killing of O'Dell?

Blackmail? He remembered one of Bone's colleagues saying that Bone wouldn't tolerate blackmail. Could O'Dell have tried . . . but Bone, if he wasn't bullshitting about the phone records, pretty much had an alibi. Of course, the phones could be finessed.

Then there was Mr X.

A Mr X who might be killing for the reason everybody suspected – to stop the merger – but who was doing it either to save his job or simply as an expression of the general feeling at the bank. But if the killer was a Mr X, he'd be almost impossible to find. And nobody knew what jobs would be lost yet. And why O'Dell, who'd taken a stand against the merger?

The killing of O'Dell, Lucas decided, had been an insane risk. Neither the McDonalds or Bone's group had enough to gain by killing her, to take the risk. If anybody had come along while the killer was going up and down in the elevator, they'd have been cooked . . .

Lucas frowned, thought about that for a minute, then called Dispatch. 'Is Swanson still at the O'Dell apartment?'

'Yes, I believe so. You want his phone number?'

'Give it to me.' He wrote the number at the top of his suspect sheet, then punched it into the phone.

'Yeah. Swanson.'

'This is Lucas. Is Louise Compton there yet?'

'Yeah, right here, want to talk to her?'

'Put her on.'

'Hello?'

'Ms Compton, sorry to bother you . . . could you tell me the exact words that Ms O'Dell said to you when the doorbell rang? Did you actually *hear* the doorbell ring?'

'No, I didn't hear the bell . . . she just said, "There's somebody at the door," and the next thing I heard was the shots.' Compton's voice was breaking up under the stress of the killing, and ranged from hoarse squawks to sudden squeaks; every word was like a nail on a blackboard.

'Was she a good friend of yours?'

'No, not socially – she was my boss. Oh, God, I can't believe . . .'

'You wouldn't know who she was seeing socially . . . in a sexual sense, I mean.'

'I . . . I don't think she was seeing anyone. Not at the moment. Not for quite a while. She has a friend over at North, but he's gay. They sort of squire each other around, when she needs an escort. Or he does.'

'And she said that Audrey McDonald had already left?'

'Yes. She said she put Audrey in the elevator, and ran right back to call me.'

'She put Audrey in the elevator.'

'That's what she said. And that's what she usually does – you know, the elevator is right by her door, she steps out to see you off. Like stepping out on the porch to say goodbye to someone.'

'And she always did that?'

'She always did for me.'

'Thank you. Let me talk to officer Swanson again.'

Swanson came back and Lucas said, 'So why'd she say "Somebody's at the door?" '

'I dunno. To get to the other side?'

'I'm serious. Why'd she say that? She's got a guard downstairs, who calls up before he lets anyone in. Or you can get up from the second-floor skyway, but you've got to have a key-card to run the elevator. At least I think you do. I noticed a key-card slot when I was riding up . . .'

'Huh. You're right. And I would have thought of that, too, in about five minutes.'

'So it had to be a friend with a key-card who was coming over unexpectedly.'

'Or somebody else who lives in the building.'

'You heard what she said about Audrey?' Lucas asked.

'Yeah, O'Dell put her in the elevator.'

'The elevator dings whenever the door opens, right?'

'So if Audrey had just stood there, and let the doors open again after they closed . . .'

'It would've dinged and if O'Dell was out there she probably would've seen the doors opening.'

'Goddamnit. See what happens if you get on there and push the *door close* button, or the *door open* button, or both at the same time. See if you can get back off the elevator . . .'

'Okay.'

'And check and see if Audrey went out past the guard or what . . . what time she left the place.'

'I already checked. She left at ten fifty-three.'

'And the guard says that's right?'

'That's what he says. He checked her out.'

'Shit.'

'Besides, if Audrey'd just made a deal, why'd she kill O'Dell five minutes later?'

'I don't know,' Lucas said. 'There could be a million fuckin' reasons.'

'I'll tell you what,' Swanson said. 'I bet it's a fuckin' boyfriend that we don't know about. Either somebody in the building she'd been screwing, or somebody at the bank. I vote for a key-card.'

'I've got the same problem with that as I've got with this firebombing of Weather. People start saying it could be random, but I'm saying if it's random, it's weird. *Anyone* could get firebombed by a random nut, but *not* Weather: not with her recent history. *Anyone* could get shot by a pissed-off boyfriend, but *not* O'Dell – not with her recent history.'

'I see what you mean,' Swanson said.

'Still: Check with the guards and see how many key-cards O'Dell had, and see if you can find them.'

'Do that,' Swanson said. 'What else?'

'Nothing else.'

'I could go over and beat up Audrey McDonald for a while.'

'Hell, just phone her old man and tell him to do it. Then you can drop by for the confession.'

'You see her leg?' Swanson asked, his voice dropping.

'Yeah, I saw her leg.'

'I once saw a stripper in a carnival who had bruises like that. Her old man beat her with a rolling pin.'

'That's some business we're going to do after we finish with this,' Lucas said. 'We're gonna haul McDonald's blubber-butt down to City Hall and put him away.'

He rang off Swanson and called Sloan. Sloan answered on the second ring: 'Sloan.'

'Can you talk?' Lucas asked.

'Not really. I could step outside.'

'Did you ask Bone about Kresge?'

'Let me step outside.'

After a moment of shuffling around and some conversation that Lucas couldn't make out, Sloan came back and said, 'Well, I'm in the can. Bone says the phone reception here is better.'

'So what'd they say?'

'Yeah, they have a relationship, and it started before her old man died – but not until after the separation. At least, that's what they say.'

'How did you read it?'

'I think they're telling the truth about that. They got together at a particular party, and a number of people know about it and know that the party is when it started. I can check all that, but I think they're probably telling the truth. One thing – I took Bone back in the kitchen to ask him about Kresge, and he said he'd appreciate it if I didn't talk about Kresge around his assistant. He said he didn't want the gossip getting around the bank, but I got the feeling that he was lying about that. I think the reason was a little more personal, and I'm wondering if he's boning the assistant?'

'One more bone joke from anybody and they're fired . . .'

'Fuck you, I'm civil service. Anyway . . .'

'I don't know; she's pretty chilly,' Lucas said.

'Really? I think she's pretty comfortable with Bone.'

Now Lucas was surprised. Sloan was the personality-reading genius in the department. 'Is that so? Huh.'

'She also doesn't have a completely solid alibi. Kresge does, sort of. She was talking to some other guy – and I get the feeling she may be boning this other guy, too – when Bone called with the news that McDonald had left and there was no deal. But this was like on call waiting. She told Bone she'd come over, and then she switched back to this other guy and told him that something had come up with the bank, and they talked about it for a few minutes. Maybe five, ten minutes, because they talked about some other stuff, too. And then she hurried right over to Bone's place and got there about twenty after eleven, and from her place, she really doesn't have time for another stop.'

'Okay.'

'And to tell you the truth, she's a pretty funky chick; I don't think she'd kill anyone. She's not crazy enough.'

'What about Baki?' Lucas asked.

'I don't know. I can't read her very well. Very pretty; and she looks at Bone like a wolf looks at a sheep.'

'Huh. You about done there?'

'Yeah. Unless you want me to torture somebody.'

'Not tonight. I'll see you in the morning.'

'Shit's gonna hit the fan tomorrow morning, dude. The *Star-Tribune* has the police guy standing outside of O'Dell's, and a business guy standing downstairs here.'

'Freedom of the press,' Lucas said.

Chapter Fifteen

Jim Bone had his head in his refrigerator when the phone rang. He picked up the kitchen extension and Kerin Baki said, 'Mr Bone, this is Kerin.'

'Jesus, Kerin, it's five-thirty. Have you been to bed?'

'No. Too much to do.' She sounded wide awake. 'Nancy Lu just called me. McDonald called Brandt out at his farm, and Brandt's asking for an emergency board meeting at ten o'clock. We've got to be ready.' Nancy Lu was the board secretary.

Bone had been drinking milk out of the carton. He swallowed and said, 'All right. Do they want the pitch today? What'd she say?'

'No pitch. They just want to sort things out. But I think you've got to go for it today. If you wait, things could get out of control.'

Bone scratched his head: 'I don't think they'd give it to me today, but we might kill McDonald off.'

There was a second of silence, and then Baki said, 'Try to be more careful with your language. You talk that way all the time, and it could cause trouble.'

Bone grinned at the phone and said, 'Yes, ma'am.'

'Bring in your blue suit with the thin chalk line – is that clean?'

'Yes . . .'

'And the red-horsy Hermes necktie and the usual shoes and so on. Also, wear jeans and one of those mock-turtlenecks and the black leather motorcycle jacket and your cowboy boots. I'm not sure which you should wear and we have to talk about that. Don't shave – you still have that electric razor in your office bathroom?'

'Yes.'

'Good. Mr Bone, I think you should leave your apartment in ten minutes and meet me at the bank in fifteen. You should be here before anybody else.'

'I'll be there. And listen. Call Gene McClure and tell him to get his ass in there. We've got to start looking at what Susan was doing. If there's anything about the murder in her computers, we've got to know about it . . . I've been thinking about it all night.'

'Yes. That's good.'

'Fifteen minutes,' he said. He hung up the phone, looked at it for a moment, said, 'Whoa,' hopped out of bed and headed for the shower. No shave? Motorcycle jacket and cowboy boots? Wonder what that was about?

Bone carried the suit and tie with a white shirt and a pair of black dress loafers into the elevator, and was met by Baki on the twelfth floor.

'Good,' she said, taking the clothes. She was dressed in a tack-sharp blue suit and her hair was perfect. 'Gene McClure is on the way in. He should be pretty quick. I scared him a little.'

'Good. Get him to me as soon as he comes in. Now. What's this about the boots and jacket?' He looked down at himself.

'We may want to reflect the image of a man who has been working all night to keep the bank going. Nobody else is in. I checked on McDonald, and he hasn't been in, so as far as anybody knows, we've been working all night. Not even McClure knows you're just coming in. I told him you were out for coffee.'

'I see . . . Listen, you gotta start calling me Jim.'

'Not yet,' she said. 'Go get your computers up, and get ready for McClure. I've got to mess up my hair.'

'Here . . .' He reached out and pulled a few strands over her eyes, a couple out at the sides: 'My God, you look different,' he said. And he thought that in the six years she'd worked for him, this was the first time he'd ever touched her, in any way. 'But you've got to try to look a little tired.'

'I am tired,' she said.

McClure arrived ten minutes later, wearing a rumpled suit over a clean shirt; the skin on his face was a scuffed pink, as though he'd scraped off his beard with an emery board. McClure was technically O'Dell's second-in-command, although his position was bureaucratic rather than executive, and he had not been part of her inner circle. Pushing sixty, he was simply waiting for retirement and enjoying himself. But as O'Dell's technical second-in-command, he was now running her department, if only for a few days.

'Jim. Kerin told me about Susan. My God . . .' Bone peered at him and realized that he was really shocked. He liked that.

'Murdered,' Bone said. 'I'm as upset as you are, but we've got some things to get straight. We've got to balance everything out, tear through everything Susan was doing. We've got to make sure she wasn't up to something . . . unusual.'

'Shouldn't we wait for the board?' McClure asked doubtfully.

'No. There's an emergency board meeting this morning at ten o'clock, and they're gonna need this information to put together some kind of response,' Bone said. Baki walked into the room with a piece of paper in her hand. 'If there's anything unusual in the record, they're going to want to know ASAP.'

'All right,' McClure said, 'I'll get some of the computer cowboys on the way in.'

'They're on the way,' Baki said, lifting the sheet of paper

so they could see a list of names. 'All of them,' Baki said.

McDonald was shaken out of bed at eight-forty-five; Audrey was up with a cup of coffee.

'What?'

'Board meeting at ten. Nancy Lu called an hour ago. I let you sleep as long as I could. You've got to be good,' she said.

'Coffee?'

'Yes,' she said. 'You go get cleaned up. I'll get your suit . . . the charcoal one, I think, since O'Dell's dead. Wouldn't that be appropriate?'

'Whatever . . .' And he staggered off to the bathroom.

The Polaris Bank's board of directors met at exactly ten o'clock in emergency session. All the members were present, plus Bone and McDonald. Bone showed up at the last minute wearing jeans, a motorcycle jacket and cowboy boots. Wilson McDonald raised an eyebrow at the costume, and turned to see if Brandt had gotten it.

Before anyone else could say anything, Oakes blurted, 'What in the Sam Hill is going on here? Jim? Wilson? Anybody?'

Wilson McDonald steepled his fingers: 'There's no reason to think that the O'Dell incident is related to the bank. I understand drugs were discovered in her apartment last night . . .'

'Drugs?' Brandt buried his hands in his face. 'Sweet bleedin' Jesus. Is the press gonna find out about this?'

'I would think that the police would make every effort to keep this private. However, I think there's a good possibility that Susan, as with any drug user, was involved with very unsavory people . . .'

'Bullshit,' Bone snapped. He was chewing on an unlit

cheroot, scowling. 'It's gonna get in the papers. I'd be surprised if it's not out by tomorrow. And her dealer was a waiter at The Falls.'

'How do you know about this drug thing, anyway?' Anderson asked querulously, looking from Bone to McDonald. And to Bone: 'How do you know her dealer?'

'The police told us about the drugs,' Bone said. 'Several of us were questioned last night. Another person told me who her dealer was. Told me in confidence.'

'We may have to know who it is,' McDonald said.

'If the cops ask, I might tell them,' Bone said. 'But right now, nobody knows that I know, except the person who told me, and the people in this room. If it gets out of this room, it'll hurt the bank and I'll want to know why it got out.' He looked straight at McDonald.

'What kind of drugs?' asked Bose, toying with a string of pearls.

'Just an old piece of hash and a little pot,' Bone said. 'Nothing serious.'

'Nothing serious?' McDonald said. This time his eyebrows rose almost to his hairline. 'Nothing serious? How can you say it's nothing serious?'

'Because it's not,' Bone said.

'I'd disagree,' McDonald said. 'I think this must be handled very carefully . . .'

'More bullshit,' Bone said. He looked at McDonald over the walnut table, his eyes glittering. 'And I'm getting pretty goddamned tired of your bullshit, Wilson.'

'Listen, pal,' McDonald said, but Bone's voice rode over his:

'First, it's *not* important,' he told the board. 'If it were heroin or cocaine or crack or methamphetamine, it'd be much more important. With this, it's a misdemeanor, and we simply issue a press release saying that we were unaware of any drug use on O'Dell's part, say it may have been related to her glaucoma.'

'Glaucoma,' McDonald said. 'I didn't know she had glaucoma.'

'Neither do I, dummy, but by the time the newspapers find out for sure that she didn't, nobody'll give a shit.'

McDonald was half out of his chair. 'You're asking to be hit in the mouth, Bone. I'm no damn dummy and I want an apology.'

Bone waved him down into his chair, closed his eyes: 'I'm sorry, I apologize. But I've been here half the night, ransacking O'Dell's files with Gene McClure. We've established that her department is apparently completely on the up-and-up. Everything is absolutely clean.'

Brandt said, 'Good going. I worried about that all the way in from the farm.'

'And we've got to stay on top of it,' Bone said. 'My assistant has prepared a press release . . .' He opened his briefcase, took out a sheaf of papers and started passing them around. 'It's all very standard, full cooperation with police, the glaucoma thing, an overnight review of her department with her top subordinates indicates exemplary management with no hints of any banking issues in the murder.'

Brandt was reading the paper, put it on the table and said, 'Excellent.'

'We're going to have to tell Spacek at Midland,' said Constance Rondeau.

'I already did,' Bone said. 'Kicked him out of bed at seven o'clock this morning, briefed him. He's issuing a press release that says that Midland is standing behind the merger proposal and that he has full confidence in the integrity of Polaris.'

'All right . . . all right,' said Anderson.

'Do you think, uh, any of the rest of us might be in danger?' Bose asked.

Bone grinned at her and said, 'That's the first question I asked when the cops came over last night.' After a bit of uneasy laughter, he said, 'The police have nothing. I can't see any connection, and no threats have been made . . . but then, O'Dell wasn't threatened, either.'

'You think we could use a vacation?'

Bone shrugged. 'That's up to you.'

The board members looked at each other, then Brandt said, 'I really don't think that's necessary. But I do think it's necessary for this board to talk privately amongst ourselves. We have some issues.'

Several of the other board members nodded, and Bone pushed back from the table and said to McDonald, 'Wilson, I think they're kicking us out.' He looked down at himself. 'And I could stand a change of clothes.'

'Not kicking you out,' Brandt objected. 'In fact, I'd appreciate it if you both would hang around for a while. I know you're both tired, so we'll give you a call in a half-hour or so. Get you out of here for the rest of the day.'

In the hallway outside the room, McDonald said, 'You called me a dummy.'

'I apologized,' Bone said. Baki was standing just behind him, prim with a bundle of papers.

'Fuck apologies,' McDonald said. 'You're going down, you prick.'

'Yeah? What's that supposed to mean?' Bone asked. 'You walking around with a little handgun, Wilson?' Bone's voice was quiet, and he looked almost as if he might be joking. But McDonald could see his black eyes, and knew that he wasn't.

'Kiss my ass,' McDonald said; and Bone, in his turn, took a mental step back. This was not the hail-fellow he knew.

Baki caught the hem of Bone's jacket and pulled. 'No,' she muttered, an inch from his ear. McDonald nodded at the two of them, then turned on his heel.

'Fat fuckin' . . .'

'Some other time,' she said. 'Did it work out in there?'

'I don't know.'

'What happened?' Audrey demanded, as soon as the door shut behind her husband.

'I damned near punched Bone out in the hallway, the prick,' McDonald said. 'Christ, I could use a drink.'

'Punched him?' Audrey was confused, and her voice turned shrill. 'Wilson, what are you thinking about? Punched him?'

'Ah, shut up,' McDonald rapped. He peeled off his coat and tie. 'Board wants us to wait around until they're done.'

'Are they going to pick someone? We're not ready. We were going to work on Bose this weekend.'

'The O'Dell thing spooked them,' McDonald said. 'I think half of them are getting ready to leave town. Hide out until it's over with.'

'But . . .' Audrey was flabbergasted. 'They said next week . . .'

'I don't know.' Wilson shrugged. He turned to look out his window, down at the street. 'Bone turned up looking like a motorcycle bum. He sure as hell didn't look like a CEO, so that's something.'

'Okay,' she said. She folded her skirt beneath her as she sat down on a plush chair. 'So we wait.'

The wait was an hour long, and seemed to take most of the day. A few people came and went; McDonald stared at a computer screen while Audrey read *Vogue*. Then Jack O'Grady came down, smiled at Audrey and said, 'Wilson, could you step back into The Room for a minute?'

Audrey patted him on the back and Wilson followed O'Grady out the door.

'Going to the Gophers game?' O'Grady asked.

'Always do,' McDonald said brightly. 'Good year, bad year, I don't care . . .'

But he trailed off when he walked through the door. Bone was already sitting at the long conference table, but this time he was wearing a dark banker's suit with a thin chalk stripe. And he'd shaved.

'Wilson, sit down,' said Brandt, and McDonald's stomach turned. He sat down. 'Wilson, we've decided we need to get a new leader in place immediately; somebody who can handle the bank and give us a single voice to speak with. We've elected you and Jim Bone to the board of directors. I'll be taking over as the board chairman, and if you'll accept the job, you'll be vice-chairman, as well as maintaining the presidency of the mortgage arm. We've asked Jim to take over as president and chief executive officer. And we've directed him to continue with the merger plans.'

Brandt looked at Bone, then back to McDonald. 'So that's it. Welcome to the board.'

'I, uh . . .' McDonald shook his head as if he'd been struck. Vice-chairman: he was dead meat. 'I, uh, thank you.'

Baki met him in the hall, eyes wide, almost vibrating with caffeine and anxiety, Bone thought, and demanded, 'Well?'

He grinned. 'I got it. Brandt is chairman, for now, and McDonald is vice-chairman. For now.'

She smiled back and six years' worth of frost melted for a moment: 'I'm very pleased for you, Mr Bone.'

'Jim.'

'Not yet,' she said; she re-frosted.

'And we have to talk about that favor.'

'Tomorrow,' she said. 'I've got some more thinking to do, and we've got some work. I should call Spacek, and tell him that you're now the man to deal with on the merger.'

'That's the first thing,' he said. 'Second thing is, we've got to start talking about how to screw the merger.'

'That's not entirely consistent with your previous position,' she said, with absolute equanimity.

'I didn't use to be the CEO,' he said. 'So let's go. We're gonna need coffee and cookies. We've got some minor receiving to do.'

'Down in your office,' she said. 'I ordered everything we'll need this morning.'

Chapter Sixteen

St Paul Police Headquarters resembles a Depression-era WPA post office, but with new windows. Lucas dumped his Porsche in a reserved parking space at the front of the building, and went inside to a glass security window, where a woman at the desk didn't recognize him, didn't care about his Minneapolis ID, wasn't sure that Lt. Mayberry had time to see him and told him to take a seat in the reception area next to a kid with green hair.

Lucas sat down, said, 'Nice hair,' crossed his legs and stared at the opposite wall. The kid, whose brain was moving in slow motion, struggled with the sentiment for twenty seconds before he said, 'Thanks, dude,' with sincerity.

Lucas waited another twenty seconds, then asked, 'What're you here for?'

Another twenty seconds and the kid said, 'Fuckin' smokin' weed.'

'Were you doing it?' Lucas asked.

'Fuckin' yeah.'

The conversation withered after that; then Mayberry pushed through the security door and said, 'Hey, Lucas, what're you doing out here?' Mayberry had a head the size and shape of a gallon milk jug, right down to the handle, which was a tiny blond pony tail tied into his hair at the back. He pushed through the security door and said, 'Come on back . . . How ya been, I haven't seen you since that goat-fuck over at Ronnie White's place.'

'Ah, ups and downs,' Lucas said. 'You heard about Weather?'

'You mean the bomb? Yeah, in the paper – and somebody said you guys busted up.'

'I don't know, we're kind of working on things.'

'She's a good one,' Mayberry said. He guided Lucas to an elevator, up a couple of floors and into a meeting room with a dozen chairs with red plastic seats, a blackboard, a wide-screen color television and a VCR. Mayberry shoved the tape into the VCR and punched a few buttons, bringing the television up. 'I looked at the tape last night . . . man, it's been a long time. I could hardly remember who was who. Anyway, Arris shows up at about 224 on the dial . . .'

He was running through the tape; at the index number 210 he stopped the tape, then restarted it at real-time speed. They were both standing to look at the picture.

'Okay,' Mayberry said, tapping the screen. 'Here we have a parade of people going by . . . lots of women, going down to the meat rack. Half a dozen guys.'

The tape was black and white, focused on a thin man with a mustache selling soda, cigarettes, bread and gasoline over a small counter in a convenience store. In the background, through a window and past two pairs of gas pumps, people occasionally walked by the store, most of them on the far side of the street.

'Okay,' Mayberry said, 'Here we come up to Arris . . . this woman goes by and there he is.' He jabbed at the screen. Arris was wearing a light-colored shirt and what might have been tan slacks.

'Pretty blurry,' Lucas said, his eyes less than a yard from the screen. 'Can't see his face.'

'Not very well,' Mayberry agreed. He stopped the tape, rewound it a few turns, and Arris rolled through the picture again, this time in slow motion. 'We got the ID by having a bunch of his friends look at it, and they picked him out by, you know, general appearance, the flappy way he walked. And the dress was right. You can see his sleeves were rolled up, and that's right.'

'Nobody looks like McDonald,' Lucas said, watching the people parade past the store.

'You sure he's your guy?' Mayberry asked.

'He's the guy we got a hard tip on,' Lucas said.

'Most of these people were going down to the rack,' Mayberry said. 'But Arris was just out for a walk, and he went on beyond it. So he was just about alone when he was shot, a block and a half further on. So if you're looking for the killer . . . he's quite a bit further down.'

'Jelly told me he didn't think it was random.'

'He's usually right,' Mayberry said.

'If it wasn't random, the shooter'd almost have to be following him,' Lucas said. 'He couldn't expect just to walk down the street and run into Arris at a convenient place to shoot. Especially not if Arris would recognize him. He'd want to come up behind him.'

'Well, Arris walked every night. Nobody knows if he took the same route every night, but his neighbors say he usually started out the same way. You want to look at this again?'

'Nah, that's okay. What about the print on the shell?'

'We know McDonald's got a fingerprint file, we've got NCIC confirmation on that – he had a secret clearance with the National Guard,' Mayberry said. 'They're supposed to be sending us something right away, but it wasn't here five minutes ago. I had Chad Ogram pull up the print file on the shell. You know Ogram?'

'Think I met him,' Lucas said.

Mayberry had been rewinding the tape, now popped it out

of the VCR and handed it to Lucas. 'This is for you. Let's go see Ogram.'

Ogram worked in a bathroom-sized office stuffed with filing cabinets. At least one clock sat on each flat surface in the office, and a half-dozen more hung on the walls. Ogram, a thin man with vanishing hair, bent over his green metal desk, his bald spot as pink as a newborn's gums.

'Chad,' said Mayberry, and Ogram sat up with a start. 'You know Lucas.'

'Yeah, hey,' Ogram said vaguely, glancing at Lucas and then bending over his desk again. 'I got the fax.'

'What do you think?' Mayberry asked.

'Well, heck,' Ogram said. 'You know there's not enough for a match.'

'Yeah,' Lucas said, 'I was just wondering . . .'

'But McDonald's right thumb matches what we've got,' Ogram said. 'We got a piece of a whorl and he's got a whorl that looks just like our piece.'

Mayberry and Lucas looked at each other. 'Are you sure?' Lucas asked.

'Pretty sure: I have to rescale the fax to get an overlay, but yeah: it looks just like it.'

'What are the chances it's someone else?' Lucas asked.

Ogram scratched his bald spot with his right middle finger. 'I don't know. Ten-to-one against. Hundred-to-one. Not enough for court, but if you come to me and say we've got a partial and a suspect, and we get this much . . . I'd say we got him.'

'Jesus,' Lucas said to Mayberry. 'This can't be true.'

'Why not?' Mayberry asked.

'It's too easy,' Lucas said. 'It's never this easy.' And to Ogram: 'I kind of need to pin down the odds.'

'I know a guy at the FBI who could give you an idea. He

fools around with that sort of math thing. Statistics and odds and chances.'

'Call him,' Lucas said. 'And call me in Minneapolis when you find out. Wilson mother-fuckin' McDonald.'

Lucas headed for the elevators with Mayberry two steps behind. Lucas pushed the call button, turned and jabbed a finger at Mayberry: 'Hey: You've got a slug, right?'

'Piece of one, anyway.'

'And the ME took a piece of one out of O'Dell – the banker woman who got shot. Let's get them together and do an analysis and see if they match.'

'Okay – you guys want to do it?'

'Sure. Send it over.'

'It'll be twenty minutes behind you,' Mayberry said. 'Hot dog, I love this. This case has been open forever.'

Lucas called Sloan from his car, said, 'We got a break in the Kresge case: get Sherrill and Del if they're around, and meet me at my office in twenty minutes.'

'Who done it?'

'Our pal, Wilson McDonald.'

'You're shittin' me.'

'I shit you not,' Lucas said. 'The problem is gonna be proving it.'

He punched Sloan off, found his notebook, looked up the number for Bone's office, and punched it in as he accelerated out onto I-94. Bone's assistant took the call: 'Chief Davenport: everybody's up in the board room right now. I think they may be picking a new CEO. So unless it's a major emergency . . .'

'Is Wilson McDonald in there?'

'Yes, of course. He's one of the candidates.'

'Thanks. I'll call back.' She had told him what he'd wanted to know: that McDonald was there, at the bank.

* * *

Sherrill was skeptical.

More than skeptical: she was absolutely nasty. 'We got diddly, Lucas. I don't care what the odds are, if it doesn't work in court, it doesn't work. And the goddamn killing is so old that there's no chance of making a case.'

'Helps to know who did it,' Del said. Sherrill had come in wearing jeans, high-top Nikes, a suede jacket and a slightly too tight fuzzy white sweater that showed her figure to exceptional advantage. Lucas, Sloan and Del were resolutely meeting her eyes, though the pressure eventually got to Del and he slumped back in his chair and looked up at the ceiling.

'C'mon, Del, look at the Cat case,' Sherrill said. 'Everybody in the office knows George Cat killed his old lady. It doesn't do any good, because we can't prove it. It's gonna be even harder with McDonald, because McDonald has every lawyer in the world.'

'Still helps to know,' Del muttered.

'Because we think Wilson's done about four of them,' Lucas said. 'If we can put together a pattern, argue it, and have semi-convincing evidence on one, a jury'll pack him away.'

'So what do you want?' Sloan asked.

'I want to tear him apart. I want to look him over with a microscope. I want to get a search warrant and pull his house down.'

'Don't think we've got enough for a warrant,' Del said.

'So let's fuckin' get it,' Lucas said. 'Sloan, can you break away from the Ericson case for a couple of days?'

'For a while,' he said.

'Ask Frank. And if he says okay, look at O'Dell again. See if there's any way McDonald could have finessed it to get into the apartment. Del, you look at Arris again. See if there's anything else. Marcy, you take Ingall. I'm going up north again, right away. I want to think about the Kresge thing again. See if I can figure out how he did it. Let's meet again tomorrow at nine o'clock. And I've got my car phone if you need me before then.'

'Why don't you get a real walk-around phone?' Del asked. 'Everybody else has one.'

''Cause then people would call me up,' Lucas said. 'And I couldn't say I must've been out.'

Sloan nodded and he and Del left. Sherrill lingered. 'You're going up north?'

'Yeah. I want to talk to . . .' His phone rang and he grabbed it, lifting a finger to Sherrill so she'd wait: 'Davenport.'

'Lucas, this is Sgt. Ogram over in St Paul. We talked . . .'

'Yeah, yeah. What'd you get?'

'I talked to my pal in the FBI and he called down to the fingerprint people and then he called me back: He says it's maybe a hundred to one against having the wrong guy.'

'So we got him.'

'You got him. And listen, that slug fragment's on the way over in a squad. Oughta be there about now.'

'Thanks. See ya.'

Lucas hung up: 'We got him . . . Anyway, I want to go up north and talk to the caretaker and walk the place a little.'

'Okay.' She turned to go, but she was going slowly.

'You got a problem?' Lucas asked.

She stopped again, looked at him and said, 'No,' and turned back toward the door. Lucas thought *Uh-Oh*. He'd never in his life gone through a little sequence like that, when the woman didn't have something to say, and one way or another, he almost always wound up getting his ass kicked.

'Okay, if you're sure.'

'I may give you a call tonight,' she said. She was nibbling

the inside of her lip, as if distracted by something. 'I do have something I sort of want to talk about.'

Lucas called Krause at the Garfield county courthouse before he left, and arranged to meet Kresge's part-time caretaker at the cabin. The trip north was a good one: quick up the Interstate, dry and fast on the back highways. The small towns were buckling down for winter: a man on a small green-and-yellow John Deere was mowing what must have been a glorious summer garden, now all brown stalks and dead leaves; a man in a camouflage jacket was shooting arrows across his back yard at two archery butts made of bundled wood shavings; an Arctic Cat dealership was running a special on snowmobile tuneups, and a close-out on Yamaha ATVs.

Krause was waiting at the cabin, stepped into the yard and frowned when he saw the Porsche slipping down the driveway. Lucas punched it into an open space next to a Ford truck, climbed out. Below the cabin, the small lake showed a collar of ice, now out six feet from the shoreline.

'Didn't recognize the vehicle,' Krause said. 'Boy, that's something; don't see many of those around here.'

'Had it for years,' Lucas said, looking back at the 911. 'I'm thinking about trading it in for something a little larger.'

'Wouldn't imagine it'd do you too much good out here in the winter.'

'Not too much,' Lucas agreed. A weathered, white-haired man in his late sixties or early seventies had come around a corner of the cabin, carrying a gas-powered brush-cutter. He put it down by the cabin steps and Krause said, 'Marlon, this here's Chief Davenport from Minneapolis, and chief, this is Marlon Wiener.'

They shook hands, and Lucas said, 'I just sorta need to walk around the place and chat for a while . . .'

'I'll leave you to it,' Krause said. 'I got some paperwork with me, I'm gonna sit inside with Mrs Wiener and drink some coffee. Holler if you need me.'

Lucas wanted to look at all the tree-stand locations. The transcripts of Sloan's interrogations had given the order in which the hunters had dispersed to the stands, but said nothing about the terrain itself.

'We got a six-wheeler here, we could ride up, unless you rather walk,' Wiener said.

'Let's walk,' Lucas said. 'They all walked the morning of the shoot, right?'

'That's right,' Wiener said.

'So tell me about Kresge,' Lucas said, as they started through the fallen leaves toward the track around the lake. 'Good guy, bad guy, what do you think?'

'Wouldn't have wanted to work for him on a daily basis – you know, right next to him,' Wiener said. 'He was all right with me. Told me what he wanted done and sometimes I'd suggest stuff, and he usually told me to do that, too. My wife'd keep the place clean, come down a couple of times a week to dust and vacuum and so on.'

'That seems like quite a lot of work,' Lucas said.

'Well, he liked to have cars in his driveway. He was always worried he was gonna be burglarized or something. Not saying that it couldn't happen. He told me once that instead of working all day on a job, he'd be happier if I'd break it up so I'd be around here every day, one time or another.'

'Did he have parties, or lots of guests? People coming and going?'

'No, not a lot of them – but he did have one big party every summer for management people at the bank,' Wiener said. 'They'd come up here and swim off the dock and drink and the kids'd fish for bluegills and everybody'd go down to the range and shoot for a while.'

'He's got a gun range here?'

'Just a gully, shooting against the end of it. You know, twenty-five feet to a hundred yards.'

'Twenty-five feet? These are handguns?'

'Yeah, and .22 rifles for the kids. You know, just fartin' around.'

'Huh. Handguns.' A handgun would be interesting, especially a big one, like a .44 Mag or a .45 Colt or a .357 Maximum. McDonald could have carried it in concealed, come back, shot Kresge, thrown the gun away. Although the ME thought the killing shot had come from a rifle, a powerful handgun might be an alternative. 'The sheriff took an inventory of guns in the cabin. I didn't see any handguns on the list.'

'I don't know, they never asked me about it. They just cleaned out the gun cabinet, and that was it.'

'Was Kresge big on handguns?'

'Naw, not really. I mean, some. Most of the handguns were brought down by the guests. City people don't get to shoot that much, and they all seemed to like it, get a few beers in them. Mr Kresge had a handgun, because I saw it: it was a Smith and Wesson .357 Magnum, silver. But I think he brought it with him, when he came up from the Cities.'

'A .357 Magnum? Or Maximum?'

'Oh, I think . . . a Magnum. Never heard of a Maximum.'

'And he brought it with him.'

'I think. Then, it's not exactly a handgun, or maybe it is . . . but he had a Contender. That should have been on the sheriff's list. That was up here.'

'A Contender?' A Contender would be perfect.

'You know, one of the . . .'

'I know Contenders. Scoped?"

'Yeah.'

'I don't think that was on the inventory.'

'Should have been. He keeps it in the gun cabinet. At least, he did. Unless he took it back.'

'We'll check that,' Lucas said. 'Do you know Wilson McDonald? Big guy?'

Wiener nodded. 'Yeah, I've seen him a time or two.'

'What'd he shoot when he came up here?'

Wiener shook his head: 'Couldn't tell you. Don't even know if he was a shooter, tell you the truth. Mr Robles, he was a shooter: he'd help instruct the kids and shoot off his mouth about everything about guns. But I think Mr McDonald was mostly a drinker. That's what I remember about him.'

They followed the shoreline around the lake to the first stand, where Robles had been stationed. Lucas went down to the stand, climbed the tree, and eased himself out onto the platform of two-by-fours.

'Did you build the stands?' Lucas called down to Wiener.

'Naw, a couple of boys up from Wyoming built 'em,' he said. 'They were joking about putting in electricity.'

The tree stand was one of the more comfortable that Lucas had been in. He could stretch his legs, lean back against the tree trunk, and still look out over the hillside edging the alder swamp. The swamp itself was dotted with stands of aspen, signs of higher ground, with a big, thick island in the middle. Here and there he could see shiny lenses of ice, where a stretch of open water lay at the surface. All around, he could make out the faint tell-tale trails threading through the brush, signs that deer were working the place. Robles' stand was uphill from what looked like a major deer interchange.

'There's a finger of land goes out into the swamp from

there,' Wiener called. 'Deer can walk right out into that stand of aspens in the middle. Man'd probably drown if he tried to follow; before freeze-up, anyway.'

'Okay . . .'

They checked all the other stands in turn, spread out over three-quarters a mile of trail, but all focused on the swamp, and pathways into it, and out of it. McDonald's stand was uphill and not far to the left of one of the big lenses of thin ice.

Suppose, Lucas thought, *McDonald had lifted the Contender from the gun cabinet in the early morning just before the group left the cabin. That would explain why it was missing. And the Contender, long for a pistol, was still short enough that he could have concealed it under a hunting parka. Then, in the dark, he walks back down the track to the hillside above Kresge's stand, waits for the shooting to begin, fires a shot killing Kresge, walks back to his stand and pitches the Contender into the swamp. Climbs the tree . . . shazam. He's up in his tree stand just like the others, and never fired his pin . . .*

'Let's·go,' he said to Wiener, as he climbed down.

'You figure anything out?' Wiener asked.

'Maybe,' Lucas said. 'What time did you get here the day Kresge was shot?'

'About ten o'clock, after I heard . . . I was supposed to come in around noon with my trailer and we'd haul any deer carcasses into the registration station and then over to the meat locker. They figured to be out of there about noon, one way or the other,' the old man said. 'The sheriff asked me about the guy the telephone man saw – the one walking along the edge of the woods – but I just wasn't around. Sorry.'

The hunter in the woods. Lucas had almost forgotten. Of course, it could have been anybody, another hunter just crossing the property to get back to his car. 'Damnit,' he said aloud. Another hunter didn't feel right; Lucas was a believer in coincidences, except when they explained too much. And if the man in the hunting coat was the killer, and if the telephone man had been right about his size, then McDonald wasn't the killer.

'Beg pardon?'

'If somebody was walking in the woods like the telephone guy said, where'd he be going?'

'Sounds like he was heading back to the cabin.'

'That'd be a problem,' Lucas said.

Krause was working on the kitchen table when he got back, a battered leather briefcase next to his foot. Mrs Wiener was washing dishes, and the odor that came from the cabin's oven was so wonderful that Lucas almost fainted with the impact.

'What's cooking?'

'Cinnamon rolls – they should be just about ready,' she said, turning from the sink. She was a chubby, pink-faced woman with kinky white hair. She took a dish towel from the stove handle, dried her hands, and opened the oven. 'Perfect,' she said.

Krause had gotten up from the table to look. 'I get the first one,' he said.

'They've got to cool,' she said firmly. 'And I've got some frosting. You all go sit down.'

Krause retreated to the table and his papers. 'Anything good?' he asked Lucas.

Lucas said, 'You know what a Contender is? Long pistol, single-shot, breaks open like a shotgun?'

'I've seen 'em,' Krause said.

'You didn't show one on the inventory of guns taken out of the house.'

213

'There wasn't one,' Krause said. 'There were three rifles and two shotguns.'

'You got a diver on your staff?' Lucas asked.

'Sure. You think you know where the gun is?'

'Maybe. It'd be nice if it were right down hill from McDonald's stand. There's a big patch of water there . . . I wouldn't be surprised if he pitched it in there.'

'I don't know about diving in swamps,' Krause said doubtfully. 'It might mess up the SCUBA gear. I can check.'

'He'll need a metal detector,' Lucas said.

Mrs Wiener said, 'There's a gun just like that, in the drawer in the gun cabinet.'

Lucas looked at Krause and Krause closed his eyes, leaned back in his chair, and said, 'Shit.' Then at Mrs Wiener, 'Excuse the language,' and then at Lucas: 'I told Ralph to take the guns out of the cabinet. I didn't check.'

Wiener said. 'Well, let's go look,' and Mrs Wiener said, 'I saw it while I was cleaning. I dusted the cabinet 'cause they left it open, and that's one place I usually can't dust.'

The gun cabinet was built into an internal wall, behind a set of shallow shelves. A key fit into a small lock that was out of sight below one of the shelves, and the entire unit swung out. Inside was an empty gun rack with space for eight long guns, and below the rack, two closely fitted drawers.

'Was this a big secret, or did everybody know about it?' Lucas asked Wiener.

'Hell, all his friends knew – all the guests. It was just supposed to hide the guns from burglars. But when he had one of those parties, the cabinet'd just be standing open.'

'Okay.'

'Top drawer,' Mrs Wiener said.

'Did you move the gun?' Lucas asked.

'No. I never touched it. As soon as I saw a gun in the drawer, I shut it.'

'She don't like guns,' Wiener said, as Lucas gently pulled the drawer open.

And there was the Contender, with a Nikon scope, sitting neatly on a black plastic pad with two boxes of .308 ammunition off to the side.

'That goddamn Ralph,' Krause said. 'He never opened the drawers.'

Lucas took a pen from his pocket, slipped it through the gun's trigger guard, lifted it out of the drawer and carried it over to the kitchen table and placed it carefully on the table. Then, using a paper napkin to unlock the barrel, and touching only the tip of the stock and the tip of the barrel, he pushed the barrel down and open. A spent shell ejected onto the table.

'Don't touch it,' Lucas said. He knelt and looked through the barrel, said, 'Yeah. Fired and never cleaned.' He looked at Wiener: 'Do you know anything about Kresge's gun habits?'

Wiener shrugged: 'He always cleaned them. Big thing, you know, sit around and bullshit about the army and shooting and chainsaws and clean the guns.'

Krause again said, 'Goddamnit,' and then, a moment later, 'That's the gun, you betcha. That goddamn Ralph.'

'Mrs Wiener . . .'

'Sophia,' she said.

'Sophia, do you have any plastic bags . . . garbage bags or anything?'

'Sure. Right here.'

Sophia produced a box of kitchen garbage bags. She stripped one out and held it open, while Lucas stuck a pencil in the barrel of the Contender and gently slipped it inside. The shell went into a sandwich bag.

'I'll have them in the lab tonight,' Lucas said. 'I'll get

somebody in to look at them right away.'

Krause was still fuming, pushing papers into his briefcase. 'I gotta go. I'm gonna find that sonofabitch and I'm going to choke him to death. He couldn't . . .'

Sophia Wiener broke in: 'You don't have time for a roll?'

Krause's eyes clicked to the tray of cinnamon rolls, cooling on the stove top, with the pan of warm frosting next to them.

'Well,' he said. 'Maybe one.'

Chapter Seventeen

The days were getting shorter, two or three minutes of sunlight clipped off each afternoon; and the sky had gone dark by the time Lucas was within cell-phone range of the Cities. He called the dispatcher, told her to locate the fingerprint specialist and get her down to the office. A half-hour out, the car phone rang and he picked it up: 'Yeah, Davenport.'

'Lucas, this is Marcy . . . Sherrill.' Her voice was tentative, as though he might not know her first name. 'Are you on the way back?'

'Yeah. I'll be at the office in a half hour. We maybe found the gun.'

'What? Where?' Her voice suggested that she was on solider ground now, talking about the investigation.

'In a drawer in the gun cabinet. In the cabin.'

After a moment of silence, Sherrill said, 'Oh, brother. I'm glad I'm not the one who missed it.'

'You oughta see the sheriff: he's talking manslaughter . . . anyway, what've you got going?'

'I'd like to stop by your office and talk about it. If you've got a minute.'

'Sure. Where are you?'

'Out in Bloomington,' she said. 'At the Megamall.'

'See you in while.'

Harriet Ashler showed up two minutes after Lucas, wearing

217

an ankle-length wool coat and a frown, and trailed by her husband: 'Dick and I were going to a movie,' she said.

'Jeez . . . Is it too late to go?'

She looked at her watch. 'If we go, we gotta be in the car in twenty minutes.'

Lucas handed her the cardboard box he'd used to transport the guns: 'A pistol and a fired shell. If there's anything on the shell, I gotta have it ASAP. If it's a matter of going over the whole pistol, that could wait until morning.'

Ashler took the bag and said, 'I'll call you in ten minutes – you'll be in your office?'

'Yeah . . .'

'We could come back after the movie and take a look at the pistol, if you're willing to pay the OT.'

'That'd be good – but tomorrow morning, early, would be okay.'

'I'll do it tonight. Dick can hang around. Then I can sleep in tomorrow.'

'I like fingerprinting,' Dick said cheerfully. He was a letter carrier and had a six handicap in golf. 'I'd just as soon watch her fingerprint as go to a movie.'

'Well, we're going to the movie,' Ashler said.

'Art movie,' said Dick, as his wife started off down the dimly lit hall. 'Made by some Jap.'

'You have my sympathy,' said Lucas.

'Coulda been worse: coulda been a Swede,' Dick said, looking after his wife. 'Gotta go: I guess I'm just a goddamn culture dog.'

Lucas headed down to his office, flipped on the lights, pulled off his coat and hung it on the antique government-issue coat rack. Then he walked up and down his ten-foot length of carpet a couple of times, rubbing his hands, looking at the phone, waiting. Wanted to call someone, but there was no one to call.

Sherrill. Where in the hell was she? If she'd been in Bloomington, she should be here. Or close. He'd left the door open, and he stepped out and looked up and down the hall. Nobody: he could hear a radio playing somewhere, a Leon Redbone piece. He listened for a moment, groping for the name, pulling it from the few muted notes flowing down the hall. Ah: *She Ain't Rose.*

Despite what Sherrill had argued earlier, knowing that McDonald was the killer was a huge advantage. If they could pull together enough bits and pieces on all the killings, they could indict him on several counts of murder, let the jury throw a couple of them out, and nail him on the easiest one. All they needed was one. One first-degree murder was thirty years, no parole. McDonald was unlikely to pull the full load. He'd die inside.

So one was enough.

Lucas hummed to himself, caught it: Jesus, he hadn't been humming to himself in months. And with all the shit happening, he should be . . . he listened to the back of his mind. No static. Not much going on back there. He let himself smile and took another turn around the carpet, looked at his watch.

And the phone rang.

He snatched it up, said, 'Davenport,' and at the same time, heard footsteps in the hall.

'This is Harriet Ashler. There's nothing on the shell. It looks like it was lifted out of the box, maybe with gloves, loaded up and fired. It's absolutely clean. Polished, almost.'

Sherrill appeared in the doorway, saw him talking. He gestured for her to come in as he said, 'Damn it: I was hoping . . . well, check the gun. I thought maybe he didn't think about the shell, just like he didn't think about the other one.'

'Not this time,' Ashler said. Sherrill stepped into Lucas' office, pulled the door shut and took off her leather jacket as Ashler continued: 'I took a look at the pistol, and I think I can see some smudges. As soon as I get back I'll start processing them. Ogram over in St Paul sent McDonald's prints over this afternoon, so I can give you a quick read.'

'Good, I'll be at home. Call me whenever.'

Lucas hung up and said, 'No prints on the shell, but there's something on the pistol. She's gonna process it tonight.'

'He'd have to be suicidal to leave prints on the pistol, but not on the shell,' Sherrill said. She tossed her coat in a corner, and the motion of the coat in the air stirred up a slight scent, something light, like Chanel Five. 'And why'd he carry the pistol back to the cabin? He could've pitched it into the woods, and who'd ever find it?'

'I don't know why,' Lucas said. He leaned back against his desk. 'But why would *anybody* carry a pistol back to the cabin? *Anybody,* no matter who it is?'

Sherrill shrugged: 'Maybe they got it there, and thought if they put it back, nobody would know.'

'Leaving a fired shell in the chamber?'

'That's a question,' she admitted.

Lucas scratched his head and said, 'We'll ask him, if we can't figure something out . . . So what's happening with you?'

She peered at him, almost as if she was near-sighted, which she wasn't. 'I've got this thing going around in my head and it won't go away.'

'Uh-oh,' Lucas said. 'I've had that problem . . .'

'No-no-no. Nothing like that. I'm not depressed. But, you know that old thing about, "Women don't want sex, women want love?" '

'What?' She was talking fast, and he was suddenly aware of how quiet the building was, how dark the hallway had been outside, and how the two of them were alone in a not-very-big office.

'Yeah, well maybe I've heard something like that.'

'The fact is, I always liked sex,' she said. 'A lot. And I haven't had any for a year-and-a-half before Mike was killed, while we were breaking up, and none since he was killed, and right now I just really don't need love, but I really would sorta . . .'

As she spoke, she was moving to his left, and he was on his feet moving to her left, in a narrow circle, Lucas edging toward the door. 'Jesus,' he said.

'Look, you don't have to,' she said. 'Where're you going? You're running for it?'

She almost started to smile, a sad, tentative smile, but Lucas only saw part of it. He flipped the latch on the door and hit the light at the same time, and in the next half-second his hands were all over her. She gasped and went a few inches up in the air, and then they were dancing around, half-struggling, mouths locked together, Sherrill's blouse coming off, and five seconds after that they were on the floor.

And ten minutes later Sherrill whispered, 'Was that loud?'

'Pretty loud,' Lucas whispered back.

'Jesus, I want to do it again.' He could only see her face dimly in the light coming through the door's glass panel. And he *thought:* This rug smells weird. But he *said,* 'My place,' and he reached out and pressed the warm palm of his right hand over one of her breasts.

'I'll follow you,' she said.

'No: come with me. We can be there in ten minutes.'

'Can't find my underpants,' she said. 'What'd you do with my underpants?'

'Don't know . . .'

She pulled on her jeans and untangled her bra from around her neck, buttoned her blouse as Lucas pulled himself together, half-turned away from each other, a small piece of still necessary privacy. Neither of them wanted the light – when Lucas was dressed, Sherrill opened the door and Lucas found her cotton underpants hooked over the top of Lucas' wastebasket. Lucas stuck them in his pocket: 'Let's go.'

'What a fuckin' terrible idea this was,' she said, as they jogged down the hall. 'Screwing your boss.' She looked at him. 'You can't screw your boss.'

'I'm not your boss,' Lucas said, 'Keep moving.'

Lucas concentrated on driving, out of Minneapolis past the dome, onto I-94 across the Mississippi and off at Cretin, south to the stoplight at Marshall. The light was a long one and Sherill was suddenly on top of him again, one hand fumbling at his belt while he tore at her blouse and finally freed her breasts, his mouth on her neck and then,

'Christ, we're a movie,' she said suddenly. He looked up, past her: a couple of St Thomas students were walking past, and one of them flashed him the V-for-victory sign.

'Gotta go,' Lucas said, as the light went green, and Sherrill subsided, but still half-turned in the passenger seat, her hand on his chest. He dodged one red light, got down toward the river, then out on the boulevard heading south. Home in ten minutes, into the garage, then through the kitchen, stumbling with each other.

'Where's the bedroom?'

She was turned around, but with an arm over his shoulder and he picked her up and carried her back, dumped her on the bed and kicked off his shoes.

'Hurry,' she said.

* * *

And later, she said, 'Man, that rug in your office sure smelled weird. What'd you do in there, anyway?'

Lucas sighed and rolled away from her and said, 'This was really a bad idea.'

'That's what I said an hour ago.'

'Yeah, well . . .'

'What?'

'So even if it's a bad idea, I wanna do it some more.'

'We should maybe wait a few minutes.'

Lucas laughed and said, 'It might be more than a few minutes.'

'I think I could cut down the turn-around time.'

'I'm sure you could,' he said. 'But you know what? I'm starving. I've got some baloney in the fridge, and some beer, and I think there's some hamburger buns.'

'Three of the major food groups,' she said. 'We'll live to be a hundred.'

'Let's go.'

'Show me the shower first.'

He showed her the shower; the turn-around time was eliminated, and the baloney sandwiches temporarily forgotten.

But they got to the sandwiches, eventually, spreading mustard over the disks of mystery meat in the light from the refrigerator, and then sat in the dark to eat them with bottles of Rolling Rock.

'I think we oughta keep this quiet,' she said finally.

'Yeah, right. We're in an office full of investigators. You're gonna walk in and you're not gonna look at me and Sloan is gonna come up later and he's gonna say, "You're fuckin' her, aren't you?" '

'So romantic. Coming over here and getting fucked.'

'Hey, you know the talk.'

She laughed and said, 'Yeah, and it's not that hard to take from Sloan. He can be a pretty funny guy.'

'He thinks you've got nice headlights.'

'I do.'

'What can I say?' he said, talking through the baloney sandwich. 'The evidence is on your side.'

'I better get going,' she said. 'My car is downtown . . .'

'Oh, bullshit,' he said. 'You're staying. I'll give you a t-shirt.'

'Lucas . . .'

'Shut up. You're staying.'

'Okay. Um, was that the last of the baloney?'

She slept on the left side of the bed, a good sign, since Lucas slept on the right. They'd settled down, talking, her hand on his stomach, when the phone rang.

Lucas glanced at the bedside clock. Ten after eleven. 'Bet it's Harriet Ashler.'

And it was. 'We've got a few bits and pieces, and a couple of good prints, but none that I can identify as from McDonald,' Ashler said. 'None of the good ones are, for sure. In fact, I'm pretty sure that none of the fragments are, either.'

'Okay.'

'Sorry to wake you.'

'No problem,' Lucas said. And he imagined a wry questioning tone in her voice. It was impossible, he thought as he headed back to bed, that anybody knew yet.

Chapter Eighteen

Eleven o'clock at night, and Wilson McDonald was savagely drunk.

Stunned by the board's impetuous decision and a patronizingly courteous afternoon meeting that Bone had called with the bank's top managers, he'd stopped at the liquor store on the way home and purchased three fifths of the finest single-malt Scotch, which he proceeded to gargle down as though it were Pepsi-Cola.

After the board decision he'd been, in sequence, angry, despairing, resigned, and finally faintly upbeat. He imagined that he might have a future in the merged bank, until Audrey dismissed the idea with such withering contempt that he lapsed back to despair.

Audrey had spent the afternoon in the back yard, wrapped in a winter parka, staring at the sky. The cold air and the hint of burning leaves – an illegal act in Minnesota, sure to be avenged by a politically correct neighbor – reminded her of the bad old days of her childhood, on the farm with Mom and Pop and Helen. Hated the farm. Hated this suburb, rich as it was. She should have had a place in Palm Beach and Malibu to go with it.

The very top job at Polaris had always been their goal and intent, the one goal that she and Wilson could agree upon, without reservation. There were other jobs that would have been as good – running First Bank, or Norwest, or 3M, or

Northwest Airlines or General Mills or Pillsbury or even Cargill – but they'd been Polaris people, and Polaris was Wilson's one real shot.

Few people outside of the top management community realized the difference between, say, President and CEO on one hand, and Executive Vice-President on the other. One was an American aristocrat, who held the lives of thousands of people in his hands, while the other was just another suit, a face, a yellow necktie. A CEO had the company plane and a car and driver; an Executive Vice-President had to fight to go business class. And the spouse took status from the CEO: Audrey'd been a half-step from becoming a duchess. Now she was a rich housewife, but a housewife nevertheless.

And the things she'd done to get here: she'd married a brutal, drunken lout, because he seemed to have a chance to go the distance. And though she'd come to love him, at least a little, somewhere down in her heart, she knew exactly what he was . . . And she'd turned herself into a self-effacing beetle of a woman, staying out of sight, out of mind, producing the perfect office parties when they were needed, at which she was never noticed, advising the lout on each and every career move . . . advising against the move to the mortgage company, where he had the title of 'president,' which he'd been so proud of at that time, but now would be fatal . . .

Early in the evening, with Wilson upstairs drinking and raving, the phone had rung, and a woman named Cecely Olene said, 'There was a police officer just here asking about Wilson. I told him that I didn't want to discuss my friends behind their backs, and would call you and tell you'd they'd been asking.'

'Well, *thank you,*' Audrey said. 'I can't imagine what they must think . . .'

'They think he killed Dan Kresge, is what they think,'

Olene said bluntly. 'And they were also asking about a lot of other people who've died in the past. George Arris and Andy Ingall. They said they have evidence. Fingerprints.'

'That's absurd,' Audrey said. 'Wilson can get angry, but he'd never in his life kill anyone. I suspect James Bone is leading them on.'

'Well, I don't know about that,' Olene said. 'In any case, I called you like I said I would. I hope things work out for you.'

And she was gone; and given that last sentence, Audrey thought, probably wouldn't be calling back. Ever. *I hope things work out for you.*

Things never 'just work out,' Audrey thought. They're worked out. Always. When Audrey lived on the farm with Mom and Pop and Helen, she'd had to take any number of harsh decisions. She took another one now, sad in her heart.

She moved around downstairs, cleaning up; watched television for a while. Wilson came down once, dripping, raving. She avoided him, hiding in the basement, running the washing machine. By eleven o'clock, he was far gone, along with two of the bottles. She went to the kitchen, poured two inches of vodka into a water tumbler, drank it down, and went upstairs to confront the Whale.

McDonald was in the oversized tub, his gut sticking up through the water level like the top of an apple pie, while the tip of his penis hung offshore of the pie, like a fishing bobber. He was reading a water-spattered copy of *Golf Digest*; off to his left, an open bottle of scotch sat on the ledge.

'Well?' Audrey demanded. 'Are you gonna drink all night?'

'Maybe,' he said. 'Don't let the door hit you in the ass on the way out.'

'You're such a pig,' she said, surveying his whale body. 'Little pathetic fucking dick floating around like an acorn. You oughta get a pair of fingernail clippers and snip it off, worthless little wart. What a sap you are . . .'

McDonald recoiled from this, astonished. They'd had their fights, but she'd never come on like this. He stared at her in stupefaction, then his face went rapidly from pink to red, and he heaved himself up, a sheet of water rolling out of the tub and onto the floor.

'You bitch,' he bellowed. 'I'm gonna beat your ass . . .'

He was fast on his feet for a fat man, but she was ready for it. She was several steps out into the bedroom, heading for the stairs, before he was out of the tub. Once he was angry enough, she knew, he'd keep coming, and he was angry enough. She ran down the stairs – the alcohol still a warm glow in her stomach, but not yet reaching toward her head – punched her sister's number on the speed-dial, listened, prayed she'd answer. In any case, Helen had an answering machine, which would do almost as well . . . She could hear McDonald thundering down the stairs, two rings, three – and then Helen, 'Hello?'

'Helen,' she screamed. 'Wilson is coming, Wilson . . .'

'Get the fuck away from there,' McDonald shouted. His face was twisted, purple, all the pent-up rage of the day now flowing out toward her. She'd never seen his face like this, not even at the beginning of the worst of the beatings she'd taken from him. But she gave him the finger and he ran toward her and when he was close enough, she swung the phone at his head like a hammer. He deflected it with his forearm, then grabbed it, but she held on, screaming, 'Let me go, Wilson, let me go . . .' while he shouted, 'Let go of the fuckin' phone . . .'

He was trying to twist the phone free, and when she held on, he stepped back and slapped her hard, knocking her down. She went face down, slamming hard into the floor, closing her eyes just an instant before impact, deliberately letting her head snap forward; felt the crunch of her nose, the taste of blood in her nose and mouth.

'Oh, Christ . . .' She tried to get up and McDonald kicked her and she went down again, and he was shouting into the phone, 'You keep your nose out of this, Helen, this is between Audrey and me, if you stick your nose into this I'll kick your ass, too . . .'

Audrey launched herself toward the living room, blood streaming from her nose; the blood left long trails across the gray tile floor and onto the rug. McDonald had hung up the phone, and was coming: she got to her feet, spotted the crystal golf trophy, picked it up and threw it at his head. He ducked, and it bounced off a bookshelf, and he turned and tried to catch it as it bounced across the floor; it was unbroken until the last bounce, when it hit the tile of the kitchen and an arm shattered.

McDonald groaned and picked up the biggest chunk of it and began blubbering: 'You fuckin' broke it; you broke my golf man . . .'

He came after her hard, then, with a balled fist. She screamed at him, 'Wilson, don't,' but he clubbed her with a balled fist, and she crashed into the music stand on the Steinway; more blood spattered across the music books, and she went down again.

'Get up,' he screamed, 'Get the fuck up . . .'

Instead, she tried crawling under the piano, where she wrapped her arms around the pedal mechanism: and a very small part of her mind assessed the damage she had taken, and was pleased.

'Get out here . . .' McDonald screamed. He'd fallen to his hands and knees, the golf trophy set to one side, and grabbed her ankle and pulled. She hugged the pedal housing, kicking at his face; he dug his fingernails into the skin of her leg, holding on, pulling, and she jerked her leg up sharply and kicked again, connecting with his hands.

'You fuckin' bitch,' he screamed, and he pivoted and began kicking her legs with his heavy bare feet, the kicks landing on her calves and thighs. She abandoned the pedals, crawled toward the other side, where a row of silk plants lined the edge of a low window. Behind her, she left traces of blood; when she'd kicked his hands off her legs, he'd peeled two-inch strips of skin away and her legs were bleeding profusely; and she was still bleeding from her nose, blowing bubbles of blood out on the beige carpet.

'Oh, no, you don't,' McDonald said, as she crawled toward the plants. He stood up and lurched to the far side of the piano, kicked one of the fake plants out of the way, and stooped over to meet her.

But she'd already reversed herself, and squirted out the other side of the piano; she spotted the broken golf trophy on the floor, picked it up and turned to face him.

'This what you want to do, Wilson?' she shrieked. She hit herself in the face with the trophy, and the edge of it cut her cheek from the corner of her left eye almost to her jawline. McDonald had been trying to get across the jumble of plants; now he stumbled, stopped.

'What the hell are you doing?'

'I'm beating myself up, so you won't have to do it,' she screamed. 'Here, I'll do it again,' and she hit herself again, slashing back at her skull with the broken edge. This drew real blood, and McDonald gawked at her.

'Now,' she said, more quietly, 'You take your turn . . .' And she pitched the trophy at him, hitting him square in the chest.

McDonald, reflexes working, trapped the trophy against his chest, still gawking at the bloody hulk of the woman ten feet away. Audrey turned and ran toward the back bedroom, and McDonald, carrying the trophy in one hand, drunk but struggling now for self-control, said, 'Jesus Christ, Audrey, I knew you were fuckin' nuts, but what the hell is this?'

Audrey pushed back out of the bedroom, carrying grand-dad's favorite twelve-gauge. She looked like a nightmare from a horror film, blood matting her hair, running down her cheek into her blouse, bubbling from her nose over her lips and chin down her neckline, and running from her legs down to her feet; she'd left a row of bloody footprints into and out of the bedroom.

'You loser,' she said, through the dripping blood.

A sad look came over McDonald's bully face as he looked into the muzzle of the gun: 'I was afraid you'd killed all those people; but I didn't want to know,' he said.

'Well, now you do,' she said.

'You don't have to kill me.'

'Wilson, that goddamned Davenport is snuffling around after you, and he's going to get you. He already knows about some of the other killings, and once he has those figured out – you'd cave in like a house of cards. My problem is, you might still be able to prove you were out of town for a couple of the killings. And I'll tell you what, Wilson, after all the shit I put up with married to a goddamn loser . . .' The booze was beginning to have an effect, and she blinked once, twice, almost lost her line of thought. '. . . after all that shit, I couldn't stand going to jail for it.'

'You don't have to,' he said, hastily. He took a step back. 'You gotta think about this.'

'I have thought about it,' she said. 'I would have had to do it sooner or later anyway.'

'You goddamn hillbilly,' he said, taking another step back.

'You . . .' She couldn't think of an answer to that, so she fired the shotgun, the load of buckshot blowing straight

231

through the broken golf trophy McDonald had moved up over his chest, through an inch of yellow fat, and into McDonald's heart. He wasn't blown backwards, the way people hit with shotguns were in the movies; he simply took another step back, tried to say something else, and then toppled.

Audrey checked to make sure he was dead, and then called 911.

'I killed my husband,' she choked; and she really choked, because she had loved him, more or less. 'I shot my husband,' she moaned. 'Send somebody . . .'

And when they said they would, she dropped the phone, tossed the gun at McDonald's sightless body, and staggered into the kitchen for another drink.

Chapter Nineteen

Lucas woke in full light, with the phone ringing again. He hopped out of bed, nearly stumbled on cramped legs, lurched through the bedroom door to the study, picked up the extension on the sixth or seventh ring and said, 'Yeah?'

'Lucas, this is Dan Johnson.' Johnson ran the overnight homicide. 'Listen, you know this McDonald guy you've been tracking?'

'Yeah?'

'We caught a call from his old lady last night. Audrey McDonald. She killed him with a shotgun.'

'What?' He heard the words, but they didn't make sense.

'Killed him,' Johnson said. 'Hit him in the chest with a goose load, range of about six feet. He'd beaten the shit out of her. There was blood all over the goddamn place.'

'Aw, man.' Lucas thought for a moment. 'Where is she right now? Audrey?'

'Over at the hospital. We got a preliminary statement from her, on the way downtown. She admitted shooting him, then asked for an attorney. Her sister Helen is here, making a statement. She says Audrey called her, looking for help, while her old man was chasing her around the house.'

'That sounds a little strange. What'd they do, call a time-out so she could use the phone?'

'Well, you gotta hear the whole story, but it holds together.'

'Okay.'

'So Helen called 911 and asked us to send out a car, that

her sister was being beaten to death. The next thing, we get a 911 from Audrey, saying she shot her old man. They were both pretty drunk, Audrey and Wilson. We got blood alcohols on both of them, the old man was 2.1, she was 1.4, and big as he was, he had to drink a shitload of booze to get up to 2.1. We got an empty fifth of scotch and another bottle with about an inch left. He had been drinking part of the afternoon and all evening.'

'You think Audrey and Helen could've set it up?' Lucas asked.

'I don't think so. You gotta see Audrey. I mean, McDonald beat the *shit* out of her. She's gonna need plastic surgery. In fact, she might be getting it right now.'

'Ah, Christ. Okay, I'll be in.'

'No rush. She won't be able to talk for a couple hours, as close as I can tell.'

Lucas went back to the bedroom, where Sherrill was still curled under the covers. 'What?' she asked.

Lucas told her: 'McDonald's dead. Shot to death by his old lady in a drunken fight. Or maybe, while her old man was beating her. Like that.'

Sherrill sat up, letting the blankets fall away. Lucas decided she was beautiful. 'How can that be right?'

'What do you mean?'

'It solves too many problems,' she said.

'Yeah.' He nodded and remembered his talk with the St Paul fingerprint specialist – remembered saying that the discovery of McDonald's prints was just too easy. 'But it happens that way.'

'The first time it happened to me was with that Bonnie Bonet chick. And that was on this case, too. Weird case . . . Are you going in?'

'Got to,' he said. He dropped down on the bed next to her. 'But not this exact moment.'

'Oh, God, morning sex,' she said. 'I never understood what men see in it. I think they just wake up with hard-ons and don't know where else to put them.' She yawned and said, 'My mouth tastes really bad. Like that drawer in *Sex* that Rigotto used to spit into.'

'Sweet image. You oughta be a fuckin' writer,' Lucas said.

'A fuckin' scribe.'

'A fuckin' hack.'

'One of those. Anyway, I got a new toothbrush you can use,' he said.

'Yeah, you would.'

'Hey . . .' He was offended.

'Sorry. I make, like, a total retraction.' She rolled her eyes.

'You should. Anyway, you could brush your teeth and then I could show you the shower again.'

She brightened. 'That's not a bad idea; I only got part of the tour last night.'

'Did we get to the soap on a rope?'

'I don't believe we did . . .'

Lucas had never thought of himself as a cheerful person, because he wasn't; he wasn't usually morose, either. He simply lived in a kind of police-world mèlange built of cynicism, brutality, and absurdity, leavened by not infrequent acts of selflessness, idealism, and sacrifice. If a cop brought a continuing attitude of good cheer to that world, there was something wrong with him, Lucas thought. His own recent problems he recognized as involving brain chemicals: he could take other chemicals to alter his mental state, but he was afraid to do that. Would the brain-altered Davenport actually be himself? Or would it be some shrink's idea of what a good Davenport would look like?

All that aside, he was feeling fairly cheerful when he arrived downtown, alone. Sherrill would not get in the car with him: she would not arrive downtown at the same time.

'If we keep doing this, they're gonna know anyway,' Lucas said.

'Yeah. Later. And that's what I want. Later.'

'But you want to keep doing it?'

'Oh, jeez, yeah. I mean, if you do,' she said. 'A couple-three times a week, anyway. Don't think I could handle every night.'

'Don't have to worry about that,' Lucas grunted, as he looked in a dresser mirror to tie his necktie. 'Another night like last night'd probably kill me.'

'You're in pretty good shape for an old fuck,' Sherrill said. She was still lounging on the bed, pink as a baby.

'If you make me think of things to say, I won't remember how to tie a necktie,' he said, fumbling the knot.

'Who picked out your suits?' she asked. She hopped off the bed to look in the closet. Not only was she beautiful, he thought, her ass was absolutely glorious; and she knew it.

'I did. Who else?'

'You've got pretty good taste.' She pulled out a suit, looked at it, put it back, pulled out another. 'I can remember, you always wore good suits, good-looking suits, even before you were rich.'

'I like suits,' he said. 'They feel good. I like Italian suits, actually. I've had a couple of British suits, and they were okay, but they felt . . . constructed. Like I was wearing a building. But the Italians – they know how to make a suit.'

'Ever try French suits?'

'Yeah, three or four times. They're okay, but a little . . . *sharp*-looking. They made me feel like a watch salesman.'

'How about American suits?' she asked.

'Efficient,' he said. 'Do the job; don't feel like much. You always wear an American suit if you don't want people to notice you.'

'Jeez. A real interest.' She was being cop-sarcastic. 'Never would have guessed it. Suits.'

He wasn't having it: 'Yeah, sorta,' he said. 'I like to watch the fashion shows on TV, sometimes, late at night.'

Now she was amazed. 'Now you're lying.'

'No, I'm not. Fashion is interesting. You can tell just about everything you need to know about somebody, by looking at their fashion.'

'What about me?'

'Ask me some other time, like three years from now.'

'C'mon, Davenport . . .'

'Nope. I'm not going to tell you,' he said. 'Women get nervous when men have insights into their personalities, and we're too early in this whole thing for me to reveal any.'

'You've had some?' Her eyebrows went up.

'Several, over the years, and more last night,' he said. 'Some of them unbearably intimate; I'll list them for you. Like, three years from now.'

'Jeez,' she said, 'What an enormous asshole . . .'

Lucas dumped the car and strode into City Hall, jingling his car keys. Sloan spotted him in the hallway.

'What happened to you?' Sloan asked.

'What? Nothing.'

'You look weird,' Sloan said. 'You look . . . happy.'

'Any fuckin' happier I'd be dancing a jig,' Lucas said. 'You talking to McDonald?'

'I was just on the way.'

'I want to watch, if that's okay.'

'Sure. It's over on the ward, at Hennepin.'

Hennepin General Hospital was just down the block and over one; Sloan and Lucas walked over in the brilliant, clear morning light, just a fresh touch of winter in the wind.

'Her lawyer says she'll make a statement,' Sloan said, as they crossed the street. 'They're trying to hurry things along, get a bond hearing this afternoon.'

'They're talking self-defense?'

'Man, it was self-defense,' Sloan said. 'I was just out at the house, there's blood all over the place. And wait'll you see her. He chopped the shit out of her head with a golf trophy. She got like forty stitches in her scalp.'

'She sure sold you on it.'

'If it's a set-up, it's the best one we're ever going to see. The ME says he's got her skin under his fingernails, and she's got big stripes on her legs where he peeled it off. Her legs are a mess, her back and ribs look like she'd been in a gang fight, her face is completely blue with bruises, except where it's cut. Her old man's fingerprints are all over the golf trophy. In blood.'

'Okay . . .'

'But just in case,' said Sloan, reversing direction, 'We should bump her a little. I was gonna get Loring to do it, because's he's such a mean-looking sonofabitch, but I can't find him. If you're gonna be around, after we get the statement, could you do it?'

'Yeah, sure.'

Bump was Sloan's private code word for *frighten*. He'd be the nice guy, and get all the basic information, but even with a voluntary statement, it sometimes helped to shake up the suspect. You could never tell ahead of time just what might fall out . . .

* * *

A tall, white-haired attorney named Jason Glass, known for handling spousal-abuse cases, a court reporter and Sloan gathered around Audrey McDonald's bed. She was propped half-upright, with a saline solution dripping into one arm through an IV. Lucas stepped into the room and looked at her. He hadn't seen much worse, he thought, where the woman actually survived. He stepped back outside the open door and leaned against the wall to listen.

Sloan led McDonald through the routine, with interjections by her attorney: yes, she was making the statement voluntarily. No, she hadn't been offered anything in return for making the statement. No, she hadn't been asked to answer police questions before her attorney arrived, but yes, she had told police that she'd shot her husband Wilson McDonald with a twelve-gauge shotgun.

As Lucas listened to her recount the sequence of violence, Frank Lester, the other deputy chief, straggled down the hall, peeked in the door and said, 'How's it going?'

Lucas shrugged: 'She ain't arguing. She says she did it. And McDonald was the guy: nothing she's saying makes it seem any other way.'

'We're getting some preliminary stuff back from the lab. Everything is consistent with what she said early on.'

'They had a history,' Lucas said. 'The question now is, can she live without him?'

'She's got a problem?'

'When I saw her, at O'Dell's, she was virtually a hand puppet. She had no personality left, that he didn't supply.'

'Well . . . you know they're pleading self-defense,' Lester said.

'Yeah.'

'If the lab comes through, I doubt she'll even be indicted.'

239

'If the lab comes through, she shouldn't be,' Lucas said. 'Speaking of the lab, did we ever get that spectrographic analysis on the slug fragments?'

'Mmm, I heard somebody say something about it. I think it's back, but I don't know what they said.'

'All right . . .'

They listened for a minute: Audrey was telling of the pursuit down the stairs, of the panicky call to Helen. 'You gonna bump her a little?' Lester asked.

'Yeah, when she's done. I'm starting to feel kinda bad about it, though,' Lucas said.

'I don't know,' Lester said, peering up at him. 'I thought you were looking pretty cheerful.'

'Yeah?'

'Yeah. You getting laid again?'

'Jesus, you married guys don't think about anything but sex.'

'That's true,' Lester said. 'Well, let me know what happens.'

Lucas nodded. 'I will.'

'And say hello to Sherrill for me. You know, when you see her.'

Sloan had gotten through the shooting, and now was working backwards: did Audrey McDonald know that her husband was suspected of committing a number of murders?

'No . . .' A little fire now, but in a prissy way. 'That ridiculous Davenport person is pushing this. Wilson would never kill anybody. He'd lose control and he'd beat me up, but sometimes I was asking for it. Last night . . . last night I just couldn't help myself, I ran into the bedroom to hide and there was the shotgun and the shells on the floor and he was coming and I knew how to load it . . .' She started rambling down the path to the shooting again, and Sloan cut her off.

'Did your husband own a pistol?'

'No. Well, yes, years ago . . .'

'State firearms records indicate he purchased a .380-caliber Iver Johnson semi-automatic pistol at North Woods Arms in Wayzata in 1982.'

'I'm sure you're right. But he never used it. He called it his car gun because he had to work down in the colored area sometimes, way back when.'

'Do you know where he kept it?'

'No, I assumed he gave it away. Or disposed of it.'

'He doesn't have it in his car now?'

'I don't think so; I think I would have known . . .'

'Do you remember how you heard the news that Andy Ingall was lost up on Lake Superior?'

'Well . . . I think somebody from the bank called and told us.'

'Mr McDonald was with you when you found out?'

'Why, yes. Somebody called him, not me.'

'You don't know if he'd been in Duluth about that time.'

'I'm sure he wasn't; it would have stuck in my mind.'

Sloan was pushing a dead-end. Lucas waited a few more minutes, listening, then breezed into the room, as though he were in a hurry. Sloan looked up and said, 'Chief Davenport . . . Mrs McDonald.'

She seemed to shrink away from him, what was left of her. Most of her face was black with bruises and subcutaneous bleeding around the cuts; a row of tiny black stitches marched up one cheek like a line of gnats; her hair was cut away on one side of her head, and a scalp bandage was damp from wound seepage.

'Mrs McDonald, I'll be brief,' Lucas said. 'We're virtually certain that your husband was involved in the deaths of Kresge, Arris and Ingall. And we're wondering how, if he killed all those people, you could not have known about it.'

'Why . . . why . . . he didn't do that.'

And her attorney, Glass, was sputtering, 'Hey, hey, hey . . . we're not answering those kinds of questions.'

'You should,' Lucas said, 'If Mrs McDonald doesn't cooperate, well, Mr Glass . . . you know how it looks. I mean, if a person has ambitions to resume her life in society.'

'What?' Audrey McDonald looked dazed, swinging her face from Glass to Lucas. 'Resume my life?'

'That's a lot of horse pucky, Lucas,' Glass said. To Audrey McDonald: 'Ignore him.'

'At your own risk,' Lucas said. 'You know how people talk.'

'People,' she said.

Lucas added, 'We will be executing a search warrant at the McDonald home this morning, looking for more evidence. But we already have substantial support for the idea that Wilson McDonald killed all three of them. And we will want to understand what your role was in the killings . . . if you had one.'

'You can't . . .'

'Mrs McDonald,' Lucas said, suddenly going soft. 'I mentioned this the other night. I recognize your voice.'

'What?' As though she hadn't heard him correctly. And Glass peered at her, a frown on his face.

'You've called me,' he said. 'You knew your husband was killing people.'

'That's utterly . . .' She groped for a word that wasn't *ridiculous*, but couldn't find one '. . . ridiculous.'

'What are you doing, Lucas?' Glass asked.

And Audrey seemed so genuinely nonplussed that Lucas, puzzled – why would she deny it now? Having helped stop him could only be to her credit, now, and he wasn't around to strike back – backed away, and tried again. 'Mrs McDonald, how often did you visit the Kresge cabin?'

'Why, why . . .' She struggled to think, 'It's so hard to *think* with these things they are putting into me.'

'You don't have to answer these questions,' Glass said. 'And I would recommend that you don't.'

'You suggest that she not tell me how often she went to Kresge's? Why wouldn't she tell me that?' Lucas asked.

'Because you might try to make your pig's ear into a silk purse, and there's no reason to help you do that,' Glass said.

'Maybe six times,' she said.

'Mrs McDonald, you don't have to answer,' Glass said. 'In fact, I'm telling you: keep quiet. Lucas – Chief Davenport – if you have any more questions about Mr McDonald, ask me first. I may advise Mrs McDonald to answer them. But she won't answer any more questions about herself.' Glass looked at the stenographer. 'Could you read that back to me?'

'Sure, just a minute.'

'No need to,' Lucas said. 'We got it, and I'm outa here. We'll be checking the McDonald house. And we may be back with more questions.' He looked straight into Audrey McDonald's eyes, held them for a second, then turned and walked out.

Glass caught Lucas in the hallway. 'What the hell was that all about?'

Lucas shrugged. 'Bumping her along a little.'

'Well, Jesus . . .' Glass scratched his head. 'You don't think she had anything to do with these things, do you? The killings? That old lady?'

'What do you think, counselor?'

'Don't *counselor* me, butthead. This is J.B. fuckin' Glass you're talking to. What I want to know is, do I have to start thinking about a defense? Or were you just blowing smoke?'

'Mostly smoke,' Lucas admitted.

'All right,' Glass said. 'How you been?'

'Not too bad . . . you heard about Weather?'

'Yeah, the bomb. Jesus. What do you think, a crazy?' Glass asked.

'We don't know. We've got no theory.'

'Shoot. Well, keep your ass down,' Glass said, and slapped Lucas on the arm before he started back to McDonald's room.

'Hey, J.B. – how old do you think your client is, anyway?'

Glass spread his hands. 'I never asked. Fifty . . . two?'

'She's thirty-eight,' Lucas said.

Glass looked at McDonald's room, then said with a hushed voice, 'No way.'

'She's got some hard miles on her, J.B. And she might not be quite what she looks like.'

Chapter Twenty

Lucas was sitting in McDonald's study, flipping through a batch of American Express statements that went back, apparently, forever. Both Wilson and Audrey McDonald were Platinum Card holders, upgraded six years earlier from the Gold. The most interesting statement involved charges on McDonald's card in the days before Andy Ingall sailed off on Lake Superior and vanished.

'The day before Ingall disappears, McDonald spends four hundred bucks at Marshall Field in Chicago. That night, and the night before, he's at the Palmer House,' Lucas said to Franklin. 'That means if he rigged the boat, he had to have done it at least a couple of days beforehand, or, if he came home that day, he had to go right up to Superior and rig the boat the night before. That seems tricky.'

Franklin, an enormous man wearing a plaid shirt and jeans, had been going through the check stubs and investment papers. 'I ain't finding anything here. It's all too general. They were pretty well off, though. He's got a trust account at Polaris with about three-point-four million divided between stocks and bonds, heavy on the bonds. Plus an account at Vanguard worth another three million, all in the stock market. And if I'm reading it right, he's got another nine-hundred thousand in stock at Merrill-Lynch. Cash in bank accounts, about twenty-four thousand, plus a money-market account with a hundred and seventy thousand . . . that's apparently a tax account.' He put the papers down, and looked at Lucas. 'I don't know. With that much – that's gotta be more'n seven million – you think he'd be killing to get even richer?'

'I asked the same thing,' Lucas said. 'The answer is, he was chasing power, not money. He was a bully in high school, he beat his wife, he killed people to eliminate competition for the promotions. He got off on power trips. He'd be running the lives of a couple thousand people if he took over the bank.'

Franklin sighed: 'I'd like to get a *nice* killer sometime.'

A uniformed cop stuck his head in the door: 'You know how you told us to find that Jag?'

Lucas nodded without looking up. According to a file he found in the house, and confirmed by the department of motor vehicles, Wilson McDonald owned a 1969 XK-E, which was not in their three-car garage.

'We talked to McDonald's old man,' the uniformed cop said. His name was Lane, and he wanted to be a detective. 'The car was in a downtown parking garage, already covered up for the winter. And guess what?'

Lucas looked up now. 'What?

Lane stepped fully into the room, held up a transparent plastic baggie. Inside, a small automatic pistol. 'Ta-ta.'

'I don't believe it,' Lucas said. He took the bag, held it up, and peered at the gun. The caliber, .380, was stamped on the slide. 'That's the one . . . you touch it?'

'No, of course not. The safety's on, and we just bagged it. Figured, who knows – if he didn't shoot it much, maybe it's got some of the same shells from the Arris or O'Dell deals.'

'Get it downtown,' Lucas said, handing it back.

'Do I get a medal?' Lane asked.

'Yeah. You'll get a size eleven medal right in the ass if you don't get it downtown.'

Lane left, and a few minutes later, Franklin, who'd fallen

into an odd reverie, sitting in an overstuffed chair with the bank statements in his hands, staring at an English hunting print on the wall above McDonald's desk, suddenly said, 'I know what it is.'

'I'm glad somebody does,' Lucas said.

'You know what's wrong with this place?'

Lucas looked around. 'Looks pretty nice.'

'There are no fuckin' books,' Franklin said. He got up, walked around the study, checking the shelves full of ceramic figurines. 'They even got a couple of bookends, with no books between them – they got these fuckin' Keebler elves, or whatever they are.'

'Hummels,' Lucas said. 'But they do have a computer.' He nodded at the Hewlett Packard crouched on the desk.

'Ain't a book,' Franklin said. 'I'm going to look around.'

Lucas finished the American Express statements, extracted the statement that showed McDonald in Chicago, and stacked the rest on the desk. Slow going. He'd just gotten up when Franklin came back: 'I could find five books in this whole fuckin' house. A dictionary, a cookbook, a bartender's guide, and travel books on California and Florida.'

'Maybe they took turns reading the dictionary,' Lucas said.

'You don't think it's weird?'

'The pinking shears thing with Del – that was weird,' Lucas said. 'No books? That's not weird, that's just a little unusual.'

'I think it's weird,' Franklin insisted. 'People with seven million, they oughta have books.' He frowned, and said, 'Hey, you know what else?'

He left the room, and Lucas trailed after him. 'There's no CD player. I don't think they've got any CDs. They got no goddamn record player, Lucas.'

'Yeah, well . . .'

Franklin turned and said, 'These people are very strange.'

He looked around the room again, spotted a studio portrait of Wilson and Audrey McDonald smiling down from another knick-knack shelf. The photo was so heavily retouched that the two of them looked like puppets. 'Look at her eyes,' Franklin said. Lucas looked. 'They follow you. Man, they are *very* strange.'

Audrey McDonald lay in her hospital bed and thought about Davenport. He seemed to know something. To know *her.* The others had shaken their heads when they saw her, had essentially apologized for their maleness in view of what another male had done to her. The hospital had provided female attendants to care for her, as if a male doctor or male nurse might somehow further the damage done.

Not Davenport. He was ready to crucify her. She would have to move on this.

She dozed for a while, in a little pain, and woke up, calculating.

The lawyer said she'd be here overnight, and then would be wheeled into court for a preliminary hearing on an open charge of murder. She would be allowed to enter a plea – not guilty – and bail would be set. If she were willing, he'd said, she could use her house as security. The assistant county attorney handling the case had already indicated that the state would have no objection, so the deal was good as done, and she could go straight home from the courthouse.

'Murder?' she'd croaked. 'They're charging . . . ?'

'Don't worry: they're already backing off,' Glass had said. 'When the police finish investigating, they'll almost certainly find that it was self-defense. Right now, it's 90–10 for no charges at all.'

So Audrey had agreed to use the house as security, and had given him a limited power of attorney so that he could get all the paperwork. She'd be out tomorrow afternoon.

And that would be the time to handle the Davenport problem.

She'd thought she was doing that when she pitched the Molotov cocktail through Weather Karkinnen's window. From what she could tell by questioning Wilson, and careful questions to others at the bank, Davenport had been the only reason that Wilson had been looked at so closely. Audrey had attacked Karkinnen in an effort to turn Lucas around – the same tactic had worked in the past, with the McKinney situation and the Bairds. And from what she could tell of the investigation's pace, and from stories in the newspapers, the attack *had* diverted him for a time. Investigators had vanished from the bank, there'd been two days of silence from the police . . . and then suddenly, they were back, and all over Wilson.

Wilson.

She sighed, and let a little tear start at the corner of her eye. She already missed Wilson. She'd known, in her heart-of-hearts, that someday she'd have to kill him, the love of her life. He would inevitably get in her way, or even become a danger to her. And he finally had. If the police had put pressure on him, he would've pointed them at her, because he was basically a coward. He had no grit. Wilson . . .

She wrenched her mind back to Davenport.

The problem with the Karkinnen diversion was that the police investigation hadn't led anywhere. The newspapers said the police were simply mystified. They'd run down every single clue and they'd found nothing at all. After a while, there was nothing left to do, so they'd gone back to Wilson and had apparently stumbled over something that pointed at the Arris killing. If they'd been preoccupied with Karkinnen a little bit longer, they might never have found whatever it was.

Now they were looking at her. Or, at least, Davenport was. She didn't quite understand why. She'd given him an answer to his question – her own dead husband.

She'd actually given him an earlier answer, the answer to who killed Kresge, but he either hadn't gotten the message, or had ignored it.

The Kresge murder weapon had the fingerprints of Kresge's caretaker all over it. He'd been the one who put it away the last time Audrey saw it. A few of the lingering party-goers had been sitting around with Kresge, talking and cleaning the guns. When they were done with each one, they'd pass it to the caretaker, who'd put it away.

Kresge had told her, on the shooting range, that she shot the Contender better than he did. That he'd never shot it at all, after the first few times. So the caretaker's prints should still be on it. But the papers hadn't had a whisper about the gun, and Wilson said nobody had even bothered to interview the caretaker. Something was screwed up, she thought. Typical. Very few people could act with her intellectual rigor . . .

Audrey was crazy and smart and she knew how to do research: she'd taken an undergraduate degree in English from St Anne's, and then, while she was pushing Wilson through law school, she'd taken a master's degree from the University of Minnesota in library science. She was still working in the library when computers moved in, and she'd more or less kept up with them over the years, and when the bank went on-line. When Davenport had become a problem, she'd looked him up in the *Star-Tribune* library node on the Internet.

And there she'd found a treasure trove.

The *Star-Tribune* had done a lengthy feature on Davenport after he'd cleared the kidnapping of a psychologist and her two daughters by a madman named John Mail. 'Davenport and His Pals' had pictured Davenport with Weather Karkinnen, with Sister Mary Joseph – whom he'd known since their childhood together – and with a variety of cops, lawyers, TV and newspaper reporters, doctors, jocks and street people, all friends of his.

The two obvious targets for a diversionary attack had been the nun and the surgeon – Davenport's oldest friend and his lover. She'd decided on Karkinnen because Karkinnen was simpler.

Audrey knew Sister Mary Joseph from her college days: the nun had been her instructor in basic psychology, and Audrey remembered her as an intense young woman with a face terribly scarred by adolescent acne. But the nun, who was still at St Anne's, lived in a communal dormitory-style setting in which intruders would be instantly noticed. An attack would be risky.

Karkinnen, on the other hand, was out in the open. Audrey had been puzzled that the year-old article implied that Karkinnen was Davenport's live-in lover, while Audrey's search had turned up different addresses, but she'd assumed there was something that she didn't know. She considered the possibility that they'd broken up, but then found an engagement announcement only a few months old . . .

So she'd gone for Karkinnen. She'd thrown the bomb through the window, concerned not a whit for the possibility that she might kill the other woman, but very concerned at the possibility of being caught. The final attack – out of the car, across the lawn, throw, back in the car, ten seconds – minimized the possibility, but it had still taken nerve.

She'd need the nerve again: but nerve had never been a problem for her. Audrey McDonald had nerve, all right.

She thought again about the possibility of going after Davenport himself. There were two problems with that: first, he was large and tough-looking, and carried a gun. He would be difficult to get at quickly, without exposing herself. She couldn't get close enough for poison, couldn't risk a gun attack; if she missed, she'd be dead. And he was a cop, so might be a little more wary than the average citizen. Further, she didn't have time to research him, as she had Arris or Ingall. And the second big problem was that killing him might lead the cops investigating *his* killing to take a harder look at his current investigations, including *her.*

A diversion would lead them away from her . . . So it would have to be the nun.

Her legs twitched down the bed, a kind of running motion, as she began working out a possible plan. She'd have to do it the minute she got out. She'd have to emphasize her injuries, complain of cracked ribs, something that wouldn't show on x-rays, but would keep her from doing anything heavy. She'd have to hobble and whimper and limp and make people feel sorry for her, and the instant she was alone, she had to go for the nun.

She'd have no trouble with this. She'd been undercover for more than twenty-five years now. She might not ever come out.

Franklin had been in a longtime 401K plan. The stocks had gone through the roof during the summer, so, like any Good American, he'd borrowed against the fund to buy a new black Ford extended-cab pickup truck, which he and Lucas walked around, Lucas shaking his head. Finally Franklin said, 'So what next? Just wrap it up? We're done?'

'Wrap it up,' Lucas said. They were standing at the curb outside McDonald's house. 'McDonald's the man, and he's dead: outa reach. I'll spend a couple days trying to figure out the firebomb thing with Weather, then maybe go up to the cabin.'

'Going up alone?' Franklin asked.

'Cut some firewood, put the snow blade on the 'Gator, haul the snowmobiles out and get them checked,' Lucas said.

'Going up alone?'

'Get the batteries out of the boat, put the boat away. Maybe figure out some way to cover it. I had some squirrels get in it last year, in the shed, and the damn thing was full of decapitated acorn shells when I got it out this spring.'

'Jesus, I wish I was single again, sometimes,' Franklin said. 'And had a cabin up north. Nothing like a little strange pussy in November.'

'If you'd asked me, I could have advised you against getting a Ford,' Lucas said. 'Anyway, see you around.'

'See you around,' Franklin said. Lucas walked back up the long driveway to the house, where he'd parked, while Franklin strolled once more around the truck, rubbing out a couple of imaginary blemishes with the cuff of his coat. 'I love you,' he said aloud. He was back at the driver's-side door, and about to get in, when Lucas arrived at the Porsche, a hundred and fifty feet away.

'GOING UP ALONE?' Franklin bellowed.

Lucas threw him the finger and got in the car.

Chapter Twenty-One

When Audrey McDonald opened her eyes the next morning, she knew something she hadn't known when she'd closed them the night before.

'Helen,' she said.

Helen had been talking to Davenport. Helen had always hated Wilson, and must have called Davenport anonymously. That's how Helen would have done it, maneuvering to get rid of Wilson without damaging her relationship with her sister — and that would explain why Davenport had thought he'd spoken to Audrey. Helen and Audrey spoke with the same soft Red River Valley accent, with the rounded and softened O's of the Swedes; they said 'boot' when they meant 'boat.'

Davenport had picked that up, but hadn't known of Helen.

But this was new: Helen had realized that people were being murdered? Believed that Wilson had done it, and had moved against him? Helen didn't keep secrets very well: give her a secret, and she usually blurted it out the first chance she had.

Audrey would have to think about this: how much did Helen know, and how much had she guessed? How early had she caught on? Had she taken any notes, mental or otherwise, that might point away from Wilson, and toward herself? And did she know about all the incidents? Did she know about McKinney and the Bairds?

When Lucas woke, he thought about Sherrill.

The woman would sooner or later be a problem; maybe even a disaster. They worked too closely, on problems too complicated, for a romance to work very well. And when the word got out – and the word would get out – there would be serious sniping to deal with. He hoped Sherrill understood that: she was smart enough, she should.

He wished she was in his bed now. He rolled over, awake, feeling fresh, pivoted and put his feet on the floor, realized that he hadn't felt quite this good for months.

And then he thought of Weather, and a touch of sadness came over him. He'd wanted to marry her. If she suddenly changed, and came back to him, he'd accept her in an instant.

But she was falling away now. Her influence was fading: he didn't think of her as much. Like Mom's death, he thought. When Lucas' mother died, of breast cancer, he'd thought of her every few minutes for what seemed like a year. Things she'd said, images of her face, moments of their life together. That was all still there in his head, and the images came back from time to time, but not like those first few months. His mother had gone gently away, and now came back only when he reached for her.

Like Weather.

He sighed, and headed for the bathroom. He was a late riser, and he looked back at the clock as he went: He wanted to be there when Audrey McDonald made her court appearance.

Audrey's attorney, Jason Glass, showed up with a woman photographer, a load of photo equipment, a pair of gym shorts and a soft halter-top.

'This is Gina,' Glass told Audrey. 'We need to take some photographs of you, showing your injuries. This is absolutely critical for the case. Gina brought some terrycloth for modesty purposes . . .'

They shot the pictures in an unoccupied hospital room, against the white drape that ran around the bed. At Gina's direction, Audrey limped into the small bathroom and put on the shorts and halter-top, carefully brushed her hair, and went out to face the cameras.

'I'm sorry,' Gina said before she started shooting. 'I should have told you to leave your hair as it was. Nobody will ever see these photos except attorneys, and frankly, we want them to look as . . . severe . . . as possible.'

Audrey nodded; she knew what was needed. She trundled back into the bathroom, and flipped her hair back and forth, stirred it around, then brushed it away from the scalp wound. In the mirror, she looked like a photo of a nineteenth-century madwoman in Bedlam. And that, she supposed, was what they wanted.

'Excellent,' Gina said, as she set up a couple of spindly light stands. 'That is just beautiful.'

When the photos were done, Glass, who'd waited in the hall, said to Audrey, 'You look like you still hurt.'

'I do,' Audrey said, deliberately vague. She peered around as though she'd lost a pair of glasses, or her shoes, and her lip trembled. 'I can't believe Wilson is gone.'

'I'm going to put you in a wheelchair before we head over to the courthouse,' Glass said. 'I think you'll be more comfortable that way.'

'Thank you,' Audrey muttered.

A man named Darius Logan was saying, 'I know I shouldn't have done it, your honor, but the dude flipped me off, you know?' when a sheriff's deputy wheeled Audrey into the courtroom, the two of them trailed by Glass.

Lucas was sitting in the back row, reading the St Paul paper. Del sat next to him, thumbing through *Cliffs Notes on*

Greek Classics. Two dozen other people were scattered around the courtroom, half of them lawyers, a couple of defendants' wives, reporters for the local television stations and newspapers, waiting for the McDonald hearing, and two or three courthouse groupies following the TV people.

McDonald looked bad, Lucas thought. Her head was patched with white bandages, stark against her gray face. She was wearing a gingham dress with short sleeves, a summer dress, really, but one that beautifully showed off the bruises on her arms and lower legs. She looked beaten, both physically and psychologically: then, as the bailiff wheeled her toward the defense table, she saw Lucas. And for a vanishingly small instant – a time so short that it must have been imaginary – Lucas felt her eyes spark. Not sparkle, but actually *spark*, as with electricity.

The judge, a prissy little blond who was known for occasional bouts of judicial intemperance, had grown impatient with Logan. He said, '. . . that's all very well, Mr Logan, but you've been here a number of times before and we're getting a little tired of it. I'll put bail at $5,000 and expect to see you back here at . . .' As he thumbed through a calendar, there was a meaty smack from the audience, as though somebody had just been punched. The impact came from the forehead of a young woman who'd just slapped herself with one heavy hand. The judge looked up and said, 'Do you have something to say, young lady?'

The woman stood up and said, 'Your honor, if we got to pay some bail bondsman seven hundred and fifty dollars to get Darius out of jail –' she pronounced it Dare-I-Us – 'where in the hell am I gonna get the money for the kids' dinners?'

The judge's eyes clicked to the face of a well-known TV reporter, then back to the woman. 'Why don't you leave Dare-I-Us in jail for a while?'

'Don't dare do that,' the woman said.

'Why not?'

'Just don't dare.'

'Okay. Sit down. Dare-I-Us, are you gonna show up for the trial?'

'I sure will, your honor.'

'All right. Bail's set at $1,000, and you've got the young lady to thank for it.'

'Thank you, your honor.'

As Bell left, the judge said, 'Call the next one,' and the bailiff called out, 'Audrey McDonald.'

'Here, your honor,' Glass called back.

The woman who'd gotten the bail reduced on Darius Logan wedged herself down a line of spectators, out to the center aisle, and headed for the door. As she passed, she saw Del, and Del said, quietly, 'Quick pregnancy.'

'Shush,' she said, and was gone. Del looked at Lucas and said, 'Didn't have any kids last week.'

'It's a miracle,' Lucas said, turning to sports.

Audrey McDonald sat hunched in her chair, her back to Lucas, as the hearing routine broke around her, speaking only two words: 'Not guilty.'

'Your honor, Mrs McDonald's attorney has offered Mrs McDonald's house as security for her appearance, and the state has no objection to that. As you may know, the circumstances around this particular incident could lead to a change in the charges against Mrs McDonald . . .'

And a while later, it was all done. Audrey waited as Glass talked to the assistant country attorney over a few details, then said, 'We've got to sign the papers and then I'm going to talk to the press. If I don't, they'll be parked outside your house, hassling you . . .'

She liked that, the press, though her face was determinedly grim.

'. . . I don't really expect you to say anything . . .' Glass was saying.

'I'll talk to them, if that will keep them away,' Audrey said.

The press caught them outside the courthouse, at the curb, where Helen Bell was waiting in her car. Glass made a short speech about spousal-abuse, said he anticipated that all charges would be dropped, then asked Audrey if she wished to answer questions.

She bobbed her head. 'Did you kill your husband, Mrs McDonald?' a woman reporter blurted.

She bobbed her head again. 'Yes,' she said weakly. 'I couldn't . . . I couldn't . . . He was hurting me so bad . . .' She touched the bandage of her scalp and peered at the camera lens. 'Oh, God . . .' A tear trickled down her cheek. 'God, I miss him. I'm so sorry . . .'

'Why do you miss him?'

'He was my husband,' she wailed. 'I wish he could come back . . . But he can't.' She grasped Glass' arm. 'I can't . . .' she gasped.

'All right, all right,' Glass said. 'She's really weak,' Glass said. 'She's got to go. I'm pleading with you all. If you have any sensitivity, leave her alone.'

'Mrs McDonald . . .'

Then she was in the car and Helen was driving them away. 'My God,' Helen said. 'My God, Audrey . . .'

'Just take me home.'

'No, no. You're coming to my place.'

'No. I want to go home,' Audrey said. 'Helen, please don't argue with me. Just take me home. Please. I just want to turn off the phones and get some sleep.'

* * *

And back at the courthouse, Lucas said to Glass, 'Quite a performance.'

Glass was staring after Helen Bell's car, turned to Lucas and said, 'The last thing I expected.'

'You didn't prep her?'

'Hell, no. I figured she was such a sadsack, we couldn't lose. I didn't think we was gonna get Greta Garbo. Did you see that tear?'

'I didn't get that close.'

'A real tear,' Glass marveled. 'Ran right down her cheek, and it was the cheek that was turned toward Channel Three. Tell you what, Lucas – if I lose this case, I'm gonna want to borrow one of your guns, so I can shoot myself.'

The house was silent: Audrey entered, listening for the footfalls of Wilson's ghost. She heard creaks and cracking that she hadn't heard before, but she'd never before listened. Helen came in behind her, tentatively. 'You're sure you'll be okay?'

'I'll be okay,' Audrey said, peering around. The police had been through the place, and though they hadn't been deliberately messy, the house looked . . . disheveled. 'I hope the police didn't steal anything.'

'Do you want me to come over tonight?'

'No . . . no. I'm going to take a couple of pills and try to sleep. I just really need to sleep, I haven't slept since before . . . before . . .'

'Okay. If you're sure you'll be all right.'

'Do you, uh . . . you used to take Prozac,' Audrey said. 'Do you still use that?'

'Well, sure. Could hardly get along without it,' Helen said.

'Do you think it would help? In the next few days?'

Helen shook her head. 'I don't think it's for your kind of problem, honestly. I could give you a few and you could try them, but I think a doctor could give you something better.'

'Maybe if I could just try a couple. If I don't sleep tonight . . .'

'Sure. We'll talk tomorrow.'

When Helen was gone, Audrey prowled through the house, already planning: she'd bundle up his suits, dump them at Goodwill and get a tax deduction. She got a notepad and wrote: ACCOUNTANT/Taxes and Deductions, and under that, *Suits*. Wilson had all kinds of crap she'd want to get rid of, starting with that XK-E. She wrote *Jag* under *Suits*. And he had a whole wall full of bullshit awards and plaques – chairman of this charity in 1994, director of that community effort in 1997. All worthless: straight into the garbage can, she thought.

So much to do.

Audrey really did hurt from Wilson's beating, and from her own enhancements to the damage. The scalp wound, in particular, felt tight, like a banjo head, and edges seeming to pull against the stitches. After half an hour of cruising through the house, she went up to the bedroom, set the alarm clock for nine p.m., and tried to sleep.

But sleep, she found, wouldn't come easily. Too many images in her head, a mix of plans and memories. If Wilson had only landed the chairmanship, none of this would have happened. She'd believed in him from the start, and the belief had only begun to falter after Kresge got the top job six years earlier. Kresge was a technocrat, and brought in other technocrats like Bone and Robles. They had no respect for family name, for fortune, for breeding or society. All they knew was how to make money. Wilson, running the mortgage division, which had always been one of the pillars of the bank, was suddenly out on a limb.

She didn't know that sleep had come, but it must have. The clock went off: she sat up, a bit groggy, realized that the room was dark. She groped around the bedstand, found the clock, and silenced the alarm. Then she touched the light and swung out of bed.

A little tension now. She went straight to the shower and stood under it, breathing deeply, flexing the muscles in her back and shoulders. Stiff. When she got out of the shower, she downed four ibuprofen tablets, then dressed: black slacks, a deep red sweater, and a dark blue jacket over the sweater. She found a pair of brown cotton gardening gloves, and pulled them on. The best she could do for night-time camouflage. Now for a weapon.

The police had been all through the house, but she remembered that when the closet rod had broken in the front closet a year or so earlier, Wilson tossed the broken dowel rod up in the rafters of the yard shed, where it lay with other scrap wood. She found a flashlight in the kitchen, let herself out the back, and walked in the dark to the shed. Inside, she turned the flash on: She could see the scrap wood overhead, but couldn't reach it. The lawn tractor was there and she stood on the seat, stretched to push the wood around, and saw the broken dowels rolling to one side. She got both of them down. One was a little more than six feet long, including the split; the other a little more than two feet long, including the sharp split end.

She carried them both back to the house in the dark, and inside the porch, gave the shorter of the two pieces a test swing. A little lighter than a baseball bat, but it swung just as well. Wearing the gloves, she rubbed both of them down with WD-40, eliminating any fingerprints.

She put both pieces in Wilson's Buick, then climbed on top

of the car hood, pulled the cover off the light on the garage-door opener, and unscrewed the lightbulb. She climbed down from the car and put the bulb on the passenger seat.

Ready. She took a deep breath, started the car, pushed the garage-door opener. The door came up, but no light came on. She backed out of the garage, lights out, then rolled down the long driveway to the street. The houses were far enough apart, and the street dark enough, that she should be able to get out without being seen . . . a calculated risk. If anyone saw her driving without lights, they'd remember it. A risk she'd take. She rolled into the street, drove a hundred feet, and turned on the lights. She'd gotten away with it, she thought.

On the south side of Minneapolis, she stopped in a beat-up industrial area and threw the longer of the two pieces of dowel rod into a pile of trash; the other waited beside the passenger seat.

St Anne's College – St Anne's College for Blond Catholic Girls, as Audrey thought of it – was a leafy, red-brick girls' college in St Paul, a short walk from the Mississippi. Davenport lived somewhere in the neighborhood, Audrey knew. The newspaper article didn't say exactly where: just the Highland Park neighborhood.

Maybe to be close to the nun, she thought.

Audrey had spent four unhappy years at St Anne's, getting finished. She'd needed the finish, with her Red River farm background. And the unhappiness hadn't counted for much, since she couldn't ever remember being happy. She'd plowed through her courses, a smart, reasonably pretty brunette, and had carefully weeded out the likely husband prospects from St James – St James College for Blond Catholic Boys.

Wilson McDonald had been the result of her four years of winnowing.

On the southwest side of the campus, the Residence squatted in sooty obscurity. A near-cube built of red brick like most of the other buildings on campus, it housed the declining numbers of the sisterhood of nuns who ran St Anne's. The newspaper article, 'The Pals of Lucas Davenport,' had mentioned that Sister Mary Joseph lived on campus, and continued to wear the traditional black habit on public occasions, including the classroom, though she sometimes went out in civilian clothing when working in area hospitals.

Audrey had never seen her in anything but traditional dress, and wasn't sure she'd recognize her in civilian clothing. Still, she thought, she could pick her out.

Audrey parked on the street, and after sitting for a moment in the dark, looking up and down, she got out, leaving her purse but carrying her cell phone, the dowel rod held by her side. She walked to the Residence along the sidewalk, and, in the dark space between streetlights, turned into the parking lot and moved quickly to the far corner of the building. She stood there, between two tall junipers, an arm's length from the ivy-twined walls – the bare ivy like a net of ropes and strings climbing the bricks – and listened. She could hear voices, but far away; and a snatch of classical music from somewhere. More of the *feel* of the conversation than the actual words and notes. The parking lot itself held only a dozen cars, most of them nun-like – black and simple; along with a few civilian cars.

She remembered this moment from the other times. The moment before commitment, when she could still back away, when, if discovered, she hadn't done anything. The moment where she could wave and say, 'Oh, hello, I was a bit confused here, I'm just trying to find my way.'

And the thrill came from piercing that moment, going through it, getting into the zone of absolute commitment.

She took the phone from her jacket pocket, and punched the numbers in the eerie green glow of the phone's information screen.

'St Anne's Residence.' A young woman's voice. Audrey had done this very job, answering the phone as a student volunteer, two nights a week for a semester, six o'clock to midnight.

'Yes, this is Janice Brady at Midway Hospital. We have a family emergency call for a Sister Mary Joseph . . .'

'I think Sister is in chapel . . .'

The chapel was in the Residence basement. 'Could you get her please? We have an injured gentleman asking for her.'

'Uh, just a moment. Actually, it'll be two or three minutes.'

'I'll hold . . .'

Then she heard more voices, closeby. A man came around the corner, said something, laughed, walked into the parking lot.

Shit. This could ruin everything . . .

The man waved, walked to a car, fumbled with his keys, got in. Sat for a moment. Then started the engine, turned on the lights, and drove to the street.

And Sister Mary Joseph was there: 'Hello?' Curiosity in her voice.

'Is this Sister Mary Joseph, a psychologist at St Anne's College?'

'Yes, it is . . .'

'There's been a shooting incident, and one of the victims asked that you be notified. An officer Lucas Davenport.'

'Oh, no! How bad is he?'

'He's in surgery. I really don't have any more information; a priest on the staff has been notified, we assumed he was Catholic.'

'Yes, he is. Is the priest doing extreme unction?'

'No, Officer Davenport is in surgery, but we thought a priest should be notified, it's purely routine in these cases . . .'

'I'll be right there.'

'If you will check with the information desk at the front entrance, not the emergency entrance, you will be directed to the surgical waiting area.'

And the nun dropped the phone on the hook.

Audrey braced herself against the wall. If the nun came out the main entrance, the entrance closest to the parking lot, and headed straight toward the parking lot, she'd pass Audrey at little more than an arm's length. Audrey would have only a moment to determine if she was alone. If she wasn't, Audrey would follow her to Midway Hospital, and try there – the nun would have to walk some distance to the main entrance, and would probably be dropped off.

She was rehearsing it all in her mind when she heard the main door open. No voices, just the *clank* of the push bar on the door, and the door opening. Three seconds later, a woman in a black habit swept by, and down the walk. Audrey instinctively knew she was alone: she was moving too quickly, with too much focus, to be with another person. Audrey swung out from behind the junipers, her heart gone to stone in her chest, a step and a half behind the nun.

And she struck, like an axe-man taking a head.

The heavy rod hit the nun on the side of the head, glanced off, hit the nun's shoulder; the woman sagged, her knees buckling, one hand going to the ground. She started to turn.

And Audrey struck her again, this time full on the head, and the nun pitched forward on her face . . . Audrey lifted the dowel rod, her teeth bared, her breathing heavy, and struck at the nun's head again, but from a bad angle: the rod this time bounced off the side of the nun's head and into her shoulder.

With building fury, with the memory of all those decades

of slights and slurs against her, with the thought of all the people who'd held her back and down, with her father, her mother, with all the others, Audrey struck again and again, hitting the nun's neck and back and shoulder . . .

And heard the *clank* of the door again, froze, looked wildly around – nowhere to run, not at this instant, this was the very worst moment for an interruption – and stepped back in the shadow of the junipers. The girl came around the corner no more than a second later, saw the nun, said, 'Sister!' and bent over her.

And Audrey struck at her, hitting the girl on the back of the head. Like the nun, the girl pitched forward, onto her face. Audrey hit her again, and again, breathing hard now. Stopped, hovered over the two motionless women for an instant, jabbed at the nun's leg with the end of the dowel rod, got no response, then scuttled away. Around the corner, onto the sidewalk, down the sidewalk to the car. Nobody on the sidewalk. Inside the car, dowel rod on the floor – a sudden touch of panic: she felt her pocket, yes! The phone was there – and the car started and she eased away from the curb.

This was always the hardest part, staying cool after an attack. With her heart beating an impossible rhythm, Audrey drove slowly off the campus, to the Mississippi, left to the bridge and across to Minneapolis.

She stopped once, on a dark street, to throw the dowel rod down a sewer. She went on, dropped the cotton gloves one at a time out the window. She hadn't seen any blood from either of the women, but it had been dark: she should burn these clothes, or get rid of them, anyway.

That would have to wait – she could wash them tonight, immediately – and throw them tomorrow.

But now, there was more to do.

Twenty minutes later, headlights on, she pulled into her

driveway, and into the darkened garage. She dropped the garage door, groped to the kitchen entrance, went inside and flipped on the light.

Upstairs, she took off her clothes, inspected them closely. Nothing she could see. Still, they'd go in the washing machine. She picked up the phone: no messages. Good.

She dialed, got Helen: 'Hello?'

'Helen . . . I just . . . can't sleep,' she said, her voice crumbling. 'I hate to bother you, have you come over here, but I'm just so blue, I'm just lying here thinking about Wilson.' She began to weep, a bubbling, pathetic wail. 'Help me.'

'Oh, God, hang on, Audrey, I'll be right there.'

'And He-Helen . . . b-b-bring a few of those Prozacs. Maybe they would help. I've got to try something.'

'I'll be right there. Hang on.'

She hung up, satisfied. Cleared her face, gathered her clothes for the wash. She might not ever need the Prozac, she might not ever need Helen coming up the drive with her lights on, to muddy any witness statements – but who knew what the future might hold. Better to work all the possibilities now, than to regret it later.

She thought about the nun, lying on the sidewalk.

Wonder if she's dead?

She never thought about the other woman at all; the other woman was irrelevant.

Chapter Twenty-Two

S herrill had brought with her a votive candle scented faintly
with vanilla, and a crystal candle-holder, and their second
night together took on the feel of college days, making love in
the yellow flickering candlelight. And Sherrill said, as they
lay comfortably warm under a sheet, 'Do you think you could
go for somebody like Candy LaChaise?' Sherrill had put four
.357 slugs through Candy LaChaise's chest during an abortive
holdup at a credit union.

'I don't think so,' Lucas said. He was lying on his back,
hands behind his head. 'I think she'd smell pretty bad by now.'

Sherrill made a quick move toward his groin and he
flinched and said, 'Don't do that, I almost killed you with my
karate reflexes.'

And she said, 'Yeah, right. Answer the question.'

He didn't have to think about it: 'Nope. She was pretty, but
she was missing a couple of links. You know those kinds of
people – basically, they're a little stupid. Maybe they don't
get bad grades in school, or maybe they even get good grades,
but somewhere, down at the bottom, they're fuckin' morons.
They don't connect with the world.'

'You remember Johnny Portland?'

'Yeah. Asshole.'

She got up on one elbow, looking down at him. 'I went out
with him a couple of times.'

Lucas turned his head to look at her: 'Jesus. Did he know
you were a cop?'

'I wasn't. This was like my sophomore year in college, I met him at this Springsteen concert. He liked younger girls, I was like twenty; he picked me up at my mom's house in a Rolls-Royce.'

'That will turn a girl's head,' Lucas said.

'He never touched me. I wasn't gonna sleep with him anyway, he was too old for me, but he never made a move. I thought maybe, you know, he couldn't.'

'There were some stories around that he sorta liked wrestling with guys . . .'

'That occurred to me, too – you know, not like I was Miss Queen of the May and everybody's drooling over me, but he was showing me off to the guys, like, "Look what I got." But he never seemed much interested in really getting me. Just showing.'

'Yeah . . . listen, don't tell anyone else you went out with John Portland. He was an asshole.'

'I think he might've been missing a couple links, too,' she said. 'And all these other missing-linkers would come around, acting like they were Robert DeNiro, or something, like wise guys, but they were really like bartenders and tire salesmen.'

'DeNiro's old man was a famous painter and DeNiro grew up with the intellectual artsy crowd on the East Coast,' Lucas said. 'Somebody told me that.'

'Really? He seems pretty real to me. Like he grew up on the streets, and I thought . . .'

The phone rang, and Lucas rolled out of bed.

'Every goddamned time,' she said, eyes following him. 'You *could* skip it.'

'Not when they call at this time of night,' he said. 'Back in a sec.' Lucas picked up the phone in the den: 'Yeah?'

She heard him pounding down the hall; it might have been

funny if she hadn't heard him virtually screaming at the telephone. Lucas thundered into the bedroom, found Sherrill pulling up her underpants, snapping on her bra.

'My pants . . .' He seemed confused.

'On the floor, by the foot of the bed.'

'My friend Elle . . .'

'I heard. She's hurt and you've gotta go,' she said. She rocked back on the bed to pull her jeans on. 'I'll drive.'

'Bullshit, you will,' Lucas said.

'I don't think you'll be in any shape . . .' she protested, but Lucas cut her off.

'I'm fuckin' driving,' he snapped. 'Shoes?'

'I think one of them is under the bed, I think I kicked one under . . .'

She was one garment ahead of him, stepping into her Nikes, collecting her revolver and purse from beside the nightstand, heading for the door. Lucas was ten seconds behind, out through the kitchen, into the garage, into the Porsche, slipping out under the garage door before it was fully up.

'Flasher,' she said, as they hit the street.

'Busted,' Lucas said.

'Better go over to Cretin, then, it's better lit and you'll hit some college kid if you run like this on Mississippi.'

Lucas grunted, downshifted and slid through a corner, punched the car two blocks down to Cretin, ignored the stop sign and cut across the street in front of a small Chevy van and gunned it again; Sherrill braced herself and asked, 'How bad is she?'

'She's bad,' Lucas said.

'Take her to Ramsey?'

'Yeah.'

'They notify Minneapolis?'

'That was one of the nuns at the Residence calling, another

friend.' They clipped the red light at Grand Avenue, barely beat the red at Summit, came up behind a line of cars and Lucas threw the Porsche into the oncoming lane, whipped by a half-dozen vehicles. 'She was just calling because she knew I'd want to know.'

'Better call Sloan or Del,' she said, digging a cell phone out of her purse. 'This is the second run at you. Until we figure out what's going on, the rest of the guys ought to know.'

Lucas risked a glance at her: she was sitting comfortably in the passenger seat, one hand forward to brace herself, the other hand working the cell phone. She was calm and composed, maybe a slight pink flush to her face. He looked back to the front, ran the red light at Randolph, burned past the golf course and dove down the ramp onto I-94.

They made a four-and-a-half minute run to Ramsey Medical Center; Sherrill hooked up with Sloan one minute down the road, filled him in. 'Tell him to find Andi Manette's home phone number and call her,' Lucas said. 'Weather's staying with the Manettes. Tell Weather about it. She and Elle are pretty tight.'

Sherrill passed the word, clicked off the phone, looked at the speedometer. 'That all you can get out of this thing?'

'No,' he said, and the needle climbed through 120.

She watched his face for a moment – a brick, a stone – then looked out at the cars flicking by. Good thing, she thought, that she hadn't driven. She'd never moved this fast on a vehicle that didn't have a stewardess.

Lucas dumped the Porsche in an ambulances-only zone and they banged into the emergency room. A startled nurse turned toward them from the reception desk, and Lucas said, 'I'm Deputy Police Chief Lucas Davenport from Minneapolis and a nun named Elle Kruger was brought in here . . .'

'Yes, yes, she's in x-ray, she just got here, the doctors are working . . .'

'Where?'

'Sir, I can't let you go . . .'

'Where?' He shouted it at her, and she stepped back and a couple of male white-coated orderlies started down a hall toward the desk.

'Hold it,' Sherrill said. 'Miss, can you tell us who the doctor in charge is? Jim Dunaway?'

'No, Larry Simone . . .'

'Okay, he's a friend of mine. Could you tell him Chief Davenport and Detective Sherrill are here asking about . . .'

'Sister Mary Joseph. Elle Kruger,' Lucas said.

'I'll be right back.'

As the nurse started down the hall, waving off the orderlies, a thin, ill-tempered man stuck his head in the door and called, 'Hey, whose car is this out here?'

'I'll get it,' Sherrill said to Lucas. 'Gimme keys.'

Lucas dug the keys out and handed them to her. The ill-tempered man raised his voice: 'I'm asking, who the hell left their car out here . . .'

'I'll move it,' Sherrill said, walking toward him.

'You goddamn well will move it,' the man said. 'Or I'll push that thing right into the wall.'

Sherrill stepped to within four inches of his face, her voice low and controlled. 'You shut your fuckin' pie hole or I will break all your teeth out,' she said. She pulled one hand back on her hip so the ill-tempered man could see the wooden butt of the .357. His eyes slid away from hers, and she pushed through the door to the car.

A balding, hatchet-faced doctor walked out of a back room,

trailed by the reception nurse. He looked around, spotted Lucas. 'Are you with Marcy Sherrill?'

'Yes. Elle Kruger – the nun – is my best friend.'

'This is Chief Davenport,' said the nurse.

'Come on back,' he said. 'Where's Marcy?'

'Outside, moving a car off the ramp. How's Elle?'

'Not good, but she's better than the other one. We've got head injury but no direct brain damage, like the girl. We've got to manage the swelling and so on, which is gonna be a problem, but I'm more worried about blunt trauma to her kidneys and liver. Somebody beat the hell out of her with what looks like a baseball bat.'

'Baseball bat?'

'Yeah . . .'

Sherrill caught up with them and said, 'Larry, how are you?' and the doc said, 'I'd like to look at that leg of yours again.'

'I think it's okay,' she said.

'Oh, I know; I just wanted to look for aesthetic reasons,' and Sherrill snorted and said, 'Aesthetic, my ass,' and he said, 'That, too . . .' and Sherrill said to Lucas, 'Larry was one of the docs that took care of me after that thing with John Mail.'

'Ah,' Lucas said, and looked wildly at Simone who said, 'Through there.'

He could barely see her. She was flat on her back, under an operating drape, her head tilted back, her head already shaven and painted with iodine-colored disinfectant. A drip flowed into her arm, and her mouth was propped open. She looked like a saint who was about to be committed to fire.

'Elle,' Lucas whispered.

'She can't respond,' Simone said. 'She might hear you, somewhere in her head, but she's too doped up to show it.'

'Gonna be all right,' Lucas said, his face a foot from her

ear. She didn't look like any Elle Kruger he remembered: separated from the habit and other paraphernalia of the church, she looked stark; and the disinfectant added a strange other-worldly touch, like an image from Heavy Metal. 'Gonna be all right, we're here with you; we're waiting.'

'Come on,' Simone said. 'They've got to finish getting her ready for the OR.'

Lucas reluctantly followed Simone out of the prep room, Sherrill a step behind him. 'You want to look at the x-rays?' Simone asked.

'Can I see anything?'

'C'mon.'

The x-rays were clipped to wall-mounted view boxes and a man in a tweed sport coat was peering at them. Simone said, 'Jerry, what do you think?'

'I've already called Jack Bornum in; we're gonna have to do them both at the same time. I'll take the kid, she's gonna go if we don't get in quick. Jack can have the nun.'

'How bad's the nun?' Lucas asked.

'Who're you?'

'I'm a cop – and her best friend. Oldest friend.'

'Whoever hit her, missed; looks like two or three blows, hard, but never quite brought it down over the top of her head, like with the kid. Everything sort of skidded off.'

'What about the blunt trauma?' Lucas asked.

The tweed man shrugged: 'I don't know; I do brains.' He glanced at his watch. 'And I better go do this one.'

'How long before the other guy gets here?'

'Five minutes, maybe. He'll be here before she's ready to go,' tweed said gruffly. 'He's a good guy, too – he'll take care of her.'

The other doctor, Bornum, arrived in the allotted five minutes, and disappeared into the back. Simone caught a knife wound to the liver area, and also disappeared. Twenty minutes later, Weather pushed through the door, with Andi Manette a step behind. She saw Lucas and Sherrill and said, 'Lucas, my God, what happened?'

'Somebody beat her up. Almost killed her,' he said. His voice got shaky and she touched his arm.

'How bad?'

'Pretty bad. They're getting her ready for the OR. They've got a neuro-surgeon working on her.'

'Oh, no . . .'

He wanted to wrap her up and hold on, but there was a wall between them: he could feel it, pressing them away from each other. 'I don't know what happened . . . in fact, I think I'm gonna . . .'

He walked over to the reception desk. 'Could somebody let me know when Elle Kruger goes into the OR, and get an idea of how long it'll take?'

'I'll check,' the nurse said.

Weather stepped closer to Sherrill and asked, 'How is he?'

She shrugged: 'Freaked out. Really freaked.'

Weather smiled, a thin, tentative smile, but a real one, Sherrill thought. 'Take care of him,' Weather said.

Sherrill blushed and nodded, then said, 'If I can.'

Lucas wandered back, and Weather said, 'The bomb through my window, and now Elle.'

Lucas shook his head: 'I can't figure it. It'd have to be somebody who knows me, to know about you two. But who? And why not come after me? And why with the bomb and now a beating, for Christ's sakes? There's too much risk involved. If they really want to get at me . . .' He rubbed his chin, wandered away, deep in thought.

A moment later, the nurse appeared in the hallway, busily stepping down toward the reception area; Lucas went to meet her.

'She's in the operating room, now,' the nurse said. 'They're just putting in the anesthesia. Doctor says he can't tell how long it'll be, anywhere from two to six hours.'

'Okay, okay . . .'

'He said she's strong,' the nurse said.

Lucas turned back to Weather and Sherrill: 'Did you hear that?'

They nodded and Weather said, 'Have you been to the scene?'

'No, that's where I'd like to go . . .'

'You guys go ahead,' Weather said. 'I'll wait here, and if anything comes up, I can handle it.'

'Thanks, Weather,' Lucas said. To Sherrill: 'You wanta come?'

'Yeah, I do.' She glanced at Weather and quickly nodded.

They'd just started toward a door when a middle-aged couple hurried in, and the woman, tightly controlled, went to the reception desk and said, 'My daughter was just hurt in some kind of accident at St Anne's and we were told she was here, but I don't see her, do you know . . .'

And Lucas shook his head at Sherrill and they hurried out: 'I didn't want to see that,' Lucas said. 'I don't need it.'

A St Paul lieutenant named Allport was running the crime scene at St Anne's when Lucas and Sherrill arrived. He spotted Lucas getting out of the car, and yelled at a patrolman, 'Send that guy over here.'

The patrolman whistled at Lucas to get his attention, and pointed at Allport. Lucas waved, took Sherrill by the elbow, and they walked along the side of the residence building to a cluster of cops duckwalking around the parking lot.

'I heard,' Allport said. 'The nun's an old pal of yours. She gonna be all right?'

'She's in the OR. So's the girl; the girl's in trouble.'

'Ah, jeez. She's some kid from the neighborhood here. One of the neighbors said her parents sent her here because she could live close to home and it's safe.'

'You figure out what happened?' Lucas asked.

'Yeah. What there is. You ain't gonna like it.'

'I already don't like it . . .'

'No-no. I mean, you *really* ain't gonna like it. There's a girl sitting in by the switchboard, she's talking to one of her friends – they're doing homework together. So a call comes in for Sister Mary Joseph – family emergency.'

'She doesn't have a family anymore,' Lucas said.

'Yeah.' Allport looked up at the night sky. 'But that's what they said. So the girl runs down and gets the sister and the sister takes the call and she listens and she freaks out and she hangs up, and she says to this girl, "Lucas has been shot; they're taking him to Midway. I've got to go." '

'*What?*'

'So she ran to get her keys and her bag and she ran back out and the girl at the phones says to the other one, "I don't think she should drive," and the other one says, "I'll take her," and she runs out. Then the girl sits there by the phones, and ten minutes later . . . or sometime later . . . another kid comes in and says there're two people hurt on the sidewalk and to call an ambulance.'

'Jesus,' Lucas said.

And Sherrill said, 'It *is* aimed at you.' To Allport: 'You know Lucas' former fiancée was firebombed last week.'

Allport nodded: 'I read about it. You had guys running all over town, kicking ass.'

Lucas looked around at the duckwalking crime-scene cops: 'You finding anything?'

Allport shook his head. 'Nope. Not a thing. We're walking around the neighborhood, looking for the weapon – a ball bat, or a big stick – but we haven't found it yet.'

'Goddamnit . . .' A thought flew through Lucas' head, quick as a scalded moth; he grasped at it, missed. He shook his head, turned to Sherrill: 'Nothing to do here. I'm going back to the hospital.'

'I'm coming.'

'You don't have to.'

'I'm coming.'

Allport, arms akimbo, said, 'I hate this shit. If the assholes want to beat each other up, or even us, that's one thing. A nun and a kid?'

In the car, Lucas said, 'Something's happening, and we don't know what it is.'

'I knew that a long time ago,' Sherrill said.

Lucas shook his head: 'I don't mean that somebody is trying to get at me, or even get at Weather or Elle. There's some kind of apparatus here. Somebody's set up a machine, and it's not some simple-minded revenge trip. It's doing something . . .'

Chapter Twenty-Three

Elle Kruger came out of the operating room just after four a.m. and the doctor, yawning, came to see Lucas, Sherrill and Weather: 'I'd say the prognosis is good – she's gonna have a few days in the ICU but there wasn't any direct mechanical damage that I could see. We've got swelling, but we're controlling it. We're going to keep her sedated, keep her quiet, so she won't be talking for a couple of days.'

'She's gonna make it?' Lucas said.

'Unless we missed something – or if there's just a further natural complication. But it's about as good as you could have hoped for, given the circumstances.'

'How about the other girl?' Weather asked.

The doc shook his head: 'She *did* have some mechanical damage. I think she's gonna live, we're just gonna have to wait and see. She might be fine, she might be . . . not so fine.'

Lucas turned away, suddenly exhausted. 'Man.'

'Let's go home,' Sherrill said.

Weather said, 'I'll be back tomorrow – every day until she wakes up.'

'You gotta ride?' Lucas asked. Andi Manettte, who'd brought Weather over, had left earlier.

'I'll get a cab. They can have one here in a minute.'

'We came in the Porsche,' Lucas said. Two seats: Weather smiled, she understood the math.

Out the door, walking to the car, Sherrill asked, 'Did Weather and Elle have some kind of relationship?'

'Yeah, they liked each other a lot,' Lucas said.

'Think Elle will like me?' Sherrill asked.

Lucas nodded. 'She likes almost everybody. You two'll get along fine.'

Rose Marie Roux talked to the St Paul chief, and St Paul put together a group of four detectives to work with two violent-crimes detectives from Minneapolis.

'You can do what you want, personally, but I want you to stay clear of these guys,' Roux told Lucas. 'You've set up this paradigm: you think these attacks on Sister Mary Joseph and Weather are aimed at you. Maybe they are, but I want to keep these guys outside the paradigm. I want them to take a cold look at it.'

Lucas agreed. 'That's smart. But I'm putting Del on the street, looking into a few things; and I'll be looking around. Sherrill, Sloan and Black are going back to homicide now that we're done with McDonald.'

Del and Lucas spent the day cruising the street, talking to druggies, thieves, bikers, gamblers – anyone smart enough to take revenge on Lucas by attacking his friends; and checking in every hour with the hospital. No change on Elle Kruger.

At the end of the day, they sat in Lucas' office, Del with his feet on the edge of Lucas' desk, Lucas with his feet on an open desk drawer, looking for new ideas.

'All day, absolutely nothing. I've never seen it this dry. Usually, there's rumors, even if the rumors are bullshit.'

'Nobody wants to get involved with a run at a cop,' Lucas said.

'Tell you the truth, *I've* been thinking of terminating our friendship, at least for the time being. Maybe take out an ad in the *Star-Tribune*.'

'I once talked to a guy, a lawyer – defense attorney – whose son was arrested for stealing some stereo gear from a Best Buy,' Lucas said. 'The kid was one of those ineffectual audio-visual freaks, didn't know which way was up. Anyway, the judge gave him six months in the county jail, and this was a first offense.'

'Oops.'

'Yeah. And this attorney tells me, he knows it was because the judge didn't like him, the attorney. Thought he was sleazy, because he did personal injury and DWI and made a lot of money at it. So anyway, the kid does most of the time, like four months, and gets out, and he's okay. But the attorney spent the whole time worrying that he was gonna hang himself in his cell or something.'

'Something to worry about, with kids like that,' Del said.

'The attoney'd go down every day to visit the kid, keep him connected. But he still worried. And what he told me was, that he decided in the middle of the kid's jail term that if the kid killed himself, he'd kill the judge. He made the decision, he worked it all out. He wasn't irrational about it, it wasn't a big macho thing. He'd just do it, and try not to get caught. The first thing he'd do was, he'd wait two years before he made his move. Wait until his son's death was way in the past. Then he'd find a way to kidnap the judge – he said that in his fantasies, he had to explain to the judge why he was going to kill him, he couldn't sleep if he didn't do that – and then he was gonna tie him up or chain him to a tree, and douse him with gasoline and set him on fire.'

'Jesus.'

'Yeah. He said he'd decided this, but when his kid got out okay, it wasn't necessary, so he let it go. He hates the judge, but he says he'll get at him politically, he doesn't have to burn him up.'

'What you're saying is . . .'

'What I'm saying is, I hope it's not something like that,' Lucas said. 'I hope it's not somebody I bumped into years ago, took care of business, didn't even think about it. And he's been plotting all this time.'

'We checked all recent prison releases.'

'That's what I mean. What if it's not recent? What if it's somebody from ten years ago, somebody I busted on a solid felony, say, who did a couple of years but figures I ruined his life and his family? And now he's coming after me, by going after my family? I mean, I might never figure out who it is.'

A tentative knock interrupted the thought. Del looked at the door, then back at Lucas, shrugged. 'Come in,' Lucas called.

A woman stepped inside. He remembered her face instantly, and her last name. He pointed a finger at her and said, 'The bridal shop, Mrs Ingall.'

'Annette,' she said.

'This is Detective Capslock,' Lucas said, 'Del, this is Mrs Ingall, her husband disappeared in that yacht up on Superior. The McDonald case.'

'Oh, sure.'

Lucas: 'Sit down. What can we do for you?'

Ingall looked doubtfully at Del, who tried to smile pleasantly without showing too much of his yellowed teeth, and sat in the chair beside him, clutching her purse on her lap. 'I saw on TV3 about your friend the nun who was attacked last night. I hope she's going to be okay.'

'She should be,' Lucas said.

'I've been bothered by it all day,' she said. 'It kept nagging at me, and nagging at me, and finally I said, "Annette, go over and talk to Chief Davenport for goodness' sake, and let him worry about it."'

'Well . . .' Lucas spread his hands, waiting, an edge of impatience barely suppressed.

'After you told me that Wilson McDonald was probably responsible for killing Andy . . .'

'Mrs Ingall, I didn't exactly say . . .'

She waved him down and continued: '. . . I was pretty satisfied, because it made a nice pattern. He killed George Arris, shooting him with a gun. Then he killed Andy, by sabotaging the yacht. And then he killed Dan Kresge, shooting him, and Susan O'Dell, shooting *her.*'

'Yes?'

'But then – this is what was nagging me – when I read about what happened with you, with your fiancée firebombed, and then this morning, with your friend the nun being hurt . . .'

'Yes, yes.'

'Look: there were two other incidents which helped Wilson McDonald's career, that nobody probably told you about, because they didn't involve anybody being killed at the bank, where it would be obvious.'

'Two others?' Lucas leaned forward, now interested.

'Two weird . . . accidents,' Ingall said. 'One involved a man named McKinney, who was in the investments department and was also competitive for promotions with Wilson. They were sort of neck and neck. This is way back, when Wilson was still selling out of the investments division, before he went to mortgages. And all of a sudden, this other man's son was killed in a hit and run accident. If I remember, he was riding home in the evening on his bike, in the summer, I think he had a paper route or something, and he was hit and killed and they never found out who did it. Anyway, McKinney just fell apart. He couldn't do anything, and when the job came up, which was right after that, Wilson got it.'

'Huh,' Lucas said. Del was looking at Ingall with interest.

'Then, and this must've been, oh, about 1990, there was sort of a bank recession going on. Lots of banks were restructuring and jobs were being cut. Wilson was one of a half-dozen people in the mortgage division as a vice-president, and people knew some jobs were going to be cut over there. The man who was in charge of the cuts was named Davis Baird, and he had an assistant named Dick McPhillips. Davis Baird didn't like Wilson, he thought he was a fat pompous oaf. He might have cut him. But Dick McPhillips was always under the influence of Wilson's father. If Davis Baird had wanted to cut Wilson, McPhillips couldn't stop it. But . . .' She paused dramatically.

'But,' Lucas said, and Del nodded at her.

'But, while they were working out the cutbacks, all of a sudden Baird's parents were killed in a fire at their cabin up north. I thought about this because of the firebomb at your friend's house. Something exploded in the Bairds' house – they even called it a firebomb in the paper, I think – and they were killed, and Baird had to take time off to deal with all of it. McPhillips was in charge of making the cuts, and he got rid of two of the five vice-presidents over there . . .'

'But not Wilson,' Lucas said.

'Not Wilson.'

'Go ahead,' Lucas said.

'So I started thinking, this took a strange mind. Not to attack the principal target directly, but to incapacitate the principal by attacking someone close to them. Distracting them in a really awful way. And I thought, you know, that's what's happening to Chief Davenport. He's investigating these murders, and suddenly his fiancée's house blows up, and then an old friend is almost killed. If Wilson McDonald weren't dead, I would say he was doing it for sure. Especially since Andy's death almost might be an accident, and Arris' death was also easy to blame on somebody else – that gang. Nothing is what it looks like.'

'Wilson McDonald is dead,' Del said.

'Yes. Shot to death,' Ingall said. 'And that's very curious.'

Lucas closed his eyes, rubbed his face. 'Jesus.'

'Do you think this line of thought might be useful?' Ingall asked.

'I don't know,' Lucas said. 'But you are a very smart lady.'

'Yes, I've always thought so,' she said.

Chapter Twenty-Four

M ost of the file on Audrey McDonald had been developed since she killed Wilson: name, age, weight, distinguishing marks. She had a number of scars; too many, Lucas thought. Her only prior contact with police had been two traffic tickets, one for speeding, one for failure to yield, which had resulted in a minor collision.

He made quick calls to the Department of Natural Resources and the Department of Public Safety: she'd never had a hunting license, never taken gun safety training, never applied for a handgun permit.

She'd graduated from St Anne's. That was interesting – she'd know her way around out there, she'd know what would happen if she called the Residence. She might even have overlapped with Elle Kruger, if just barely. He made a note to ask. After college, she'd worked as a librarian, then with a couple of charitable organizations.

He mulled over the file for a few minutes, then glanced at his watch. Almost time to see Elle. But first he picked up the phone book and looked up Helen Bell, Audrey's sister. She was listed in South Minneapolis. Not expecting too much, he punched in her phone number. She answered on the second ring.

'I'd like to come talk to you about the whole case,' he said, after he introduced himself.

'I . . . thought it was just about done,' Bell said. He noticed her voice immediately: she sounded like Audrey, who sounded like the woman who'd called him to press him on McDonald.

'Well, we haven't settled the Kresge thing,' Lucas said. 'I just want to come over and chat. Get some opinions.'

'Okay. I'll be here the rest of the day.'

Three nuns, all in traditional dress, were perched on chairs in Elle's room, watching a young nurse change a saline drip. When Lucas stepped in, easing the door closed, one of them chirped, 'Hi, Lucas. She's awake.'

Lucas stepped around the beige curtain that masked Elle's bed from the outside, and looked down at his oldest friend. They'd gone to Catholic grade school together, goofing along the sidewalk, her long golden hair shimmering in the autumn sunlight, her blue eyes happy, smiling at him . . . His first clear memory of a female other than his mother. Now, her head was swathed with bandages, her face bruised, showing yellow disinfectant, her eyelids drooping over blue eyes that seemed more hazy than happy. She smiled weakly and he thought she looked wonderful.

'You look terrible,' he said. 'Like somebody beat the daylights out of you.'

'That's funny,' she mumbled. 'I sort of feel that way, too.'

He touched her foot. 'You're gonna make it.'

'Yes, probably. Do you know what happened?'

'Pretty much. You got a phony phone call. Somebody pulled you out of the building, and ambushed you.'

'I don't know,' she said. 'I can't remember much after about six o'clock, but that's what I've been told.'

'How bad is the memory thing?' He swallowed as he said it: he didn't need bad news, not about Elle.

Again she smiled weakly: 'Just a couple hours of amnesia, nothing unusual. I've taken a few tests: there's no impairment. Permanent impairment.'

'All right,' he said. 'All right.'

'The other girl . . .'

The other girl would live. She smelled vanilla when a nurse wiped her arm with an alcohol swab; smelled fried eggs in a glass of apple juice, celery in oatmeal. When asked to read aloud from a chart, she'd read quite well – except that she'd read some words backward, pronouncing them correctly in their backward form.

'She could recover,' Elle said. 'I feel so bad that she was running after me . . .'

'Nothing you could do,' Lucas said.

'Does anybody have any idea who might've done it?' A shadow of fear in her eyes, something he'd never seen before.

He shook his head. 'Not yet.'

They talked for ten minutes before Elle's eyelids grew heavy; Lucas kissed her on the cheek, with much approval from the squad of nuns who perched like blackbirds on their row of red leatherette chairs. Before he left the hospital, he talked to her doctor for a minute, picked up a pack of x-rays and some pre-operative photos at the radiology department.

The Hennepin County Medical Examiner's office was just down the street from police headquarters, connected by what the cops half-seriously referred to as the secret tunnel. Lucas dumped his car in one of the cop slots on the street, stopped to tell Rose Marie Roux's secretary that he'd be out of town the next day, and then took the tunnel to the ME's office. He showed the photos and films to one of the forensic pathologists.

'Probably right-handed, and probably not too tall,' the ME said, sucking on an illegal Winston. 'The blows all hit on the side and back of her head, rather than coming down on top. But if it were a man, swinging flat, like a baseball bat, he

would've knocked her head off. This looks more like somebody coming down, but from a relatively low swinging
position.'

'Possibly a woman?'

The ME pushed his lips out and blew a capital O. 'Could
be. Whoever it was, wasn't all that strong. Jumping somebody
from behind, with a club – a strong guy would have killed her,
hitting her like that.'

'Huh.'

Lucas had seen Helen Bell at the arraignment of her sister,
and had been struck by how little they resembled each other,
in the sense of a total package, for two women who looked so
much alike. Audrey at thirty-eight was a beetle, hunched,
fussy, dressed all in earth colors, her movements small and
nervous. Bell at thirty-four was not exactly a butterfly, but
seemed even in the restrictive circumstances of a legal hearing
to be much more outgoing, much more like a woman in her
thirties. Her hair was touched with color, she wore a bit of
makeup, and at the arraignment, she'd worn a pretty red silk
scarf with a conservative blue business suit; and she'd smiled.

Helen Bell lived in a small white house with green shutters,
backed onto an alley, a shaky-looking garage standing behind
the house. Lucas left his car in the street and walked up the
narrow seventy-year-old sidewalk to the front door and
knocked. Bell was there in a minute, smiling nervously when
she opened her door and, said, 'Chief Davenport? Come in.'

The living room had a just-vacuumed look, and magazines,
mostly about home-making, were stacked carefully on a coffee
table. 'Coffee?' she asked. 'It's only microwave instant.'

'Yes, that'd be nice.' The voice again: this was the tipster,
all right. Lucas mentally kicked himself: he'd known that
Audrey McDonald had a sister.

'Decaf or regular?' She was bustling around, making sure he was comfortable; he felt as though he was on a first date.

'Whatever you have . . . regular is fine.'

She went to get it, and he looked around the small living room, checked a shelf of paperbacks: self-help, mostly. How to succeed in business. 'Where do you work?' he called.

He heard the door slam on the microwave: 'Fisher Specialties down in Bloomington. You know – truck accessories. I'm in charge of the orders department.' She came out of the kitchen carrying two mugs of coffee. 'Sit on the couch – I'll take the easy chair.'

'Any children?'

'A daughter. Connie. She should be home from school any minute.'

'I wanted to talk to you about some background involving the death of Dan Kresge and then later, of Wilson McDonald . . .'

'Are they going to drop the charges against Audrey?'

'I don't know, I don't work in that area,' Lucas said. 'Mrs Bell . . . did you write to us about your brother-in-law? Call me on the phone?'

She looked too surprised by the question; she wasn't surprised, but she acted as though she was, her eyebrows going up, her head cocking to one side. 'Why . . .'

'I can get phone records, if I want to,' Lucas said. 'And there's nothing at all illegal about what you did. You were simply recommending an investigation.'

She took a sip of coffee, then ran the index finger of her free hand around the rim of the cup. After a second, she said, 'Yes, that was me. You'd already figured it out, I guess. But it couldn't be from the phone – I called from Rainbow.'

Rainbow was a supermarket. Lucas shook his head: 'It's just your voice. You sound a little, I don't know – Canadian.'

'Aboot,' she said.

He nodded. 'The first time I talked to your sister, I thought she was the one who called. So: how long ago did you decide Wilson McDonald was killing people?'

'I . . . thought there'd been a lot of deaths, to get him where he'd gotten. But it was only when Mr Kresge was shot that I was really sure. You know that Mr Kresge was going to merge the bank . . .'

'Yes.'

'And Wilson's job was gone. I mean, *Gone*. Then Mr Kresge gets killed, and Wilson's job was saved. And maybe he's even in line for Mr Kresge's job. That was too much. There'd been too many of these things.'

'How long had he been beating your sister?'

'He beat her up before they got married,' Helen said. 'She told me that later.'

'Then why'd she marry him?'

'Because she loved him,' Bell said simply. 'She still loves him.'

'That's a very odd relationship.'

'A kind of co-dependency,' Bell said. 'You know . . . never mind.'

'No. Say it.'

'My father, before he died, used to beat up my mother. And Audrey. And he would've started on me, if I'd been old enough. And somehow, I think that did something to Audrey's brain – she thinks women *deserve* to get beaten. I mean, she'd never say that, but way deep down, I think she might feel it. I used to plead with her to leave the man.'

'Where do you come from? You and Audrey?' He knew, but if could get her rolling, anything might come out.

'Oxford. It's up in the Red River Valley,' she said. 'The closest big town is Grand Forks.'

'Sugar beets?'

'No, we never really farmed. We lived just outside Oxford – we could walk to school – and my dad was a mail carrier. Both of my grandfathers were farmers, though. Dad grew up on a farm, and so did Mom, but he just wasn't interested.'

'Your folks still live up there?'

'No, they both died. My father died when I was little, when I was ten, that was . . . twenty-four years ago, now. Just about this time of year. Mom died four years later. In the spring. After Mom died, I went to live with my Aunt Judy in Lakeville and Audrey went to college. She went to St Anne's.'

'I know . . . listen, I assume that you didn't talk to us directly because you didn't want to offend your sister. Or alienate her. Is that right?'

Bell nodded. 'You know, she kept talking about how she loved him and what a great provider he was, but I really thought he was an animal and that sooner or later, he'd kill her. He was a killer. You said on the phone that the Kresge thing wasn't finished yet, but you know, it really is. Wilson killed him. Maybe I should have come forward earlier, but . . . I wasn't sure. And he was my sister's husband.'

'The good provider.'

'Easy to laugh off if you're a police officer, down here in Minneapolis,' Bell said. 'But if you were poor in Oxford, Minnesota, and we pretty much were, then "good provider" isn't something you laugh at.'

Lucas glanced around: 'Are you married? Or . . .'

'Divorced,' she said. 'Four years now.' She shook her head at the unstated question. 'Larry never laid a hand on me. We just found out that we weren't very much interested in each other. We were dating when I got pregnant, and we got married because we were supposed to.'

'All right,' he said.

293

They talked for a few more minutes, then Lucas stood up. 'Thanks.'

'What about Dan Kresge? Are you all done now?'

Lucas shrugged. 'I don't know. There doesn't seem much more to look at. We'll keep picking at little corners, but there's not much left.'

'I'm glad that man's gone – Wilson, not Mr Kresge. I know it's a sin, but I'm glad he's gone.'

Lucas had just taken a step toward the front door when the door opened, and a slender teenager stepped in, dressed head-to-foot in black, carrying a black book bag. Her hair was blond, no more than an inch long, and a tiny gold ring pierced one eyebrow. She looked quickly at her mother, then to Lucas, gave him an assessing smile and said, 'My. This is a studly one.'

'Connie!'

'He *is* . . .' Slightly seductive, intended to tease her mother.

'Please! This is Chief Davenport from the Minneapolis Police Department.'

'A cop? You can't be asking if Aunt Audrey really killed him – she admits it,' the teenager said. She dropped her book bag in the entry. 'I don't think she killed anyone else.'

'We're just making routine calls,' Lucas said.

'The chief of police makes routine calls?'

'I'm not the chief, I'm a deputy chief,' Lucas said. 'And sometimes I make routine calls, if the case is important enough.'

'We were just finishing here,' Bell said.

'Well, good luck with Aunt Audrey,' the girl said. 'The meanest woman alive.'

'Connie!' And Bell looked quickly at Lucas: 'Connie and Audrey don't get along as well as they should.'

'She is such a tiresome little bourgeois,' Connie said, rolling her eyes. 'The only interesting thing she ever did was kill Wilson.'

'Which was, when you think about it, pretty interesting,' Lucas said.

Connie nodded: 'Yup. I gotta admit it.'

Lucas smiled at her, deciding he liked her. The girl picked it up, and smiled back, a touch of shyness this time. Lucas said to Bell, 'If anything else comes up, I'd like to give you a call.'

As Lucas passed Connie, he picked up just the slightest whiff of weed; he glanced at her, and she picked *that* up, too. Smart kid, he thought, as he walked down the sidewalk.

Thinking: more dead people. Audrey's parents, dead and buried.

From his car phone, he called Sherrill: 'I'm gonna run up to the Red River Valley tomorrow, up by Grand Forks. Can you go?'

'Yup: this is my weekend. Can we stay overnight in one of those sleazy little hotels with the thin walls and fuck all night so the people can hear us on the other sides of the walls?'

'I don't know about all night . . . maybe, you know, *once*.'

'I'll start practicing my moaning. Call me tonight.'

The phone rang a minute later, and he thought it was Sherrill calling back. It was Roux: 'See me when you get in,' she said.

Rose Marie Roux was working on the budget when Lucas stepped in. 'Sit down,' she said, without looking up. She worked for another moment, humming to herself without apparently realizing it: she was happy doing budgets.

'So,' she said eventually, dropping her yellow pencil and linking her fingers. 'Are you sleeping with Marcy Sherrill?'

Lucas got frosty. 'We're seeing each other. I don't think it's much of anyone's business what happens . . .'

'Lucas, for Christ's sakes – are you living in a goddamn cave?' she asked in exasperation. 'A deputy chief of police can get away with sleeping with one of his detectives only if . . .'

'She's not one of my detectives,' Lucas said. 'I don't have any regular supervisory control . . .'

'Oh, bullshit – she works for you when you need her. And besides, the media won't give a shit about technicalities. You're a deputy chief, she's a sergeant. I don't care – I really don't. What I was about to say is, a deputy chief can get away with sleeping with one of his detectives only if he's very, very careful. Not secretive, but careful. Now: You left a message that you were going off to this place . . .' She looked at a notepad. 'Oxford. Tomorrow. Up in the Red River Valley? Were you planning to take Sherrill?'

'I thought . . .'

'If you take her, she's gonna have to take vacation time. Or she puts in her regular hours, and you go up on her days off and she doesn't get paid at all.'

'Look . . .'

'No, you look: I'm not trying to save *her* ass. I'm not trying to save *my* ass. I'm trying to save *your* ass. I can guarantee you that if you go up there with her, and she's paid for it, and the press finds out, you'll wind up being fired. I'd back you up, but it wouldn't do any good – you'd get it in the neck anyway.'

'Maybe we just oughta forget the whole thing,' he said. 'Me'n Marcy.'

She softened a quarter-inch: 'I didn't say you gotta do that. But you've got to be discreet, and you've got to be politically careful. She can't be on the payroll when you're off together.'

'All right,' he said. 'That's it?'

'Elle Kruger seems to be doing okay.'

'I was just talking to her, and her doctor. She's gonna have a lot of pain for a long time,' Lucas said. 'But her brain wasn't affected. At least, not as far as they can tell. Motor is all right, memory, language.'

'Nothing on it?'

'Nothing yet. But that's why I'm going up to the Red River. There's a question about whether Audrey McDonald might be involved.'

Roux's genetically-enabled left eyebrow went up: 'Seriously?'

'Seriously. We might have the edge of something pretty interesting,' Lucas said.

'Okay. But remember what I said about Sherrill.'

'She's off the next couple of days. We should be all right.'

'No expense accounts, no meals, no nothin' . . .'

'Nothing,' he said. 'Not a nickel. For either of us.'

'All right,' she said. 'Good luck.'

'With Marcy? Or the case?'

'Whatever,' she said.

Lucas, back to his office, called the county attorney's office and asked Richard Kirk, the head of the criminal division. He waited for a moment, and Kirk came on: 'What's up?'

'How long can you hold off on a decision about Audrey McDonald?'

'Why?' Just like a lawyer.

''Cause.'

'Just like a fuckin' cop: *'cause*,' Kirk said. 'Anyway – we're gonna take McDonald's story to the grand jury and let them decide. That's the democratic way, and also lets our beloved county attorney off the hook if something goes wrong.'

'So when do you go to the jury?'

'Next Wednesday, but it'd be no problem to hold off for a while. We could present the basic case Wednesday and hold the decision for the meeting one after that.'

'That'd be good,' Lucas said. 'Some odd stuff has come up.'

'So we'll do that – and don't surprise us at the last minute.'

'Okay. And tell your boss to hold off any speeches to the Feminist Fife and Drum Club, about it being an obvious case of self-defense.'

'Okay. But if something happens, call me, so we know which way to lean,' Kirk said.

'I'll call.'

'Goddamnit, Davenport, you're old enough to know. . .'

'What?'

'. . . That too much investigation will screw up a perfectly good case.'

Chapter Twenty-Five

M organ Bite had such a beatific look on his face as he stood at the edge of the Bite Brothers parking lot, at the end of the line of black Cadillac limousines, still holding the check, that Audrey McDonald actually thought of killing him; actually thought that after she received all the money she was due, after all the legal matters were cleared away, after all the police were gone, she might come back some night and murder the man, simply for the pleasure of doing it.

Bite was speaking in clichés: '. . . able to achieve such a natural appearance that the loved one seems to be undoubtedly present among us . . .'

She wanted to say, 'Yes-yes-yes,' and run away down the sidewalk; she limped instead, putting on a stunned expression, as though she might at any moment suffer a relapse. Though, now that she thought of it, Bite might find a relapse attractive, given his profession.

'. . . not regret this in any way, and do not hesitate for a moment to call me at any time, day or night, with any concerns . . .'

She'd just given him a blank check to handle Wilson's funeral – well, blank to the tune of $25,000, which he thought would be adequate to protect Wilson's image in the business community. Whenever she'd mentioned anything having to do Wilson's death, Bite had seemed intimately aware of every detail, while somehow remaining unaware that she'd had anything to do with it. Come to think of it, she sort of liked that. Maybe she wouldn't kill him.

Well: she could decide that some other time.

Audrey McDonald came with a full set of the negative emotions: hate, anguish and anger, pain, fear, dread and loathing were her daily bread, illuminated by an active imagination. Love and pleasure were not quite a mystery. She thought she might have loved Wilson, and her parents, and even Helen. She felt pleasure with the prospect of money – not with what it could buy, but the lucre itself; she loved handling it, reading account statements. She had talked Wilson into buying a hundred gold coins, American Eagles, which she kept in a box in a cubbyhole in the kitchen. Once a week she would take them out and handle them, so smooth, so beautiful and cool to the touch.

And she certainly felt pleasure with the prospect of killing.

Killing was the most interesting thing she'd ever done, and that alone was a powerful attraction. Added to the attraction was the simple reality that a killing was always done to decrease her own fear – fear of poverty, fear of helplessness, fear of low status – and to increase the amount of money she would someday have. So far, she hadn't killed idly: so far, she'd always made a profit on her killings.

But it was dread that hung over her fifteen minutes after she left Bite Brothers, as she pulled the car to the curb in front of her sister's house. Helen had been talking to Davenport again: she'd called to confess it, and to admit that she'd written to Davenport that Wilson had killed people.

But Wilson hadn't. She had.

And if Davenport was still sniffing around, he might trip over something inconvenient. She was beginning to fear the man, not because he seemed to be particularly bright, or especially hard-driving, or even mean, but because he simply wouldn't go away. Now he was visiting Helen. This was all supposed to be done with. What did he want?

Helen was standing in the doorway as she limped up the sidewalk. Putting on the limp.

'I'm sorry,' Helen said. 'He was hurting you so badly that I don't think I had a choice.'

Audrey nodded abruptly and let Helen take her coat at the door. 'Still hurt,' she mumbled. And she looked terrible. The bruises were going yellow, and her hair, unwashed since the attack, looked like sticky pieces of dirty brown kite string.

'Let me get you a coffee,' Helen said, bustling around.

'Why aren't you working?' Audrey asked. Audrey hadn't worked since Wilson's second promotion, the one that carried him into mortgages. She'd always talked about Helen's having a 'career' in a way that made both Helen and her ex-husband feel like ragpickers.

'I had personal time coming, and since the fight with Wilson, I thought . . . I just thought I ought to be around,' Helen said from the kitchen. She appeared a moment later with the coffee. 'How are you?'

Audrey shook her head: 'I still hurt. I still feel like I've been in an auto accident . . . and Wilson . . .' She sniffed.

'When's the funeral?'

'They released him today. His father's secretary called and said his father wanted to handle the funeral, but I said no. I would handle it. It's at Bite Brothers, day after tomorrow, at two o'clock.'

'I'll take you,' Helen said.

'Thank you. I think we should go in Wilson's Lexus, though.'

'No problem; I'll come over to your place with Connie, and we'll all go together in the Lexus.'

They talked for a few minutes about the funeral, sipping

the coffee as they talked. Then Audrey asked, 'What all did Detective Davenport want to talk about?'

'Oh, he just figured out that I was the one who wrote the letter about Wilson,' Helen said. 'And he wanted to know why I thought Wilson did it.'

'You know, I'm not sure Wilson did all those things,' Audrey said tentatively.

Helen looked away, flushing just a bit; this embarrassed her. 'Oh, Audrey . . . I know you loved him.'

'Yes. And sometimes . . . I don't know.'

'What?' Helen asked. Audrey almost never opened up. Now she seemed about to.

'I sometimes wondered myself. Something you don't know – and please don't tell Detective Davenport this, I mean, Wilson is gone – but I began to wonder myself. And after Andy Ingall disappeared on his boat, well, Wilson was gone the night before. He came home at three o'clock in the morning, and he'd been drinking, and we had an awful fight. And the next day, Andy sailed away. That's when I began to wonder.'

'You should have said something,' Helen said.

'I . . . really did love him,' Audrey said. 'And he loved me. Nobody ever loved me before, no man did. I'm not so good-looking as you are . . .'

'Oh, shut up, Audrey,' Helen said. 'As soon as this is all over with, we'll take you to a friend of mine for a make-over, and you'll be amazed. You'll have guys coming around. You've got the whole rest of your life to look forward to.'

'Unless they send me to jail,' Audrey said piteously.

'No way,' Helen declared. 'I asked Detective Davenport about that, and he said that the county attorney was ready to declare that it was self-defense. Which it obviously was . . .'

Audrey perked up a bit at that. 'Maybe I could do a make-over,' she said, brushing some of her sticky hair away from her face. 'That would be good . . .'

'So you'll be okay?'

'I think so. I have to go, now, there's more funeral things to be done. I talked to Wilson's father; he seemed to think the whole thing was like a bad business deal. I was afraid he'd hate me. But he didn't seem any different.'

'Well, you know the old man,' Helen said. She'd met him two or three times at the McDonalds' house; he was, she thought, a spectacular horse's ass. 'Though usually, they say that having a child die is the worst thing that can happen to a person.'

'Not for that old man; he is a monster,' Audrey said.

'I was just talking about our folks with Detective Davenport,' Helen said. She'd gone to get Helen's coat from a chair, and didn't see her sister jerk around toward her.

'What?'

'Oh, you know, we were just talking, nothing serious,' Helen said, as she held the coat.

'I mean, about them dying, or just that they were gone?'

'Nothing, really – just something that came up in passing.'

He *was* sniffing around. Audrey didn't push it, because it seemed unlikely to produce much, and she didn't want Helen wondering about the conversation. But she would have to think about this. Go after Davenport directly? That was one possibility, as long as it wouldn't push more investigators her way. As for Helen, she had to do something to interrupt this relationship with Davenport, which was altogether too cosy.

All this was going through her head as she went through the forms of departure, ending with, 'So you'll be at the house at noon?'

'Noon,' Helen said. 'And if you need anything before then, call me. Please. This is the reason I took the time off.'

When Audrey pulled away from the curb, Helen was still at the door. Audrey touched the horn, emitting a polite Japanese tone, and thought, '*Connie.*'

And no time like the present.

She drove to a Rainbow supermarket, looked up Child Protection in the phone book. 'I don't want to give you my name – I'm a teacher at South High and I'm going out of channels here – but there's a student named Connie Bell who has been smoking a great deal of marijuana and I've heard from another student that she gets it from her mother; and I've heard that she and her mother have been fighting, and that Connie has been beaten up several times by the men who hang around with her mother. Thank you.'

She hung up.

Connie smoked marijuana – Helen had confessed that. Helen had told Audrey weeks before that she'd slapped Connie after an argument over marijuana. There was just enough truth in her call to cause Helen some inconvenience. That was all Audrey needed for now: for Helen to look away from Davenport.

Chapter Twenty-Six

Marcy Sherrill was banging on Lucas' door at seven o'clock. He stumbled out to open up, his hair still a mess from the night, wearing a t-shirt and jeans, one sock on, one sock off; his alarm had gone off ten minutes earlier.

'You look terrible,' she said cheerfully. 'I got up early and went for a run.'

'God will someday strike you dead for that kind of behavior,' he said. He was not a morning person. 'If I could only get the glue out of my eyes.'

'Quit pissing around; let's get going,' Sherrill said. 'I'll drive. You can sleep, if you want.'

He perked up, but just slightly. 'If you drive, I might survive.'

'So, I'll drive,' She said. 'C'mon, c'mon. Go.' He turned back to the bedroom and she slapped him on the butt.

'Christ, it's like having a coach,' he grumbled, but he tried to hurry.

Minnesota is a tall state; Audrey McDonald's home town, Oxford, was in the Red River Valley in the northwest corner, on land as flat as the Everglades. They took Lucas' Porsche out I-94, Sherrill driving the first two hours, giving it to Lucas, then taking the car back four hours out. Sherrill was a cheerful companion, not given to long stretches of silence. As she chattered away about the landscape, the various road signs and small towns, the river crossings, animals dead-on-the-road, Lucas began to wonder what, exactly, he was doing with her. He began to check her from the corner of his eye, little peeks at her profile, at her face as she talked. Over the years, he'd had relationships, longer or shorter, with a number of women, and in the transition zone between them, had often felt ties to the last woman even as the ties to the new woman were forming.

In this case, there were more than simple ties back to Weather. Weather had been something different – the love of his life, if Elle Kruger wasn't – while Sherrill was much more like the other women he'd dated: Pretty, smart, interesting, and, eventually, moving on.

He wasn't sure that he wanted a relationship with a woman who'd be moving on, especially when she really wouldn't be out of sight. Sherrill was a cop, who had a desk right down the hall from his office: even when he wasn't trying to see her, he saw her four or five times a day.

'You sighed,' she said.

'What?'

'You just sighed.'

'A lot of shit going on,' Lucas said.

She patted him on the leg. 'You worry too much. It's all gonna work out.'

They followed Interstate northwest to Fargo, crossed the Red River into North Dakota, took I-29 north past Grand Forks, then recrossed the Red into Minnesota on a state highway to Oxford.

'Starting to feel it in my back,' Sherrill said to Lucas. Lucas was behind the wheel again. 'Probably would've been more comfortable in my car.'

'Yeah, I'm getting too old for this thing, I need something a little smoother,' Lucas said. 'Good car, though.'

'Too small for you. Though you'll probably start to shrink

a little, as the age comes on. You know, your vertebrae start to collapse, your hair thins out and sits lower on your head, your muscle tone goes . . .'

'You go from a 34-C to a 34-long . . .'

'Ooo. That's mean. But I kinda like it,' she said.

They passed a sign warning of a reduction of speed limits; Lucas dropped from eighty to sixty as they went past the forty-five sign. Past a farm implement dealer with a field of new John Deeres and Bobcats and antique Fords and International Harvesters; past competing Polaris and Yamaha snowmobile dealerships, both in unpainted steel Quonset huts; past a closed Dairy Queen and an open Hardee's, past a Christian Revelation Church and a SuperAmerica; and then into town, Lucas letting the car roll down to forty-five by the time they got to the twenty-five sign. Past a red-brick Catholic Church and a fieldstone Lutheran Church and then a liquor store, that may once have been a bank, built of both fieldstone and brick.

'Just like Lake fuckin' Wobegon,' Sherrill said.

'No lake,' Lucas said. 'Nothing but dirt.'

'If I had to live here, I'd shoot myself just for the entertainment value,' Sherrill said.

'Ah, there're lots of good things out here,' Lucas said.

'Name one.'

Lucas thought for a moment. 'You can see a long way,' he said finally, and they both started to laugh. Then Sherrill pointed out the windshield on the left side of the street, to a white arrow-sign that said, 'Proper County-Oxford Government Center.'

The Proper County Courthouse and Oxford City Hall had been combined in a building that resembled a very large Standard Oil station – low red brick, lots of glass, an oversized nylon American flag, and a large parking lot where a grassy town square might once have been. Lucas spotted three police cruisers at one corner of the parking lot, and headed that way.

'Watch your mouth with these people, huh?' Lucas said, as they got out of the car.

'Like you're Mr Diplomat.'

'I try harder when I'm out in the countryside,' Lucas said. 'They sometimes resent it when big city cops show up in their territory.'

The Oxford Police department was a starkly utilitarian collection of beige cubicles wedged into a departmental office suite twenty-four-feet square. The chief's office, the only private space in the suite, was at the back; the department itself seemed deserted when Lucas and Sherrill pushed through the outer door.

'A fire drill?' Sherrill asked.

'I don't know. What's that?' An odd, almost-musical sound came from the back; they walked back between the small cubicles, and spotted a man in the chief's private office, hovering over a computer. As they got closer, they could hear the *boop-beep-thwack-arrghh* of a computer action game. Sherrill gave Lucas an elbow in the ribs, but Lucas pushed her back down the row, walking quietly away. Then, 'Hello? Anybody home?'

The *boop-beep-thwack* stopped, and a second later a young man with a round face and a short black mustache stepped out of the chief's office.

'Help you folks?'

'We're looking for the chief of police, or the duty officer . . .'

'I'm Chief Mason.' The young man hitched up his pants when he saw Sherrill, and walked down toward them. Lucas took out his ID and handed it over. 'I'm Deputy Chief Lucas Davenport from Minneapolis, and this is Detective Sherrill . . .'

He explained that they had come up to review documents and interview people who might have any information about the death of George Lamb, Audrey McDonald's father, twenty-four years earlier. The chief, who had been staring almost pensively at Sherrill's breasts, started shaking his head. 'I been a cop here for four years; nobody in the department has been here more than twelve. Better you should go up and talk to the county clerk, she might be able to point you at some death records or something.'

'Second floor?' Lucas asked.

'Yee-up,' the chief said.

The county clerk was even younger than the chief, her hair dyed an unsuccessful orange: 'Okay, twenty-four years. About this time of year, you say?'

'About this time.'

'Okay . . . we're computerizing, you know, but all this old paper is hard to get on-line,' she said, as she dug through a file cabinet. 'Here we go. George Lamb? Here it is.'

'You got anything in there on an Amelia Lamb? George's wife? Four years after George?'

She went back to the cabinet, dug around, then shook her head. 'Nothing on an Amelia.'

She straightened up, stepped to the counter, pushed a mimeographed form across the counter at them, said to Marcy, 'I really like your hair,' and Marcy said, 'Thanks. I just got it changed and I was a little worried about doing it . . . used to be longer.'

The death form was filled out on a typewriter, and signed by a Dr Stephen Landis. Lucas scanned the routine report and asked, 'Is Dr Landis still practising here?'

'Oh, sure. He's over at the clinic, right down the street to Main, take a left two blocks.'

Marcy looked over Lucas' arm: 'Heart attack?'

'That's what it says.'

'You know, Sheriff Mason would've been a deputy back then, I bet he would know about it,' the clerk said, reading the file upside down. She tapped a line on the file with her fingertip. 'This address isn't right in town – it's out at County A – so they would have been the law enforcement arm involved in a death.'

'We just talked to a *Chief* Mason,' Sherrill said. 'They're not the same guy?'

'Second cousins, though you could never tell,' the clerk said. 'Sheriff John Mason's grandparents on his father's side, and Chief Bob Mason's great-grandparents on his father's and grandfather's side, are the same people, Chuck and Shirley Mason from Stephen.'

'Thank you,' Lucas said. 'Where can we find the sheriff's office?'

'Down the hall all the way to the end.'

As they left, Sherrill asked, 'Are Chuck and Shirley still alive?'

'Well, sure,' the clerk said. 'Hale and hearty. 'Course, they'd be down in Arizona right now.'

The sheriff was out, the receptionist said, but if it was a matter of importance, he'd be happy to come right back. Lucas identified himself, and the receptionist's eyebrows went up, and she punched a number in her telephone. A minute later, the phone rang, and she picked it up and said, without preamble, 'There're some Minneapolis police officers here, looking for you.'

The sheriff was a chunky, weathered man, going bald; he

wore an open parka and was carrying a blaze-orange watch cap when he stepped into the office five minutes later.

'You want to see me?'

'Yes,' Lucas said. He introduced himself, produced his ID, and mentioned the death of George Lamb.

'George Lamb? You mean about a hundred years ago, that George Lamb?' The sheriff's voice picked up a hint of wariness.

'Twenty-four years,' said Lucas.

'Come on back,' the sheriff said. And to the receptionist: 'Ruth, go get Jimmy and tell him to come back, too.'

To Lucas, 'You folks want some coffee?'

'That'd be fine,' Lucas said. They were passing a coffee pot in a hallway nook, and Sherrill said, 'I'll get it. Sheriff? Sugar?'

As the sheriff settled behind his desk, and Sherrill brought the coffee, Lucas said, 'We're sorta digging through the background on Lamb. The county clerk said you were around at the time, I don't know if you'd remember it or not.'

'Yeah, I do. He used to be a mail carrier outa here, he had the rural route. Died of a heart attack. Why're you looking into that? If I might ask?'

'We've got a case going on in the Cities, woman just shot her husband,' Lucas said. 'She's charged second-degree, but that could get dismissed as self-defense. We're looking into all the deaths that have been associated with her, and we found out that both her father and mother died young . . .'

'I know the woman,' the sheriff said. 'Audrey McDonald. Used to be Lamb. Been reading about the case in the *Star-Tribune*. What the heck is a chief of police doing way up here on a case like that?'

'Actually, uh, Marcy and I are friends,' Lucas said, tipping his head toward Sherrill. 'We were both working the case, and we sorta wanted to get away for a weekend . . . and we were sorta curious about Lamb.'

The sheriff glanced at Marcy and then back at Lucas, nodded as if everything were suddenly clear. 'I didn't take the first call on Lamb, but when we got word that somebody out there was dead, I came in,' the sheriff said. He spun in his office chair, looking out of the office window toward the back of a line of Main Street stores. 'This was early in the morning. I mean, real early, like four o'clock. He was dressed in gray long-johns, and he was laying on the kitchen floor. One of the girls had called us – Audrey, I think, the other one was still pretty young – and the two little girls had their mom out in the living room, and she was sitting on the couch all wailing away. And Lamb was deader'n a mackerel. It was his practice to wake up in the morning by breaking a raw egg in a double-shot glass, then pouring the glass full with rye, and drinking it down. We found him laying on the floor in a puddle of rye, with the egg all over his face. Took him off quick.'

'Egg and rye. That'd open your eyes, all right,' Sherrill said.

'Spoze,' said the sheriff. Another man, tall, lean as a fence post, ten years older than the sheriff but with a full head of hair, propped himself in the office doorway.

'You wanted me?'

'Yeah, Jimmy, come on in . . .' The sheriff introduced Lucas and Sherrill and said, 'They're checking around about the time George Lamb died down there on A. You remember that?'

'Yeah. Long time ago. Don't quite see what you'd be checking on. Dropped dead of a heart attack.'

'Was there anything unusual about the circumstances?' Lucas asked. 'Something to make you wonder if it was more'n a heart attack?'

The sheriff shook his head, and Jimmy scratched his head and said, 'Well, no. Not really. The population up here is older'n average – not much to hold the younger people anymore – so we see a lot of heart attacks. Probably once or twice a week we get a call and a fair number of times, the victim is dead before the ambulance gets there. I probably seen a few hundred of them in my time, and . . .' He shrugged. 'Soon as I saw him, I thought, *Heart.*'

'Shoot,' Lucas said. 'How about the mother? Amelia?'

The sheriff shook his head. 'They left here after George died – sold the place off and moved down to your territory, I think.'

'Really?' Lucas shook his head ruefully. 'You know, I never asked. I just assumed . . .' Lucas glanced at Marcy, then said to the sheriff, 'I didn't see a motel coming in. Is there a place we can stay?'

The sheriff seemed to relax a half-inch. 'North out of town a half-mile, there's the Sugar Beet Inn. Real clean place.'

'Good enough,' Lucas said. They all stood up and Lucas shook with the sheriff and Marcy said, 'Thanks for the coffee.'

And then they were outside and Lucas looked up at the building and said, 'That's the goddamnedest thing, huh?'

'He seemed a little tense,' Marcy said.

'They oughta be a little tense,' Lucas said. 'They're covering something up.'

They were at the car, and Marcy looked at him over the roof. 'All right, you got me. How do you know they're covering something up?'

'Because they both remembered the details of a heart attack twenty-four years ago. What he looked like lying on the floor. Gray long-johns. The egg and rye thing . . .'

'I might have remembered that, the egg and rye. 'Cause it's unusual.'

'Audrey's name . . .'

'They could have remembered that from reading the paper.'

Lucas shook his head: 'Why? She didn't change it until she married McDonald, eight years after her father died. You think they were tracking her?'

Marcy nodded. 'All right. They remembered too much. What do we do next?'

'We go over and jack up the doctor.'

'You notice how I'm being the nice little housewife and sweety-pie? Get the coffee, girl-talk about hair, let it pass when you hint to the good sheriff that we're up here for a little whoopee?'

'It's making me nervous,' Lucas said. 'The pressure'll start to build. Sooner or later, you'll explode.'

'That could happen,' she said.

Dr Stephen Landis couldn't see them until the end of his patient day, at four o'clock.

'You can come right here to the clinic,' the nurse said. 'Four o'clock sharp. He has some patient visits to make out in town, starting at four-thirty, so you'll have about twenty minutes.'

'You mean, he actually goes out and visits people?' Marcy asked.

'Of course.'

'Amazing.'

Back on the street, Lucas looked at his watch: an hour to kill. 'Let's go see the undertaker,' he said.

The undertaker was a roly-poly young man in a plaid suit: he didn't remember the case because he was too young. 'Dad might remember, though,' he said. 'He's out in the garage . . .'

The senior undertaker was a pleasant fellow, dressed in

cotton slacks and a v-necked wool sweater. He was in the back of the mortuary's heated garage, hitting golf balls into a net off an Astro-Turf pad.

'Yep, I remember Mr Lamb,' he said, slipping his five-iron back into his golf bag. 'Actually, I don't remember Mr Lamb as well as I remember the daughter . . . the older one.'

'Audrey,' Sherrill said.

'Don't remember her name. Audrey could be right. I do remember that she handled all the arrangements. Her mother came along, of course, but it was Audrey who settled everything.'

'Cremation, I understand,' Lucas said.

'Yes, it was. Quite a bit cheaper, you know. I applaud that, by the way. The family didn't have a great deal of money, and with the breadwinner gone, they had to watch their nickels and dimes. The young woman marched right in the door, said we could forget about a big funeral, they didn't have the money, and that she wanted the body cremated. Period. No argument allowed.'

'Did she pick up the ashes?'

'Yup. In a cardboard box. She said they didn't need an urn, they were planning to scatter them over the family farm.'

'Tough kid,' Lucas said.

'That she was,' said the senior undertaker. 'Never saw a tear from her, except once when the sheriff happened to come by while they were making the arrangements, and then she couldn't stop bawling. That was the only time.' He took another iron out of his bag. 'What do you know about the two iron?'

'If only God can hit a one iron, then it'd probably take a prophet to hit the two,' Sherrill said.

The senior undertaker looked at her with interest. 'You're a golfer.'

'A little,' she said. 'My husband was a two-handicap.'

'Was?'

'He died.'

'Ah. That *will* play hob with your handicap,' he said cheerfully. Then, 'Do you think that young lady – Audrey? – do you think she might have killed her father?'

Lucas looked at Sherrill and then back at the senior undertaker. 'Why would you ask?'

'Well, because you're here, obviously. And because there was something very cold and unpleasant about that young girl. It crossed my mind when we were setting up the funeral arrangements that she cared less for her father than she might for a clod of dirt. When she came to pick up the ashes – and she drove herself, by the way, and she was too young to have a license, I'm sure – I watched her from the window when she went back to the car. She opened the car door and tossed the box in the back seat like you might toss an old rag. There was something in the way she did it. I thought at that very moment that the ashes might never make it to the family farm. That they might not make it further than the nearest ditch.'

'But she was bawling about it, you said.'

'Oh, and very conveniently, with the sheriff.' The senior undertaker shook his head. 'You see a lot of very strange things in this business, but that has stuck in my mind as one of the strangest. No. Not strange. Frightening. I locked the doors for the next few weeks. I would dream that the little girl was coming for me.'

'He died of a heart attack,' Dr Stephen Landis said. Landis was a roughneck fifty-five, with sparkling gold-rimmed glasses and heavy boots under his jeans. A stuffed mallard, just taking wing, hung from the wall of the reception room, while a nine-pound walleye was mounted over his desk in his private office. 'He'd been having some problems – cardiac insufficiency – and he wouldn't stop drinking or smoking. I told him if he didn't stop, that he was gonna have a heart attack. And one day he keeled over. Drink and cigarette in hand.'

'He was smoking when he went?' Sherrill said.

'Still had the cigarette between his fingers,' Landis said.

'But you didn't do an autopsy?' Lucas asked.

Landis shrugged. 'There didn't seem to be a reason to do one. He'd been sick, it seemed apparent that it was the onset of a heart problem. And then he had a heart attack.'

'Aren't you required to do an autopsy when the person didn't die under a doctor's immediate care?' Sherrill asked.

'Not then. Back then, not everything was regulated by the legislature yet. You could use your judgment on occasion.'

'Did you ever treat Mrs Lamb?' Lucas asked, injecting a slight chill into his voice.

Landis' eyes drifted away from Lucas'. 'I may have seen her a time or two, but the Lambs moved away, you know . . .'

'Did you ever treat her for injuries that might have been inflicted by her husband?'

'No, I didn't. Well – you probably heard this from somebody else, or you wouldn't be asking the question. There were rumors that George used to knock her around. And I had her in one time, and she had some bruises that looked like they might have come from a beating. She said she fell down the stairs. I doubted that, but the bruises were old and . . . I let it go. Maybe I shouldn't have, but she wasn't interested in talking about it.'

They sat in silence for a moment, then Lucas said, 'No sign of anything but the symptoms of a heart attack.'

'Not that I could see.'

'And you examined the body carefully.'

'I examined it. Briefly.'

'No tissue cultures.'

'No.'

'You never came to suspect that anything unusual might have led to Joseph Lamb's sudden death.'

'No. He had heart trouble. If anything, I was expecting a heart attack.'

Outside, Sherrill said, 'I see what you mean – another case of remarkable memory. Lamb had a cigarette between his fingers when he died.'

'There's something here,' Lucas said, turning to look back at the front of the clinic. 'I have trouble thinking what it might be.'

'Maybe she's some kind of town philanthropist and gives them money or something, so they protect her,' Sherrill suggested.

'Have you seen her? She doesn't look like she'd give a nickel to a starving man. And if it had been that, somebody would have mentioned it.'

'So what do you want to do?'

'Let's go check into this motel. Get some dinner.'

Lucas always expected a certain amount of awkwardness when he and a new woman friend got around a bed, and the room at The Sugar Beet Inn was basically a queen-sized bed, a television set and bathroom; along with the built-in scent of disinfectant. Sherrill wasn't quite as inhibited: she pulled off her jacket, tossed it on the chair, jumped on the bed, giving it a bounce, then hopped off to check the TV. 'I wonder if they have dirty movies?'

'Give me a break,' Lucas said. 'Come on, let's find a restaurant.'

'Too early. It's barely five o'clock. I wanna take a shower

and get the road off me,' she said. 'You wanna take a shower?'

'If we take a shower, we'd probably wind up on the bed, dealing with sexual issues,' he said, injecting a tone of disapproval into his voice. 'We're here on business.'

'Quit bustin' my balls, Davenport,' she said. She pulled her sweatshirt over her head. 'But if you want to sit out here and wait . . .'

'I suppose we'd save water if we both got in there.'

'And water is precious out here on the prairie.'

'Well. I mean, if it's for the environment . . .'

The desk clerk at the Sugar Beet told them two restaurants would be open: Chuck's Wagon, a diner, and the Oxford Supper Club, which had a liquor license. They drove down to the supper club and were met at the entrance by a cheerful, overweight woman with hair the same tone of orange as the county clerk's, and a frilly apron. She took them to a red-vinyl booth and left them with glasses of water and menus.

'That hair color must be a fashion out here. She looks like a pumpkin,' Sherrill whispered.

'Mmm. Open-face roast beef sandwich with brown gravy, choice of potato, string beans, cheese balls as an appetizer, and pumpkin or mince pie with whipped cream, choice of drink, $7.95,' Lucas said.

'You ever hear of cholesterol?'

'Off my case. I'm starving.'

Lucas ordered a martini, to be followed by the roast beef sandwich; Sherrill got the Traditional Meatloaf with a Miller Lite, up front. They ate in easy companionship, talking about the day, talking about cases they'd worked together and what happened to who, afterwards. Touched lightly on Weather's case. Lucas got a Leinenkugel's and Sherrill got a second Miller Lite, to go with the pie. They were just finishing the pie when Lucas felt the khaki pants legs stepping up to the table. He looked up at two sheriff's deputies, two men in their late twenties or thirties, one hard, lanky, the other thicker, like a high-school tackle, with the beginning of a gut.

'Are you the Porsche outside?' asked one with the gut.

'Yeah. That's us,' Lucas said.

'So you're the guys from Minneapolis.'

'Yeah. What can we do for you?'

'We were just wondering if you're done here,' said the lanky one. His voice was curt: his cop voice.

'I don't know,' Lucas said. He was just as curt. Across the table, Sherrill had swivelled slightly on her butt so that her back was to the wall, and her legs, still curled up, projected toward the deputies. Their attitude was wrong; and other patrons in the restaurant had noticed. 'We didn't get very far today. We weren't getting a lot of cooperation.'

'We were just talking over at the office about how everybody was cooperating, and you were being pretty damn impolite about it,' said Gut.

'Not trying to be impolite,' Lucas said. Swiveling a bit, as Sherrill had. 'We're trying to conduct an investigation.'

'Yeah. I bet you were investigating the hell out of this chick up to the Sugar Beet,' Gut said.

Sherrill said, 'Hey, you . . .' But Lucas held up a peremptory finger to silence her, and she stopped and looked at him, then Lucas said to Gut, 'Fuck you, you fat hillbilly cocksucker.'

Gut looked at the slender man, who stepped back a bit and said, 'Let's cool this off,' but Gut put his fists on the table and leaned toward Lucas and said, 'If you said that outside, I'd drag your ass all over the goddamn parking lot.'

'Let's go,' Lucas said. 'I'm tired of this rinky-dink bullshit.'

Lucas tossed a twenty on the table and followed Gut toward

the entrance; the lanky man said, 'Hey, whoa, whoa,' and
Sherrill said, 'Lucas, this is a bad idea . . .'

But six feet outside the door, Gut took a slow, short step,
feeling Lucas closing behind him, spun and threw a wild,
looping right hand at Lucas' head.

Lucas stepped left and hit the heavy man in the nose,
staggering him, bringing blood. As Gut turned, bringing his
hands up to his face, Lucas hooked him in the left-side short
ribs with another right; when Gut pulled his arms down, Lucas
hit him in the eye with a left, the other eye with a right, then
took the right-side short ribs with a left, then crossed a right
to the face. Gut was trying to fall, staggering backwards, got
his back wedged against a pickup truck and Lucas beat him
like a punching bag, face, face, gut, face, ribs, face, face, like
a heavy workout in the gym.

Lucas felt it all flowing out: the frustration with Weather,
the attack on Weather and Elle, the uncertainty, the depression.
And heard Sherrill screaming, flicked somebody's arm off his
shoulder, was hit from the left and turned, almost punched
Sherrill in the forehead, felt another man moving behind him,
spun, and saw the lanky man covering Gut, holding his hands
in front of him, shouting something . . .

The world began to slow down, and Lucas backed up,
hands up, Marcy pushing him, shouting. He could barely hear
her. 'Okay,' he said finally, through the roaring in his head.
'Okay, I'm done.'

Marcy faded in. 'You're done. Are you done?'

'I'm done . . .' He dropped his hands. They were dappled
with blood, and blood from Gut's nose was sprayed across his
shirt. He said, 'This shirt's fucked.'

Gut was stretched on the ground next to the pickup running
board, groaning, the lanky man leaning over him, saying,
'Breathe easy. Come on, you're okay.'

But he wasn't okay. He said, 'I can't, I can't, I can't . . .'
Every time he tried to sit up, he moaned, holding his sides; he
was blowing streams of blood from his nose. 'We better get an
ambulance,' the lanky man said. 'Get him over to the clinic.'

'Can you call from your car?' Sherrill asked.

'Yeah, I can do that,' he said, as if the concept were new to
him. He hurried to the squad car, parked at the edge of the lot,
pushing through a narrow ring of spectators. As he went,
Marcy asked, quietly, 'Are you okay?'

'Yeah, yeah, he never touched me,' Lucas said.

'That's not what I meant.'

He looked at her: 'Yeah, I'm okay. I sorta let it all out,
there.'

'I'd say.'

The lanky deputy was back, said, 'The ambulance'll be
here in a minute.' Then to Lucas, 'I ain't gonna try to take you
in, 'cause we all got guns, but you're under arrest.'

'Bullshit,' Lucas said. 'You two came here to try to push us
out of a murder investigation and he took the first swing. If I
don't get some answers, I'll get the goddamn BCI up here and
we'll tear a new asshole for your department. You two are
gonna be lucky to get out of this with your badges.'

'We'll see,' the lanky man said. 'Why don't you go on
down to the courthouse? I'm gonna get the sheriff in. And
you're not helping around here.'

'Why don't you just come up to the Sugar Beet,' Lucas
said. 'We've got a big room.'

A siren started down in the town, the ambulance. The
lanky man looked at Sherrill and then at Lucas. 'All right.
We'll see you up there.'

'This is just fuckin' awful,' Sherrill said, on the way back to
the motel.

'The fight?' That was odd; she'd always been one of the first to get in.

'Not the fight. The way the fight turns me on. You could bend me over the front fender right now, in front of all those people, I swear to God. Whoo. But you sorta hung me up, there, dude. I don't think I coulda taken that skinny guy.' She was vibrating, talking a hundred miles an hour. 'Maybe I could have slowed him down. Didn't take you long with the fat guy, that's for sure. Man, if the skinny guy had gone for his gun, though, I'd of had to do something, and we coulda wound up with dead people out there. Whoa, whatta rush. Man, the fuckin' adrenalin is coming on, now. It always comes about ten minutes too late.'

Lucas grinned at her: 'About once a year. It cleans out the system.'

'What're you gonna tell the sheriff? I mean, we could be in some trouble.'

Lucas shook his head. 'There's something going on. We know it, and now they know we know. I think we might learn something.'

'Jeez – I wish I hadn't used you up before dinner. I'm serious, here, Lucas, I could really use some help.'

'We might have a couple minutes.'

'It won't take long . . .'

The sheriff showed up a little more than an hour later. Lucas was walking back from the Coke machine with a Diet and a regular Coke, his hair still wet from another shower, when they arrived in two cars: the sheriff, the older deputy named Jimmy, the young, lanky man from the restaurant, all in the sheriff's squad car, and Dr Stephen Landis in a two-year-old Buick.

Lucas continued to the room, pushed through the door, said, 'They're here.'

323

Sherrill tucked her shirt in: she'd been worried the room would smell too much like sex, which she thought would seem perverted so close to the fight – which Lucas told her *was* perverted – so she'd turned up the shower full blast, cold water only, and sprayed it against the back wall of the shower stall. Now the room smelled faintly of chlorine, with a hint of feminine underarm deodorant. 'We're ready,' she said, looking around. 'Put your gun over on the nightstand. That'll look nice and grim. I'll keep mine, but I'll let them see it.' She was wearing her .357 in the small of her back.

He nodded: 'You could be good at this.'

She came over and stood on her tiptoes and kissed him on the lips. 'Remember that,' she said.

The sheriff knocked a second later. Sherrill opened the door and let them in.

'Damn near killed him,' the sheriff said. He was standing in front of the dresser, looking at Lucas, who was sitting on the bed, his back to the head board. The other three men were standing near the door, while Sherrill stood at the head-end of the bed, near Lucas. 'He could still be in trouble.'

'Bullshit. I cracked his short ribs and busted his nose. He won't be sneezing for a month or six weeks, that's all,' Lucas said.

'That's a fairly clinical judgment,' Landis said. 'You must've done this before.'

'I've had a few fights,' Lucas agreed.

'In all my time as sheriff, I haven't had a man hurt that bad, except one who was in a car accident,' the sheriff said. 'We're talking to the county attorney to see if an arrest would be appropriate. We don't want you going any place.'

'We're leaving tomorrow, I think,' Lucas said. 'But we'll be available down in Minneapolis. I'm gonna talk to a couple of friends over at the Bureau of Criminal Apprehension, maybe a guy in the attorney general's office. About coming up here and deposing you people on the murder of George Lamb: to ask you why you've been covering it up all these years. Why you'd send a couple of cops to roust us, in the middle of a murder investigation that you'd been reading about in the *Star-Trib*.'

The sheriff shook his head: 'We didn't send anybody to roust you. These idiots thought of it themselves.' He tipped his head toward the lanky man, who shrugged and looked at the curtains covering the single window.

'The thing is, we can take care of Larry,' the older deputy drawled. 'Cops get beat up from time to time. The real question I got – not the sheriff, just me – is whether you can be talked to. Or if you're just some big city asshole up here to kick the rubes.'

'I've got a cabin outside a town half this size, in Wisconsin. The sheriff's a friend of mine, and he's been bullshitting me about moving up to run for the office when he quits, and I've thought about it. I've worked with a half-dozen sheriffs all over this state and Wisconsin, and this is the first time I've had trouble,' Lucas said. 'You want some references?'

'Already made some calls,' the older man said. After a few seconds' silence, he said, 'You want to talk, or do we do this all legal?'

'Talk,' Lucas said.

The sheriff looked at the older deputy and said, 'You think?'

'Yeah, I think.'

The sheriff nodded and said, 'The thing is, we don't know whether or not George Lamb was murdered. But he might have been.'

'There were some problems at the time, with the way the death happened,' the older man said. 'Happened way too early in the morning. He got up early, for his job, but not in the middle of the night. It looked to us like he'd gotten sick the evening before, and they'd let him lie there until he died.'

'He came to see me twice in the month before he died. He was feeling sicker and sicker, and at first I thought it was the flu. He'd had some diarrhea, he'd had some episodes of vomiting, dizzy spells and so on. We'd had some flu going around at the time, and it fit,' Landis said. He pulled a chair out from the dresser/desk and sat down. 'I gave him some antibiotics for a lung infection he'd developed – nothing serious, he was coughing up some phlegm with pus in it. And we had an argument the second time he came in, and he never came back. Then he dropped dead. *Could* have been a heart attack.'

'But you don't really think so,' Lucas said.

Landis shook his head. 'I think maybe it was rat poison. Arsenic. The thing is, when I went out and looked at this body, he had a rash, a particular kind of rash that flakes off the skin when you've been taking in arsenic for a while.'

'You didn't take any tissue samples?'

'If we'd taken tissue samples, and sent them to a lab, then the fat would be in the fire,' Landis said. 'Other people would know about it . . .'

'You didn't want other people to know?' Sherrill asked.

The sheriff took off his hat, smoothed his hair back, and said, 'My daughter went to high school with the Lamb girls. And the older Lamb girl had a reputation as knowing way too much about sex for a girl her age. Then, a couple of months before George died . . .'

Landis picked it up. 'The mother brought in the older girl, Audrey, to the clinic. Said she'd been fooling around with one of the boys at school, wanted me to keep it quiet, but wanted her tested to see if she was pregnant. She wasn't. But I gave her a little standard lecture that I gave back then, about staying out of trouble, about saying "no" to boys, about using some protection . . . She sort of went along with the lecture until she got tired of it, then she got up and left,' Landis said. 'As she was going out the door, she turned and *looked* at me. The look was like ninety-five percent hate and fear. And she said, "That's all fine and good, but not relevant in my case." '

'Not relevant in my case,' the sheriff quoted. 'Hell of a line for a kid that age. The fact is, George had been fu . . .' He glanced at Sherrill. '. . . having sex with her.'

'When I told you that his wife had some bruises,' Landis said, 'I was telling you the truth. But not all of it. The woman had been beaten from head to foot.'

'The whole goddamn house was a reign of terror,' the sheriff said. 'Steve told me what he thought was going on. I talked to the sheriff at the time, Johnny James, and he told me that there was nothing to do, unless somebody complained. So I caught up with George on his mail route one day and said if I ever heard of him screwing that little girl, I'd kill him.'

'Did he believe you?'

'I don't know, but he should of, 'cause I would of,' the sheriff said. 'But it never came up, because he dropped dead.'

'He was lying there on the floor, looking okay, except for this rash,' Landis said. 'We knew he'd been screwing at least the older girl, and maybe the younger one, too; we knew he'd been beating the bejesus out of his wife. So the question was, do we do tissue samples? Didn't have to. No requirement.'

'Steve came and talked to me, and we said, "screw it." Leave it alone. And we did. Shipped George off to the funeral home. And that was the end of it, until you showed up this morning.'

They all thought about that for a moment, then Lucas rubbed his chin and changed the subject: 'That fat kid I beat up,' he said to the sheriff. 'He's gonna be nothing but a pain in the ass for you. He's gonna be in trouble for the rest of his career.'

'He's had a couple problems,' the sheriff said.

'You oughta get rid of him before it's too late. And this guy,' Lucas said, nodding at the lanky man. 'He rode along a little too easily. He's gotta learn to stand up. He wanted to stop the whole thing, but he couldn't get the job done.'

'I learned something,' the lanky man said.

'I hope the hell you have,' the sheriff said. To Lucas: 'What do you think?'

'I think if you recast exactly what you told me here tonight, you'd have a perfectly good story if you ever had to go to court to testify. You know, that you thought it was a heart attack at the time – still think it was possible – but sometime later worked out that it might have been a poisoning. But by then it was too late, the body had been cremated. That kind of thing happens all the time. That's why we have exhumations.'

'You think we might have to testify?'

Lucas stood up, yawned, stretched. 'We're putting together a circumstantial case. So you might have to. But we've got a way to go, before we get anything together.'

'But her husband . . . the papers say he was beating her, just like her father beat her mother. It seems to me there might be some justification.'

'We're looking at eight murders and several ag assaults over the last ten years, including a couple of out-and-out executions of absolutely innocent people,' Lucas said.

After a moment of stunned silence, the sheriff said, 'Eight?'

Lucas nodded.

'God in heaven.'

And Landis stood up and looked at the sheriff and said,

'Old George did a lot more damage than we knew about. You shoulda killed him.'

The older man pushed himself away from the wall. 'So what're we going to do about tonight?'

Lucas shrugged. 'Nothing happened to me. If you guys want to say nothing happened, nothing happened.'

The sheriff took a quick eye-poll, then nodded to Lucas: 'Nothing happened.'

'If we need to talk to you again, an assistant county attorney'll be calling,' Lucas said. 'I'll give you a warning call ahead of time.'

'I appreciate it,' the sheriff said. 'I'd also appreciate it if you'd get the hell out of my town.'

'We're going tomorrow morning,' Lucas said.

'And I surely wish you hadn't taken Larry out in the parking lot. I'm always short-handed when the snow starts to fly.'

'Sorry.'

'But not too sorry,' the sheriff said.

'Not too,' Lucas agreed, and grinned at him.

The sheriff showed the faintest hint of a smile, and eased out the door. The older man was the last to leave, and at the threshold, he turned and looked at Sherrill, and then back at Lucas. 'I once had a woman looked just about like that,' he said to Lucas. 'When I was just about your age.'

'Oh yeah?'

'Yeah.' He gave Sherrill a long look, and said, 'She flat wore me out.'

'Better to wear out than to rust,' Sherrill said, from her corner.

'Yeah.' And he laughed, a nasty laugh for an old codger, and closed the door.

Chapter Twenty-Seven

The sun was only two or three fingers above the western horizon, the evening rush already starting, when Lucas and Sherrill dropped past the Dunwoody exit on I-394, zigged a couple of times and rolled into downtown Minneapolis.

'Now *that* was a road trip,' Sherrill said, enthusiastically. 'Fightin', fuckin' and detectin'. So what's next?'

'I've got to work tomorrow,' Lucas said. 'You're working, right?'

'Yeah – but there's not much going on. I could probably get away to help, if you needed me . . .'

He shook his head: 'Better not. I told you about the little talk with Rose Marie.'

'I might have a little talk with Rose Marie myself,' she said with a flash of anger. 'Pisses me off.'

'Probably wouldn't help.'

'It'd make me feel better,' Sherrill said.

'Do what you want,' Lucas said. 'And when you get a minute, send me a memo on the whole sequence up there in Oxford. All the details. Make a copy for yourself. Take both copies over to the government center, have them notarized for date, but don't let anybody read them.'

'Just in case?'

'Can't tell what's gonna happen yet.'

'When you say all the details, you want the part where I said, "Oh my God, put it in, put it in?" '

'I don't remember that,' Lucas said.

330

'I think you were looking at your watch. We're gonna have to talk about that, by the way.'

Lucas shook his head: 'Christ, I'm beginning to understand what that old guy meant.'

'What old guy?'

'You know, the old deputy, who once had a woman like you. "Flat wore me out," he said.'

She looked at him critically: 'You still got a little good tread on you.'

Lucas kissed her good-bye outside City Hall – what the hell – and went down to his office, whistling, picked up the phone and got the brrnk-brrnk-brrnk message signal. The mechanical operater said there were six: all six were from Helen Bell, frantic, accusatory.

'Did you do this with Connie? Did you call Child Protection? Why? Why? Please, please call me . . .' and 'Why aren't you calling? Did you do this? I'm getting a lawyer, goddamn you . . .'

He punched in her phone number and the phone at the other end was snatched up halfway through the first ring. 'Hello?' Still frantic.

'This is Lucas Davenport. What happened with Connie?'

A moment of uncertain silence. 'You didn't have anything to do with Connie?'

'Mrs Bell, I haven't even thought of Connie since I last saw you. I was out of town all day yesterday and today, I just got back and got your messages.'

'They came and got her,' she wailed.

'Child Protection?'

'Child protection, child welfare, whatever they call it. They say I gave her marijuana and beat her up and I never did any of that, she's my baby, I don't understand, they said some teacher called, but I can't find anybody at her school.'

'Let me make a call,' Lucas said. 'I know a woman over there who might know something.'

'Please, please get her back.'

Lucas talked to her for another minute, then hung up, found Nancy Bunker's name in his address book, and punched her number in. She was just leaving.

'Yeah, I know about it. Doesn't look like much. The girl said her mother slapped her once during an argument, open hand, no injury, more like a girl fight. Said she's used some marijuana around school but that was what the fight was about. Her mother was trying to stop her.'

'So what're you doing with her?'

'Well, she's out at a foster home right now; we usually keep them a couple of nights, just to make sure. She'll be home tomorrow.'

'Huh.'

'What's your interest, Lucas?'

'Did you ever find the teacher who called in the information?'

'No, it was anonymous, but you know how it is – we don't take chances if there're reports of physical abuse. Especially drugs and physical abuse. And we want to get the kid off to a safe place, where she feels safe about talking about it . . . So, what's your interest?'

'I think you were deliberately set up to mess with the kid's mother. She's a source of mine in this Kresge murder case.'

'Really? Set up?'

'I think so. I don't doubt that the kid smokes a little dope, but then, so did you.'

Bunker laughed. 'Yeah, the good old days. So what do you want me to do?'

'How about releasing the kid to her mother? I'll pick her up, take her home.'

'Damn it; I'd have to sit back down and turn the computer back on . . .'

'Another little tragedy in your life.'

'You gotta be over here in ten minutes,' Bunker said. 'I'm trying to catch a bus.'

'Taking a little undertime, today?'

'Nine minutes, now.'

'Be right there.'

The foster home was in Edina, west of Minneapolis. Lucas picked up the papers for the foster parents, and on the way out, slowed by traffic, Lucas called the Medical Examiner's office and got an investigator on the line. 'I'm looking for a file on an Amelia Lamb. About twenty years old.'

'Nothing here, Lucas. Are you sure of the name?'

'Last name I'm sure of, the first name, I don't know, there may be an alternative spelling.'

After a few more seconds, the investigator said, 'Lots of Lambs, but nothing like an Amelia.'

'Can you get into the state death certificates from your computer?'

'I'd have to call, I could get back to you.'

'Could you do that? This is kind of important.'

The ME's investigator was back five minutes later. 'You want Dakota County, and specifically, you want Mercy South. You want that phone number?'

'Give it to me.' Lucas got the number, the date of Lamb's death and the attending physician, and scribbled it all in his notebook. He called the hospital, spent five minutes working his way through the bureaucracy, and was finally told by an assistant director that he could see the records if he brought a subpoena with him.

'Even if the woman's dead?'

'It's our policy,' she said.

'It's a pain,' Lucas said. 'But I'll get one for you. What's the name of your director out there?'

She gave him the name and he said, 'Ask him to stick around the house tonight, we don't want to have to have a cop run him down. We can probably get the subpoena out there before midnight.'

'Really? I think he and his wife are going to the chamber orchestra.'

'Well – he should be home before we get the subpoena. If we do get it earlier, we'll just ask the orchestra people to page him during the concert.'

'Hang on.'

And *she* was back in five minutes: 'The director tells me that I was misinformed. Since Mrs Lamb is dead, and you're a police officer conducting an official investigation, we can show you the records.' She sounded faintly amused.

'Gee. Thanks. That's really nice. Will somebody be in your records department, about seven o'clock?'

'There's always somebody there. Around the clock.'

'Tell them I'm coming . . .'

Connie Bell started crying when she saw Lucas. She had a small bag with her, and the foster mother patted her on the shoulder, and Connie said, 'Did you do this?'

'No.'

'Then who did?'

'I don't know,' Lucas said, leading the way to the car. 'But it was pretty mean.'

'My mom is really upset, I thought she was going to fight those people last night, I've never seen her like that.'

'Why don't you call her?' Lucas said. 'There's a phone in the car.'

Connie called, told Helen that she was on the way home, and that Lucas was bringing her. She handed Lucas the phone and she said, 'Thank you, thank, thank you . . .'

And when they arrived at Helen's home. Helen ran out and wrapped up her daughter, and they both started crying again and after a moment, Lucas said, 'Could you send Connie inside to get cleaned up? I'd like to talk to you for a moment.'

Connie went, Helen watching her running up the steps.

'Do you have any feeling who might have done this?' Lucas asked.

'There was a literature teacher she had last year, who hated Connie – and several other kids, too. If this was last year, I'd say her. But I can't believe that she'd wait a whole year. I've been racking my brain . . .'

'This is not the way they do things in the school system,' Lucas said. 'They've got a whole bureaucratic procedure they follow, and it's all very routine. This was strange, right from the start. I don't think it was a teacher at all. Could you think, really hard, about who it might be?'

'Okay, okay . . . but you're scaring me. Why?'

'Because it might be related to something else. Anyway, think about it. If you come up with anything, you've got my number.'

'Okay.' She stepped close and gave him a hug. 'Thanks.'

Traffic was beginning to ease as he headed south, down to Dakota County, finally to Mercy South. He went in through the emergency entrance, was directed by a nurse to records, and found a dark-haired young woman sitting in a pool of light from a desk lamp, in an otherwise dark room full of file cabinets and computers. Her feet up next to a computer, she was engrossed in a Carl Hiaasen novel. A stack of what looked like thick textbooks sat on the floor.

'Good book?' he asked in the silence.

She jumped, turned, saw him, looked down at the book and said, 'Yes, as a matter of fact.' She looked at the photo on the back cover. 'And this Hiaasen is a yummy little piece of crumbcake, if I do say so myself . . . You'd be Officer Davenport, and you need some records.'

'That's right.'

'I'm supposed to Xerox your credentials,' she said. She went for the double-entendre: 'You'll hardly feel a thing.'

'Young women these days,' Lucas clucked. He gave her his ID, she Xeroxed it, and said, 'There's not much in the computer file – mostly just the bare bones. If you want to look at her actual file, we don't have the paper anymore, but it's on fiche.'

'I'd like that, if I could.'

'Sure.' She found the right fiche, set him up with a reader, and went back to the novel.

The file was short, and echoed the Oxford's doctor report of symptoms on George Lamb. Amelia Lamb suffered from flu-like symptoms – gastric discomfort, sporadic vomiting. She saw the doctor twice, the visits two weeks apart. The discomfort had increased in the two weeks, and he ordered a number of tests. He noted that her blood pressure was high and that she had been asked to come in for a series of blood pressure tests, but there was no indication that any blood pressure medication had been prescribed. Four days after the second visit, she was brought to the hospital by ambulance, and was reported dead on arrival. The report noted that the daughter reported that she'd been suffering chest pains, but had refused to come to the hospital because of cost, and she'd called only after her mother had collapsed.

'Relative reported that final collapse was accompanied by

severe chest pains and rapid loss of consciousness. Myocardial infarction indicated.' There was no mention of a rash.

Lucas looked at the woman with the book: 'Is there a doctor around that I could talk to? Who'd have a little time?'

'I'm a fourth-year med student,' the woman said. 'What's the question?'

'Look at this blood pressure,' Lucas said. 'Should she have been on medication?'

The woman bent over the screen, read the report, and said, 'She would now. That's definitely way high. But back then, the drugs weren't so good. You'd have to talk to somebody older, who'd remember. But back then, she might not have been.'

'All right: then look at this. On her second visit, they do some tests. But the tests never show up in the records.'

The woman bent over the screen again, skimming through the records: 'You know what?' she said finally. 'It looks like she died before the tests could get back. So when they got back, they probably just tossed them.'

'Huh. And the body was sent directly out to a funeral home.'

'Yup.'

'Why wouldn't they do an autopsy?'

'Again, they didn't do them so often back then. Not for hospital deaths. And, uh, you'd have to keep this under your hat . . . Or at least, not say I told you. I've noticed this in other records . . .'

'Sure.'

'You see this funeral home?' She tapped the screen. 'The predecessor organization to this hospital, which was called Dakota Mothers of Mercy, had a deal with the funeral home. If the relatives didn't express a preference, they'd send the bodies out to this place, and the hospital would get a . . . consideration.'

'A kickback.'

'An emolument. If they sent them into Hennepin, for an autopsy, the body was up for grabs.'

'So there would be a bias against autopsies,' Lucas said.

'Unnecessary autopsies.'

'You shoulda been a lawyer,' Lucas said.

'Not enough money in it.' The woman tapped the screen: 'Here's something else for you. The insurance company called about it. That's the code for Prudential.'

'They called?'

'Yup. That's what that is – the files were sent out in response to a request from Prudential.'

'They send them out to Prudential, but they're gonna make me get a subpoena?'

'This was a long time ago,' the woman said. 'Things were really different.'

The woman went back to the novel while Lucas made notes. When he was finished, he shut down the screen and gave her the fiche. 'Thank you very much,' he said.

She looked up from the desk. 'Do you think if I, like, Xeroxed my breasts and sent a copy to Hiaasen with my phone number, he'd call me up?'

'Certainly worth a try,' Lucas said. 'In fact, I'd recommend that you do it. How else will you know? If you don't, you could be like two ships, passing in the dark.'

'Cops are weird,' she said. But as Lucas left, she was looking at the Xerox machine.

Lucas drove toward home, thinking it all over: he'd call Prudential in the morning, hoping that they'd still have a record of the call. In any case, they must have paid somebody some money, if they bothered to make the call. He'd bet that Audrey was the recipient.

As he crossed the Mendota Bridge, he noticed, for the second or third time, that there was no noise in the background of his brain: no chattering. He'd caught himself whistling again. In the last twenty-four hours, he'd gotten thoroughly laid, hugged by Helen Bell and double-entendre-ed by a nice-looking medical student.

'Glacier's breaking up,' he said aloud. 'Ice is going out.' He wasn't sure what it meant, but it felt right.

Chapter Twenty-Eight

Sherrill saw him walking in, came down to meet him, took his hand. 'Can I take you to dinner tomorrow night?'

'Sure. But things are starting to cook with Audrey McDonald. Shouldn't mess us up, but if something comes up . . .' He was fumbling with his keys, opened the office door. She stepped in behind him.

'Tell me about it,' she said. 'About Audrey.' He told her, and she said, 'Goddamnit. If we weren't sleeping together, you could just come down and tell Frank that you need me to work on this, and I'd get another neat case to work on. Now, we'd sorta have to jump through our asses.'

'Nothing happening yet, anyway,' he said.

'Well, if you're going out to shoot somebody, call me,' she said, as she went out the door.

'Do that.'

Three calls: to Prudential, to the doctor who signed the death certificate, and to the funeral home who handled Amelia Lamb's body.

Prudential was cooperative, but the right guy would have to get back.

The doctor was cooperative, but had no memory of the event at all. 'I was doing a surgical residency and working part-time as an emergency room doc,' he said. 'I worked emergency rooms for seven years and must've signed five hundred of those things. Maybe a thousand. I'm sorry, but I just don't remember.'

The funeral home was confused, but a woman with a quavery, elderly voice finally found the record: Amelia Lamb had been cremated.

'Shit,' Lucas said aloud.

'I beg your pardon?'

The Prudential guy called back a half-hour later, as Lucas was pulling together records on the murders proposed by Helen Bell, as well as the two proposed by Annette Ingall.

'We paid $6,400 on George Bell, which was not an inconsiderable sum at the time; and then four and a half years later, we paid $15,000 on Amelia Bell. That insurance policy had been in effect only three years, which was probably why we called the hospital on it,' the Prudential man said.

'Who was beneficiary on the Amelia Bell policy?'

'Uh, let's see . . . Um, this is an older form . . . an Audrey Bell. Apparently her daughter.'

'Not Audrey and Helen?'

'No, just an Audrey.'

'How about on George Bell?'

'That was . . .'

'Huh. Did Amelia Bell have to take a physical?'

'Um . . . Passed okay.'

'Anything about high blood pressure?'

'Nope. But this form isn't specific – you'd have to see the original doctor's report, and that was so long ago . . .'

'Do you have the doc's name?'

'Yup.'

But the doctor was dead. His son, a dentist, said his father's records had been transferred to other doctors when he gave up his practice, and records not transferred had been stored for ten years, then destroyed.

'Shit.'

'I beg your pardon?'

Lucas went back to the records for an hour, and finally came to a push-comes-to-shove point. If Audrey was guilty of all of this, then she must have killed O'Dell. But according to the investigative records, signed off by Franklin and Sloan, she left the building before O'Dell was killed. That was confirmed: she logged out of the building at ten-fifty-three. Two people visiting their son in the building, who had logged out after her, confirmed that they had left just as *Nightline* was ending. *Nightline* ended a couple of minutes before eleven, and they were shown as logging out at eleven, while O'Dell was confirmed killed at eleven-oh-two.

It was possible, of course, that Audrey was a master burglar and that she had some way of getting into a building with a security desk in the lobby. Or that she had somehow obtained a key-card for the elevator. But the first of those possibilities seemed laughable, while the second was only barely reasonable – she wouldn't have had much time to plan the killing of O'Dell, unless the killing was part of a long-range plan.

He thought about that for a moment. Maybe she did have a long-range plan. Maybe she had access to everybody she might ever need to kill. Then he shook his head. Couldn't think that way. If she was working off a long-range plan, which had somehow involved getting home keys for all her possible victims, then she was a perfect killer and they were out of luck.

He glanced at his watch, punched up his computer, and wrote a memo, with copies to Frank Lester, head of the investigative division, and Rose Marie Roux.

Halfway through, a sheriff's deputy called from Itasca County. 'You called yesterday about the Baird case?'

'Yeah, thanks for calling back,' Lucas said. 'How well do you know the case?'

'I was lead investigator,' the deputy said. 'I pretty much know it all.'

'I understand it was a firebombing,' Lucas said. 'A Molotov cocktail.'

'Yeah, that's right. A mix of gas and oil in a gallon jug,' the deputy said.

'Was there anything weird about the bottle?' Lucas asked.

After a moment of pregnant silence, the deputy said, 'Like what?'

'Like scoring? Like with a glass cutter?'

Another beat. Then, 'How'n the hell did you know about that? We never put it in the report . . .'

When he was done with the memos, Lucas printed them and walked them down to Roux's office and left them with the secretary. Homicide was just down the hall, so he stopped by.

Sherrill was at her desk: 'Lunch?'

She was sitting next to Sloan, who was eating a corn-beef sandwich. 'If you don't think people'll think you're fucking me,' she said, just loud enough for Sloan to hear.

Sloan never flinched. 'Let's go,' Lucas said. And to Sloan: 'Have you got an hour, in an hour or so? To go over to O'Dell's place, and look around?'

'Sure.'

Lucas and Sherrill walked down the street to a cop hangout, got sandwiches, and Sherrill said, 'I hope I can get past this wise-mouth stuff with you. I've been a wise-ass ever since we got together and I'm having a hard time getting off that wavelength.'

'I'll recite you a poem some time,' Lucas said. 'It makes

women feel all gooshy and tender; they roll right over on their backs.'

'You just did it to me.'

'What?'

'Wise-assed me. I heard you read poetry. I always thought it was neat. Now you wise-assed it.'

'Yeah.' He looked up at her, serious now. 'I'm sorry I wise-assed it. I do like poetry, and I do like reading some of it to women.'

'Say a poem to me.'

He thought, and then said, slowly, 'It was Din, Din, Din you limpin' lump of . . .'

'Get the fuck out of here,' she said. 'You did it again.'

'We gotta do something about this,' he said, grinning at her. 'I really am serious. We've got to have at least one honest talk. Penalties for any wise-ass remarks.'

'Tomorrow night. For dinner.'

'Tomorrow,' he agreed.

Sherrill's phone rang, and she took it out of her purse, listened, and handed it to him: 'Rose Marie. Christ, she knew right where to call.'

Lucas put the phone to his ear. 'Yeah?'

'I didn't interrupt a tender moment, did I?'

'Yeah. I was about to bite into a cheeseburger.'

'I called Towson about your memo. He wants to meet.'

'It's too soon.'

'No, it's not. I'm sending a copy over for him to read. You should get over there at two o'clock. Frank is gonna go along. From the memo, I don't think we're likely to get her unless she kills somebody else. So you guys are gonna have to figure something out.'

Lucas dropped Sherrill back at the office, picked up Sloan,

and they walked together over to O'Dell's apartment building. The security guard recognized Sloan and sent them up.

'The basic problem is, if you go down in the elevator, you can't get back up without a key-card,' Sloan said. 'Even if you have a key-card, there's a monitor camera in the elevator, so a guard might recognize you . . . not that they spend a lot of time looking at the monitor,' Sloan said, as they got in the elevator.

'So she gets off at another floor . . .'

'Nope. Can't get off at another floor. If you get in at the lobby, you can go to any one floor. If you get in at any other floor, you can only go down to the lobby. Unless you have a key-card.'

'How about the fire stairs?'

'The doors are locked in the lobby and the skyway. From those floors, you can't get in without a key, you can only get out. And you can't get out on any floor except the lobby or the skyway, even if you have a key.'

'A key, not a key-card,' Lucas said.

'That's right – like a Schlage.'

'How close do they track the cards?'

'They know how many each person is signed out for. O'Dell had three, two for herself, and one for her father, who lives way the hell out in South Dakota. We found her two cards, and her father still had his when he was here to pick up the body. So that was all of hers. But somebody else in the building? Who knows? There are almost three hundred cards out. I suppose we could try to find all of them . . . I'd guess a few are missing. The problem is, figuring out how the McDonalds might have gotten one.'

'Huh. If it was all arranged ahead of time, we're fucked, anyway. What if she had to do it off the top of her head? Maybe a day's thought?'

Sloan shrugged. 'You figure it out.'

They got off on O'Dell's floor, and Lucas stood with his back to the door of her apartment. 'She went down first, then she had to get back up to kill her.'

'Right.'

Lucas looked at the elevator: 'Even if she's got a key-card, there's a problem coming back up to kill O'Dell. She can't guarantee the guard won't look at the monitor out of sheer boredom, if he sees movement on the screen. If he does, she's dead meat. He's just seen her leave, and now she's going up to kill somebody. Therefore . . .'

'She doesn't use the elevator, she uses the stairwell,' Sloan said. 'She has a Schlage key for the door in the skyway. She signs out of the building, runs across the street to the skyway, goes up, walks across the skyway to the skyway fire-door, uses her Schlage to get into the stairwell, walks up here. Where you have a problem: she can't get out of the stairwell. There's no key at all that'll get you out of the stairwell onto another floor. You can only get out in the skyway or the lobby.'

Lucas worked on it for a moment. 'Like this,' he said finally. 'She knows she doesn't have the votes to make a real deal with O'Dell: she claims she's got them, but Bone says she didn't, and she knows she doesn't. She's come here specifically to kill O'Dell – she knows that when she gets here. She can't just sneak up and do it, because she doesn't have any key. She doesn't have anything. So she calls O'Dell to talk about making a deal, and her only purpose is to get into the building. So she gets out of the elevator, and right when she arrives, before she talks to O'Dell, she walks over to the fire-door, opens it, takes some duct tape out of her purse, tapes the lock, walks down the stairs to the skyway, opens that door, tapes it, and then comes back up here and rings the doorbell.

'O'Dell answers it, they talk, the deal falls through, and she leaves. O'Dell sees her into the elevator, and she goes down through the lobby and signs out,' Sloan said.

'Then she runs across the street, comes up into the skyway, goes in through the taped door, runs up the stairs, knocks on the door, and boom. She has to do it then – even though she knows we'll look at her – because she can't count on the tape being left on the door for more than a short time.'

'Which explains something,' Sloan said. 'O'Dell told Louise Compton that there was "somebody at the door," which meant that she didn't know who was at the door, which meant that she didn't know who'd be arriving. She wasn't expecting anyone, like a boyfriend. There was no easy explanation for that knock, at least, not in her mind.'

'So Audrey shoots her, checks her to make sure she's dead, runs back down the stairs, carefully pulling the tape off the locks . . . and goes home.'

'Fuckin' cold, man,' Sloan said.

'She *is* cold. I wonder if she was cold enough to wash the sticky stuff off the doors, when she pulled off the tape? She'd need acetone, or something,' Lucas said.

They were both staring at the fire-door. Sloan reached out to the door knob, pulled the door open, bent forward to look at the lock tongue, then knelt. Lucas squatted beside him.

'Looks like sticky stuff,' Sloan said. He tapped his index finger next to what looked like gray tape residue.

'Wonder how many movers have gone in and out, using tape?'

'Up this high? None. That's why the elevator's so big. And I think this stuff would wear away, if the door was opened and closed on it enough. So it's probably fairly new.'

'Let's get crime scene over here,' Lucas said, standing up. 'And let's get a search warrant ready, see if we can find some tape at her place that matches this sticky stuff – if the lab guys can make a match like that.'

On the way back down in the elevator, Sloan said, 'It's a reach.'

'*She's* a reach. She looks like Old Mother Hubbard and she's really the Wicked Witch of the West.'

The Hennepin County attorney, Randall Towson, his chief deputy, Donald Dunn, and Richard Kirk, head of the criminal division met with Lucas and Frank Lester, deputy chief and head of the investigative division.

'You're telling us she's a serial killer,' Towson said.

'Everything points to it,' Lucas said. 'I'm not sure we could prove it to a jury.'

'Make the argument.'

'You've all seen the memo. The major point is this: we have too many unusual deaths. First, her parents. She benefited directly from the death of her mother – a $15,000 life insurance policy that her sister apparently didn't share in. She probably got insurance from the death of her father – her mother was weak, and Audrey seemed to be running things, even then, as a kid. We also have four obvious and un-questioned murders: George Arris, shot in the back of the head in St Paul; Daniel Kresge, who, you all know, was shot while deer hunting last week; Wilson McDonald, who she admits shooting to death, and Susan O'Dell, who was shot to death in her apartment. Audrey McDonald was the last person known to have been with O'Dell.'

'I'd think that would almost be exculpatory, from what I get from your memo,' Kirk said. 'She could prove that she was out of the building before the killing happened.'

'Things have changed in the last hour, since I wrote the memo,' Lucas said. 'Detective Sloan and I have worked out a

---

way she might have done it. There might even be the possibility of some physical evidence . . .'

'How . . .'

He explained quickly about the duct tape, then said, 'Let me finish this other thought,' Lucas said. 'In addition to her parents and the four outright murders, we also have four mysterious deaths: Andy Ingall disappeared and has never been found after a supposed boating accident; eleven-year-old Tom McKinney was killed while riding his bicycle; and Mr and Mrs Sheldon Baird were burned to death in their cabin. We also have two aggravated assaults in the past two weeks. One was on my former fiancée, Weather Karkinnen; her house was firebombed, you've probably read about it. Normally, I wouldn't suggest that there was a tie, but I would here. You can read the full reasoning in the memo – Audrey has a history of attacking people to distract, as well as to eliminate, and I believe that's what she did here. We even have some evidence for this.'

'And it is . . .'

'When Mr and Mrs Baird were burned to death, investigators found the remnants of a glass jug in their front room, and the glass had been scored to make sure the bottle broke on impact,' Lucas said. 'That feels like a pro job – but it happens that when my fiancée was firebombed, remnants of bottle used in that bombing show the same kind of scoring.'

'Jesus Christ,' Towson said.

'Then, last week, another friend of mine was attacked, Sister Mary Joseph, from St Anne's College. As it happens, Audrey McDonald knew her. And presumably knew where she lived, and attacked her for the same reason she attacked Weather. To get me off her back.'

'And you can show that she benefited from all of these,' Dunn said.

'She benefited financially from the killings of her father and mother – in addition to the money, she may have killed her father because he was sexually and probably physically abusing her, and she got rid of him. All the other deaths were done to push her husband's career: when you put them down in outline form, you'll find that he benefited from each of the other deaths . . . look at page three of the memo, there's a chart.'

'What about her husband?'

'I think her husband was killed because we were getting too close, and he was a rather notorious coward. If he knew about the killings, he might have ratted her out, if there was pressure. Also, she inherits if she's found not guilty of murdering him. Running through his files after he was killed, we figured he could be worth about seven-eight million.'

'I see one problem,' Towson's deputy said, snapping the paper with his finger. 'If I remember right, you guys had elected Wilson McDonald for the Kresge killing. Looking at this, I ask myself, couldn't McDonald have done all of these? We know he was a brutal asshole. Look what he did to his own wife.'

'It's worse that that,' Lester said. 'St Paul's got a partial print, probably made by McDonald, on a shell from the gun that killed Arris.'

'Not good,' said Towson.

'No – but all that proves is that McDonald loaded the gun. I'll also say that when O'Dell was shot in the head, it seems that the bullet might have come from the same gun. We can't prove the gun-slug connection, because the slug, a hollow-point, came apart in her head, and there was nothing left but fragments. But a spectroscopic analysis of the metal from the slug in O'Dell's head, and from the traces of a slug in the Arris killing, suggest both came from the same batch of lead.

We also have the gun – taken out of a car owned by McDonald, but not driven by him since September – and the clip was full. But all the shells had his prints on them but the last two. The lead from those two came from a different batch, but the lead from the shells in the lower part of the magazine came from the same batch – probably the same batch – as the slugs that killed Arris and O'Dell.'

'You'd drive a jury nuts with this stuff,' said the criminal division guy.

'There's another point here. I think I can demonstrate by the recorded times of some cell-phone calls that Wilson McDonald couldn't have killed O'Dell. And if he couldn't have killed her, then somebody else who knew where the gun was, must have. Audrey McDonald. And like I said, I think we can show how it was done.'

'But you can't definitively prove that was the gun that killed O'Dell.'

'No.'

'That's a problem,' Towson said.

They all sat in silence for a minute, then Kirk said, 'Pattern.'

Everybody nodded. Dunn said, 'Pattern, plenty of motive, we knock down any sympathy she might get with the killing of her mother . . .'

'Which is more than balanced off by the fact that her mother apparently stood by while her father was fucking her,' Kirk said. 'The defense puts a weeping woman on the stand who denies doing anything, but points out that if she did – which she didn't – it certainly would have been justified, a fourteen-year-old girl getting the ol' pork trombone from her own father. Matter of fact, if I was the defense attorney, I'd make the mother an accomplice. If Audrey's as smart as this stuff makes her, she wouldn't need too much of a hint to come up with something pretty lurid.'

'Which, if we could drive a wedge between Audrey and her sister, we might get the sister to refute . . . is the sister as whacko as Audrey?'

'No. But there was a complaint filed with Child Protection a couple of days ago that she beat her daughter and gave her dope,' Lucas said.

'Aw, Jesus.'

'But not justified,' Lucas said. 'In fact, I think Audrey filed it.'

'Goddamn this woman.'

'I'm sure He will,' Lester said drily. 'But it'd be nice if we could get a few whacks in first.'

Towson leaned over his desk, looking at his deputy and the head of his criminal division: 'I'll tell you what, boys. We're faced here with the usual sloppy police work that virtually ties us hand and foot, even as we have to take our cases before drooling liberal judges who don't wish for anything finer than putting criminals back on the street where they can rape our Cub Scouts. However . . .'

'I wish I'd said that,' Lester said.

'Part of a speech I'm writing,' Towson said. 'Seriously, Lucas, do you think she's gonna kill anyone else in the next few days?'

'I don't know who'd it be,' Lucas said. 'Me, maybe – but I'm careful.'

'You *be* careful,' Towson said. 'She apparently likes guns . . . Now listen. I'm looking through this memo, and I'm convinced. A trial is something else. Give me another few days' work on this thing. Nail down that stuff about O'Dell. Give me something harder. Work out a really tight timetable, and find a way we can put her there to pull the trigger. And anything else. Even people willing to suggest that she did it. We need more hard evidence: anything would help.'

'What're you going to do?'

'I'm thinking that we might charge her with everything,' Towson said. 'All the murder counts, all the ag assaults. Put all the evidence together, argue the pattern. Then, probably, we'll lose most of them. But we'll have a chance of getting her for killing her husband, if we can make it part of the pattern. Because she's admitted it. The jury might let her go on the other ones, for lack of specific evidence, but we might get her on at least second degree, and maybe first, on her husband.'

'She was pretty beat up,' Lucas said. 'They took pictures.'

'We can handle that, if we can make the other things clear enough. If we get her on just second degree on her husband, and then whisper sweet nothings to the judge, he could blow off the guidelines, depart upward on the sentence and put her away for twenty.'

They all looked at each other, then Kirk said, 'Right now, Lucas, I'd say it's sixty-forty against. It'd be nice if you could come up with something a little stronger. Give us another twenty percent, or so.'

'It'd be nice,' Towson said.

'I'll hit her tonight with a search warrant on the duct tape, maybe look for a glass cutter,' Lucas said.

'Talk to us,' Towson said. 'We want to know every move from here on out.'

Chapter Twenty-Nine

A udrey McDonald was packing Wilson's suits into cardboard boxes, after carefully noting labels, estimated cost – which she'd have to confirm with the tailor – and condition, all toward a tax deduction. The accountant had recommended a donation to Goodwill.

She didn't like the idea of Goodwill, but she did like the idea of the tax deduction. Still, she was muttering to herself as she did it. Shaking her head. Wilson had spent a fortune on clothing, and now she'd get only a fraction of it back. Nothing for the underwear. Perfectly good boxer shorts, and some bum was going to get them.

'So reckless,' she muttered. 'Just didn't care. Just didn't care what you spent on this. Look at this. Fourteen, fifteen, sixteen pairs of undershorts. Why would you need all those undershorts? You could have gotten by with three pairs, or five pairs. Sixteen pairs of undershorts. Look at this. This is silk. Silk undershorts?'

She was counting them again when the headlights swung into the driveway, glowing through the bedroom drapes. Helen? She hadn't called. She always called before she came. But who else? She went to the window and looked down.

Lucas and Sherrill waited as Sloan pulled into the driveway with Del in the passenger seat; a squad car followed a few seconds behind Sloan, with two uniformed cops. Lights shone from several windows in the house, both upstairs and down, and Lucas handed the warrant papers to one of the uniformed cops, who walked up the stoop, rang the doorbell and knocked.

'All glass cutters, all packages of tape, all one-gallon glass jugs, all guns, cartridges and/or cartridge parts, to include gunpowder, primers, brass and bullets, all credit card records or billing statements involving gasoline purchases,' he read, in the light coming through the window in the door. There was no answer, so he rang again, then opened the storm door and pounded. Still no answer.

'What do you want to do?' he asked.

'We're going in,' Lucas said. 'Let's not break anything yet. Let's check the garage doors.'

The front door rattled and the cop at the door stepped back. A moment later, Audrey McDonald stuck her head out. 'What?' she croaked. She looked worse than she'd looked in court: the bruises on her face were a sickly bluish-yellow, with small reddish splotches. She still wore the bandages on her head, and her visible hair looked like broom straw.

'I'm sorry, ma'am,' the cop said. 'We have a search warrant for your house, for certain items.'

He handed her the papers, and she took them, peered at them querulously. 'A search warrant? Can you wait until I call my lawyer?'

'No, ma'am. You're welcome to call your attorney, of course, but the warrant is served and we'll have to come in.'

Her eyes drifted past the cop to Lucas, who'd begun to feel sorry for the woman: but when her eyes landed on him, they hardened into small black diamonds, like a cobra's, and he leaned back, though he was ten feet from her. 'Okay,' she muttered, breaking her eyes away. 'But do I have to do anything? I feel awfully bad.'

'You just go sit down, and we'll do all of it,' the cop said.

She disappeared inside and the cop looked over his shoulder

at Lucas. Lucas said quietly, 'Keep an eye on her. She's not what she looks like.'

The McDonalds had a small cluttered workshop area in one corner of the basement, nothing more than an old chest of drawers with two, two-by-eight-foot sheets of three-quarter-inch plywood screwed together to make the top of a small workbench, and a couple of steel shelving units with plastic boxes for storage.

Lucas had seen the workshop the first time in the house, after Wilson McDonald was shot. He went straight to it, checked all the tools. No glass cutter. He found a roll of black plastic electricians' tape, which he bagged, but that seemed unlikely to be the tape they wanted. He walked once around the basement, looking behind the water heater, the furnace, through racks of paint cans and a pile of hoses and miscellaneous gardening equipment: no gallon glass jugs.

Del was working the kitchen. When Lucas came back up the stairs, he said, 'Got lots of tape. Duct, plastic mending, bunch of it.'

'Good. Bag it up,' Lucas said. 'Check the wastebaskets and her car, see if you come across any small balls of tape that might be the right length. Two would be good.' He went on through the living room, found that the carpet had been removed. Wilson McDonald's blood hadn't seeped through to the wooden floor, which looked freshly waxed.

Sloan had run quickly through the bedroom, not expecting to find much, and had moved on to a large, first-floor guest room which had a walk-in closet the McDonalds used for general storage. This was where Audrey McDonald had gotten the shotgun with which she'd killed her husband. The closet was jammed with motoring, golf, and boating equipment, all of it apparently belonging to Wilson McDonald. The homicide cops investigating the shooting of Wilson McDonald had taken the gun and shells, but hadn't dug into the back of the closet. Sloan hauled everything out, found nothing of special interest, and then, as an afterthought, was patting down the weather gear, life jackets, golf and hunting jackets.

Just as Lucas walked in, he felt a heavy lump in the pocket of a golf jacket, and manipulated it out through the layers of cloth. Box of cartridges.

'Gimme a bag,' he said to Lucas.

'What is it?'

'Boo-lets,' he said.

Lucas held the transparent plastic bag and Sloan manipulated the box into it. Lucas turned the box on its side and read, '.380 Remington. Excellent.'

Sloan stood up and said, 'It'd be nice if her prints were on the box.'

'Yeah, but I'm not holding my breath.'

One of the uniformed cops stuck his head in the door: 'Del says, no glass cutter in the kitchen. No gallon jugs, either.'

'Okay . . . check the garage.'

At the end of an hour, they still had no glass cutter or gallon jugs, but did have nine rolls of tape and the box of cartridges. Sherrill had been going through the house files again, and had pulled out a stack of Amoco credit car receipts; the McDonalds shared a single account, but the cards had separate numbers. 'If they go back far enough, look for credit card charges in the Duluth area in the days before Ingall disappeared,' Lucas said. 'We found an Amex charge in Chicago, the day before, for Wilson . . .'

'They go back that far . . .' She started flipping through them.

A little more than an hour after the search started, McDonald's attorney showed up. 'What's going on?'

Lucas said, 'Search warrant. Mrs McDonald has a copy. She's in the TV room.' He pointed him through to the TV room, and Glass asked, 'You really think there's something going on here?'

'I ain't doing it for the exercise,' Lucas said. 'You've got a problem, I think.'

Glass wandered off to find McDonald, and the uniform cop came back from the garage: 'No jugs, no glass cutter.'

'Gonna have to give up on the jugs,' Lucas said. 'The glass cutter could be anywhere, if she didn't throw it away. Anybody look in the silverware drawer?'

Del looked at the cop, and they both shook their heads.

'Watch this,' Lucas said. He pulled open drawers near the sink, until he found the silverware drawer, then pulled that out all the way and stirred through the silverware. Nothing. Same with the cooking utensils drawer. Nothing.

'Fuck it,' he said, pushing the drawers shut.

'The guy is a genius,' the uniform cop said to Del, who nodded.

Sherrill came out of the back, carrying an Amoco billing statement. 'Got something,' she said.

'Duluth?' Lucas asked hopefully.

'No. But Audrey filled up on successive mornings, the day before Ingall disappeared, and the day he disappeared. So sometime in that twenty-four hours, she drove off a tank of gas.'

'Huh,' Lucas said. 'She could've been filling somebody else's car, or Wilson's car.'

'Wilson filled up that night.'

Lucas nodded: 'All right. That's something. That's a straw, and we need straws.'

'And that's about all we got,' Del said. 'I'd bet you anything that door in O'Dell's apartment was taped with duct tape, and we found duct tape, but I bet there's a roll of duct tape in every goddamn house in the city. A jury's gonna blow that off.'

Glass had been walking back through the house, Audrey McDonald limping along a step behind him, and he heard Del's last comment: 'Jury's gonna blow off what?' he asked.

'Just . . . nothing,' Del muttered.

'Mrs McDonald says she thinks you, specifically, Chief Davenport, have targeted her for a personal attack. We'd hate to think that was true.'

'You know that's bullshit,' Lucas said to Glass – and then his eyes skipped beyond Glass to Audrey McDonald, who was peering at him with her snake's eye.

'It *is* true, and I know why,' she said. 'Because if you can pin something on me, then Wilson's father will inherit, and his father and his father's friends run everything down there at City Hall.'

Lucas was shaking his head: 'I don't even know Wilson's father.'

'Oh, bullshit,' she snapped, picking up Lucas' word. But she looked so gray, so old-lady-like, that hearing the vulgarity tripping so easily from her tongue was almost shocking. 'There's no way that he's going to let McDonald money get out of that goddamned family.'

'Mrs McDonald . . .' Glass cautioned, but Lucas was becoming interested. Audrey McDonald was not quite visibly shaking, but he could sense it in her: she was very close to the boil, but he didn't know what would happen if she did tip over the edge. So he pushed a little.

'Mrs McDonald – can I call you Audrey?'

'No, you may not.'

'Audrey, we know you killed your father, and we know why. We even know why you killed your mother, I'm sorry to say. For the money. It's not so clear that you killed all the others, but we think we've got a pretty good list, and stuff is beginning to turn up.' He picked up a bag on the kitchen counter, with a roll of duct tape sealed inside. 'You didn't use this duct tape on Susan O'Dell's doors, did you? Because if you did, our lab will be able to tell . . .'

'Lucas, Lucas . . .' Glass was sputtering, but Lucas wasn't looking at him. He was watching Audrey, the gray-faced, self-effacing little brown beetle, who was shuffling up to her attorney's elbow, then past him, and she said, 'My parents, my parents . . .'

'. . . and we know you went to Duluth the day before Andy Ingall disappeared, and that you fired that Contender pistol of Kresge's, the one that killed him, and . . .'

And Audrey launched herself at him, so quickly that Lucas was surprised, unable to quite fend her off without hurting her. Her right hand, hard and bony as a crow's foot, caught the skin at the side of his throat and when he wrenched away he felt her fingernails slicing through the skin; then Sherrill had Audrey around the waist and heaved her back, and Glass wrapped her up. 'You fucking . . .' Audrey hissed, still struggling to get at him, her black eyes fixed on Lucas. 'You fucking . . . you talk to that fucking sister of mine . . .'

'Jesus, Lucas, you're bleeding,' Sherrill said.

'Get me some toilet paper or something,' Lucas said, watching Audrey McDonald as her struggles subsided.

'Gonna ruin your shirt,' Sherrill said, coming back with a box of tissue paper. She pulled out a wad of tissue and pressed it against his neck.

'Worth it,' he said, watching Glass wrestle Audrey McDonald back toward the TV room. He looked around. 'Are we about done here?'

'Another hour, if we really think that glass cutter is here somewhere,' Del said.

'Keep looking,' Lucas said. 'I'm gonna take off.'

'I better come along,' Sherrill said. 'You're pretty cut up.'

'All right,' Lucas said. To Del, 'You and Sloan figure it out from here.'

'You going home?' Del asked.

Lucas could feel the blood seeping through the tissue. 'No. I'm gonna go talk to that fucking sister of hers.'

Helen and Connie Bell were watching television when Lucas and Sherrill arrived. Helen opened the door, smiled at Lucas, nodded at Sherrill, then frowned and said, 'Good God, what happened to you? Are you hurt?'

'Um . . . your sister scratched me. Sort of blew up.'

'Why? Well . . . come in. Why were you talking to Audrey?'

Connie Bell turned backward on an easy chair to listen to the conversation: Lucas, Sherrill and Helen were standing in the entryway, and Lucas said, 'I've got some fairly bad news, I think. Uh, maybe you'd rather get it in a more formal way . . .'

'No, no, no, tell me.'

Lucas nodded. 'We think it's possible that, uh, your sister may have committed some of the murders you listed in your letter to me.'

Helen took a step back, one hand going to her throat. 'Audrey? Oh, no.'

'Could we, uh, could we sit down, I just have a couple of things,' Lucas said.

'The couch.'

They stepped into the front room, and Lucas and Sherrill sat on the couch while Helen leaned against the chair where Connie was sitting. Lucas said, 'If you want Connie to go do homework or something . . .'

'No way,' Connie said. To her mother: 'I'm old enough to stay.'

Her mother looked at her for a moment, then nodded. 'You can stay.'

Lucas looked at Sherrill, and then asked, 'When you were younger, was there ever anything . . . did you think anything was odd about the way your father died? Or your mother.'

Helen looked at them in stunned silence, then said, 'My father was an evil man. We don't talk about him.'

'We know about, uh . . . we know about Audrey,' Lucas said.

'What about Audrey?' Connie asked.

Lucas looked at Helen, who blinked rapidly, shook her head, then turned to Connie and said, 'My father molested us when we were children. Audrey, mostly; but I got some of it, too. He never made me do anything with him, like he did with Audrey, but it was coming. He'd . . . handle me. But Audrey was four years older and that protected me.'

'Jeez,' Connie said.

'Do you remember the night your father died?' Lucas asked.

Again, Helen seemed stunned. Then she nodded, slowly. 'I didn't know what was going on until the sheriff came – Mom wouldn't let me get out of bed. But I knew my father was sick, that's what they said up the stairs to me, Mom and Audrey.'

'Was he sick for a while, or was it a sudden attack?' Lucas asked.

'He was sick for a long time, I think, more than a week . . . I don't know, exactly, I was only ten . . . but for a long time. Then the night that he died . . . God, it was cold, it was already snowing up there, that's one thing I remember about it. The wind used to whistle through that old farm house. It was a bad place. And I heard him having a terrible argument with Audrey, before I went to bed. We slept in the same bedroom, Audrey and I . . . Then, I don't think anybody went to bed. I heard him groaning, and in the bathroom, that's the last thing I remember about him – being in the bathroom. Then he was quiet, and then I think I went to sleep, and the next thing I knew, people were banging around and cars were coming, and he was dead.'

'Had Audrey ever come up to bed?'

Helen looked down at her daughter, then at Lucas. 'I don't think so. I don't think she ever came upstairs that night. She was downstairs, I think, taking care of him . . .'

'Huh. Okay. What about your mother?'

'Mother was . . . ruined . . . by my father. It was like there was no person left. I used to think, this is what a slave would be like, after they beat all the resistance out of him. "Do this," "Yes master," "Do that," "Yes master." She was like a rag.'

'And she died . . . was Audrey there when she died?'

'Yes. We both were. I think she had the flu, she was sick to her stomach, and sometimes she'd start vomiting, and Audrey would keep her in bed and spoon-feed her. And then one night she passed out, and Audrey called the hospital. She died on the way.'

'Your mother and father were both cremated,' Lucas said. 'Was that Audrey's idea?'

'Yes.'

'You didn't keep the ashes, by any chance.'

'No . . . Mom used to walk over to a park that was a mile or so from our house, down here in Lakeville, and we didn't know any cemeteries, so Audrey just said it would be nice to sprinkle her around the trees in the park, she'd be there forever as part of the trees.'

After a moment of silence, she said, 'You think she killed them? Poisoned them, or something?'

Lucas nodded. 'I think it's very possible. The insurance payments . . .'

Helen shook her head: 'There wasn't any insurance, as far as I know.'

Lucas said, 'Huh.' Then, 'What happened after your mother died?'

'Well, we couldn't stay together. Audrey was barely eighteen, and so I went off to my aunt's home until I was of age. She got a scholarship and went to college. I worked my way through a tech school, a business course . . . and then she married Wilson and everything.'

Lucas said, 'I know this probably comes as a shock. But, if it would be possible . . . and I honest-to-God think you should do this . . . if I come over with a stenographer and an assistant county attorney, could we sit here some night this week and go over the whole thing? Your whole history? In a really detailed way.'

Helen said, 'I can't believe that Audrey . . .'

'Yes, you can,' said Connie. 'I told you, she's a mean old witch under all of that pretend stuff.'

'Connie . . .' Her mother looked a warning at her.

But Connie said to Lucas, 'Why'd you want to know about grandma's ashes?'

'Well, just a thing,' Lucas said.

'What thing?' Connie persisted.

'If your grandmother was poisoned, a lab analysis of ashes might turn something up.'

Connie looked up at her mother, and Helen frowned at her and said, 'What?'

'How about that lock of hair on her picture? You said you cut it off the day she died.'

Helen put her fingertips to her mouth. 'Oh, that's right. I'd forgotten, completely.' To Lucas: 'Would a lock of hair help?'

Lucas shrugged. 'I don't know.'

Sherrill, who'd been sitting quietly, finally chipped in. 'The doc up in Oxford thought George Lamb was killed with arsenic. If Amelia was killed the same way, and it sounds pretty similar, then it would show up in hair.' They all looked at her, and she said, 'I read about it.'

Lucas turned back to Helen.

'Could we have the hair?'

Chapter Thirty

At ten minutes after midnight, Audrey was still packing. The cops had gone, taking a small box of miscellaneous junk with them. It wouldn't amount to anything, she thought. Tape? Everybody had tape – though she wished she'd taken a minute to clean those doors after killing O'Dell. But she'd never even thought of it.

On the bright side, she *had* thrown away the glass cutter. It was lying somewhere on the shoulder of I-94, gone forever. On the down side, she hadn't thrown it away after she'd bombed the Bairds. She'd thrown it away after she'd hit Karkinnen, but only because she hadn't thought she'd need it again. She hadn't *thought* about evidence.

She hadn't thought about it since the cremation of her mother. With all the other killings, if she'd been caught, she would've been caught, and that would have been that. There hadn't seemed any point in worrying about evidence, except in the most gross ways – don't leave any fingerprints, don't buy any guns.

She'd have to start thinking.

She'd gotten to Wilson's sweaters. He'd spent a fortune on sweaters, though they'd made him look the size of an oil tanker. He'd thought they made him look like a football lineman; in fact, they'd made him look even fatter than he was. 'Three hundred dollars for a sweater. I remember when you told me that, I couldn't believe it. Three hundred dollars. And it's not just the three hundred dollars; if we'd saved it, if we'd put it in Vanguard, it would have tripled by now.'

Lights in the driveway. She froze. Cops again? She drifted for a few seconds: she hated the police: that Davenport, he was the devil in this deal. A year from now, if she could find a gun, she'd take care of him, all right. Give it a year or a little more, and then one night, maybe in January, when people's doors were shut and windows were closed, she'd wait by his house. If she could find a gun like the one she'd used on Kresge: now that was a wonderful gun. Wonderful . . .

And snapped back. A car in the driveway. She hurried to the window, looked down, and saw Helen walking across the driveway toward the front door. Helen? She hadn't called.

A thought struck her. Helen had been talking to Davenport again. She turned and hurried toward the stairway, as the doorbell rang downstairs.

Helen looked strange: ordinarily neat, her hair was in disarray, her face pinched, her mouth tight. She didn't take off her coat, but simply stood in the entryway.

'I don't really know how to ask you this, Audrey. I'll just tell you what Chief Davenport told me. He thinks you killed Mom and Dad. Poisoned them. I told him I didn't think you did, and then I thought about it all evening and finally thought I better come over.'

'Mom and Dad? Mom and Dad? Do you think I killed Mom and Dad?' Audrey was horrified, even as the small kernel in the back of her brain hardened around her secret knowledge.

'I . . . don't think so,' Helen said, but her eyes drifted away. When they came back, she said, 'Chief Davenport thinks that's why they were cremated. To cover up.'

'That's ludicrous,' Audrey snapped. 'Davenport is all tied up with Wilson's father; they're trying to keep me from the money. Wilson's money will go to his father, you know, if they decide I've committed a crime. That's all it is: it's about money.'

Helen looked at her for another moment, a little too coolly, Audrey thought, then said, 'Okay. I just had to ask. Chief Davenport asked me not to talk to you, so please don't mention it but I had to come over and ask you.'

Audrey turned away, and started wandering back toward the kitchen, as though disoriented, as though saddened by this sisterly betrayal. 'You must talk to him all the time,' she said.

'Only three times,' Helen said. 'He doesn't seem like a bad man.'

Audrey spun: 'Oh, snap out of it, Helen,' she snarled. 'You never figured out how things work. You sit down there and sort your little auto parts and the world just goes by. You should ask yourself someday, "What happens when I get old? What happens when I'm trying to live on Social Security, when nobody wants me anymore?" Helen, you just don't have any idea.'

Helen turned to the door. 'Don't worry about me; just worry about yourself, Audrey . . . by the way, after Mom died – did you know this? I think you did – I took a lock of her hair to put with her picture on the piano. Chief Davenport took it with him. He's going to have it analyzed by the laboratory.'

'Well: I'm sorry to see you lose your precious lock, but at least it'll show she wasn't poisoned,' Audrey snapped.

'I hope so,' Helen said. 'Audrey, when all this is done, we've got to sit down and talk. So much stuff happened when I was a kid, I never got it straight.'

'I'll set you straight,' Audrey said. 'Come back when it's done.'

Helen left, the heavy door wheezing shut behind her: Wilson had insisted on the special door, three inches thick, saying, 'It's the first thing people will know about us.' Two thousand dollars for a door . . .

'Fuck,' she said aloud, wrenching her mind away from Wilson. A lock of hair! Could it really be analyzed, or was it a game that Davenport was playing with her? Was there any way to find out?

Maybe the Internet, though it seemed far-fetched. She went to the library, waited impatiently to get on-line, brought up the Alta Vista search engine, and typed in: ARSENIC+HAIR.

Almost immediately, she got back a list of articles, and her heart sank. The first one was, improbably, on Napoleon. She opened it, and it referred to arsenic content in Napoleon's hair. Shit. She went to the next one, something to do with analysis, and it also mentioned arsenic in hair. Hair.

She punched the 'off' button on the computer, and the computer's fan moaned as it closed down. The computer didn't like that, she thought. Didn't like to be up and running, and then cut off.

Fuck the computer.

Arsenic and hair. She had to do something, and do it quickly.

Chapter Thirty-One

Lucas went to lunch with Del, who said, 'I can't shake free of this opium thing. A couple of the old ladies have been calling every day, wanting to know what we're gonna do.'

'That's your problem, thank God,' Lucas said. 'Go over and talk to Towson or one of his guys, see what they want to do.'

'They want it to go away,' Del said. 'So does Rose Marie. Nobody wants to deal with it. I don't want to deal with it anymore. Hell, I'm going on vacation in two weeks. I'm finally getting my shot at Cancun. But now these old ladies, they want something done.'

'Why? Tell them to keep their mouths shut and everybody'll forget it,' Lucas said.

'They're not thinking that way. They've all been getting together in these fuckin' . . . covens. They think they've got to pay their debt to society,' Del said morosely.

'Jesus. Well, you asked for it,' Lucas said brightly. 'I feel for you, pal. But when that doc told you about it, you coulda walked away.'

'Ah, man, you gotta find a way to help.'

'Not me.' Lucas laughed, and thought, *My God, I think I just chortled.* 'I'm not narcotics. Go talk to the guys down there.'

'They treat me like I got the plague . . .'

'That's 'cause you *got* the plague,' Lucas said. 'I don't want to hear about it.'

'Fuck me,' Del said, moodily. 'I wasn't cut out for this.'

Lucas laughed again, said, 'Nobody is. Sixty old ladies? Is that what it is? You poor fuck. You're dead meat.'

Del looked at his watch. 'That lab report is about due.'

'Let's get back,' Lucas said.

'You think you got her?'

'It's almost too much to hope for,' Lucas said. 'When Helen said she had a hair sample, my teeth almost fell out.'

Lucas had a message when he got back: 'Call Davis.' Davis Ericson worked in the state crime lab. He punched in the number, and Ericson picked up.

'What'd you get?'

'Lucas. Tell you what, I've never seen this before. Not in real life.'

'What? You got arsenic?'

'The hair is stiff with it,' Ericson said. 'She must've been eating it for a month before she croaked.'

'Goddamnit, Davis.'

Lucas punched in the county attorney's number, waited for three minutes, and Kirk, the chief of the criminal division picked up. Lucas explained about the lock of hair.

'If Helen can swear that it came from her mother, then that might do it,' Kirk said.

'That's where Helen says it comes from.'

'Give me her name and address. We'll set up an appointment for a deposition.'

'What about Audrey?'

'Easiest way to do it, is, we'll talk to the judge, and have bail revoked on the killing of her husband. And then before tomorrow's bail hearing, we'll get an arrest affidavit put together on her mother, and arrest her on that. Maybe boost the charge on her husband to first degree.'

'So how long is that gonna take? The bail revocation?'

'Mmm . . . we'll have to get some stuff in writing. If you'll set out the circumstances of obtaining the hair sample, and describe the lab test – just in general terms – and walk it over here, I'll have a secretary put together an affidavit and we'll have the judge sign it this afternoon. If you can get your memo over here in an hour, we'll have it done by the end of the day.'

'And then we pick her up.'

'Yup. We could have her inside for supper.'

'Excellent,' Lucas said.

Audrey had been up most of the night, packing. She wanted to have it done in case she was rearrested, so that Wilson's clothing wouldn't still be hanging in the closets when she got back. She was eradicating the sight of him.

And she would probably be rearrested, she thought. If Davenport really had that hair, he would probably be coming for her in the next day or two. How long would a lab take? She had no idea. But she was certain it couldn't be done before nine o'clock in the morning.

By seven-thirty, with four hours out for sleep, she was done with the packing. After a last quick check around, she hauled the boxes down to the front entry, and stacked them. After a quick shower and a change of clothes, she went to the library, fired up the computer, brought up Word and wrote for half an hour, editing and re-editing as she worked. Satisfied, she dumped the document to a floppy disk, put it in her purse.

At nine o'clock, she was out of the house.

The Gold Bug was a custom jewelry boutique on the south side of Minneapolis. A half-dozen craftsmen worked out of a small common smelting area, with actual fabrication of jewelry done in separate shops on a wing off the smelting area. She'd been there once before, with a ladies' tour group from the country club, to look at gold jewelry and how it was made.

She hadn't bought any gold, but she'd found the tour interesting.

A tall, bony redheaded woman was working at the desk, looked up and said a cheery, 'Hello,' as Audrey tentatively poked her nose through the door.

'Hello. Are the shops open?'

'Sure. Go on down. Do you know . . . ?'

'Yes. I've been here before.'

Audrey scuttled away down the wing, walked past the open fire-door that led to the smelting area, slowed, looked inside. A sign beside the door said, 'Please come in and watch; but please be quiet.'

One man was working at an exhaust hood; three other hoods were vacant. He looked up, focused on her.

'I'm sorry,' she said. 'Is it . . . okay?'

'Sure. Come on in. I'm just smelting a little gold, here.'

She walked in with her purse clutched in front of her, an old lady. She'd have to work on this image, a little, she thought. If she got in the newspapers, perhaps she should look younger . . .

The goldsmith had gone back to his work, a small crucible that he worked with a torch; she couldn't see exactly what he was doing, but didn't particularly care. She wasn't interested in gold work. With her eyes fixed on the torch, she drifted to another one of the exhaust hoods. The table beside it was empty. Goddamn it. She passed behind him, now looking around at the equipment, then turned so she could watch him from the other side. He was vaguely aware of her, she thought, but he was used to being watched, and paid no real attention.

She moved up to the next exhaust hood, and saw the bottle.

That was it. She stood next to the table, and when he momentarily turned away, his back more toward her, she reached carefully out, picked it up, and slipped it into her coat pocket. It was small, no bigger than a shotgun shell or an old iodine bottle. With the bottle in her hand, she moved closer to him.

'Very interesting,' she said finally, as he finished a small pour into what looked like a lump of plaster.

'Simple enough, after you've done it a while,' he said.

She had no idea of what was going on, said, 'Thank you,' and still looking carefully around the smelting room, drifted out the door. She stopped at two of the shops, looking at their small display cases. Then, glancing at her watch – it was already past ten o'clock – she headed for the door.

'Have a nice day,' the redhead said, as she left.

You betcha.

Twenty minutes later, after a quick stop at a drug store to buy a pack of razor blades, she fixed the pill in the parking lot of a Burger King. First, she took one of the Prozac capsules she'd gotten from Helen, carefully pulled the cap apart, spilled the drug into the palm of her hand and flicked it out the car window. Then she took out the bottle she'd stolen from the Gold Bug and looked at it. The simple label said, *CAUTION*, and below that, in small letters, *Sodium Cyanide*. And below that, *Poison: If ingested, get physician's help immediately. For industrial use only.*

When the club ladies had visited the gold workshop, one of the goldsmiths had joked about using the cyanide to purify recycled gold. The same stuff Hitler's boys had used to kill themselves, he'd said. She hadn't known exactly what he was talking about – purifying the gold – but she remembered what he'd said about Hitler's boys.

The cyanide was an off-white powder, innocent enough. She poured a little on the sandwich box, cut it up with the razor blade, then carefully refilled the Prozac cap with the cyanide. Then she slipped the top back on the cap: not bad. If you looked at it closely, it wasn't quite right. But who looked at pills that closely?

She wrapped the pill in a napkin, and put it on the car seat; the sandwich box she carried to a trash can, and pushed it inside. A pay phone hung on the wall just inside the Burger King door, and she went in, and dialed Helen's number. Helen should be working, Connie should be at school. No answer. As a double-check, she got the number of the auto-parts place from directory assistance, called, and asked for Helen. Helen answered a second later, and Audrey clicked off as soon as she recognized her sister's voice.

Helen's house was no more than ten minutes away. If she tried to do something subtle, to sneak in, she'd probably draw more attention in the neighborhood than if she barged right in. She parked on the street, waited until she could see no one on the sidewalk, then hurried up the walk, through the outer porch, and rang the doorbell. No answer. She leaned on it the next time, ringing for a solid minute. Nothing.

Good.

She took her keys from her purse, found the key for Helen's house, opened the door and went inside. The house was deathly quiet. She went straight through to Helen's bedroom, to the corner where she kept her computer. Switched it on, took the floppy disk from her pocket, went to the *My Documents* folder. Helen had written a note to herself two months earlier, but the computer would update the time to show the last entry. Audrey slipped the floppy in the drive, brought up the text she'd written that morning, pasted it into the earlier note. Then she cut the text of the note itself, and checked her work.

'If I die . . .' the note began. 'I'm sorry about everything! I killed those people, not Audrey! But Audrey was my only support, and I had to do something if Wilson was going to move up at the bank! If Wilson had lost his job all those years ago, what would have happened to Connie and me? Without the money from Audrey, we would have been on the street! My former "husband" is good for NOTHING!!! But I didn't kill Mr Kresge! I think that must have been an accident! And Chief Davenport, if somebody shows this to you, yes, I called you. I could no longer stand the way Wilson was treating Audrey! I was afraid he would kill her! I thought you would do an investigation and his treatment of her would come out and nobody would ever know it was me that called you, and Audrey could keep helping me, because now, if they got divorced, she'd get all kinds of money! Connie – I love you. You go stay with your Aunt Audrey, because she really loves you. I'm sorry for all of this!!'

And at the bottom of the note, she'd left all the fragments of sentences that she'd pushed while editing: 'I fearedilling heraaacidenikill treeting Wil;sIonMisterKresge Without money I got from Audrey'

It would, she hoped, look like a practice note; she was especially proud of all the exclamation points. Helen used them everywhere, as though they were periods.

She closed the file, shut down the machine, put the disk in her purse and headed for the bedroom. Helen carried a pill case with a chiming clock to remind her to take the pills; she took one at noon every day. The Prozac bottle itself she kept in the bedroom, in her bureau drawer. Audrey found the bottle, unscrewed the top, looked inside. A dozen pills. Carefully unwrapping the cyanide pill in the napkin, she let it drop on top of the pills in the bottle, and replaced the bottle, shut the drawer.

Out of the house: she'd been inside no more than ten minutes, she thought. As she drove away, she moved in the car seat and felt the cyanide bottle in her pocket. She should ditch it somewhere, she thought. But she liked the idea of it. A bottle of death. She thought about it for a while, then stopped in a park, where a thin shell of woods surrounded a small drainage lake. She stepped just inside the tree line, picked out a good-sized oak, walked over to it and sat down. Probed the ground with her car key: damn. Frozen.

She looked around, spotted a culvert protruding from the edge of an embankment. She walked over to it, pushed the bottle well under the culvert. The bottle should be safe for years, she thought. Does cold weather affect cyanide? She had no idea.

Now, she thought, standing up.

Where are you, Davenport?

Chapter Thirty-Two

Two uniformed cops with a warrant stopped by the McDonald house at four o'clock, and found it empty. Audrey McDonald's car license-plate number was put on the air, along with a description. She was eating at Baker's Square Restaurant, having waited impatiently all afternoon. Two cops went by while she was inside, but she missed them all going back home. At seven, the uniformed cops swung by her house again, and saw lights.

Audrey McDonald came to the door.

Sherrill called: 'We're supposed to go out to dinner tonight.'

'Damn it, I'm sorry – but we're busting Audrey McDonald right now,' Lucas said.

'All right. Tomorrow for sure.'

'Tomorrow.'

Audrey was processed through the county jail, then taken to an interview room to wait for her attorney. J.B. Glass arrived a half-hour later, a little white wine under his belt. He found Lucas waiting outside the interview room with Sloan, and said, 'What the hell happened?'

'Your client's a serial killer,' Sloan said laconically.

'What, Sugar Pops or Shredded Wheat?' Glass said.

'Her mother and father for starters,' Lucas said.

'You're *really* telling me I've got a millionaire client who might be a serial killer?' Glass asked in a hushed voice. He rolled his eyes to the heavens, the view toward which extended twenty-eight inches to the basement ceiling. 'I don't want to seem cynical, but . . . thank you, Jesus.'

Then he was all business: 'I want privacy with my client.'

'She's in the room,' Lucas said.

'Have you talked to her?'

'Nobody's talked to her,' Lucas said. 'She opened the door to her house and said, "I want my attorney." Nobody's said a word to her since, except: "Stand up, sit down, turn to the right." '

'Good,' Glass nodded. 'I'll tell you though, it's gonna be a while before you can see her.'

'We can wait,' Lucas said.

They waited. Glass talked to her for a half-hour, asked Lucas if he could get a couple of cans of Diet Pepsi-Cola for them. Lucas walked through the dark hallways to a Pepsi machine, got two cans, walked back, passed them through the door.

'Thanks,' Glass said, as he shut the door.

Another twenty minutes passed, and then Glass opened the door and said, 'Come in.'

Sloan led the way, carrying a portable tape recorder. Lucas nodded at Audrey. She fixed him for a moment with her cobra eyes, then broke off and looked down at the table. When Sloan was ready, and had a cassette running, he said, 'This is a preliminary interview with Mrs Audrey McDonald, in the presence of her attorney, Jason Glass, conducted by detectives Sloan and Davenport.'

He ran the machine back to make sure it was working, replayed the statement, pushed Record again, added the time and date, and turned to McDonald.

'Mrs McDonald, you have been rearrested after the revocation of your bail granted after the killing of your husband

379

Wilson McDonald . . . the bail revocation, however, is based on what we believe was the murder of your mother, Amelia Lamb.'

'I did no such thing. I loved my mother,' she said, calmly.

'Mrs McDonald, did you know that your sister saved a lock of your mother's hair after she died?'

'Yes, I knew that.'

'We had the hair sample analyzed by the state crime laboratory, Mrs McDonald, and the hair was found to contain amounts of arsenic which would be lethal to a human being.'

'I don't know anything about that,' she said.

'Um, do you know where she lived – Mrs Lamb – at the time she died?' Glass asked Lucas.

'In Lakeville.'

'Have the police inspected the house they lived in?'

'Not yet.'

'It was a very old house – you find arsenic all over the place in those old houses. It's in the wallpaper, the paint, people used it all the time to spray for bugs. Mrs Lamb may have had arsenic in her hair, but there's no reason to think that my client put it there. In fact, she did not.'

'Did you get large insurance payments from both the death of your father and your mother, Mrs McDonald?' Sloan asked.

'She won't answer that,' Glass said. He looked down at Audrey. 'That's something we've got to look into ourselves, before we start discussing it.'

'Did you use the insurance payments to put yourself through St Anne's, where you met Sister Mary Joseph?' Lucas asked.

Glass shook his head: 'We'll refuse to answer that.'

'We have gray duct tape from your house with only one set of fingerprints on it,' said Sloan. 'The adhesive on the duct tape matches exactly adhesive taken off the door locks outside

Susan O'Dell's apartment. Did you put that tape there, Mrs McDonald?'

'No, I did not.'

The questioning went on for half an hour, Audrey growing more and more angry. Finally, she turned to Glass and said, 'How much longer do we have to do this?'

'You want to stop now?'

'Yes.'

'Then we're done,' Glass said. To Sloan: 'No more questions.' Sloan looked at Lucas, reached out to the recorder. Before he could turn it off, Audrey hissed at Lucas, 'You think you're so smart, but you just don't understand anything.'

Sloan froze, then, as unobtrusively as possible, let his arm slide sideways and rest on the table next to the recorder. Sometimes you got the best stuff after the formal questioning was done.

'I think I do,' Lucas said. 'I've talked to your friends, I've talked to your sister. We don't have every piece, because you got rid of some of them. But there's enough left to hang you, Audrey.'

'So dumb,' she said. She stood up, and turned toward Glass. 'Will there be another bond hearing?'

'Yes, tomorrow morning.'

'Gonna cost you a little more, this time,' Lucas said. 'And when we finish all the paper on your mother, we'll just pick you up again. It'd be easier just to stay put. Mr Glass could arrange for your sister to watch your house.'

'My sister . . . my sister,' she said. She pushed her hands up through her hair, as though she were about to tear it out. 'My sister gave you a lock of mother's hair?'

'Yes.'

'That was good of her. And my sister told you about this whole murder idea in the first place, didn't she?'

Lucas looked at Sloan, then nodded. Glass opened his mouth to say something, then shut it.

'And did my sister tell you that all those years when I was supposedly killing these people, her sole support came from us? From Wilson and me? That we gave her cash to keep her head above water? That if Wilson didn't do well, if he lost his job or lost a promotion, that she'd be hurt as much as we would? Did she tell you about our father feeling her up, about finding a box of rat poison in the machine shed and pouring it into Dad's whiskey? Did my sister tell you all of that? Did she tell you about fighting with Mom about screwing boys out by the cornfield in Lakeville? And more than that, screwing them for money? Did you look at everything you have, and ask, "What if her sister did it?" And did you ask, if you send little Audrey McDonald off to prison, if she could tolerate it? I'll answer that for you: I'm claustrophobic. I wouldn't last a year in a prison. I'd find some way to hang myself. And then who gets my share of the money? My sister? That's what she thinks . . .'

Lucas was astonished: at that moment, he believed that Audrey believed. She was utterly convincing, a beetle-hard, scuttling young-old woman. 'Jesus,' he said.

'We gotta stop,' Glass said convulsively. 'We gotta stop this.'

He put an arm around Audrey to stop her: and for a moment, the woman's dead-cobra eyes gave something away, a spark, something almost like humor. Then the moment passed, and she was as sullen as ever.

Lucas looked after her as she left: what was this all about?

Lucas and Sloan stopped at a greasy spoon on the way home, Lucas following Sloan out in separate cars. As they walked inside, Sloan said, 'What if the sister did it?'

Lucas shook his head: 'No way.'

'Why not?'

'She was too young to kill her old man; I don't care if he was groping her. But the big thing is, why would she ever risk calling attention to that whole string of killings? Even if she blamed them on McDonald, there was always the possibility that McDonald would be able to prove that he didn't do it . . . and if he could prove he couldn't do any one of them, then all of them would be in question. Nope. Whoever killed these people – Audrey – is too smart to have called attention to them.'

'But what . . . what if she saw Wilson McDonald going down, and shot Kresge specifically to pull McDonald down, so that Audrey would get his money. And then, when you get on top of Audrey, she decides to sacrifice Audrey? I mean, what if she's three layers back, waiting for Audrey to die in prison? Or even planning to poison her if she's acquitted?'

'No fuckin' way,' Lucas said. 'You gotta know the people.'

They found a booth, ordered beer and fries: 'She scared the shit out of me, man. And I'll tell you what, Glass was looking at that tape machine like it was solid gold,' Sloan said. 'Anybody who listens to that tape is gonna believe her, too. Like a jury.'

Lucas shook his head again: 'Not if they listen to Helen at the same time. Helen is just . . . an innocent. She picked up on McDonald because the pattern became so clear to her over the years. She talked to them often enough that she knew when a promotion was up, and then she'd read about some guy from the bank being killed, and then it'd turn out to be a guy in McDonald's department. Nope. She even waited longer than she should have. And why in God's name would she offer her mother's hair? If she knew her mother had been poisoned . . .'

They ran over it for another hour, building the case against Audrey. In the end, Sloan said, 'You'll have to admit, most of it could be built the other way.'

'Naw: jury'd never go for it. And remember, she killed her old man.'

Sloan shook his head. 'Just wish there was some way to pry the sisters apart. Put one of them in Kansas while somebody's getting killed in Minnesota.'

As Lucas put the beer bottle to his mouth, the light went off in his head: 'Oh, shit,' he said, the bottle frozen in front of his face.

'What?'

'In the Arris killing. We never looked at that tape for women.'

'Huh. Where's the tape?'

'My place. St Paul gave me a copy of it, and I left it at my place.'

'Can I come along?'

They stuck the tape in Lucas' VCR, and the bad picture came up on the screen. They watched Arris go by, followed by several women, and then, a minute later, another woman, walking rigidly down the hill. 'There she is,' Lucas said.

'That's fuckin' Helen,' Sloan said.

'No, no, that's fuckin' Audrey,' said Lucas. He ran the tape back. 'Look at the way she walks.'

'Looks like fuckin' Helen to me.'

'Remember, this is eight years ago. Audrey'd be thirty. Helen would only be in her mid-twenties . . . They look alike, but that woman is not twenty-six.'

Sloan was on his hands and knees, peering at the screen. 'Goddamn. Could be Audrey.'

'Is Audrey,' Lucas said.

'Selling it to a jury'll be hard,' Sloan said. 'You'll get one dumb shit on there who'll believe nothing but his own eyes, and his eyes'll say it's Helen.'

'I wonder if we can get this enhanced somehow,' Lucas said. 'Maybe the feebs?'

'I don't know... tell you the truth, if there was a way to ditch the tape, I'd do it. It confuses things. But now that I keep looking at it, I think you're right. She moves like Audrey does. She *scuttles*.'

The phone rang as they ran through the tape one last time. Sherrill. 'Did you get her?'

'Yeah, I think – but it's gonna be a close call,' Lucas said.

'You want me to come over and comfort you?'

He didn't, especially, but he said, 'Come on over.'

'Nah. You don't sound like you mean it,' she said. 'Tomorrow night, though.'

And she was gone.

'Fuckin' cop-women,' Lucas said.

'That's what you're doing,' Sloan agreed.

'Fuckin' was an adjective, not a verb,' Lucas said.

'Could've been a verb,' Sloan said.

Sloan left, and Lucas sat in his study for a while, doodling, running through the case in his mind, looking for loose ends. He didn't find many, except to note that they'd have to re-interview half the people who worked at the bank. They'd have to find witnesses who saw Audrey McDonald firing the Contender pistol; they'd have to find witnesses who would testify about promotions, and who was competitive for them . . .

He finally trundled off to bed, lay restlessly, for a while, finally fell asleep.

* * *

In the morning, he moved sluggishly around, looked at the clock: already nine. He dressed, stopped at a fast-food place for French toast, then headed downtown. He called the county attorney's office and got Kirk.

'Had the bail hearing yet?'

'Yeah. The judge was a wee bit skeptical about the arsenic. J.B. did a pretty nice job. We got the bail up to a million, but she was ready for it.'

'She's out?'

'Twenty minutes ago,' Kirk said.

'How about the arrest warrant on her mother?'

'We're slowing down on that. J.B. brought up this stuff about the old house they used to live in, and we heard about this business with her sister, so we're gonna have the house checked and depose the sister. I mean, we've got her on a million, I don't think she'll run.'

Sherrill dropped by at mid-morning, carrying a doughnut and two cups of coffee. 'She's out, I hear.'

'Yeah,' Lucas said in disgust. 'I'll tell you what: if she was a black guy with a record, she'd be washing dishes in Stillwater by now.'

'Sloan told me about that whole rap about her sister: that's pretty weird.'

'Yeah, I don't understand that,' Lucas said. 'It's a fucked-up defense. You put Helen on the stand, the truth is gonna come out.'

'You don't think there's any chance that Audrey's telling the truth? That it's Helen?'

'No, I don't.'

'The one thing that's hard for me to get over, is her appearance,' Sherrill said. 'She's only five years older than me . . .'

'Really? I thought you were sixteen . . .'

'Shut up. I'm being serious. The thing is, if you take the attack on Elle, where somebody beat her up with a ball bat, who do you think would be most likely to do that? Helen, who looks pretty active, pretty good shape, still young? Or Audrey, who looks old, slumped over?'

'Whatever she looks like, she's only thirty-eight,' Lucas said. 'She . . .'

He stopped, put a hand to his forehead. 'What,' Sherrill asked. 'A stroke.'

'Aw, man,' Lucas said. He picked up the phone book, talking fast: 'I think this might have gone through my head the night we were at St Anne's, the night Elle got hit, but it went away; it's like it *was* a stroke . . .'

'What, what?'

'If Elle takes the phone call, and grabs her keys, and runs out the door and gets jumped . . . whoever called her must've been standing right there. Must've been calling from the bushes. Must've used a cell phone, not a pay phone. All the other tips we've had have come from pay phones, it must've blocked me off or something . . .'

Sherrill snapped her fingers: 'Phone records.'

'Absolutely.'

The man who could get the records was away, but was expected back before lunch. In the meantime, the company would try to reach him, to hurry things up.

Lucas said to Sherrill, 'If this pans out, she's dead meat.'

'What if it's Helen's phone?'

'That'd be a problem,' Lucas said.

'So we wait?'

'We wait.' Lucas looked at his watch. 'Shouldn't be more than an hour or so.'

* * *

Del stopped in: 'I'm being haunted by these old ladies,' he said.

'Tell them if they insist on going to jail, they'll be raped by bull dikes,' Sherrill suggested.

'I think some of them are gonna need to be rehabbed,' Del said. 'They're all getting different lawyers; there's gonna be fifty-eight lawyers to deal with.'

'Too bad the pinking-shears thing wasn't fatal,' Lucas said nastily. 'Think how much better off you'd be.'

'That's the truth,' Del said sincerely. 'Jesus, what a mess.'

'When're you going to Cancun?' Sherrill asked.

'Two weeks,' he said. 'Hope this is done by then. I'd hate to have it hanging over my head for the whole time I'm down there.'

'The thing is,' Sherrill said, after Del had gone, 'What if Helen really loves Audrey – they've been through a lot together, and they're sisters – and decides to help her out? What if we go talk to Helen, and she starts taking the fifth? Audrey gets on the stand, blames everything on Helen, and Helen refuses to talk . . .'

'I don't think that would happen. Audrey killed their mother and . . .'

Lucas trailed off and Sherrill said, 'What? Again? Something else?'

'Yeah. What if Helen wasn't here to defend herself?'

Helen was working at the auto parts place. Lucas found the name in the Yellow Pages, called her. 'You've got to take time off, and meet us at your house,' Lucas said. 'I'm sorry, but this is critical for both you and Connie. I'll talk to your boss if you want.'

Lucas took the Porsche. Sherrill, getting the go-ahead from

Frank Lester, trailed in a city car. The bomb squad was ten minutes behind her, a crime-scene crew a few minutes behind that.

Lucas thought of the lie that Audrey had told during the interrogation, how harsh, straightforward, how *honest* it seemed. But not unrehearsed. And there'd been smugness about her when they'd come to take her away. She must have known that whatever case she could make against Helen would be denied by Helen, and that Helen's denials might even be provable in some cases. She might have understood that Helen was simply more believable than she was. She might even have understood that finding a hank of hair with arsenic in it didn't mean much unless Helen was there to swear that the hair had been taken from her mother . . .

She must have deduced that the police case rested squarely on Helen; and that if Helen were dead, Audrey had all kinds of defenses available.

And that little spark in her eyes, that smugness at the very end.

She thought Helen was out of it.

How would she do it? She'd used firebombs, guns, and poison. Guns were out, because she couldn't have known that she'd be free. Some kind of bomb was possible. Some kind of poison.

Helen arrived: resisted. 'I know Audrey. She would never do anything like this. Never. We've been together since we were children.'

'Mrs Bell – we're pretty sure she killed your mother and father . . .'

'She says she didn't,' Bell said stubbornly.

'We think she did. And if you don't think there's any chance, why did you give us that lock of hair?'

'I . . .'

'Believe what you want,' Sherrill said gently. 'But just let us look. If we're wrong, no harm has been done.'

No bomb.

The bomb squad went in with sniffier equipment, found nothing. They checked the furnace and gas water heater for tampering or gas leaks. Nothing there, either.

'Pills,' Lucas said. 'What kind of pills do you take? Aspirin? Something in capsules, I think . . .'

'Prozac,' she said. 'I take Prozac.'

'Where do you keep it?' Sherrill asked.

'In my bedroom.'

She got the bottle of Prozac and they poured the pills out on a clean garbage bag on the kitchen table. One of the crime scene techs had a hand glass, and Lucas used it to look at the capsules. After a minute, he shook his head. 'I don't see anything.'

'We do have aspirin,' she said. 'Not in capsules, though.'

'We could take a look,' Lucas said.

'And I've got some antibiotics left over from a cold last winter. And there're some of those timed cold pills, now those are capsules, I think.'

'We'll take them all,' Lucas said. 'The problem is, we don't want anything Connie would take. How about food? Is there any food that is absolutely yours, that Connie wouldn't eat?'

'I've got some of that diet drink, but the cans are sealed . . .'

'We better take a look,' Lucas said.

'Look: I've got to get back to work,' she said. 'Since it's not a bomb, maybe we could do it this evening?'

'I suppose,' Lucas said. 'Jesus. it's gotta be something.'

'Unless you're wrong about her.'

'I'm not wrong,' Lucas said. 'I've got some things . . .'

He heard the tinny music in the back of his head, but didn't react until he noticed Helen looking at her purse, a peculiar expression on her face. 'What?' he asked.

'That's my pill box,' she said. 'I keep a pill box in my purse, it's got a little alarm clock, so I always take my pill at the same time every day. I just filled it up this morning.'

Lucas picked up the purse, clicked it open, found the pill box. The box was playing 'My Bonnie Lies Over the Ocean.'

'Push the button to stop it,' Helen said, as the two guys from the crime-scene crew stepped up to Lucas to look at the box. Lucas carried it into the kitchen, dumped it on the garbage bag.

'Gimme the glass,' he said.

He spotted the pill in a half-second: 'Got it.'

'No.' Helen didn't believe it.

'That goddamn pill has been messed with,' Lucas said. He handed the glass to the crime-scene man. 'What do you think?'

The crime scene man squinted through the glass: 'And guess what? There's nothing better in the world than gelatin for picking up a fingerprint.'

'There's a print?' Lucas asked.

'A piece of one, anyway,' the crime-scene man said. 'Gimme a Ziploc, somebody.'

'No,' Helen said. 'No.'

They pulled the capsule apart with forks, avoiding what appeared to be a fingerprint smudge. White powder spilled out. Lucas pulled apart one of the Prozac capsules from the bottle. 'It's different stuff,' he said.

The lead crime-scene tech got down close to the table, an inch from the white powder, barely inhaled, then straightened up, wiping his nose.

'What?' asked Lucas.
'Almonds,' the tech said. 'That stuff is cyanide.'

Chapter Thirty-Three

Lucas called the county attorney from Helen Bell's house, told him about the pill: 'All right, that's it,' Towson said. 'Pick her up. We'll put her away this time. No bail. No nothing.'

Lucas hung up and nodded to Sherrill: 'We're gonna go get her. Want to follow me over?'

'I'll ride with you,' she said. 'You can always drop me back here to get the car.'

'Let's go,' he said. 'We'll get a squad to meet us there.'

Four miles out, Dispatch called and said a man from ATT-Wireless was on the phone.

'Patch him through,' Lucas said.

'There're dozens of calls from that account in the past week,' the ATT man said. 'What was the time and date?'

Lucas gave it to him and said, 'Look for a 699 prefix.'

After a moment's wait, 'Here it is. Here it is, by gosh.'

Audrey was talking to a Fidelity account manager when the phone rang in her purse. 'I better take that,' she said, pleasantly. She was wearing her best, acting the banker's wife: she wanted to get the money out of Fidelity before some legalism held it up. If she could get the cash and stash it somewhere, she would be good for at least a few years, no matter what else happened.

'Let me get the rest of these numbers,' the manager said. She was a young woman dressed in a nice Ann Taylor suit, with a pretty silk scarf, nothing flashy, nothing too expensive. Audrey approved; maybe Fidelity wasn't throwing her money away on exorbitant salaries.

Audrey answered the phone on the third ring and Helen said to her, 'Did you do it?'

And Audrey could hear Connie in the background, saying, urgently, 'Mom, hang up. Hang up.'

'Do what?' Audrey said calmly, though she knew.

'You'd know, if you did it.'

'That Davenport's been there again, hasn't he?' Audrey asked. 'May I speak to him?'

'He's gone,' Helen said. She choked on the words, and Audrey heard Connie say, 'Mom, I'm gonna hang this up. You shouldn't . . .'

And the connection was gone. Audrey looked at the phone for a moment, then punched the power button and turned it off. Davenport had found the pill. She wouldn't need to talk to Helen again.

As she walked out through the Fidelity office, she met the young manager on her way back: 'I'm sorry,' Audrey said. 'I've got something of a family emergency. I have to go home.'

She drove back toward her house on remote control. She didn't have access to any serious money, so running was not a possibility. And with Helen alive, she didn't really have many options left. She could think of precisely one.

'I can die,' she said to the car. She was overwhelmed with a feeling of sadness, not for herself, but for the world. She'd be gone. The world wouldn't have her anymore. 'But they'll see then,' she told the car. 'That's when they'll see.'

The car seemed to steer itself, but she knew where it was going: North Woods Arms, in Wayzata. The gunshop was a small place, a door beside a picture-window, the window laced-over with security bars disguised as wrought-iron curlicues. The area beside the door and around the window had weathered-wood siding, to simulate a North Woods cabin; small Christmas lights blinked in the window, around a festive display of nine-millimeter pistols.

A bell rang above the door as she walked in, and the owner looked up from a magazine. 'Hello.'

'Hello,' Audrey said, glancing around at the rack of long guns. 'I'm looking for a gun for my husband for Christmas.'

'You've come to the right place,' the owner said pleasantly. 'Do you know what you're looking for, or . . .'

'Yes.' Audrey unfolded a piece of yellow notebook paper. She'd thought that would be a nice touch. 'A Remington 870 Wingmaster twelve-gauge shotgun.'

'No problem,' the owner said enthusiastically. 'You know what he's going to use it for?'

'Ducks, I guess. He mostly hunts ducks. And geese.'

'No problem . . .'

She took the 870 along with two boxes of No. 2 shells. The store owner took her check, carried the boxes out to the car and said, 'Tell your husband I said, "Good hunting." '

'When I see him,' she said, and got in the car. The store owner thought that was an odd thing to say, he would mention it to his wife that night.

Lucas and Sherrill had gotten to the McDonald house before Audrey, and a minute before two patrol cops in a squad car. Lucas knocked on the front door, got no response, and while the uniforms waited in front, they walked together once around the house. Nobody. Peering through the deck windows, they saw no sign of movement or light. Back in front, Sherrill rang the doorbell again. Lucas said, looking up at the bedroom windows, 'Nobody's home. Feels too quiet. I hope she's not running.'

They were standing in the 'L' made by the front of the house, the living wing to the front, extending to the left, the three-car garage swinging off to the right. 'Maybe put out a call on her. Or we could just wait,' Sherrill said. The uniforms were leaning on the front fender of their squad car, chatting.

'I hope she's not looking for Helen,' Lucas said. And thought about Elle Kruger and his jaw tightened. 'Or anybody else. By God, I'd like to be there to bust her; but maybe we'd better . . . Whoops. There she is.'

Audrey turned into the bottom of the driveway, saw the Porsche and the police car at the top. She reached up and pushed the garage-door opener. The shotgun rode beside her, muzzle down, in the passenger foot-well, the butt resting against her hip. She'd loaded four shells, as many as it would take, and had two more loose on the seat for reloading.

And she was ready for it. On the way home from the gun store, her vision had seemed to narrow: on the highway, she could see only the road itself. On the driveway, she could see only the garage door, until she made the little left-then-right loop that could take her into the garage. Then, she looked out the passenger-side window and saw Davenport walking toward the garage, and her vision narrowed to a small point: Davenport's face. A mean man, she thought. Harsh. A man like Daddy.

When the garage door started up, the two uniformed cops pushed away from the fender of their squad car, and looked down the drive. Audrey rolled slowly up the drive, made a little jog that took her straight in toward the far door. Lucas and Sherrill started walking toward it from the front stoop, and the two uniform cops started toward it from their parking spot at the edge of the driveway. The back of Audrey's car had just cleared the inside of the door when it started down again.

Lucas turned and said, 'Side door.' Sherrill followed him toward an access door at the near end of the three overhead doors, just ambling along without thinking about it. Lucas opened the access door and stepped into the semi-dark garage, which was getting darker as the end door dropped the last couple of feet. 'Mrs McDonald,' he said.

Audrey heard that, and looking left, saw Davenport step inside the garage. He was standing in a shaft of light from the open access door. She grabbed the shotgun with her right hand, took a second to make sure the safety was off, then opened the door with her left hand, pushed it out with her feet and pivoted out of the car. The shotgun was long and awkward, and she had to maneuver it around the car's roof post. Still, once it was out, it came up smoothly, and she saw the surprise register on Davenport's face and heard him scream a word and saw a violent motion and then the muzzle was coming down . . .

The dome and door lights came on in Audrey's car as she opened the door; and with that light, Lucas could see the shotgun barrel as it came up. Sherrill had come in behind him and he screamed, 'Gun,' and batted her sideways as he went down behind a Lexus. At the same instant, the shotgun blew a foot-long finger of flame at him, and the wall behind exploded in a shower of drywall plaster.

BAAA-OOOM.

The sound came after the lightning flash – a long time after, it seemed, though he was suspended in air when he thought that. Then he was on the floor, groping for his pistol, dragging it out of the holster, rolling along beside the Lexus, and the shotgun lit up the garage again, blowing glass out over his head. He'd lost track of Sherrill, lost track of everything: the thunder of the shotgun was magnified in the enclosed space, and the lightning of the shots was now the only illumination, aside from the feeble dome light from McDonald's car.

Audrey had been blinded by the muzzle flash; she hadn't expected that, but she expected Davenport to be falling, so she dropped the muzzle of the weapon as she pumped it, and convulsively jerked the trigger again. Glass shattered and she registered a voice, screaming; and a surge of confidence ran through her. Got him. Now to finish him.

'Light.' Lucas heard somebody screaming; his mind processed it as Sherrill, but he couldn't tell what she was saying. 'Top.'
BAAA-OOOM.
Three shots; and Audrey was getting closer, walking toward them. But some shotguns only held three shots. Was she reloading? Was this a four-shot chamber? And then suddenly, the overhead lights were on and he saw, from the corner of his eye, Sherrill scrambling away from a light switch, a gun in her hand. And at the same time, from his spot on the concrete floor, saw Audrey's ankle behind the back bumper of the sport-ute. He pushed his hand forward, couldn't see the front blade of the pistol but squeezed off a shot. Twelve feet: and he missed to the right. Audrey did a little hop step, and he heard her pump, and a shotgun shell bounced off the floor and he adjusted a hair to the right and pulled the trigger again.
And this time, he hit her.
Audrey screamed and went down, and suddenly, her face was there, looking under the cars at him. And the barrel of the shotgun was pointing at him, too and she was moving it toward his face. He rolled behind a tire as she fired, and the tire

soaked up the blast; but he could feel the air torn apart beside him.

She'd be dealing with recoil; she might be reloading. He didn't think it, but knew it, and pushed himself just to the right and extended his arm again, still unable to find the front sight in the shadow under the car, but he was close, and her face was there, and he was tightening his grip on the trigger and she was moving the barrel back to him . . .

Sherrill dropped on her like a meteor. She'd crawled over the sport-ute, and dropped from the roof. She landed with her feet behind Audrey's neck, smacking Audrey's head face-down into the receiver on the shotgun. Lucas jumped up and ran around the end of the car and caught Sherrill's hand coming up with the pistol in it. 'No, no . . .'

'What?' Sherrill looked confused.

'We got her.'

Audrey wrenched her shoulders and neck around, looked up at them, dazed, blood running down her lips and across her teeth. 'Who are you?' she asked.

One of the cops outside was screaming, 'Davenport, Davenport, talk to me . . .'

'We got her, we got her, we got her . . .' With his foot, Lucas pushed the shotgun under the sport-ute, out of reach. 'She's hit,' he said to Sherrill. 'Let's get her outside.'

'I'll get the doors . . .'

Lucas got his arms under Audrey's back and knees, and picked her up as best he could; then the three garage doors started rising simultaneously, and light flooded into the garage.

The uniformed cops were there, pistols drawn. They reholstered as they saw Lucas carrying Audrey.

'Jesus Christ,' one of them said. 'What was that?'

'Shotgun,' Lucas grunted. 'She's hit. Get an ambulance out here.'

'Put her down on the driveway, Lucas,' Sherrill said. 'Let's get her flat. One of you guys, you got a blanket in your car? She'll be going into shock . . .'

A cop got a blanket, spread it on the driveway and Lucas put Audrey on it. She seemed only semi-conscious, though her eyes were open. He stood up. 'Damn,' he said. 'That was a little too close.'

Audrey said something. Sherrill heard it, said, 'What?'

She said something again. Sherrill said, 'What?' and bent over the other woman.

And as she put her head close to the other woman's face, Audrey lifted her hand, and despite her awkward position, hit Sherrill in the eye with her fist, knocking Sherrill flat on her butt.

'Knock that shit off,' one of the uniformed cops yelled at Audrey, stepping over her, and she unballed her fist and turned her head away, her eyes softly closing. Sherrill had crawled away, one hand to her eye. 'Aw, man, that hurts.'

Lucas looked at it: 'You're gonna have a mouse. And a hell of a black eye.'

Audrey mumbled again. They both turned to look at her, eight feet away, flat on her back, and her cobra eyes caught Lucas. And suddenly she smiled, a big, toothy smile with bloody teeth.

Lucas felt the hair rise on the back of his neck. He turned back to Sherrill, who looked up at him and shook her head once: 'Fuckin' nuts,' she said.

Chapter Thirty-Four

S herrill said, 'So Krause thinks maybe she *deliberately* let
the lineman see her so we wouldn't suspect Wilson. And
then *she* called to tell us about the lineman, because we were
digging at Wilson.'

'Smart woman,' Lucas said.

'Nasty,' said James T. Bone, who was just settling into
Lucas' visitor's chair.

'I gotta go,' Sherrill said. She stood on her tiptoes, black
eye nearly gone, kissed Lucas on the lips, said, 'See you
tonight,' and, 'Bye, Mr Bone.'

When Sherrill closed the door, Bone looked sleepy-eyed at
Lucas and said, 'White fuzzy sweater and chrome revolver in
a shoulder holster. My heart almost stopped.'

'Wearing my ass out,' Lucas said comfortably.

'I know how that goes,' Bone said.

Bone said, 'Audrey . . . is she gonna fight it?'

'Her attorney's a friend of mine,' Lucas said. 'He says she's
crazy as a loon. Maybe she is. She even denies buying or
firing the shotgun, even though we had four witnesses, the
receipt in the car, and the gunshop guy identifying her. He
says she's having trouble remembering anything after the death
of her husband. A shrink's looking at her now.'

'Is she faking?'

Lucas shrugged. 'I don't know. She's smart, that's pretty
clear. But her whole life has been a nightmare. I think it's

possible that she never did know the difference between right and wrong.'

'And if the court decides she's nuts?'

'She'll go off to the state hospital.'

'What if she's not nuts?'

'Then we have a trial, and we've got her.'

'Huh.' Bone looked out the window at the street. The weather had turned gray, and small flecks of snow bounced off the window. Although it was only three in the afternoon, most of the passing cars had their headlights on. A week after the fight in the garage, the world was beginning to settle down again. 'I'd feel a lot better if I knew she was going away for a long time; like forever. I'd hate to see her get out of a hospital in a couple of years.'

Lucas nodded: 'So would I.'

Bone had the bank: of the top five Polaris executives in October, only two had made it to the end of November, Bone and Robles. 'I've got my assistant winding up O'Dell's affairs here. I talked to her father – he's having trouble dealing with her death.'

'Death of a child,' Lucas said. 'Just 'cause they're grown up, doesn't make it any easier.'

'No, I don't expect it does,' Bone said. Then, 'Have you seen Damascus Isley lately?'

'Not since we had lunch together a while back.'

'I saw him at the bank. We talked a little basketball ... He's on a strange diet, a Big Mac every day with popcorn.'

'He told me he was thinking about it,' Lucas said. 'I hope he can stick it out.'

'I think he will. He was on the diet for one week, he told me, and lost eighteen pounds. He knows that won't keep up, but when he got on the scale after the first week, he said his wife went out to the bedroom and cried for fifteen minutes. Outa joy, I guess. He was freaked out. I don't see any way he'll relapse.'

Bone said, 'This Audrey McDonald thing has torn me up.'

'Yeah?' Lucas had an archaic typewriter tray in his desk, just the right height for feet. He pulled it out and put his feet up.

'Yeah. I was gonna run a major bank some day. But it wouldn't have come this soon, if Audrey hadn't blown old Dan Kresge out of his tree stand.'

'Won't you be out of a job, if the merger goes through?'

'Sure. But some problems are cropping up with the merger,' Bone said, showing a thin smile. 'The road might not be as smooth as it looked. Even if it happens, once you're running a place, you can usually go someplace else, and run that. It's the breakthrough to the top that counts.'

'Sloan talked to you about your relationship with Marcia Kresge . . . I'd think that might have been a dangerous relationship for somebody trying to get to the top,' Lucas said.

'Eh . . . it's easier in a private company. You don't have to deal with elections and all your insane bureaucratic rules. I doubt Dan would have cared; he probably would have been amused. Marcia wasn't any more of a potential problem for me than Miss Fuzzy-Sweater is for you. Besides, that's all done.'

'All done?'

'Yeah.' Bone seemed mildly embarrassed and turned to look out at the street again. 'You met my assistant, Kerin Baki.'

'The glacial blonde.'

'Yeah. When the whole scramble started, after Kresge was

killed, she started working to get me the top job. She did everything right: pretty much managed the whole show. And when I asked her what she wanted out of it, she said she wanted a favor from me. But she wouldn't tell me what it was until after I got the job.'

'And you got it.'

'Yeah. So after things settled down a little, when Audrey McDonald was arrested, I got her in my office and asked, "What's the favor?" '

Baki had been a little uncomfortable when he pressed her, Bone said, but finally sat down and outlined what she wanted. Basically, she was tired of living alone. She wanted to find a man who was as smart as she was, who worked as hard as she did, and had similar interests. That was difficult.

'What she wanted from me,' Bone said, as Lucas started smiling, 'is she wanted me to take her around – just as a friend, as an associate – and introduce her to guys I knew in the banking and investment communities who might be candidates.'

'Just as a friend,' Lucas said.

'Yeah. "Mr Bone," she said, "I don't have a chance to meet many people like that, socially, because I'm always here. And I know this sounds a little cold and a little calculating, but I don't have many more years to go if I want to have children and a normal home life." ' Bone said, mimicking Baki's precise soprano. 'And she pushed her glasses back up on her nose, which is about the only thing that's ever been wrong with her – her glasses slide down.'

'Yeah,' Lucas said. 'She's, like, vulnerable.'

'I said, "Okay," ' Bone said. 'I could understand that. So I took her around to a couple of places, a couple of outside meetings she wouldn't normally have gone to, and she made quite an impression on a couple of guys. I got some calls asking about her status . . . I told her about them, and she was pretty interested.'

'You chump.'

'You know how the story comes out?'

Lucas knitted his hands across his chest and said, 'Let me guess. You decided to take her out for a dinner . . .'

'. . . dinner meeting.'

'And then you have to take her home afterwards.'

'I just went up for a minute; I'd never seen her place.'

'And you didn't come out for a while.'

'Quite a while.'

'And the glacier melted.'

'You might say that . . . And she's told me I've seen the last of Marcia Kresge,' Bone said. 'She also mentioned a couple of other women that I had no idea that she knew about.'

'What about the kid thing?'

Bone shrugged. 'I always thought, "Maybe, you know, with the right woman . . ." '

The phone rang, and Bone stood up. 'I gotta go,' he said, but Lucas held up a finger: 'Hang on a second.' He answered the phone. 'Hello?'

'Lucas, this is Del.' Del was on a cell phone; his voice sounded like he was shouting through a hollow log, with a roar in the background.

'Yeah. What's going on?'

'Aw, I'm calling from the plane . . .'

Engine roar. 'That's right,' Lucas said. 'Cancun. I forgot. Have a good time.'

'If anybody comes asking for me, tell 'em, ten days, would you?' Del shouted.

'Sure.'

'Nobody's come asking yet?'

'Not to me,' Lucas said. 'Should they?'

'Can't hear you too good. See you in ten days,' Del shouted. And hung up.

Lucas looked at the phone, puzzled, then hung up, and said to Bone, 'We play a little ball at the Y on Wednesday nights, bunch of cops, a few lawyers. Sort of a cross between basketball and hockey – you know, no harm, no foul. If Kerin'll let you, you're invited.'

'Yeah, that'd be nice,' Bone said. 'Maybe Isley'll be around in a year or so.' They shook hands and Bone said, 'See you.'

He went out the door, but ten seconds later was back: 'Uh, there's some people here to see you,' he said.

'What?'

'Some . . . people,' Bone said.

Lucas, frowning, stepped out in the hallway. He wasn't sure until later of the exact number, which was twenty-four, but he knew at a glance that there were a lot of them.

Old ladies.

Gathered like a flock of curly-haired, white-fleeced sheep, each clutching a purse and what seemed to be a brand-new gym bag. One of them, a sweet-looking grandmotherly woman with a trembling chin, said, 'We've come to turn ourselves in.'

'In?' Lucas asked. And Bone said, 'Gotta go.' And left.

'We're the opium junkies,' the grandmother said, and the other women nodded. 'Del said our best chance for leniency was to come down and surrender to you.'

'Sonofabitch,' Lucas said. He looked in at his phone as the grandmother recoiled; Del was probably halfway to Mexico.

'I beg your pardon?' she said, clutching the gym bag more tightly.

'Nothing. Stay right here,' Lucas said. 'Don't move. I'll be right back.'

He trotted down to the chief's office. 'No, Rose Marie's

gone,' the secretary said. She seemed to be biting the insides of her cheeks.

'Where?'

The secretary had to struggle a bit to get it out: 'Cancun.'

Lucas looked at her, a hard look, and she put her hands to her face. He turned on his heel and headed down toward violent crimes. He imagined he heard explosive laughter coming from the chief's office just before the door closed behind him.

In violent crimes, Loring was sitting on an office chair, peeling a green apple with a penknife. 'Seen Frank?' Frank Lester was the other deputy chief.

'Nope.'

'How about Sherrill?'

'Nope. They left. Together.'

'Together?'

'Yeah. They said they were going to Cancun.'

'You sonofabitch,' Lucas said hotly.

'What?' Loring asked, surprised. 'What?'

'You know what.'

'No, I don't know what.' He really seemed confused. On the other hand, he lied well. 'What?'

The heads of intelligence and narcotics were gone. Nobody knew when they'd be back. Sloan and Black were missing, Franklin was gone.

On one of his trips past the old ladies, the grandmother said bravely, 'We brought our things.'

'Your things?'

They held up their gym bags. 'Toothpaste and pajamas and so on. For the slammer.'

'Aw, Jesus Christ,' Lucas said.

He finally went back to Loring, got him out in the hall,

explained the situation. '. . . surrendering, and I want you to help with the processing . . .'

Loring was backing away. 'Fuck that,' he said. 'They're yours.'

'They're not mine,' Lucas shouted. But Loring was running toward the exit. 'Goddamnit, get your ass back here. Get back here . . .'

Loring was the last of them.

Lucas walked back toward his office, where the little flock gathered with their purses and the gym bags, awaiting justice. All up and down the hallways, the doors were closed.

Nobody home, except him.

'Is there a problem?' grandma asked.

POCKET
BOOKS

This book and other **Pocket** titles are available from your bookshop or
can be ordered direct from the publisher.

0 7434 2895 1	**Last Man Standing**	**David Baldacci**	£6.99
0 7434 0846 2	**Absolute Power**	**David Baldacci**	£6.99
0 7434 1555 8	**Chosen Prey**	**John Sandford**	£6.99
0 7434 1556 6	**Mortal Prey**	**John Sandford**	£6.99
0 7434 6823 6	**The Third Option**	**Vince Flynn**	£6.99
0 7434 6825 2	**Transfer of Power**	**Vince Flynn**	£6.99

Please send cheque or postal order for the value of the book, free postage
and packing within the UK; OVERSEAS including Republic of Ireland
£2 per book.

OR: Please debit this amount from my VISA/ACCESS/MASTERCARD:

CARD NO: . . . .

EXPIRY DATE: . . . .

AMOUNT: £ . . . .

NAME: . . . .

ADDRESS: . . . .

. . . .

SIGNATURE: . . . .

Send orders to SIMON & SCHUSTER CASH SALES
PO Box 29, Douglas Isle of Man, IM99 1BQ
Tel: 01624 677237, Fax: 01624 670923
E-mail: bookshop@enterprise.net
Please allow 14 days for delivery. Prices and availability subject to
change without notice